OFF THE GROUND

CATHERINE RICHMOND

❧ Created with Vellum

For Dad - This Ercoupe's for you!

Because you are my help, I sing in the shadow of your wings.
Psalm 63:7 NIV

PROLOGUE

"SWANKY." Miss Sackett, school librarian and girls' basketball coach whistled. "Corrie's papa has some heavy sugar."

"Hope Miss Klemfuss doesn't hear you." Mac maneuvered his Tin Lizzie between a Pierce Arrow and the Chrysler parked on either side of the road. One scratch would cost his next paycheck.

Miss Sackett blew a raspberry. "We can sling slang to our heart's content. No one invites the school secretary to their graduation party."

He lowered his voice. "Miss Klemfuss hears all, sees all, knows all."

"Class of twenty-nine! More than fine!" chanted three fellows in slacks and shirts as they crossed the road. None wore a suit coat or tie. Mac let out a breath. He'd borrowed a light-brown suit from Mr. Smooth's closet. The cuffed slacks fit well, but the double-breasted coat was too big in the shoulders. He'd leave it in the car.

"Which house is it?"

Miss Sackett peered at the library catalog card on which she'd written Corrie's address. "The big white one. Go ahead and park."

"I'll let you out by the front door." He inched past another long touring car. Who in Omaha could afford a Duesenberg? "Haven't spent all winter coaching your basketball team to have you hurt your leg again."

"Ankle's better than new." She poked him with her cane. "Park now or I'll bean you right in the kisser."

Mac squeezed into the next spot. "What's your hurry?"

"You got to take your shot before the other guy."

"What other guy? What shot?"

"Mac McFarland, you're not fooling anyone. You've been carrying a torch for Corrie since the day you met."

Uh-oh. Did everyone know? Mac's face heated as he ran around the car to help Miss Sackett out. "You were in surgery that day." Which was how Mac had ended up as the substitute coach.

The older woman glanced at the house and whistled. "How Corrie grew up unspoiled is beyond me."

The mansion commanded the large lot. Mac counted fifteen windows on the front alone. Flowers bloomed along walkways. The United States, Nebraska, and Central High flags fluttered from a pole in the middle of the manicured lawn.

The librarian yanked her cloche over her gray curls, smoothed her skirt, and straightened her blouse, all in Central purple. She marched across the grass, holding her cane like a battle sword. "It's graduation day. Corrie's no longer a student, no longer subject to the rules of Central, no longer off limits. Ask her for a dance and a date. Don't forget me when you send out wedding invitations."

"As if her father would let her marry a Montgomery Ward's clerk," Mac muttered as they followed a group of students around the house.

She cocked an eyebrow in his direction. "Play your cards right, and you'll be running a jewelry store."

"Corrie has three brothers, one working in the family business."

"Three brothers ..." Miss Sackett stopped, her head tilted. "When the oldest was a freshman, their mother was always at school. She worked the circulation desk for me, served punch at National Honor Society receptions, decorated for dances. With the second boy, she began skipping school. By the third son, she'd show only for special events. I haven't seen Mrs. Tinley once during the four years Corrie's been at Central. Not once." The librarian looked from side to side, then leaned close. "Scuttlebutt in the teachers' lounge notes the country club opened four years ago."

It wasn't right to run someone down while enjoying their hospitality, so Mac tried to find something positive to say. "Corrie's brothers helped teach three-man defense and watched one of our games."

"Let's say hello then."

Jazz music drew them along a brick path to parklike backyard.

Beneath an awning, a seven-piece band belted out the latest hits to dancers on a basketball court. A chef cooked on a grill and uniformed waiters tended a buffet next to the house. Guests gathered at round tables.

Miss Sackett whistled again. "The Tinleys put on the Ritz."

"All this from a jewelry store?"

"I hear Papa has done quite well in the stock market." Miss Sackett pointed to the crowd hopping to "Ain't She Sweet." "No need to babysit this old woman. Cut in and make your move."

"I'll find you a chair and some food."

Fingers strong from typing hundreds of catalog cards pinched his chin. "Scram, you sap, or I'll give you the bum's rush."

Mac grinned and headed for the dance floor.

"Good to see you, Mac!" Ernie Tinley, smartly dressed in a white suit, pumped Mac's hand. "Still with Montgomery Ward's? Let me introduce you to the Brandeis family. Move you up in the world."

The luxury department store's motto was "Everything you want is at Brandeis." But right now, everything Mac wanted was on the dance floor. Not that he'd say that to one of Corrie's brothers. "Maybe later."

"Hey, Coach!" Mary Frances called.

Mac raised his arm—half in greeting, half in dismissal—as he worked his way through the party guests. Eyes on the goal, he'd told his team. His eyes were on Corrie. She spun across the dance floor, curls bouncing and skirt swirling. The Charleston was perfect for her long legs.

Miss Sackett was right—Mac could declare his intentions now. Or at least see if Corrie would be willing to date. She'd been giving off signals these past few months. They'd even talked a few times, real conversations, nothing to do with sports.

The captain of the boys' basketball team steered Corrie across the floor. *Traveling!* Mac wanted to shout. *Hit the bench!* The kid raced to the far edge, bouncing Corrie's outstretched arm as if dribbling, then pivoted her around. Corrie laughed, the bright sound carrying over the tune.

Here she comes! Twelve feet, ten feet, eight. Mac stepped onto the floor. He tapped the boy's shoulder, nodded his thanks, then pulled Corrie closer than the Charleston required, his arm around her trim waist.

"Mac! Am I ever glad to see you!" She snuggled even closer and planted a too-quick kiss on his cheek. Her scent of Woodbury soap, "The Skin You Love to Touch," had his head spinning.

"Let's make plans!" he said into her ear.

Her smile widened into a big grin and her eyes sparkled. "Let's!"

The band brought the song to a stop with a loud chord.

"Ladies and gentlemen," the bandleader shouted through the megaphone. "Mr. Tinley requests the presence of his honored guests at the barn, where he's going to give Miss Corrie, the new graduate, her gift." The band played a jazz rendition of "Pomp and Circumstance."

"C'mon!" Corrie dashed for the large red building as if running for a basket. Mac lost her in the crowd. A pair of elderly women tut-tutted, fanning themselves with lace handkerchiefs.

"Walk, Cordelia Elizabeth!" Her mother shook her head. "That girl."

"Whaddya think, Coach?" Corrie's teammate Jackie joined Mac. "Every other father gives his girl a wristwatch. Or a typewriter if she's college-bound. So what is Mr. Got Bucks giving his little princess?"

Corrie's father had enough money to indulge his youngest, his only daughter, her every whim. "A car."

Jackie narrowed her eyes. "A yellow roadster."

Would a girl with a new roadster date a fellow with a jalopy? She didn't seem to mind riding in it to basketball games. "A horse."

"A white Arabian." Jackie lit a cigarette. "Or a motorcycle. Those sweet little Indians are really fast."

Mac hoped not. Fast wasn't safe.

Corrie bounced up and down, hugged her father, and untied the giant pink ribbon on the door handles. Her older brothers slid them open. Late afternoon sun lit a metal circle, a long wooden shaft, and black cylinders. Fuselage, wings, landing gear.

Jackie gasped. "An airplane."

No. Not an airplane. Anything but an airplane.

Mac turned and pushed through the crowd to escape. But one glimpse had set off his nightmare.

The engine revved and spewed black smoke. The flimsy plane shuddered. Part of the tail snapped off. Wind screamed in the wires. Faster and faster it came, nearly straight down. The pilot's head bobbed. Pull up, Henry! Get out! The plane slammed into the ground. The impact vibrated through Mac's body. With a whoosh, fire engulfed the fragile airframe. The hot smell of gas, oil, and burning flesh choked him.

Someone called his name, but the roar of the fire muffled their voice. Clear of the crowd, Mac broke into a run. He made it to the corner of the neighbor's house, where he lost his breakfast in a hydrangea bush.

CHAPTER
ONE

EARLIER IN THE *School Year*

More than two years had passed since Mac's high school graduation, but the worn brass door handle, creaking wood floors, and smell of chalk dust reduced him to the quivering rank of student. His feet marched to the office. His mind scrambled for a plausible excuse … even though he wasn't late. Ah the carefree days of high school, when his biggest worry was—

"Horatio McFarland, not another step."

Mac flinched. Only one person at Central ignored his request to use his nickname. "Please, Miss Klemfuss—"

The pear-shaped school secretary narrowed her eyes. "You think you can prowl the halls, ruining the reputation of our girls? Not on my watch."

Coach hurried to run interference. "McFarland's here to help."

"I know what he's here for." Klemfuss knew everything. She jabbed her stubby finger at Mac. "You may have graduated, Horatio, but the rules of conduct are still in force. One step out of line and–" The stubby finger slashed across her wattle neck.

"Gotta go. Team's waiting." With a glance over his shoulder to make sure they weren't followed, Coach walked him up the steps to Central's afterthought of a gym on the fourth floor. "Thanks for pinch-hitting, Mac. Surgery went well. Sackett should be back later in the season."

"It's an honor, sir." He hoped the bigwigs at Montgomery Ward's would be suitably impressed.

"C'mon in and meet your team." He yanked open the door to room 425. High windows lit the empty space. "Now where'd those girls run off to?"

Girls? When Coach asked if he'd volunteer, Mac had been thinking of boys' golf or track. Coach hadn't said anything about girls.

The older man stomped down the girls' staircase to the landing. He pounded on the small wood door of the restroom. No response. Grumbling under his breath, he continued to the third floor, peeking in every classroom until, "You'd better not be sneaking a smoke."

"Look!" An unmistakably female and excited voice called. "Over there!"

Mac peeked around Coach. Yep, girls, all right. Two of them.

Mac had waited on female customers, but they were women—wives, mothers, friends of his mom, wearing flower-print dresses down past their knees. Not teenagers with bobbed hair, bare arms extending from sleeveless blouses, long legs stretching from shorts.

The dark-haired one ground out a cigarette on the windowsill, then tossed it outside. The lighter-haired one bounced and pointed to the sky.

What was she— Oh no. A low whine of an engine grew louder. It roared past the high school, a double-winged deathtrap like the one that killed Henry. The plane circled the school, then headed northeast. Mac turned away, gut hurting as if he'd been punched.

"Unless it's Lindbergh himself, we're not canceling practice." Coach herded them back to the room. "Where's the rest of the team?"

Legs stretching and curls bouncing, the light-haired girl raced up the steps then ran circles around the room, arms wide. "I want to fly! Up there in the big beautiful sky!"

Sure it's beautiful, right up until the crash. No sensible parents would let their daughter do something so dangerous. And the high windows in the gym would keep them from plane watching.

The brunette sauntered—with wiggling hips—up to Mac. Her kohl-rimmed eyes gave him a once-over. "Who do we have here?"

Two more girls hurried in, out of breath, chorusing their apologies.

Coach gave his trademark loud clap. "Okay, team. Miss Sackett's out for a few weeks, so Mr. McFarland's going to coach you. Good luck. Make Central proud." Then he was gone.

Leaving Mac standing alone on the gym floor, surrounded by …

Girls.

"All right! We have a coach!" Miss Light-Brown Hair handed him a clipboard and whistle. "I'm Corrie, running center. This is Thelma, jumping center; Mary Frances, forward; and Jackie, guard. Our other forward, Halleen, had to watch her little brothers."

"While her mother goes to the hospital to pop out another kid." The dark-haired smoker, Jackie, rolled her lips out with a loud burst.

"Her mom sewed our uniforms," Mary Frances whispered.

Jackie squinted at him. "Were you on the boys' team a while back?"

"You're thinking of my brother." His older, more athletic, and better-looking brother, Mr. Smooth, who continued his famous basketball career at the university. A bead of sweat ran down Mac's neck. Injuries acquired when Mac had pulled Henry out of the airplane wreck, ended his time on the court. Coach had felt sorry for him and let Mac be the team manager.

"Familiar. Recognized. Recall." Thelma wagged her finger. "Store. Shop. Montgomery Ward's!"

"Uh, yes." Where the big bosses in Chicago had put the word out —only civic-minded men involved in their community would be promoted.

"You're no teacher," Jackie said in a dismissive tone. "Do we have to call you 'mister'?"

"Uh, yeah. Or no. It's okay to call me Mac." He glanced at the door, but the coach hadn't come back to rescue him. "Is this everyone?"

"Ruth, other guard, is …" Corrie exchanged a look with Thelma.

"Under the weather. Indisposed. Out of action," Thelma said.

"She'll be back Friday," Corrie said.

One of those female things then. Mac kept his gaze down.

"And our sub Evelyn, had a bad permanent." Mary Frances grabbed the ends of her hair. "She'll be back when her hair grows out."

How was a team supposed to play with only a half dozen girls? Girls with no height and little interest in basketball. "Okay, then." Mac flipped the whistle's lanyard over his head. It caught on his ear. He reached to untangle it and dropped the clipboard.

Jackie snorted.

His pale Celtic skin blushed too easily, which made him even more embarrassed. He frowned at the toothpick dangling from Jackie's bottom lip. "Take a ball to the face and you'll get an extra hole in your lip."

Thelma nodded. "Pierced. Impaled. Skewered."

Corrie handed him the clipboard. "Last month we played the juniors, sophomores, and freshmen."

"Beat the freshmen fourteen to nine, the sophomores twenty-two to zip," Jackie said.

No mention of the juniors. Must not have gone well.

"Our first tournament game is Friday, against Benson," Corrie said.

Benson's boys won the championship every year. Mac had never heard anything about their girls' team. Or any girls' team, for that matter.

"Catastrophe. Tragedy. Annihilation."

Jackie raised an eyebrow at Thelma. "Swallow a thesaurus?

"Pea brain. Blockhead–"

Mac had to stop this before he found out what girls did instead of fist-fighting. "Okay, pair up for passing drill. Dribble three times before passing. Each of you take a shot, then back to the other hoop."

Mary Frances managed a weak throw in Jackie's general direction, but the brunette didn't adjust her pace to meet it. The ball drifted past, hit the wall, and rolled into the corner. Mary Frances picked it up, ran to the free-throw line without a single dribble, and tossed the ball underhanded in the general vicinity of the basket.

Jackie pointed east. "If you want good girls' basketball, try Iowa."

They moved like puppies, bouncing around without any plan or purpose. Except the dark-haired one, Jackie. She strolled down the court, ignoring the rest, until Corrie shot a pass into her arms. A flip of Jackie's wrist sent the ball swooshing through the net.

Thelma's throw bounced off the backstop and beaned her right in the nose. Even though it wasn't bleeding, practice ground to a halt as the girls decided who would walk their center to the school nurse.

Was it too late to forfeit … the entire season?

———

Corrie watched their *handsome* new coach hurry down the boys' staircase. He moved with the light-footed ease of a good dancer.

"He don't know from nothing." Jackie kicked the ball into the corner. "Doesn't even know girls aren't supposed to run full court. Benson's going to mop the floor with us."

Thelma slammed her ball into the bin. "Thrashed. Mincemeat. Skunked."

"Probably drives a Tin Lizzie." Jackie led the way into the girls restroom. "He's got that fuddy-duddy, boring smell to him."

"We won't have to take the bus." Mary Frances untied her Spaldings.

"Oh I don't know." Corrie ran her hands under cold water, then patted her face and neck as she considered their substitute coach. As lean as Lindbergh. He had that noble, lonely air about him too. Dark hair like Ramon Novarro's in *The Flying Fleet*. A curl on his forehead like Gary Cooper in *Wings*. His deep voice cut through the team's whining. More mature than the boys wandering the halls of Central.

Corrie raised her arm. "He has the potential to be a real sheik. Dibs."

Jackie swatted her. "He'll be a sheik on the day you get drunk."

Thelma giggled. "Spifflicated. Ossified. Plastered."

"I thought you had your heart set on Lindbergh." Mary Frances yanked a comb through her perm.

"He proposed to the daughter of the ambassador to Mexico." Corrie kicked off her shorts.

Jackie laughed. "She's head over heels for *Tailspin Tommy*."

Corrie saved every episode of the comic strip. "Call me Cockpit Corrie. No one wants a tailspin." She buttoned her blouse. "When's the next dance?"

"You want to ask Mac? Awfully forward." Mary Frances gulped. "And I hate to be a killjoy, but teachers aren't allowed to date students."

"He's no teacher." Jackie brushed her hair with a slow stroke. "Goody-Two-Shoes has a crush. The most interesting news to hit Central all year."

"Careful." Mary Frances bit her thumbnail. "The rule probably applies to coaches. If you get in trouble now, they won't let you graduate."

Corrie made eye contact with each of her teammates. "So who's brave enough to ask Klemfuss for me?"

"Terrified. Petrified. Terrorized."

Mary Frances crossed herself. Twice.

Jackie shuddered. "Even Boss Dennison and Al Capone get the heebie-jeebies when it comes to Klemfuss."

Corrie pulled on her tweed skirt. Four more weeks of basketball. Somehow she had to find out if they were allowed to date. But first she had to get Mac interested.

CHAPTER
TWO

THE EXPRESS DELIVERY man arrived at the freight door before the store opened. "Where do ya want this?"

Mac followed him to the alley. A large crate sat in back of the truck. "Inside." Where else? "Need help carrying it?"

The driver rubbed his chin. "Well, ya see, it's leaking."

A dark-orange puddle seeped from the corner of the box.

"Is that oil?" Mac stuck his finger in it. It didn't feel like oil.

"I wouldn't–"

Too late. Mac brought his finger close to his nose and got an eye-watering whiff of ammonia. "What's in here?" Mac popped the latch, opened the top, and released a barnyard reek. Morning's light showed long, furry ears, round backs, and puff-ball tails. "Rabbits?"

The animals in question responded by thumping and hopping in circles.

The delivery man read the invoice. "Got you pairs of Havanas, Himalayans, New Zealands, and chinchillas. Although who knows what you'll end up with, them does and bucks all mixed together."

Uh-oh. "Who ordered them?"

"B. Pavelka. Probably going to turn 'em into hasenpfeffer."

Eat them? A black and white rose up on his hind legs, ears pivoting and nose wiggling. A jolt of queasiness hit Mac. "Why didn't you deliver them to Mr. Pavelka?"

"Order says he'll pick them up."

"I'll call him."

The driver helped Mac carry the crate in, then left. Mac opened the lid again. "Aren't you supposed to come with a pamphlet?" he asked, generating a burst of ear flapping. A few scraps of well-chewed paper littered the crate along with their droppings. "You ate your instructions." The rabbits hopped in circles, leaping over and landing on each other. "You need more space and food and water." Mac found a chipped enamelware saucer on the returns shelf, filled it with water, and set it in the crate. The rabbits backed away from his arm, except the black one who rubbed his head against Mac's hand. "You're soft." Mac tried to pick him up, but he shot into the corner. "Okay, I'll call your new owner. Drink your water."

B. Pavelka hadn't put a phone number or address on his order. The man hadn't ordered hutches or fencing, so the store didn't have his name on file. Calls to every Pavelka in the phone book had Mac wishing he knew a few words of Czech. Soon the store would be full of Pavelkas or full of rabbits. How were the critters?

Wet. They'd stepped in their saucer, dumped it, then mixed the water with the mess in the crate. Mac grabbed a large cardboard box, then tried to move the rabbits. One of the white ones scratched his wrist, and another nipped his finger, drawing blood. Wearing work gloves, Mac got them all, squirming and kicking, into the clean box. Now—

"Time to open," said the furniture salesman.

Mac filled the cash registers, unlocked the door, and set the sandwich board announcing the day's sale on the corner of Twenty-Fourth and Farnum.

"Eek!" Mrs. Eischied shrieked from the women's department. "There's a rat in the store! A big furry rat!"

Oh no. Mac raced down the aisle. "It's a chinchilla."

The woman stood on a chair. "I know what I saw."

"Please keep your voice down." The last thing Montgomery Ward's needed was a rumor that the store had rats. "It's a customer's order."

She turned down the volume to police-siren level and pointed to a shelf of hats. "There it goes!"

Mac dove and missed. At least it was Saturday and the boss was off.

"There's a rabbit chewing on the telephone wire," yelled the appliance salesman.

"Catch it," Mac called as a black one scooted between his legs and raced behind the bicycles.

"Rabbit chewing invoices," the guy in automotive yelled.

"Catch it." Good riddance to paperwork. But ... how did they all escape? A black-and-white one disappeared under a washing machine. Would there be any rabbits left when Mr. Pavelka arrived?

"Mrs. Eischied, please stand by the door to a make sure none of the animals escape."

"Mr. McFarland, I am *not* getting off this chair."

"Good morning, Mac." A young woman in a green V-neck sweater and matching skirt gave him a confident smile. "Want some help?"

How did this pretty girl know his name? Oh, wait. The basketball team. Fast, light on her feet, agile Corrie. Could he use her help? "And how!"

———

Corrie planned to drop off the basketball rules, then skedaddle. Shopping with Mother meant slogging through Brandeis and Kilpatrick's, trying on boring dresses. But at Montgomery Ward's, there was yelling, shrieking, and rabbits.

Mac sprinted like a basketball player, his hair mussed and tie flapping, hot on the heels of a zigzagging white bunny. A sable one streaked by them both.

Corrie put her coat and copy of girls' basketball rules on top of a chifforobe. What a nifty opportunity to impress Mac. "How many are loose?"

He winced. "Maybe as many as eight."

A gray one with a fluffy tail scampered along the men's counter.

"Are any of them squirrels?"

"That's a chinchilla. We should catch those two first. Mrs. Eischied thinks they're rats." He pointed to the woman standing on the chair, then hurried to the back room. "Let me get you some gloves. They bite."

Corrie grabbed a broom and handed Mac an old towel.

"Yes, they all escaped." Mac nodded at an overturned cardboard box, then handed her a pair of work gloves.

Corrie ran—whee! Mother never let her run in stores—for the automobile department. The chinchilla climbed to the top of the tire display. Corrie nudged it off with the broom. "Catch!"

Mac held out the towel and the little fellow dropped right in. "Got it! I'll put it in the crate."

"I'll find the other."

Mrs. Eischied shrieked, "Housewares!"

A crash of enamelware confirmed her sighting. Corrie dashed over, but the chinchilla jumped to the shelf with glassware. "Come here, little one." She held the broom in front of it, hoping it would hop on for a ride. Instead it squirmed into the corner, pushing a china teapot to the edge.

"Careful," Mac said in an undertone.

"I got this." Corrie took the towel.

Mac reached, and the little monster panicked, dashing for the other end of the shelf. The teapot landed in the towel. "Two points."

"At least." Mac kept his eyes on the troublesome ball of fur.

The rodent leaped for the dish display. Mac made a midair grab and it let out a shriek. "No, no, Mrs. Eischied's the only one allowed to make that sound."

A black-and-white one rubbed his chin on the leg of a davenport. Corrie placed her hand on its back, scooped it up, and headed for the back room. "It's okay, baby bunny."

"So that's how you do it."

"If they hold still." She added it to the crate.

The appliance salesman had the other black and white cornered under a washing machine. Corrie tried to persuade it out with the broom, but it scampered under a stove. When it dashed for a heater, Mac made the catch.

A customer in a cowboy hat arrived, and Mrs. Eischied yelled, "Close the door before the rabbits escape."

"You're having a rabbit roundup?" the cowboy asked.

Mac nodded. "By any chance are you Mr. Pavelka?"

"Not me. You might want to grab that one." He nodded toward the display of irons, toasters, and fans, where a white rabbit industriously gnawed a cord. Mac grabbed the bunny. "I know you're hungry, but the Blue Line model is not on your diet."

A clatter sent Corrie running to the hardware department. A sable bunny had tipped over a bin of nuts and bolts, then chomped wallpaper samples as if they were potato chips, then raced behind the paint cans.

Mac crouched at the other end of the shelf. "Come here, rabbit."

Nose twitching, the bunny took a step toward Mac, then turned around and hopped twice toward Corrie. It went back and forth, a few hops closer to one then the other, never within reach.

"Smarter than it looks." Mac's lips twitched.

"But not smart enough." Corrie moved a couple paint cans, slid the broom into the hidey-hole, and pushed the sable rabbit into Mac's hands.

"Where do you want 'em?" The cowboy had a white one tucked under his arm like a football.

Mac took them back to the crate. "Only one more black rabbit missing."

"By the curtains." Mrs. Eischied pointed. Corrie, Mac, the cowboy, and the rest of the salesclerks followed. "Heading for the fabric."

The rogue dashed full speed past radios and automotive batteries into a rolled carpet.

Mac grabbed the end of the roll and lifted. Scrambling and scratching, the rabbit slid out into Corrie's hands. "What a fast little ball of fur you are. Have you considered playing basketball?"

Mac thanked the customer and his staff, then returned the bunny to the crate. "Two, four, six, eight. All here." After all that chaos and racing around, he hadn't broken a sweat or lost his cool. He gave Corrie a wide smile. "How'd you get to be such a swell rabbit wrangler?"

"My brothers and I used to have a pet bunny, Peter Rabbit. He'd lead us all on a chase for hours and somehow manage to bite through the telephone wire any time he was on the lam." She reached into the crate and petted one. "So how did you end up with them?"

"Customer order. They dumped the water I gave them."

"Do you have …" She found a clean, but dented metal ashtray on the returns shelf. "They won't be able to tip this over, although they will step in it. I'll go pick them some dandelions."

Mrs. Eischied announced, "Your rabbit customer is here."

A middle-aged woman in a faded housedress marched a boy in worn overalls to the crate. "This," she said, speaking slowly and giving the boy's ear a yank. "This is Bobby Pavelka."

Mac nodded at the woman, then addressed the boy. "These are the rabbits you ordered."

A smile lit the boy's face and he reached for them. His mother yanked him back with a torrent of a language Corrie didn't recognize.

"I'm sorry," Mac said. "I don't speak Czech."

The boy's bottom lip trembled. "She said no."

"You didn't have permission"—Mac gentled his tone—"before you put in your order?"

The boy shook his head. A tear rolled down his cheek.

Corrie had seen her father and brothers work with customers at their jewelry store, so she recognized the skill and kindness in Mac's conversation with these two. He talked up an easy payment plan, offered to let the boy work off his debt, and reviewed the advantages of owning rabbits, although his voice wavered when he mentioned meat and fur. He even offered to deliver them and give mother and son a ride home. But he couldn't change the fact that the Pavelkas lived in a third-floor apartment without a yard.

"No, no, no." The mother shook her head and towed out the tearful child. As the glass door closed, he collapsed into a puddle of sobs.

Mac pressed a fist over his mouth for a moment, then turned to Corrie. "I don't suppose you and your brothers would like more rabbits."

Corrie cuddled a sable one. He was softer than velvet. "Sorry. Mother put the kibosh on any more pets."

"I can't send them back. Who would take them? Rabbits are on the same page as Boy Scout equipment in our catalog. Maybe I'll call the troop leaders and see if any want to take on a project."

"The Nebraska Humane Society's close, on the other side of Creighton."

"They'd become someone's pets instead of meat. Great idea."

Mac telephoned and the rabbits were picked up minutes later. He mopped the floor. "So what brought you to Montgomery Ward's this morning, Corrie?"

"You mean it's not always an adventure here? This is the most fun I've ever had in a store." Corrie gave him the handout of girls' basketball rules. "Here I brought you a gift."

Mac took the pages without looking at them. "You are a gift."

The store around them faded, leaving Corrie alone with Mac. His hazel eyes warmed as they stared into hers. His dark-brown hair, ruffled from herding rabbits, curved across his forehead. He leaned closer, giving her a hint of his salty scent.

"I mean …" He shook his head and looked down. After a moment, he peered up through long eyelashes. "You're gifted with rabbits. Thank you." He blinked at the paper in his hand as if trying to remember what it was. "And thank you for the rules."

Mac had a store to run. And Corrie had a paper on the Peloponnesian War due Monday, plus a date with what's-his-name tonight. "Glad to be of assistance." She sounded too much like Mother. Better scram before she turned into a complete dimwit.

He escorted her to the door. "We work well together, Corrie."

Together? As in dating? Her heart did a happy dance. "And how."

His mouth curved, hinting at a dimple on his left cheek. He saluted her with the rolled-up paper in his hand. "These next four weeks of basketball are going to be swell."

She smiled back. "See you Monday morning, Coach."

CHAPTER
THREE

MAC STOOD OUTSIDE THE GIRLS' restroom, listening to giggles, whispers, and Jackie's hoarse cough. How was he supposed to get them into his car? He didn't even know how to call them—Girls? Team? Everybody?

Lord, isn't there an easier way to become a Montgomery Ward's manager?

"Bet he caught his tie in a cash register." Jackie laughed.

"Or another bout of escaping rabbits." Corrie opened the door and burst into a big smile. "He's here."

"And not wearing a tie." Mac put his hand on his chest, where his heart did a step-hop.

Corrie yelled behind her. "Let's go, team!"

The girls filed down the stairs, wearing their uniforms of white cap-sleeve shirts and dark purple shorts.

"Looking good, team," Mac said, unleashing complaints about perms, pimples, and the lack of pockets in their shorts. *Not another word about their appearance ever again*, he promised himself. He held the door open to the parking lot. "Going to be a squeeze."

The girls spotted his Tin Lizzie and groaned. Not that the Model T didn't deserve criticism, but Mac preferred to be the one throwing mud. "It'll get us there." He hoped.

"What is this, the first Ford ever made?" Jackie asked.

"More rust than paint." Halleen picked at a loose flake.

Maybe he shouldn't have washed it. Dirt evened out the color.

"Junk. Heap. Lemon."

"Say a prayer, Mary Frances."

"C'mon, girls." Corrie waved the clipboard. "We've got a game."

Corrie and Jackie sat beside him. The other five piled in back. Fabric ripped and someone said oops. Mac hoped it wasn't his roof. Or one of the girls' shorts.

The engine banged to life. Mac climbed in beside Corrie and headed out of the parking lot. Girls. Mac had girls in his car. Every inhale brought a dizzy mix of Cashmere Bouquet, Woodbury, and Palmolive.

"Montgomery Ward's needs to give you a raise." Jackie braced as he turned onto Dodge Street.

"You be sure to suggest that." What was it about Jackie that got his goat? Mac concentrated on avoiding the many potholes signaling spring in Omaha. Another sign of spring—raindrops—hit the windshield. If it turned into a downpour, he'd have to pull over.

"We're getting wet," howled the back seat.

"There's window covers under the seats."

The car rocked as the girls snapped the covers to the canvas roof.

"Man, is it hot in here. Ever burn your tootsies, Mac?" Jackie pulled her feet back from the firewall.

"Roasty toasty." Corrie warmed her hands by the engine. "I should have brought marshmallows. We could have made s'mores."

Chatty basketball players steamed up the windows. Mac wiped the windshield with his sleeve.

"Beats the bus," Corrie said. "And we need to beat Benson."

Yes, stop fussing about the car and focus on the game. "What do you know about their team?" Mac asked.

The back seat agreed Benson's girls were country bumpkins who could lift a hay bale with one hand and wrestle bulls for fun. As they debated whether Benson's team would be meaner than South's, Mac turned up Walnut Hill. His Ford hiccupped and his stomach plummeted. He'd forgotten to fill the tank. If they were late, they'd have to forfeit, which might be best—

Corrie patted the steering wheel, brushing his hand. "C'mon, Tin Lizzie. You can do it!"

Mac made a U-turn in the middle of the street, pushed the middle pedal, and put the car into reverse. A Chevrolet honked and whizzed past them. Then a Dodge left them in the dust.

"Humiliating, embarrassing, mortifying."

"Getting the job done," Mac said. Although his hot face agreed with Thelma's assessment. "Look behind us, team. Make sure I don't hit anyone."

Jackie leaned out the passenger side. "Flock of chickens and goats."

Mary Frances peered out the back window. "There's nothing in the road. Lying is a sin."

Halleen monitored the driver's side. "More to the left. No, too far."

Finally they crested the hill. Mac made another U-turn and continued, the engine banging away.

"You're not out of gas?" Corrie asked.

Mac tipped his hand to illustrate. "On hills, the gas goes to the back of the tank instead of in the engine."

"Oh, so backing up brings the gas to the engine." Corrie tilted his hand forward, her touch nearly sending him careening off the road. "My father's car doesn't do that."

"I suspect your dad's car isn't this old." Mac parked at Benson.

"He likes to buy a new one every year."

Every year? What business was her dad in? Whatever it was, he'd been successful. "Okay, team, let's go win our game."

Unfortunately, winning wasn't on the agenda.

———

"Snuffed out." Thelma groaned. "Exterminated. Annihilated."

"Well I never," Halleen huffed. "Can you believe they wouldn't let us have a few measly points? Incredibly rude."

"Bandage, anyone? Mercurochrome?" Ruth rattled her first-aid kit.

"I could use a drink," Jackie said, "and I don't mean java."

Mac turned the ignition switch to battery, put his hand on the throttle, and stepped on the starter. *Please, Lord, these girls have had a bad day.* The Ford started on the first try. *Thank You, Jesus.* The only good thing about the game was that few people had witnessed their humiliation. Mothers and boyfriends of the Benson players, he guessed.

"I prayed." Mary Frances fanned herself with his copy of the girls' basketball rules. "I asked St. Sebastian to help us."

"St. Jude is the one for lost causes." Evelyn pressed her hands to her shorn head. "Although he didn't do a thing about my perm."

Jackie coughed. "Even God can't help this team."

They needed a pep talk. Mac cleared his throat. "With practice—"

Corrie's soft fingers touched his wrist. Whoa. "Turn right."

"Right?" While Corrie touched him? He glanced at her from the corner of his eye. "But Central is—"

"Got any cash?" She let go, and he could think again.

Mac gulped. "A little. Why?"

Corrie pointed toward the two blocks of businesses that comprised Benson's downtown. "There's an ice cream shop next to the theater."

"It's a tradition," Ruth said. The rest of the back seat agreed.

The sign, Bensonette Confectionary, covered most of the storefront. "Better than a pep talk." Oops, he hadn't meant to say that out loud.

Corrie giggled. "You can polish your pep talk tonight. Give it to us when we show up a half hour early for practice tomorrow morning."

"Half hour?" Halleen groaned. "I can barely get out of bed as it is."

"Mean. Rotten. Slave driver."

"You gotta be kidding—"

Corrie grabbed the whistle from Mac's neck, giving him a second to block his ears, and blasted through the whining. "With the ice cream Coach is buying us, we'll have plenty of energy to run all morning."

Grumbling fizzled out. Mac parked, facing downhill. If the car wouldn't start when they left, the girls would have to push it. They climbed out and headed inside. Mac checked his wallet—yes, he had a few bucks—then raced to open the door.

Someone was coaching this team and it wasn't him.

———

Corrie led the team across Maple, but Mac raced ahead and held the door. A gentleman. Good. Mother fussed over her brothers' manners. Boys were so hard to train.

The shoebox of a store had a candy-filled display case running its length. Artie had brought her here one hot summer evening when the crowd lined the sidewalk all the way to the movie theater. But today, with chill of winter hanging on, the team had the store to themselves. "Remarkable Girl" played on the radio. Corrie would like to be remarkable in Mac's life. She kicked-stepped forward and back, then hop-turned, her best Charleston moves. "I love to dance. Don't you, Mac?" *How's that for a hint? Fellows need bright lights and a three-story marquee to catch on.*

Unfortunately Mac was busy studying the menu board, so all Corrie got out of him was a vague hum.

The store clerk eyeballed them and gave a low whistle. He stage-whispered to Mac, "Seven dolls on a date? What's your secret?"

Mac turned red.

Mary Frances piped up, "We're a basketball team and he's our coach."

"She can't help being honest," Halleen explained. "She's going into a convent after graduation."

"You want a date?" Jackie fluffed her hair and fluttered her eyelashes at the clerk. "What time you busting outta here?"

"You've got homework," Mary Frances said.

Jackie struck a pose. "Who cares. I'm heading to Hollywood."

"Single dip cones for everyone." Mac straightened. "Please."

The fellow turned his attention to scooping.

Thelma sidled up to Mac. "Strategy. Plan. Tactics."

Jackie pointed. "Get that girl an ice cream quick, before she kills me with synonyms."

Why couldn't they stop fighting and behave for once? Corrie ducked behind Mac and gave the girls a glare.

"You're right. We need a plan." Mac turned to Corrie. "What's next on the schedule?"

Ah, he'd figured out she was the one to ask. Now she just had to make herself indispensable for the rest of his life. "North High."

Mac paid for their cones and a roll of Necco Wafers. He peeled open the paper package, shook the pieces on the counter, and separated them by color. "Listen up, team. The best defense is control of the ball." He held up an orange wafer. "If the other team never gets their hands on it, they won't have the chance to take a shot. Ever tried a three-man defense?"

How clever of Mac to teach while the girls were busy eating. He explained the strategy while moving the pieces around—green for Benson, purple for Central, of course.

Ruth let a drip roll down her knuckles as she informed Mac, "But we don't have any men on our team, much less three."

"Oooh. Three men on a date would be fun." Trust Jackie to give basketball strategy a lewd twist.

Mac ignored the naughty comment. "Those fellows watching the game were Benson's championship team. My guess is they've been teaching their winning techniques to the girls. What do you know about fake and feint?"

"Faint? That went out with corsets." Evelyn made Mac blush again.

"F-e-i-n-t. Pretend to go one direction, then run the other."

"Bluff. Deceive. Trick." Thelma finished her cone too soon.

"Benson went all sneaky-tricky," Halleen said. "Such poor sports."

"Worked for them." Mac pocketed the candy. "We can do it too."

"Sneaky?" Jackie narrowed her eyes and nodded. "I like sneaky."

Mac opened the door and they trooped back to his car. "Monday's practice, divide into teams and give it a try. By the time I get to school, I want to see a recognizable three-girl defense."

Horsefeathers! None of the other girls would remember what Mac told them—their minds were off getting ready for tonight's dates. And Corrie had been so busy admiring Mac's long fingers, she didn't remember a word he said. He'd peg her as a dimwit, for certain. Who could— Ah, she knew exactly who would help her. She'd be a three-man defense expert in no time. Corrie smiled. "You got it, Coach."

CHAPTER
FOUR

"ANYONE HOME?" Mac wiped his feet to keep Mom's brick-patterned linoleum clean, then entered through the kitchen door. Only the ticking hall clock answered. *You're late ... you're late.* Mom would be home any minute. He lit the oven and loaded it with the meatloaf from the icebox and potatoes from the cellar. Running the laundry at the hospital wore Mom out—she should come home to a hot meal. Mac counted off half his pay and tucked it into the old butter crock. Maybe he couldn't give her a vacation, but at least he'd make sure she had a rainy-day fund.

Mac sat at the telephone table and found his brother's team list. He picked up the receiver and heard the buzz of the dial tone—always a good start. Mr. Smooth was at college, but the rest of the team still lived in Omaha. Mac started with Lou. "Hey, I need some basketball players to demonstrate technique. Could you meet me at Central's gym in the morning?"

"Basketball season's over, Mac. Wait ... Coach conned you into helping with the girls' team? What a sap!" The line echoed with laughter, then the loud click of hanging up.

Frank taught at Brownell Hall, a girls school, so Mac figured he'd understand. "Haven't you heard?" Frank squawked. "The Amateur Athletic Association wants to ban girls' basketball. Too competitive. Causes the girls to suffer nervous fatigue. Erodes their womanliness. Even First Lady Mrs. Hoover says the girls are playing too hard. Shut it down, Mac!"

If anyone seemed high strung, it was Frank. As far as Mac could tell, the girls on the team were plenty feminine. Especially that Corrie. None were in danger of nervous breakdown. Mac tried the next fellow.

Clarence managed to sound sorry. "I'd love to help you out, but I got a job at the Ford plant, making Model T's. My shift starts at seven."

No answer at Raymond's.

Tom's father told Mac that Tom had moved to Texas.

Phil's wife answered for him. "No and no. He's got twin daughters here at home. Any playing he does will be with his own girls."

Mac headed out on his bicycle. The setting sun flickered through budding trees onto the quiet neighborhood of tidy houses. Lit windows showed families gathered around the table for dinner. Ten years ago, before the Spanish influenza, that had been the McFarland family.

Two streets over he found some fellows shooting hoops, but they would only help Catholic high schools. The men at the park played like thugs with lots of elbow jabs and cursing—not a good influence. The kids with a peach basket nailed to a garage were too young and didn't handle the ball any better than his team.

His team? When did he start thinking of them as *his*?

An older woman, her hair in a bun, crossed the street.

"Long day?" Mac asked

Mom managed a weary smile. "Every bed full. Must be running a sale."

As she changed from her uniform to a housedress, Mac set the table. Toward the end of supper, she asked, "As the kids say, what's eating you?"

"We—" He corrected himself. "The Central girls got thrashed."

"What went wrong?"

He lifted a shoulder. "Nothing went right."

"Does Mr. Montgomery Ward's care if the team loses?" Mom passed him the cookie jar. "Will he find out, far away in his Chicago office?"

"Probably not." Mac picked out an oatmeal cookie. "Probably wouldn't care if we—er, they win either."

She refilled his milk glass. "When you're a store manager, you'll be supervising young women. Take this as an opportunity to practice giving instructions, correcting mistakes, setting a respectful tone." Her chapped hand patted his cheek. "Be brave and don't let it worry you so much."

Why worry? The team may not matter to Montgomery Ward's, but it did matter to one enthusiastic running center with light-brown curls.

———

"I'm home!" Corrie dropped her schoolbooks and coat in the foyer.

Light glowed from the living room. The floral wallpaper, velvet davenports, and heavy drapes were gone, replaced by lemon-yellow moiré wallpaper, pale-green loveseats, and sheer drapes. The painting over the mantelpiece, of Mother as a Gibson Girl, had been replaced by a mirror reaching to the ceiling. Mother had redecorated *again*. For this she'd missed her daughter's induction into the National Honor Society and the annual senior play. Corrie blew out a breath. If she ever had children—hopefully with Mac—she'd show up for them.

The hall tree held the day's mail: *Collier's*, *McCall's*, three more wedding invitations from her brothers' friends, and—eureka!—the latest *Flying Aces*. "Who wants to teach me a three-man defense?"

"Like to teach you pick up after yourself, little one." Mrs. Zukas peeked out of the kitchen, unleashing a zephyr of roast beef and pineapple upside-down cake. She wore a flowered dress instead of the maid's uniform Mother thought their housekeeper ought to wear. Mother must be out.

"Yes, ma'am." With a wink, Corrie grabbed her belongings. "Can you teach me three-man defense?"

Mrs. Zukas narrowed her eyes, but her mouth twitched with a barely suppressed smile. "But of course."

"Where's the boys?"

"Is it my job to keep track of them?"

"Like no one else in the whole world can." Corrie grinned.

"Upstairs, downstairs, and out in the barn."

"And Mother?" Who could spoil any plan of Corrie's with a single raised eyebrow. "No, let me guess. Library committee? Playing bridge? Women's Relief Corps?"

"Golfing at the country club with your papa. Back in half an hour."

"Meet you under the hoop in two shakes." Corrie dashed to her room and tossed her books on her bed. They promptly slid to the floor. Mother had replaced her nubby white bedspread with a pink satin one. Applesauce. She raced across the hall. "Artie? Arthur?"

Her next oldest brother sat up in bed, stuffing the latest issue of *True Detective* under his pillow. "Pipe down, little one. I'm right here."

Little one? She was only an inch shorter than Artie. But now, when she needed his help, wasn't the time to remind him. "Put on your sneakers. I've got to learn a three-man defense before tomorrow morning."

Artie glanced out at the setting sun. "We'd better get moving."

They found Ernie in his basement workshop, tinkering with a silver necklace. He'd wired six old lamps to light his jewelry bench.

"Oooh, I love this shade of blue." Corrie picked up a gemstone from its box. "Is it a sapphire?"

"Nope, it's a black diamond." He gave the stone a second glance. "Looks more blue at the moment. Thought I'd try it in this choker."

"How about a basketball break?"

He rubbed the back of his neck. "Absolutely."

Harry had escaped from his Union Pacific office early and taken advantage of the spring sunshine to polish the Pierce Arrow. As they pushed it back into the barn, Corrie popped behind the wheel to steer. "Think Dad will let me drive to church Sunday?"

"Not if Mother has anything to say about it."

"Maybe if you're ready on time, little one."

"Pick her some flowers." Ernie pointed to the pansies lining the driveway.

"Nope, the gardener planted those last week." Harry wiped the handprints off the fenders. "Besides, it's my turn."

Corrie grabbed the ball, dribbled for the hoop, and sank her shot. If only Mac could see her now. "It's your turn to make me an expert in three-man defense!"

"No, that's my job." Mrs. Zukas caught the rebound with a grin. "*Paskubek!* Gather around, and I will teach you the secrets of defense."

————

"Come on," Mac urged his Model T as it struggled up the hill and around the construction zone for the art museum, to the imposing edifice of Central High. "You're as good as any big six in the lot." A gleaming Pierce Arrow sat next to the entrance. Who could afford that? Mac backed into a spot so he could roll his jalopy down the hill to Ward's when practice ended. He pulled his whistle over his head, grabbed his clipboard, and hurried to the gym.

An older woman and three fellows stood on center court surrounding Corrie. Of course she collected boys like nobody's business. And right now his business was to coach her.

Corrie spotted him and burst into a sunny smile. "Mac. My brothers came to help us out this morning."

"Your ..." Whew. "... brothers."

Corrie introduced Harry, Ernie, and Artie. "And this is Mrs. Zukas. She played basketball in Lithuania and taught us."

"McFarland? Any relation to the senator?" Harry asked.

"The minister at Dundee Methodist?" Ernie asked.

"The guy on the north side whose wife divorced him for buying too many cars?" Artie asked.

"No, yes, and no," Mac answered.

Close up, Mac could tell they were too old for high school. And too well dressed. They sported custom suits, silk ties, and polished shoes. The Pierce Arrow had to belong to them. Their handshakes were firm, teeth straight, posture confident.

"Handsome, elegant, princely." Thelma heralded the arrival of the rest of the team.

Mrs. Zukas clapped. "And now, three-man defense." She took over so quickly, Mac wondered why she hadn't gotten the coaching job. And how had Corrie made friends with a Lithuanian basketball player?

"We'll walk through it first," Mrs. Zukas said.

"Who knew Corny Corrie had such delicious brothers?" Evelyn fluttered her eyelashes.

Jackie tugged Artie's tie as she passed. "Whatcha doing later, Daddy?"

Mac blew his whistle. What else could he do with a girl like that? Mrs. Zukas talked them through the drill as Corrie held the ball. At first the brothers let her keep the ball, but on the third run-through, Artie grabbed it, ran, and sent it swishing through the net.

"He ran the full court." Halleen stomped her foot.

"He's playing boys' rules because he is a boy." Jackie looked him up and down, then grinned. "A mighty spiffy boy."

Artie chased his rebound.

"If you do not want him to get points, do not let him have the ball," Mrs. Zukas said.

Ernie pulled out his handkerchief, and a chain clattered to the floor.

"What's that?" The girls gathered around, practice forgotten.

"A necklace I've been working on." Ernie scooped it up.

"Ernie works in Father's jewelry store." Corrie pointed to the gemstone. "The diamond lost its sparkle."

"That's a diamond?" Jackie squinted. "It looks like an onyx."

"It needs a different setting." Ernie stuffed it into his pocket then gave Mac an apologetic look. "Back to practice."

The brothers ran the drill with his team on offense. The girls seemed more intent on flirting than playing.

"Keep your eyes on the ball!" Mac shouted.

Something blue streaked onto the court, swept the ball from Ernie's grasp, and sent it through the net with a swish. "And that's how it's done."

The group stared, open-mouthed, at the short woman in a hospital laundry uniform.

Corrie recovered the quickest. "Who are you? And will you teach us how to do whatever you just did?"

Mac cleared his throat, rattled by a jumble of pride and embarrassment. "This is Mrs. McFarland, my mom. She played basketball for Central ..."

"A while back," Mom finished. "I taught Mac how to play."

Corrie made introductions. "We'd love for you to teach us."

"This is the only time I can get off work, so pay attention." Mom reviewed a few basic principles of ball control and footwork. "You can't grow taller than the other team, but you can play smarter."

Six girls and Mom held their own against Corrie's brothers and Mrs. Zukas. Mom scored the most baskets.

The early bell rang.

"Off to work," Harry said. His brothers nodded and put on their suit coats. None of them had broken a sweat, but Mac had soaked through his shirt while standing in place. "Can we give you a ride, Mrs. McFarland?"

"No need. It's only a few blocks downhill, Twenty-First and Howard. I work at Clarkson."

"Perfect," Artie said. "It's on our way. I'm at Mutual, Ernie's at the jewelry store, and Harry's at Union Pacific."

Mrs. Zukas linked arms with Mom. "You will come with us."

"Do you have room for me?"

The door shut on their laughter.

Mac glanced at the clock. "Three-minute game. Corrie, Thelma, and Halleen versus Jackie, Evelyn, and Ruth. Where's Mary Frances?"

Their other forward raced in. "Sorry. Novena."

As excuses went, it wasn't the worst. "You're on Ruth's side." Before an argument burst out, Mac tossed the ball in the air. Corrie caught it and passed to Halleen, who promptly handed it off to Evelyn. Mac blew his whistle. "Pass to someone on your own team."

"How am I supposed to remember?"

Boys would take their shirts off or turn them inside out. Mac swallowed. Not an option with girls. Mac restarted the game. Evelyn blocked two of Corrie's shots, but Corrie sank three on rebounds. Mary Frances missed. And missed again. And again. Her prayers must have been about something other than basketball.

The hall door banged open. "Ho—" Miss Klemfuss started to yell his name, wiping out the last particle of respect the team might have for him, but fortunately the second bell rang. The team raced for the restroom, leaving him alone with the school secretary.

Cowards.

She charged across the gym floor, finger pointing, neck quivering. She would have raised her chin if she had one. "I know all about it. I know what you're doing down here. Corrupting our girls with all those men. And that fancy car."

"And my mother."

"And your—" Her eyes narrowed. "What?"

"Mom, a team member's brothers, and a Lithuanian basketball player."

The pointer finger lowered. The outside corner of her left eyebrow twitched, and her mouth pursed as she revised her attack. "Is that so?"

Mac fought to keep his expression neutral. He'd graduated. What could she do to him? Other than her usual hanged, drawn, and quartered. She gave a dismissive shake of her head. "And what's this about you and Central's girls in the same car?"

"I drove the team to and from the basketball game with Benson. We'd be glad to take a school bus if you'd–"

"First of all"—her stubby finger jabbed—"I've been against this from the beginning. Intramural games provide sufficient exercise. Competing against other schools causes girls to become overly excited."

"They seemed restrained after the loss."

"Don't you sass me, Horatio. Second, the budget doesn't allow for the extravagance of a school bus. You may drive the team, the whole team. But don't let me catch you alone with just one girl. I know all about what you degenerates do in cars." Her scowl deepened. She stepped close enough to poke his chest. "No dating, no dancing, no drinking. Understood?"

"Yes, ma'am." Foul breath and fear had his eyes watering.

"If even one of those girls misses class Friday for that senior-sneak-day nonsense, I will make them all stay after school next week, and I will ban them from any further outside activities. Playing hooky means no playing basketball." Jab. "Am." Jab. "I." Jab. "Clear?" Jab.

"Yes, ma'am. Excuse me. I have to go to work." Mac scooted around Klemfuss, raced down the steps, hopped in his car, and rolled down the hill to Ward's. No old bats in the alley where he parked. Whew. He checked under his shirt for bruises. None on the outside.

His heart ached though. Of course, no dating. He knew that. But a great girl like Corrie would be going steady or engaged by graduation.

CHAPTER
FIVE

THE GIRLS SQUEEZED into the restroom on the landing to change.

"Nifty having help this morning." Halleen wadded up her gym uniform.

"And how," Evelyn said. "Mrs. Zukas and Mrs. McFarland have the moves."

"I told those fellows I'd show them a night on the town." Jackie sashayed across the tile floor. "They'd never stick a girl with the tab."

"You'd date all three at the same time?" Mary Frances wet the ends of her hair, trying to make a Clara Bow curl on her cheek.

"Together or one at a time." Jackie shimmied. "Fun either way."

"Gold digger," Thelma hissed. "Pushover. Vamp."

Jackie hip-bumped her. "I believe the *Register* needs a thesaurus."

Evelyn frowned in the mirror and pushed down on her hair. "Wish my perm looked better. We could double date."

"Or triple date." Ruth kicked off her sneakers. "I'd like a ride in their Pierce Arrow."

"Let me tell you all their bad habits." Corrie inched the door open and listened to the tirade from the gym. "What's Klemfuss's beef with Mac?"

"Probably her beef with everyone—he's breathing." Jackie lit a cigarette.

"Put that out before Klemfuss smells it." Mary Frances pressed her palm under the faucet and sprayed her teammate.

"Nuns aren't supposed to hose sinners."

"Like I want detention from now until I enter the convent."

"Jesus spit on people." Ruth bandaged Thelma's blister.

"Never heard that in Sunday school." Jackie blew a smoke ring.

Mary Frances fanned the air with her shorts. "As if you ever went."

Halleen peered over Corrie's shoulder. "She's giving him an earful."

Tirade complete, Mac dashed down the steps. Corrie closed the door, hoping the school secretary wouldn't smell the smoke. Klemfuss's screech rang in the stairwell as she mounted her broomstick and cackled all the way down to the office.

Corrie slumped against the wall. "Two months until graduation."

"What's got you all balled up, Miss Cheery-Face?" Jackie stubbed out her ciggy.

"No dating." Halleen tied her shoes. "Klemfuss closed the bank."

"And your fellow's one of those rule-following types." Jackie smoothed her plucked eyebrows, then struck a pose worthy of *Photoplay*. "Perfect match for Goody Two-Shoes, except for sitting by herself at the movies."

"But he's not my fellow, and that's the problem." Not even Mother's latest shopping success, a sky-blue sweater and skirt set from Brandeis, perked her up. "I'm nothing but some kid who plays basketball." Same as home, where her family always saw her as the incompetent baby.

Jackie gave her a slow smile. "Play your cards right and he'll be wrapped around your finger by graduation."

"I'll help," Ruth and Halleen chimed in.

Corrie bit her lip. "I'm no sheba."

"You could be." Jackie wiggled her little finger.

"Okay." Corrie nodded. "What do you have in mind?"

———

"You jughead!" The boss's yelling echoed as Mac entered Montgomery Ward's through the alley. "How many times do I have to tell you?"

"Good morning, gentlemen." Mac stuck his head into the office.

The boss pounded his cigar into the ashtray. Clarence, the night man, grabbed his mop and escaped.

"Mac." The boss's scowl twisted into a smile. "How'd the game go?"

"Hope Chicago isn't expecting a winning season."

"Only a good deed."

"Say, Mac." The boss motioned him closer to the desk. "Investing yet? Got your share of Wall Street?"

Sweat popped out beneath Mac's collar. "That March episode—"

"An adjustment. Smart fellows buy in when the market hiccups like that." He made a grabbing motion, as if the money hung in the air, ripe for the taking. "Jump in with both feet. You'll be sorry if you miss this opportunity. Don't worry about money. Headquarters is expanding from two hundred thirty stores to fifteen hundred by the end of 1930. You'll have your own store, bet on that." The boss gave a firm nod.

"I'm saving for a new car."

"Old one still won't start when the engine's hot?" The boss waved a fat hand. "Time the market right and swap your Ford for a Packard. Surprise the girls with a touring car."

"Yessir. It would certainly be less crowded." And it'd be nice to get an attaboy instead of griping from the team. Although … he liked having Corrie next to him on the seat.

"Speaking of cars, you're in automotive today."

Uh-oh. "Ed's wife sick again?"

"Had to let him go." The boss banged a stack of time cards on the desk. "Missed too many days work. Wasn't pulling his own weight. Montgomery Ward's is a business, not a charity. Got an ad in tonight's newspaper."

"Okay." Gut churning, Mac headed for the sales floor. How would Ed feed all his kids without a job? The thick stench of rubber tires didn't do anything for Mac's stomach either.

Yes, Ward's was a business. But managers shouldn't be despots. When Mac had his own store, he'd run things differently.

———

"We play Tech tomorrow, so let's scrimmage," Mac said.

"Scrimmage?" Mary Frances asked. "What's that?"

"A practice game. Let's go through the three-man—"

"Three-girl," Ruth said. "We're girls."

As if he could forget. "All right. Three-girl. Where's the rest?"

"Thelma went on a choir trip to Nebraska City," Corrie said. "Halleen has to stay with her brothers while her mom takes the baby to the doctor, and Evelyn's not feeling well, but she'll be fine tomorrow."

Fine tomorrow? He didn't want to know. "So how–"

Jackie jabbed her thumb at Ruth and Mary Frances. "We'll play defense. You and Corrie will be offense."

"No fair–" Ruth started, but Jackie stopped her complaint by shooting daggers from her eyeballs.

Corrie grabbed the ball and sank it before he could think of another solution. "Two points!" She fired the rebound at Mac.

He caught the ball and dribbled in for his shot, only to find Jackie in the way.

"Mac!" Graceful arms waved under the basket. He passed and Corrie landed it. Mrs. Zukas had taught her well. Mom had said the older woman was the Tinleys' housekeeper.

"Defense!" He seized the rebound and passed to Corrie. Long legs brought her to the top of the key in seconds. She bounce-passed to him, and he made another basket.

Corrie played like a boy, taking chances, moving fearlessly, dribbling low, jumping high. But she was all girl. She carried herself like a dancer, balancing lightly on her toes, twirling her turns, and curving her arms. He could watch her all day.

Her sparkling eyes met his and time stopped. This girl, this amazing girl, looked at him and called his name. How did that happen?

The others ganged up on her. Mac ran in close, and she handed it off. He made the layup.

"Now we're cooking!" Corrie patted his arm as she ran for the rebound.

Mac grinned, feeling like a million bucks. Energy hummed through him. He could run and sink baskets all day long with Corrie by his side. He hadn't felt this good since ...

... Since before Henry crashed.

The ball left his hand and dropped, missing the net, rim, and backboard. The three on defense hooted, but Corrie said "Next time" as she dribbled past.

Eyes on the ball. Mac's next shot swished through the net as if it'd been greased. But his focus stayed on Corrie—her grin when he made a basket, the sparkle in her eyes as she passed to him, the way the corner of her lips tucked in when she shot. They conquered the defense, building up points. The rest of the team dimmed, until only Corrie—

The early bell sounded.

The girls headed to the restroom, fussing about Tech, needing a nap, needing a shower.

Corrie paused in the doorway. She glanced back, her head tipped and her neck long. "Good game, Mac," she said, her voice soft and low. With a flicker of long eyelashes, she winked, then followed her team.

The floor hummed, vibrating up his legs and through his heart.

He could fall for a girl like Corrie!

———

The final buzzer sounded on another defeat. Their team shook hands with Tech's girls, then raced off the court.

"Quick, Corrie. Change clothes."

"No, do her makeup first."

"I brought a towel."

Tech's captain propped an elbow on their fancy metal lockers. "What are you girls cooking up?"

"Nothing," Ruth said. "Need a bandage?"

"Beat it." Jackie blocked the captain.

"In case you don't know, this is our locker room." The rest of their team clustered around the captain.

"And a lovely locker room it is. Wish we had one." Corrie had to settle this before a fight broke out. She squeezed around Jackie and whispered to the Tech girls, "They're trying to help me get dolled up so I can attract a certain sheik."

The captain studied her. "Yeah? Let's see. Such a crowd to pick from. Could it be the one with glasses or the one with the mustache?"

"None of your beeswax," Halleen said.

Mary Frances pointed at Corrie. "Those are her brothers."

Jackie raised her nose. "At least we got someone other than our moms to show up."

The team captain crossed her arms. "You've got a crush on your coach."

Plucked eyebrows raised all around.

"Yeah, Mr. Average. No accounting for some girls' taste, is there?" Jackie pulled Corrie to the mirror where Evelyn.

"I like the way his hair curls around his ears," Corrie said as Halleen helped her out of her uniform.

"He needs a haircut," advised a Tech player.

"No haircut before I run my fingers through those curls." Corrie perched on the stool.

"Part her hair lower on the side," suggested another Tech player. "So her bangs dip over one eye."

Evelyn applied powder and rouge. Ruth drew a dark line around her eyes, then added two coats of mascara. Halleen painted her lips into a deep-red bow. And the other team gave advice.

"Ready for Hollywood," Tech's captain pronounced.

Hollywood? All she wanted was Mac. "Seems like a bit … much?"

"Not yet." Jackie held up a vase-shaped bottle of golden liquid.

"Shalimar?" Halleen recognized it. "Where ever did—"

"My dates have dough." Jackie dabbed the scent behind Corrie's ears and on her wrists.

"Unfasten your top button and do this." Mary Frances leaned forward and squeezed her elbows together.

"Nuns aren't supposed to know about sex appeal," Corrie said.

"I go to the movies." Their future novitiate fluffed her hair. "Don't forget to play with your curls, flutter your eyelashes, and smile a lot."

"And flatter him. Lots of compliments."

"Girls. What's taking so long?" yelled a Tech mom from the doorway.

"Gotta go." Corrie peeked at the mirror again. Who was that flapper?

Jackie steered her out the door. "Mac will never know what hit him."

Which was exactly what Corrie was worried about.

———

Mac sat on the running board of his jalopy and glanced at his watch again. What did girls do in the locker room? If his little sister had lived, he might have some idea, but instead all he had was Mr. Smooth, a leading man without effort. And Mom—but she barely took a moment, always hurrying between work and home.

Central had lost again, 17 to 13. But they'd remembered the three-girl defense. If they could break their habit of calling their shots—

"Where'd our cheerleaders go?" Evelyn's voice carried across the lot.

"Back to work," Corrie said.

"Nifty having someone rooting for us."

"And how."

The girls piled in. Over the oil and gasoline mix of the car, over the smell of soap, rode a different scent. It wasn't the powdered roses perfume favored by his customers. It was more exotic, spicy—

Jackie leaned around Corrie. "We going to sit here all day? Let's go get some ice cream."

Mac stuck his head out the window, gulped in non-scented air, and fired up the car. The engine ran like a three-legged horse. "Where to?"

"Blake's."

"Myer Dillon's."

"Liggett's."

"Beaton's it is." Mac picked the drug store on the way back to school. "We handled the ball better this week. Next week, when we play–" He peeked under the brim of Corrie's cloche and almost ran off the road. Makeup?

"South High," pronounced bowed and reddened lips.

"You passed Beaton's," chorused the back seat. "There's a spot."

Mac made a U-turn in the middle of traffic. His face heated, probably as red as Corrie's lips. *Stop!* No thinking about lips. Where was that bucket of ice water when he needed it? Where was—cue the doom music—Miss Klemfuss? If she caught Corrie in makeup, her mother would be called. Klemfuss wouldn't hang out in the drugstore, would she? Only if Beaton's sold eye of newt.

He followed the girls to the soda fountain to a storm of whispering and giggling. Even the girl behind the counter got pulled into the action.

Mac joined the line behind Corrie, where he couldn't see her lips. "What's going on?"

"Uh, school stuff." Corrie exchanged glances with Jackie, then she tipped her head back and fluttered her Theda Bara eyelashes. "I mean, what do you think is going on?"

"I never know." He kept his gaze on the menu board.

"Oh, I'm guessing you know plenty." She leaned closer, enveloping him in the scent of magic carpets and domed temples, of Egypt and Nefertiti. He was Douglas Fairbanks in *The Thief of Bagdad*: athletic, clever, and worthy of a princess. Her voice lowered to a purr. "I'm guessing you know how to make a girl look real good on a dance floor." She extended her arms, her bare arms, and shimmied side to side.

Mac couldn't move, couldn't breathe, couldn't think. Fortunately, the counter girl asked Corrie for her order, and she turned back into her normal self. The team took their cones to the long corner table. With more giggling and whispering, they changed seats as if they were playing musical chairs. Mac sat across from Corrie.

"When we play South High ..." Mac looked everywhere except at Corrie. "We'll continue the three-girl defense, but not call out our moves."

"A girl's got to keep some secrets." Corrie's tongue slid out from those lips and swept up her ice cream.

Mac propped the clipboard in front of him and reviewed the game. "Swell shot from midcourt, Thelma. Nice shot from under the basket, Mary Frances. Good taking control of the ball, Jackie."

"Call it like it is—stealing." Jackie grabbed the clipboard. "And how many jump shots did our captain make?"

Corrie leaned on the table, causing some funny business with the top of her blouse.

"Two?" Mac closed his eyes, but he couldn't erase the skin and curves he'd seen. "No it was more. Sex, uh six." His face caught fire. Giggles flared into whoops of laughter, hopefully keeping the other customers from hearing his slip. "If Klemfuss doesn't kill me, your parents should."

"We'll defend you," the team agreed. "Three-girl defense at your service."

"I'll wait in the car."

The team straggled out a few minutes later, and Mac drove them back to Central without further disgrace. The girls headed inside, Evelyn and Ruth to French Club, Thelma to edit the *Register*, Mary

Frances to Big Sisters, and Jackie to the theater to work on the set for *The Queen's Husband*. Corrie stayed on the seat beside him. She twisted her fingers together.

"Are you wearing greasepaint for the show?" Mac kept his hands on the steering wheel. He'd turn off the car and jump out if he thought there was half a chance it would start again.

"No, it's not for the show."

"You've got to go before Klemfuss–"

"I heard what she said to you. No dating." She slid out but held onto the door. "That's why the girls taught me to vamp."

Did she mean … Could she think … No, impossible. Mac blinked and heaved in another breath, hoping to clear enough perfume from his head so he could think clearly. "I appreciate the effort, but I've always thought you were waterproof." He used slang for a face that didn't need cosmetics. He should stop before he dug himself in any deeper. "It's not necessary."

Heavy eyelashes blinked. The red mouth curved as she caught his drift. "Until graduation then."

CHAPTER
SIX

CORRIE BOLTED from Mac's car and raced for the school entrance. The expression on his face had been nothing less than disgust. He wouldn't even look at her. Forget dating—he never wanted to see her again.

Jackie grabbed her arm. "Well?"

Corrie shook her head, unable to talk over the basketball-sized lump in her throat.

"Klemfuss has him running scared." Jackie dragged her down the lawn. "Well, no sense letting all our makeup go to waste. Let's blow."

"Aren't you working on the play?"

She huffed. "Those stuffed shirts wouldn't give me a role. All they let me do was paint sets. Finished last week."

"I've got Honor Society–"

"Seniors are supposed to be unreliable. Helps the juniors take charge." She pointed to the yellow trolley cresting the hill. "Race you."

Basketball practice had given them good speed. They dashed across Dodge Street, earning a "Great gams!" from a guy in a sweet little roadster, and jumped onto the streetcar.

"I'm starving," Corrie announced. Mother wasn't there to tell her a lady never referred to her body. She dug through her purse and found a nickel. "Let's stop by Harry's office, see if he'll buy us a hamburger."

Jackie snorted. "Someone's buying dinner and it's not your brother."

A flash in the sky caught her attention. "Look, there's an airplane. Let's go to the airport."

"No streetcar. Nothing to eat there." A block past the Orpheum, Jackie nudged her out of the seat and they jumped off. "Gonna catch some fun."

Corrie followed her down an alley and into a storefront with a pool table and a Coca-Cola cooler. A kid idly pushed the balls with his cue. Was this a pool hall? Mother had warned her brothers about pool halls, but Corrie didn't see why. Nothing happening here. Nothing to eat either.

"Hey, Barley. This is my friend Corrie."

"Hey, Jackie. You're the first girls tonight." The boy reached under the pool table. "Potatoes."

Potatoes? Where? asked Corrie's stomach.

Jackie pointed her to the telephone on the wall. "Tell your mom you're staying with me tonight. Working on your music appreciation homework."

"I'm not taking music appreciation."

"You are now."

Artie answered, saving Corrie from having to lie to Mother or Mrs. Zukas. She whispered, "I'm visiting a pool hall with Jackie."

Artie hooted. "Who's this? Can't be my sister, Miss Goody Two-Shoes."

"I'll be home in the morning."

"Mother and Father won't be back from Kansas City until Sunday, so go ahead, but don't take any wooden nickels."

Corrie followed Jackie down a dark hall. "There's no food here."

Jackie knocked on a door.

A rectangle opened to the hardest eyes she'd ever seen. "Yeah?"

"Potatoes."

The door opened to a hall lit by a bare bulb. The hard eyes belonged to a fellow twice as muscular as any football player on Central's team. He let them through, then returned to his chair and detective magazine.

Corrie dogged Jackie along a hall, around a corner, and down a flight of steps to a damp hall. "It smells nasty like–"

"Stop acting like a baby, will you?"

The next door slid open to a room with paneled woodwork, carpet, and lamps hanging in a smoky haze. A counter ran along one end in front of a small kitchen. A saxophone player warmed up in the opposite corner. A half dozen men looked up from their tables. None looked familiar.

The nearest raised his glass. "Jackie's here. Start the party."

The rest of the men—older fellows in their thirties and on up—cheered. One took a seat behind the trap set, and another picked up a clarinet. They played "Hitch Up the Horses." Jackie was right—the music was good.

"Is this a speakeasy? A juice joint?" What would Mac think? What if they were raided? What if she was arrested? Good thing Harry had friends at the courthouse; he knew how to deal with trouble.

"Don't be a flat tire," Jackie said over her shoulder, then kissed the cheek of the man who toasted her. "John. It's been too long."

"What'll you have?" The fellow went to the counter.

"A couple hamburgers. I'll have a gin rickey, and my friend …" Jackie sent her a glance, but Corrie couldn't think of a single drink at the moment. "… will have a bee's knees."

The drink tasted like a pine tree dunked in orange juice. She set the glass on the bar.

"How about a dance?" A fellow drew her onto the floor. He had a touch of gray at his temples, but his build was trim and he knew his Charleston. She'd partnered with men she didn't know at the country club, friends of her brothers. This stranger had no connection to her family—how daring!

Jackie and her fellow joined them on the floor. The band finished "The Brush Stomp" then started a slower song. The man reached for her, and she stepped back. "My hamburger's probably ready."

"Sure, doll. I'll buy you a hamburger."

"I've got—" She reached into her purse.

"Didn't Jackie tell you? Your money's no good here." The man guided her with a touch to her back as he retrieved her drink and food, set some money on the counter, then steered her to a table. She felt like quite the lady, with all his attention.

Seeing as how he was kind enough to buy her a hamburger, Corrie figured she should introduce herself. She stuck out her hand. "I'm Corrie–"

He pressed a pine-scented finger to her lips. "No last names."

"Oh, of course." He must think she was a nitwit.

"Call me John."

"Sure." Was every man in this joint was named John? She couldn't ask the usual questions, like where he worked or who his family was. "So have you ever been up in an airplane?"

He laughed and leaned back in his seat. "My, aren't you a gutsy doll. No, I haven't. Have you?"

"Twice. I rode in a Jenny when I was a kid." Her stomach growled. Corrie bit into her hamburger and burned her mouth. She reached for her drink and took a gulp. Her tongue cooled, but the bitterness increased with every swallow. She wiped her mouth, leaving a lipstick print on the paper napkin. A paper napkin— Mother would be scandalized. Now, what were they talking about? Oh, airplanes! "Last summer I rode in a Standard with a one-eighty horsepower Hispano-Suiza engine, like Lindbergh flew."

"Don't suppose Lindbergh was your pilot."

"No, he was flying the Caribbean and Central America. And taking the *Spirit of St. Louis* to the Smithsonian." What fun. Mother never let her rattle on about airplanes.

John slid her glass closer. "So where'd you go on your flight?"

"Up the Missouri. You could see all the way to Fort Calhoun. It was so beautiful." The hamburger was awfully dry. Corrie took another gulp of her drink. Worse with every swallow. She should have ordered a ginger ale. "The pilot did a wingover."

"A wingover? You went upside down?"

"Oh no. You do a steep climb, then turn and dive." She demonstrated with her hand, another behavior Mother frowned on. What would Jackie say? Corrie turned toward the dance floor, but the room tilted. She grabbed the table. Where was Jackie? Her friend had been dancing, but the girl on the dance floor was blond. "Where did my friend go?"

"Don't worry. She's having fun." John waved to the bartender. "Let me buy you another drink."

"No, thank you." Corrie blinked, trying to bring the room into focus. "I need to find Jackie." *Concentrate. That's a man. Another man. Man.* Where was she? There, getting her cigarette lit by— Applesauce! That's Tom Dennison. Boss Dennison was the big cheese in Omaha, known for gangsters, gambling, bootlegging, murder, and prostitution. Prostitution? Jackie could be sold into white slavery. Corrie had to get her out of here.

John handed her another drink. "Try this. You didn't seem overly fond of the first one." He sang to the band's "Yes Sir, That's My Baby."

"No, I need to–"

"I'll ask the band to play 'Charlie Is My Darling' in honor of Lindbergh and we'll dance."

"Thanks, but I got to …" What did she have to do? Something important. Why couldn't she think? Oh yes, save Jackie. Corrie stood. The room swayed. She sank back to the chair. Lying down seemed like a good idea. But not here. Not with Boss Dennison hanging around. Need to get home. But how? She couldn't walk. Her tummy hurt.

"Don't worry, my vamp." John's cold fingers slid up her arm. "I'll take good care of you."

———

The telephone rang as Mac tuned the RCA Radiola. "I'll get it," he said so Mom could keep her feet up as she listened to Montgomery Ward's Riverside Hour. He hurried into the hall and answered.

"Is this Mac?" The voice cracked. "This is a friend of Jackie's. You gotta come get her and Corrie. Now."

"What's wrong? Who is this?"

"Don't matter." The kid fired off directions, then hung up.

Mom put down the sock she'd been darning. "Montgomery Ward's alarm go off again?"

If he told her where he was going, she'd worry. But if he didn't tell her, she'd worry more. So he told her.

"Down there?" Her eyes widened. "Is someone trying to frame you, make you a fall guy?"

"My mom the detective." Mac swapped his slippers for shoes. He didn't have any enemies, except Klemfuss, and this wasn't her style.

Mom tipped her head toward the radio. "The St. Valentine's Day massacre hitmen are still on the loose."

Rumors about Al Capone blew through town as often as thunderstorms. "If the girls are in trouble …"

Mom drummed her fingers on the arm of the chair. "Wouldn't Corrie call her brothers?"

He shrugged. Vanity had him hope she'd called him first. More likely, she hadn't been able to reach her brothers. Mac grabbed his jacket and headed for the door.

"I'll be praying for you. And for the girls."

"Appreciate it."

Clouds raced past the moon, tree branches whipped across street-lights, and last fall's leaves skittered on the pavement, as if the whole night was on edge. A handful of people hurried out of the Orpheum, but otherwise the city was empty. Mac found the laundry and turned in as the kid had directed. His feeble headlamps showed a narrow alley. No janitors on smoke breaks, no trash bins, no broken furniture. Almost as if it had been swept clean. Engine noise echoed off the brick buildings. He wouldn't hear the machine gun that took him down.

Be anxious for nothing. He wiped his hands on his slacks. *God, please make this nothing.*

A small figure peeked from a recessed doorway. Corrie and Jackie, followed, hanging on to each other. As he braked, Mac caught the stench of cigarettes, hooch, and perfume. The kid reached for the front door.

"Back seat," Mac told him. Wouldn't surprise him if Klemfuss had Boss Dennison under her thumb. "Sorry. Can't shut the car down."

He reached to help Jackie. Her foot missed and she tipped face first onto the seat, knocking off the fedora she'd been wearing over her cloche. "Mac, you are a sh-sh-sheik."

Corrie pushed her friend over, then climbed in. The carefully applied makeup had smeared—Mac should have brought her a wash-cloth. "Ab-show-lute-ly." In spite of the barfly smell, Mac wanted to grab Corrie and hug her. She was safe. She was alive.

"Beat it." The kid closed the door and slapped the rear fender.

Mac accelerated down the alley as fast as he dared, then turned onto Thirteenth Street. "Where to?" He glanced over his shoulder. They weren't being followed.

Jackie leaned against Corrie, eyes closed and mouth slack. Corrie blinked, her eyebrows pulling her lids open. No wonder inebriation was called "owled."

"Jackie's hush, hows, house." She rested her forehead on her arm. "Twenty-Sick, Stick, Six, and Joe, Joan, Jones? Can't talk."

"What did you have to drink?" Mac headed west. "Corrie. You've got to stay awake. Do you know Jackie's address? What her house looks like?"

"Apartment."

"Well, that narrows it down," Mac said, earning a giggle.

With a heave and a sigh, she pushed herself upright. Holding onto the seatback with both hands, she declared, "Why drink? Is... terrible."

"Are you going to be sick? I can pull over." Although in his jalopy, it wouldn't make much difference.

"No. I ... will ... not ... upchuck." Each word required extensive deliberation. "Fresh ... air ..."

"So want to tell me what happened?"

"No." But she did.

Brick duplexes lined Twenty-Sixth and Jones. "Which one?"

Corrie shook Jackie awake and repeated Mac's question.

Bleary eyes scanned the neighborhood. "Don't live here no more."

"Where?" Mac tried not to shout. "What's your address?"

"Twenty-Ninth and Mason." She promptly fell back asleep.

Mac headed south. After a few blocks, Corrie pointed to a two-story building with a well-lit porch. "There."

He stopped under the streetlight. "You could have been arrested or attacked, or somebody could have slipped you a Mickey."

"I know." A tear melted more of her makeup. She sniffed and he passed her his handkerchief. "I wanted ... an adventure."

Jackie pried open her eyes. "Yep, home sweet home. Mac, I take back everything I ever said about you." She clung to the light pole.

"Don't forget your fedora." Mac handed it to her.

"It's John's." Giggling, she lurched to the door.

"I'll drive you home," he told Corrie. Even Klemfuss would agree that she was better off with him than wandering the streets after dark.

"I'm staying with Jackie tonight." Corrie staggered to the sidewalk.

Mac leaned out the window. "Corrie, if you want an adventure, try something safe next time."

Her head tipped toward the sky. Mac tightened his grip on the controls. If she wobbled, he'd jump out and catch her—even if his flivver never started again. Corrie's mouth crooked in a half smile as she glanced back at him. The streetlight caught the fire in her gaze. "If it's safe ... how can it be an adventure?"

———

"Corrie." Jackie shook her shoulder. "You gotta get outta here."

"Boss Dennison?" Her tongue had dried up and her words come

out in a croak. Her eyes wouldn't open either. "He sold us into slavery?"

"What are you talking about?" Her friend sounded awfully awake.

Corrie's eyelids pried apart. Why was the room so bright? "We're in police custody?"

"No, you nitwit. My apartment. Remember, Mac drove us home last night."

Mac had been their hero. When his jalopy chugged down that alley, she'd wanted to cheer.

"You got drunk, and he turned into a sheik." Jackie laughed until she coughed. "Wish you smoked so I could bum a ciggy off you."

Jackie was out of cigarettes? Corrie hoisted herself upright with a groan. The swaybacked davenport hadn't done her body any favors. In the next apartment, a baby cried and a harsh voice screamed for quiet. The curtain fluttered, bringing in humidity and the stench of liver and onions. Her stomach did a loop-de-loop. Corrie raced to the bathroom.

The phantom of the opera's ugly sister stared back from the speckled mirror. Kohl and mascara deepened her eye sockets. Upholstery had embossed rouge into her left cheek. And her hair ... Corrie hoped she hadn't lost her hat. "Do you have any cold cream?"

Jackie handed her a dishcloth and a scrap of pumice soap, the kind her brothers used after working on the car. "Hot water's on the fritz."

Which meant no coffee. Ugh. The mug on the sink had a disreputable amount of scum, so Corrie cupped her hand and wet her tongue. Ah, better. The makeup went down the drain with the top layer of her skin. She shuffled to the living room.

Jackie stared out the window. "You gotta get outta here."

Corrie peered over her shoulder. No gangsters, only kids playing basketball in the street. "I'm going ... I'm going." Home where the coffee was hot, the sheets clean, and the air smelled of furniture polish.

"Get out of Omaha." Frightened eyes met hers. "Find your adventure."

"We nearly got bumped off last night."

Jackie shook her head. "After graduation."

"You're heading to Hollywood."

"Can't." Dark eyes puddled with tears. Jackie had been angry before, but she never cried. She held out an empty El Producto box.

"Your money?" The money she'd been saving since she was six years old. On New Year's Day, the stash had grown to over a hundred dollars.

Jackie nodded and pressed her fist to her mouth.

"Maybe it fell out. I'll help you look."

"Mom's latest con man, a big shot in the stock market, ran off with her dough." She dropped the box to the floor. "And mine."

"Maybe he'll bring it back."

"Yeah, and I'm Alice in Wonderland." Jackie slumped.

Corrie sat beside her. The cushions tilted, tipping them together. "What's his name? Maybe my brothers could find him–"

"Long gone. Believe me, I've asked around." Jackie poked Corrie's shin with her toes. "His name was John. Didn't you learn anything last night?"

"Plenty. Hope to never have another lesson like that." Corrie groaned and stretched. "Artie likes you. He'll loan you train fare, and you can pay it back when you hit it big. Or get a job here, work during the day, and act at the Playhouse at night."

"Corrie." Jackie grabbed her arm. "Your family has money. They don't run with crooks. You can do anything you want. Go have an adventure."

"But I haven't quite figured out what to do yet."

"You've been dreaming up crazy ideas since kindergarten." She waved her hand. "Pack up your car and go camping in Yellowstone."

"I don't have a car."

"Ask your dad." She huffed, starting another coughing fit. "Move to Polynesia and run around barefoot all year."

"But I like Omaha."

"You can visit. Join the circus and do bareback tricks on your pony."

"Where do you come up with these?"

"From you."

"Right now my idea of fun is going home and changing into clean clothes. Want to come?" she asked to be polite.

"Gotta work."

"You found a job already?"

"Taking tickets at the Muse. As close to Hollywood as I'll ever get."

"You'll get there. Someone will discover you." The Muse? Corrie would have cheered if her head didn't hurt. "That's the movie theater across the street from Ward's. I should get a job there, keep an eye on Mac."

Jackie plopped Corrie's hat on her head. The brim cut the glare, changing the pain in her head from an axe to a kitchen knife. "Horsefeathers. You haven't listened to a word I said."

"Yes, I have." She buckled her shoes. "I need a plan." The cat's meow of plans, something so daring, everyone would realize they'd been underestimating her. As soon as this buzzing in her head went away. No, wait. She leaned out the window. The buzzing came from a biplane circling the city. "That's it! I'll fly you to California!"

"Then you can fly in the movies." Jackie smiled. "You're the one who went out to Aksarben to watch the airplanes and got a ride."

"No one else had three dollars." The Jenny had smelled of leather, oil, and excitement. They had bounced across the grass and into the sky, so high that her brothers looked like ants.

"And rode in that other plane."

"Ernie took out a want ad in the *Omaha Bee* and got a ride." The Lincoln Standard was larger, holding four passengers. While her brothers pointed out landmarks on the ground, Corrie had studied the plane, watching the ailerons tilt the wings into the wind.

Corrie hugged Jackie, then headed out the door. "I'll get Artie to drive me down to the airport so I can start taking lessons."

Corrie hauled her sorry self to the streetcar stop and headed home.

Home? Something was wrong at Jackie's. Corrie leaned against the window of the trolley, closed her eyes, and tried to think. Every other time she'd spent the night, her mom had woken them up singing and dancing when she stumbled in after midnight. She'd left her shoes and stockings on the living room floor, draped her feathered headband on the doorknob, crowned the lamp with her necklace. But this morning, the apartment was empty, the kitchen cupboards as bare as Old Mother Hubbard's.

Jackie's mom had taken Jackie's money and run away, leaving her without enough for groceries or hot water. Corrie would talk to her brothers—they'd know how to help. She stumbled off the trolley and trudged home.

The housekeeper spotted her slogging up the driveway. "Good thing your mother's away."

"Good morning, Mrs. Zukas." Corrie shuffled through the kitchen, the black-and-white tile rippling under her feet. Bessie Smith sang

"T'ain't Nobody's Business if I Do" on the phonograph. Unfortunately Mrs. Zukas still considered Corrie her business and blocked her way. Corrie raised her right arm. "I promise never to do it again if you lower your voice."

"No deal." The housekeeper held up three slips of paper. "Some fellow named Blair Adams wants to take you to the Benson for *The Cameraman*. I told him you already saw that one, on account of Lindbergh being in it. Paul Wiemer asked you to *In Old Arizona* at The Circle, and John Rogers has *The Coquette* at the Paramount in mind."

Corrie shuddered. She never wanted to see anyone named John again, even if he was senior class president and the most popular guy in school.

"Wash up, then come eat."

She stuffed the slips into her pocket. "Thanks, but I'm not hungry."

The housekeeper crossed her arms in her don't-argue-with-me pose. "Start with toast and coffee, then follow with aspirin. *Paskubek*."

Corrie hauled herself up the stairs, regretting Mother's choice of a geometric-patterned carpet. She filled the tub and sank wishing she could rinse her memory as easily as she washed her body. Nasty men. She scrubbed the bar of Woodbury over her arm where "John" had touched her. She didn't want to be anybody's doll, especially his. She dumped half the bottle of Mulsified Coconut Oil shampoo on her head and sudsed furiously. Nasty cigarette smoke, stinking up her hair and making her eyes water. Nasty hooch, fogging her brain. Never again.

"C'mon out, prune." Artie called from the hallway. "I want to hear about your career as a pool shark."

"If you promise to take me to the airport."

"Deal," he growled. "Spill it."

"Didn't play a single game." She dried off and wrapped in her kimono, then raced for her bedroom. "Danced to some good jazz though."

Artie's eyes bugged out. "Where did Jackie take you?"

She closed her door, leaving him in the hall. "Somewhere beneath Thirteenth and Harney."

"Underground?" He gasped. "That's—"

"I know. Call me Carrie Nation. I've sworn off it. So don't tattle." She pulled on a pair of Artie's outgrown pants and an old middy blouse.

He slapped his palm on the wall, jiggling the picture frames where covers of *Popular Aviation* magazine replaced prints of Edgar Degas's ballet dancers. "Corrie. You could have been–"

She opened her door. "Yes, that's what Mac said."

"McFarland?" Artie jerked his chin. "He doesn't seem like a boozer."

"He's not. You weren't home last night, so I called Mac." Or rather the kid had, since Corrie couldn't make heads or tails out of the phone.

He scrubbed his palm against his forehead. "I worked late, Dad stuck Ernie with inventory, and Harry took Dorothy Jasperson to the movies."

"Say, about the movies and Jackie–"

Mrs. Zukas yelled up the stairs, "Lunch is on the table."

"Bend my ear while we eat." Artie put a hand on the newel-post. "Glad you lived to tell about it, little one."

Corrie grabbed her shoes. She paused at her dressing table and opened her scrapbook of heroes. Photos from movie magazines showed Ramon Navarro from *The Flying Fleet* and Richard Arlen and Buddy Rogers from *Wings*. Newspaper clippings heralded the Waco dropping a football at the University of Omaha's homecoming game last October, and Elinor Smith's and Bobby Trout's endurance records. Corrie ran her hand over an empty page.

This space reserved for Mac McFarland.

CHAPTER
SEVEN

MAC WATCHED the team climb into his jalopy. Corrie gave him a clear-eyed smile, radiant as always, no worse for her experience at the speakeasy. Jackie slumped against the far door, paler than usual. The three in the back, Thelma, Mary Frances, and Evelyn—

"Wait a minute. Where's Halleen and Ruth?"

"Halleen's sick and Ruth's taking care of her." Mary Frances didn't look up from her algebra homework.

"No sub." Mac frowned. "We'll have to forfeit."

"Mac." Corrie speared him with her straight-shooter gaze. "We're all suited up and ready. No one cares how badly we lose. Let's play."

Should he worry about the girls collapsing from nervous exhaustion, as the experts cautioned? Or let them play? He scanned the back seat, getting nods from Mary Frances and Evelyn.

"Absolutely, affirmative, agreed," Thelma said.

Jackie stared into space, but raised her thumb.

"I'd rather play than ask Miss Klemfuss to call North High." Mac slid onto driver's seat beside Corrie. Someday he hoped to snuggle and sing, "Side by Side." But today, with Klemfuss's x-ray vision always a threat, he kept his distance. Heading out, he launched into his pregame pep talk. "Don't wear yourself out right away. Save energy for the fourth quarter. Signal if you need a time-out. And we can always call the game—"

Corrie's gentle shoulder nudge left him wanting more. "Mac, we promise not to faint on you. We are the big six of girls' basketball."

"Big five. If we had six, we could rotate." He glanced over, wishing he wasn't driving so he could study her face up close, and caught her sassy grin. "Hit 'em with all your cylinders, no matter how many you've got."

They arrived as North's team of twelve ran a warm-up drill with military precision. All their players towered over Thelma, Central's tallest.

Corrie led the team onto the floor, whistling "Ain't We Got Fun."

"That all you got?" A North player snickered as they took positions for the tip-off.

"Hey, batter, batter, swing!" Corrie yelled.

The North players gawked at Corrie. The referee tossed the ball. Thelma jumped and hit it to Jackie, who sank it. All least it wouldn't be a shutout.

Corrie ran up and down the full court, long legs jumping and spinning, blocking a dozen shots. She kept up an endless patter. She sang "Where Oh Where Have My Little Points Gone" and the chorus of "Keep It on the Sunny Side." She told knock-knock jokes. Laughter didn't keep North from scoring. Seconds before halftime, Corrie seized the ball and handed off to Jackie for two more points.

In the third quarter, Corrie passed to Jackie again. The ball bounced off the hoop. Corrie jumped and pushed it through the net. In the fourth quarter, the tallest North player leaned back for a long shot. Corrie swatted it to Evelyn, who passed to Jackie, who scored again. Finally the buzzer sounded.

"That was the most fun." The North players gave them a round of applause. "You girls are lollapaloozas."

After a stop for ice cream, they headed for Central. Corrie conked out with her head on his shoulder, her arm against his. Soft curls brushed his neck. As far as his nose could tell, she hadn't broken a sweat. Even such a slight contact warmed him, made him want more. Mac wished he could wrap his arm around her, but he needed his right hand to work the accelerator. And of course Klemfuss would bump him off if he did anything so improper.

Evelyn shook her as they pulled into Central's parking lot. "Corrie, wake up. It's your brother."

Ernie sat on the school steps. The red ribbon on his panama hat matched his tie. Too bad he hadn't found them half an hour ago. The

Tinley brothers could afford sundaes for all. Mac parked and the girls jumped out.

"What's up?" Corrie plopped beside her sibling.

Ernie scanned the circle of females, then heaved a resigned sigh. "It'll be in the morning newspaper. We were robbed."

Corrie's face paled. "Was anyone hurt? Is Father all right?"

"No shots were fired." Ernie studied the tips of his oxfords, making Mac wonder what he wasn't saying. "They smashed the display cases, swept everything into a bag, then left."

"Law, cop, officer?"

"Yes, the police came, but it happened so fast, I couldn't give much of a description."

"My dad says Chicago is sending all their crooks here."

"My dad says it's all those foreigners, especially the Italians."

"Oh yeah? My dad says the bootleggers are branching out."

Ernie stood and pulled Corrie to her feet. "Well, your dad says he wants you home now. Mother's in a tizzy."

"Wait … they nabbed my black diamond, didn't they?" Corrie bit her lip and blinked back a tear. He passed her his handkerchief.

Corrie dried her eyes. "Not that the black diamond was mine, and of course I'm thankful you're okay, but …"

"There's others where that came from." They climbed into the Pierce Arrow and headed west on Dodge Street.

If Mac was a movie hero, he'd figure out some way to get Corrie's black diamond back.

"Got any dough?" Jackie put out her hand.

Mac handed over the change from their visit to the Palace Candy Kitchen and she took off for the streetcar stop. "Where are you going?"

"Don't even think about it, McFarland." She waved over her shoulder. "You'd be pumped full of lead before you could say Boss Dennison."

Jackie couldn't stop him, but the name of Omaha's crime boss could.

———

Headquarters had no idea the chaos unleashed by inventory. Mac's feet ached, his right hand cramped, and his shoulders burned. All he wanted was a few bites of leftover meatloaf and a soft pillow.

But instead of the usual single lamp in the living room, the entire house was lit. On the porch, girls danced to "Sweet and Hot." Beyond the streetlight's puddle, fellows passed a bottle. A couple canoodled in the rumble seat of a roadster. Any minute the police would pull up and haul them to the clink, and Mac could kiss his promotion goodbye.

"Hey, it's the baby brother, all growed up! Hiya, sweetheart." A blonde with kohl-rimmed eyes grabbed Mac. Her red lips planted a kiss on his cheek with a fog of gin and bitter perfume. "Where ya been, baby?"

Mac's brain turned over slowly. Her name was Dorothy, but she wanted to be called Dottie. "Where's Mr. Smooth?"

"You call your brother Mr. Smooth?" Dottie hooted and slapped the air as if the nickname was the funniest thing she'd ever heard, increasing Mac's estimate of the amount of hooch she'd consumed. "You are so funny. He says you're a bluenose, but you are very funny. Such a funny boy."

Deciding it would be faster to look for his brother than wait for Dottie to sober up, Mac took a step toward the house. The girl grabbed his arm. "Dance with me, baby. Nobody's danced with me all night. You can't leave a girl like me all alone."

Mac pried her fingers off. "I'll find my brother."

Rubbing lipstick from his cheek, Mac squeezed through the crowd into the house. The living room furniture had been pushed to the walls and the rug rolled up. A new phonograph sat on Mom's radio. Girls danced the Charleston, a cigarette in one hand, a drink in the other, spattering the wood floor. So much for sleep.

Mom stood at the stove frying hamburgers. Her hair had slipped halfway out of its bun. Grease stained her apron. "Guess who's home!" she yelled.

"Your college student. Where is he?"

Mom waved toward the backyard. "Isn't this a great party?"

"You worked all day. Aren't you tired?" Mac put his left, less sore hand on the back of her neck and rubbed. Stiff as a statue.

She shrugged. "We don't have much chance for fun."

"Hamburgers!" Some fellow took the full platter to the living room.

They'd go broke feeding these moochers. Armed with a flashlight, Mac stepped into the backyard. "I'll welcome him home."

The beam reflected off the octagonal lenses of a college man's eyeglasses. "Don't point that at me."

"I'm looking for my brother."

The fellow glanced at the garage. "Don't be a buttinski."

Mac yanked the light cord inside the garage and got an eyeful. Yipes. The poor Tin Lizzie would never be the same.

Mr. Smooth looked up from his sheba of the moment. "It's the kid."

"Beat it," Mac told the girl, who scrambled to straighten her dress. "Dottie's looking for you," he said while she was still in earshot.

Mr. Smooth sprawled on the back seat. "College will loosen you up."

"Yeah, look where it's gotten you." As if Mom could afford more tuition. Besides, Mac had plans involving Corrie as soon as she graduated. He aimed the flashlight at his brother's eyes. Mr. Smooth had an edge, but he hadn't reached the fully lit stage yet. "It's almost midnight."

"Party time. How about that great phonograph I brought home."

"You're not on campus anymore. This is Mom's neighborhood."

"She's not complaining."

"And she won't, until the cops haul us all off."

"They won't." Mr. Smooth grinned and jabbed his thumb at his chest. "You're looking at the newest member of the Permits Department."

Mac slumped on the doorframe. Crime boss Tom Dennison ran the Permits Department. Businesses made "campaign contributions" and payments to the "police benefit fund" or their licenses were yanked. "You kidding me?"

Mr. Smooth propped his legs on the seat back and took a swig from an unlabeled bottle. "No more poorhouse for me. I'm riding this stock market to the stars." His cashmere vest and wide-legged, cuffed trousers defined snappy dresser. He waved Mac off with a blasé flip of his wrist. "Scram, kid. I'm taking care of Mom now."

———

"Oh good, Jackie's not here yet." Corrie raced into the girls' restroom. "Where's Halleen? Never mind. I'll call her later. Listen, I've come up with the best idea. But first I have to tell you the bad news."

Evelyn leaned toward the mirror, plucking her eyebrows. "It's too early in the morning to talk so fast."

"Betcha Corrie's mom lets her drink coffee," Ruth said.

Mother was still in bed this early, but no one needed to know that. Corrie dropped her voice to a whisper, bringing the girls into a huddle, and filled the team in on the situation at Jackie's.

Mary Frances chewed a fingernail. "Jesus said to love our neighbors, but my mom won't let Jackie in the house."

"Slippery. Sleazy. Shady."

Ruth bit her lip. "Same here. I don't know why your mom lets you—"

Because Mother didn't know what Jackie's life was like, and Corrie would keep it that way. "I know … I know. So we're throwing a benefit—"

Evelyn sighed. "Corrie, your heart's in the right place, but she won't accept charity."

"If we have a drawing and all enter Jackie's name—"

The door creaked and Jackie plodded in. "What kind of trouble are you cooking up?"

"Nothing," the team said in unison.

"I've come up with a great idea to date Mac before school gets out." Corrie motioned her into the circle. "Well, Artie and Ernie helped too. Field Club has their opening dance at the end of the month."

Jackie slumped onto the bench. "Sorry. My limousine's in the shop."

"They agreed to let us have a dance before they open, to give their orchestra a chance to practice. No dinner, but we can buy Cokes. This Friday, seven to nine. My brothers said they'd come and bring their friends. So put out the word, everyone you know."

"If Klemfuss finds out—"

"It won't matter. It's not a school function." *C'mon, team. It's a great plan.*

"I gotta work," Jackie said.

A great plan until reality hit. "Please ask for the night off. I need your help getting ready."

Jackie met her gaze with tired eyes. Finally a flicker of a smile crossed her lips. "Gotta get you all dolled up. Yeah, I'll ask."

A basketball bounced off the door. "Time to practice!" Mac called.

Corrie ran into the gym. "Great news, Mac! We're having a dance Friday." She cut him off before he could come up with a lame excuse. "You've got to come. It's a benefit for the basketball team."

He launched the ball, sending it swishing through the net, then gave the girls a fierce look. "If we beat South High."

Beat South High? No chance ... unless Mary Frances prayed. It could happen. Anything could happen. Corrie grinned. "You're on!"

———

Two steps into the gym, Mac realized something had changed. Everything had changed. If girls had a gauge—and they desperately needed one—it would read lower than ever. Monday's excitement about the dance had evaporated like yesterday's rain. Today they sat on the bench. Corrie and Evelyn had their arms around Halleen who boohooed into a soggy handkerchief. Ruth rubbed her back. Mary Frances worked her rosary. Thelma perched on the floor in front of Halleen and patted her sneakers.

If they were boys, Mac would blow his whistle and they'd practice and forget their problems. But they weren't, any way he looked at them, boys. "What's wrong?"

"I *have* to get married," Halleen wailed.

Oh. Mac glanced over his shoulder, but no girls' basketball coach limped through the door. He sat beside Corrie. "Should I say 'congratulations' or 'I'm sorry'?"

Halleen blew her nose. "It's not that I don't want to get married. Eddie and I have been going steady since our sophomore year."

"Steady Eddie got too hot and heavy." Jackie slumped against the wall.

"I wanted a nice wedding. A lacy dress with a veil. You'd all come and I'd carry flowers and ..." She stopped talking to sob.

"So what happened?" Mac whispered to Corrie.

Jackie's laugh turned into a cough. "How wet behind the ears are you?"

Mary Frances stopped praying. She managed to look down her

nose at Mac even though she sat below him. "Even I know where babies come from."

"As many as you Catholics make, you oughta." Jackie put out her cigarette.

Thelma filled him in. "Knocked up. In the family way. With child."

Halleen? He'd pegged Jackie as the most likely to get in trouble, not polite and proper Halleen. How many ways could these girls make him blush? Uh-oh. Could she play basketball while pregnant? Without their forward, they had no chance against South High. As if they had any chance. Mac cleared his throat. "I mean, what happened to your wedding plans?"

"We have to marry at the courthouse the day after graduation."

"Graduation's on a Saturday," Corrie said. "At eight pm."

"The Monday after, then. I wanted a little fun. You know, party, dance, honeymoon trip to Denver." She hiccuped and held out her chapped hands. "Now I'm going straight from diapering little brothers to diapering my own—" She sobbed.

"Let's have a party anyway," Corrie said. "We'll have it at my house. Mother loves parties."

"Babies are a blessing from God." Mary Frances passed her a dry hankie. "You'll fall in love with him when he arrives."

"Mary Frances, you're going to be a good nun. Halleen, you'll be a good mom." Mac's efforts at consoling led to more tears.

Jackie slumped against the wall. "And I'll be a legend in Hollywood," she said with a distinct lack of enthusiasm.

"What are the rest of you planning after graduation?" Mac asked, abandoning all hope of basketball practice but desperately searching for a way to cut off the waterworks. "You're all seniors, right?"

"I'm going to Boyles Business College," Evelyn said.

Mac had seen their building. "Down Harney at Eighteenth."

"Clarkson College for nursing," Ruth said.

"Thelma got accepted to the University of Nebraska," Corrie said.

"Congratulations. Have you picked a major?"

"Journalism. English. Education."

Should have known. Mac focused on Corrie, which he always wanted to do. "And you? Are you headed to college too?"

Corrie smiled. Not a phony flapper face, but a genuine happy glow. She looked up at the ceiling. "I'm going to—"

The hallway door slammed open, and Miss Klemfuss stormed in.

"What sort of misbehavior is going on down here? This is supposed to be basketball practice, but I haven't heard one bounce all morning."

If the school secretary had sonic hearing, like her relatives the vampire bats, Halleen would be kicked out of school. Mac stood and picked up the ball. "We're having a ... strategy session."

Klemfuss swooped down on Jackie. "You're smoking."

The brunette held out her empty hands with a couldn't-care-less shrug. "I quit."

The index finger jabbed Halleen next. "And you've been crying."

"Sick."

"Do I have to call your mother?"

Halleen straightened and forced a smile. "No, ma'am. All better."

"I have an announcement. Miss Sackett will be returning to Central tomorrow. I'm sure"—Klemfuss paused to give Mac the evil eye—"I'm sure you're all as relieved as I am." The school secretary scowled at their bare legs. "In my day, girls were modest. Sleeves covered our arms and stockings came right up to our unmentionables. We did not allow men to watch our games, much less coach us."

Jackie dared to ask, "*You* played basketball?"

The secretary's pointed nose raised, making her look even more like an offended pig. The index finger whipped in Jackie's direction. "I *will* be calling your mother, Miss Schnackel, and tell her you've been smoking." Klemfuss somehow managed to slam the swinging door as she flounced out.

Miss Sackett's return meant Mac could concentrate on training the new salesman in Ward's automotive department. He wouldn't have to worry about ballplayers who got pregnant, or spoke only in synonyms, or turned into an enchantress in the locker room. No need to worry about how badly South High would beat them, what the girls would do to embarrass him, or how his car would add to his humiliation.

Ruth whistled. "Klemfuss played basketball?"

"Tiny. Little. Short."

"I can't imagine her moving fast enough."

"When the game first started," Corrie explained, "the court used to be divided into nine sections. Girls weren't allowed to leave their space or run and dribble."

"Sounds like playing catch. Boring," Evelyn said.

"Uh... Coach?" Corrie said. "Mac?"

"Yes." He didn't turn around.

The rest chimed in. "If you wouldn't mind–"

"I think–"

"You'd better–"

Corrie stood beside him. "We don't know how Miss Sackett's feeling."

Mary Frances stood next to her. "We've prayed for her recovery."

"But she probably won't be up for much," Ruth finished.

"She's a great coach and all, but she doesn't know about the three-girl defense," Evelyn added.

Jackie leaned on the wall and crossed her legs. "Not to mention she's never taken us out for ice cream."

Never? Hadn't they told him ice cream was a longstanding Central tradition? And he'd believed them, sap that he was.

Halleen blew her nose and gave him a damp nod.

"Might as well finish out the season." Mac tried to be casual, but his heart yelled whoopee and he couldn't keep from smiling.

"You're the cat's meow," Corrie said, making him feel like a big cheese. "Okay, team, dribble drill."

Thelma raised both arms. "Problem. Complication. Snag."

"Now what?" Jackie passed the ball and Thelma caught it for the first time all season.

"Full. Stuffed. Packed."

"Mac's car isn't big enough," Evelyn interpreted. "Where are we going to put Miss Sackett?"

CHAPTER
EIGHT

"GOOD THING YOU CAME BACK," Corrie told Mac when he arrived at the gym Friday afternoon. "Miss Sackett isn't here."

"What's wrong?"

"I don't know, but Mary Frances is praying for her."

"Attagirl." He nodded at the rest of the team. "Let's win this for Miss Sackett!" He lectured on strategy the ride down Twenty-Fourth Street to South High. He smelled of aftershave, the same scent her brothers wore for dates. Was Mac trying to impress her? "Play the ball and not the man."

"We're not playing against men," Ruth pointed out.

"Repeat. Redundant. Rerun."

Jackie reached into the back seat and swatted Thelma. "Says you, you big parrot."

"Keep control of the ball," Mac continued. He never went on and on like this. Maybe he wanted to win and dance with Corrie as much as she did.

Inside South High's gym, they were met by four girls, none taller than five feet. The shortest introduced herself as the replacement team captain. "The rest of the team was barred from outside activities because they played hooky on senior sneak day."

"We should use only four players too," Mary Frances said. "To be fair."

The girl shook her head. "Play full team. We're good at losing."

"Not as good as us," Jackie muttered.

Central High won 24 to 6.

Corrie invited the South High team for ice cream and for tomorrow night's dance, but they declined. The girls headed to the car, but Corrie lagged behind. For a moment, she and Mac were alone in the parking lot.

"Tonight's dance." He swung the whistle, looping it around his finger. "Will you save one for me?"

"Only one?" She tipped her head, stepped close, and slid her hand into his. "I'm hoping for more."

"More?" He blinked. Then his mouth curled into a warm smile and he squeezed her hand. "How about that. I am too."

———

Toes tapping to the orchestra, Corrie surveyed the Field Club ballroom from her perch by the entry. Spring had finally arrived, so the boys were down to shirtsleeves, and most girls wore short-sleeved summer frocks. Corrie's dress had a bow at the neck, two flounces on the skirt, and large purple and green blobs on the white fabric. Mother said it was like one worn by actress Norma Shearer. Corrie wondered if Norma's itched too.

Central had the best turnout, of course. Most of her senior class, the underclassmen, and a good bunch of alumni kicked up their heels to a frantic "Brush Stomp." Basketball players from Tech and North had brought their friends, but only the team captain from Benson and her boyfriend showed. No one from South came—probably stinging from their loss yesterday. Halleen was missing, confined to home until graduation, poor bunny. Corrie's mother and her squad of chaperones hovered around the edges of the room, making sure no one crossed the boundaries of propriety.

Let's see, a hundred dancers at a quarter each... Mrs. Zukas would say no sense counting pennies before the dance was done.

Two classmates stumbled in, rebounding off the doorframe and into each other. Robert Cunningham and Robert Carlberg had been inseparable since kindergarten. In elementary school, they'd been known as the Bob C twins. In high school, when Cunningham shot to six foot three and Carlberg stopped growing ten inches below him, they became known as Mutt and Jeff. "Did you hear? We got into University of Nebraska!"

"Both of you?" Corrie asked. Jeff managed top grades with no effort, but Mutt squeaked by on his charm. "What are you going to study?"

"Girls with a minor in beer." From the smell of their breath, they'd already started. "We're rooming together."

Jeff pointed to his tall friend. "The coaches promise to put his size to work."

"Is that wise?" Corrie had seen Mutt trip in every sport Central offered. In football he'd tackled their own quarterback. In basketball, his butterfingers had sent the ball into the opposing forward's eager grasp. His foot caught on the edge of the wrestling mat and he'd slammed his opponent before the match started, disqualifying himself. He'd fallen over hurdles, golf clubs, tennis rackets, and baseball bats. After he'd tangled in the pool rope, Coach sent him to the debate club for his own safety.

Jeff waved aside her concern as he paid for both of them. "He'll be fine now he's done growing."

Mutt clasped her hand and leaned close. "Will you be my sheba?"

Jeff grabbed her other hand. "Cash or check, baby vamp?"

Corrie had realized long ago these two had picked each other. "Sorry, boys. Best I can do is offer you a dance, say, in an hour?"

"It's a deal!" They raced off to find a few fresh toes to step on.

Corrie watched from the safety of her post as they wrangled a pair of wallflowers from Tech onto the floor. Even goofs had plans for after graduation. She knew what she didn't want: a boyfriend whose only goal was smuggling giggle water into football games while wearing a raccoon coat. Sure, serious students like Thelma headed to the university too. But endless hours in lectures sounded boring. Scratch college from the list.

When Corrie had asked her parents about flying, Mother had scheduled her for golf lessons. Golf turned out to be Mother's way to dangle her in front of wealthy single fellows at the country club. Those silver-spoon boys held no interest. Not like—

The door to the parking lot opened and Mac led in an older woman with a cane. Corrie ran to hug her. "Miss Sackett! Thank you for coming!" She beamed at Mac, considerate and honorable Mac, over the woman's shoulder.

"After missing the South game yesterday, I have to redeem myself. Besides, I couldn't refuse the offer of chauffeur service from the gallant Mr. McFarland here." Miss Sackett lowered herself into the chair Corrie had vacated. "You kids go enjoy yourselves. I'll watch the money box."

How little polite conversation was necessary before Corrie could whisk Mac onto the dance floor? "I didn't realize you knew each other."

Miss Sackett propped her foot on the base of the table. "Mac helped out in the library after—"

"Excuse me. I'd better move my car." Mac hurried outside.

As the door closed, three young men in argyle vests and checkered knickers sauntered in from the golf course. "Hiya, doll," said the one with the look-at-me swagger. Where had she seen him before? In the movies? He had wide shoulders and thick hair like Gary Cooper. He braced an arm on the door frame and leaned over to peer down her blouse, nearly knocking her out with cigar and whiskey breath. "Got you a nice little dance going on."

"We're raising money for the Central High girls' basketball team."

His up and down scrutiny had Corrie squirming. He lowered his voice. "Is that so? Are you a player?"

"I'm the running center."

"My position too. At the university." He grabbed her hand. "Let's see what moves we can make on these boards."

"I'm waiting for—" Corrie motioned toward the door, hoping Mac would hurry and save her from this man with his speakeasy ways.

"It's not nice to make a doll wait." The fellow dropped a five-dollar bill into the money box. Miss Sackett started to count out his change, but the fellow shook his head. "For my friends. And for a dance with the loveliest doll in Omaha." He swept her onto the floor.

Oh for heavens sakes, what was she worried about? It was only a dance. It brought Jackie five dollars closer to her dream. Nothing could happen with Mother on guard.

But it did. Somehow, by his signal or mind reading, the band finished their peppy Charleston and segued into a slow foxtrot. Joe College pulled her too close. He rubbed his leg against hers, and his fingers explored her back. His friend circled by with a girl from Corrie's French class. *He* kept his hands where they belonged. The cheeky one spun her, and his hand slid, inching under her bra.

Enough. Where was Mother when she needed her? Heading for the ladies' room, of course. Now what? Who could she pass him off to? Jackie would know how to deal with him. Where had she gone?

"Hey, doll." The fellow brought his face close. He'd better not try a kiss. "Anyone ever tell you to keep your eye on the ball?"

"I believe my coach may have mentioned it." *Ah, there's Jackie with Artie.* Perfect. "As well as how to pass to a teammate." Corrie spun away from those naughty hands, gave her friend a wide-eyed look, and grabbed her brother. "Whew."

"McFarland getting fresh?"

"What? No, that wasn't Mac."

"That's Mac's older brother, Mr. Smooth."

"Uh-oh." That was it—the family resemblance. He'd played for Central back when Ernie did. But he was too handsome, too impressed with himself, too sure of his welcome. He gave her the heebie-jeebies in a way Mac never had. Corrie hurried to Miss Sackett. "Where's Mac?"

The older woman grimaced. "I'm not sure. He took one look at the dance floor, announced he had a family emergency, and left."

Oh no.

———

Mr. Smooth had an instinct for making Mac's life miserable. Like the time he'd given Mac's bike to the orphan boy down the street, winning friends all over the neighborhood but depriving Mac of his wheels. And the way he kept his clothes in perfect condition, but his hand-me-downs were stained and shredded. And the way he'd finished all the food in the house late last night, leaving Mac only the heel of the loaf for breakfast.

So how had his brother learned that Mac liked Corrie? And that Mac wasn't allowed to date her? His brother charmed everyone. He probably even had Klemfuss in his back pocket. Klemfuss and Mr. Smooth in cahoots. Mac should volunteer to open a Montgomery Ward's in Maine.

His brother had a slapdash approach to life, scheming and dreaming, ready to party when the needle touched the record. A girl would fall for it until she found herself another act in his circus, another ride at the carnival of his life. That good-for-nothing better not treat Corrie bad.

Entering Ward's, he greeted the boss. "Any word about the new stores?"

"Nope." He handed over a thick stack of statements. "Did you follow up on these past-due accounts?"

Follow up? This was the first Mac heard of the problem. He gritted his teeth and took the pile. "I'll get right on it." He went to his desk, behind the clothing department, and sorted the accounts by amount. His bookkeeping teacher said the little debts didn't make much difference, so start with the big ones first.

"Doesn't anyone work in this store?" asked a matron whose complexion Ward's called "Tea Rose."

Mac stowed the paperwork in his desk drawer. "Yes, ma'am. How may I help you?"

"I meant a woman. I want a *female* sales clerk."

"Of course." Mac headed down the main aisle. New fellow in automotive, another in appliances. He excused himself to ask the manager, learning both Miss Ogle and Mrs. Eischied were out sick.

"Handle it." The boss waved him off. "If you want to be a manager, you have to handle everything."

Mac refrained from pointing out he was still only a sales clerk. The manager was paid to deal with irate customers. He returned to the woman.

The customer's complexion deepened to "Cardinal." "I need a female sales clerk. What do you know?"

After one girls' basketball season, Mac could safely say "nothing." Women were a mystery. Figuring the customer wasn't looking for shoes, he strolled into the lingerie department. "I'm trained in every department. How may I help you?"

Her face now "Jockey Red," the woman whispered, "I need a maternity foundation."

Mac stepped behind the counter and opened the drawer. This wasn't the way Mrs. Eischied worked, but measuring the customer would make him turn "Scarlet." "We have three different styles in many sizes. And a dressing room."

"Thank you," she said, then waited for him to leave.

Mac returned to his desk. The most expensive account was for engagement, wedding, and gents' rings in "True Sweetheart"-style.

The purchaser was a fellow from Mr. Smooth's class. Mac reached for the telephone and froze.

What if his brother asked Corrie out? He'd realize she was worth giving up his crazy ways and propose. What if Mr. Smooth *married* Corrie?

Mac would open a Montgomery Ward's in Timbuktu.

CHAPTER
NINE

GRADUATED AT LAST!

After making her try on everything in Brandeis, Haas Brothers, and Kilpatrick's, Mother had finally agreed to a soft-green sleeveless dress with a flip at the hem. The round neckline showed off the family pearls. Corrie twirled in front of her mirror. How far would her skirt go up before her knickers would show? Or ... why not wear basketball shorts? Corrie fluffed her bob and touched up the Tangee lipstick Mother let her wear.

"Got your glad rags on?" Artie pounded on her bedroom door. "Guests pulling up. Get your little self downstairs before Mother blows a gasket."

Corrie yanked on a stocking. A giant snag raced down her leg. Never mind. Off they went in a ball under the bed. She unclipped her garters, shoved her feet into pumps, and dashed out.

"I'm not little. I'm graduated." Corrie sashayed past. She leaned into the stairwell. The rattle of dishes and silverware drifted up with the aroma of grilled beef. For now, the entry hall was clear. She rode the banister down. "Whee!"

"Still a kid." Artie hopped onto the rail and followed, landing with a thump behind her.

"Cordelia Elizabeth Tinley. Arthur Haverford Tinley!" Mother gave Corrie a glare and Artie a whack with her notebook. "Set a good example for your sister–"

She started in on her standard lecture, then spotted the display.

Corrie had arranged her diploma, National Honor Society certificate, and the Sunday *World-Herald*'s full-page photograph of the Central girls' basketball team on the hall tree. Corrie held her breath, waiting for Mother to say she was swell.

Mother scanned the photograph with a frown, then shoved her notes in the drawer. "If only you'd gone out for golf."

Corrie blinked. What did she have to do around here for an atta-girl? If she ever had children—she thought of Mac with a flutter—she'd celebrate every accomplishment.

Mother pointed toward the backyard. "Artie, go check on the barbecue and tell the band to start. No, band first, then food. Corrie, let me take a look at you. Nice touch with the lipstick." She gave her a head-to-toe inspection, smoothing her hair, straightening her necklace, turning her around. "Cordelia Elizabeth, what are you wearing under your skirt?"

"The minister's here."

"The instant we finish greeting the Portlands, you will take off those basketball shorts. And no arguing." Gracious smile fixed in place, Mother opened the door. "Good afternoon, Reverend. Excellent sermon this morning." She chitchatted the family down the hall to the terrace, motioning behind her back for Corrie to go upstairs. But Father's golfing buddies arrived, then their neighbors, and most of her National Honor Society chapter.

Where was Mac?

Ernie sauntered in carrying a cup of punch.

"For me?" Corrie took a sip.

"If you don't mind some dog drank out of it."

"As long as it wasn't a skunk."

Ernie greeted a couple from his class, then whispered to her, "Found a box on the porch this morning. The jewelry stolen in the robbery."

"Are you kidding?" Dealing with three brothers honed Corrie's skill in spotting lies, and this wasn't one. "All of it? The black diamond?"

"Everything but the black diamond. I'm sorry, little one."

"I'm not little." She kicked toward his shin, intentionally missing to keep his slacks clean. "How'd you get the loot back?"

"Apparently your friend Jackie knows some interesting people."

He opened his jacket. A Union Pacific ticket peeked from his pocket. "Have her find me."

Corrie had a sudden flash of her friend talking to Boss Dennison at the speakeasy. Did her friend have a word with the crime boss?

A stream of Lithuanian flowed from the kitchen as Mrs. Zukas directed her family in serving the food. Harry pointed a celery stalk at Corrie. "Mother wants you. She filled your dance card with stockbrokers, accountants, and a seminary president."

"Riveting company, I'm sure. If you see Mac, tell him to cut in."

"Your basketball coach? Got something going under Klemfuss's nose?"

"Her nose is no longer my concern."

Harry shuddered. "Says you."

The girls' basketball team arrived. Corrie walked them to the terrace, leaving Jackie with Ernie. Before she could join the buffet line, the boys' team captain pulled her onto the dance floor.

"Is this the one?" the band leader yelled to her. "Waltz now?"

"No! Not till I give the signal."

The fast Lindy Hop had her flying across the floor, passing a blur of faces. Her partner spun her, setting off gasps from the old ladies' corner. Wait—was that Mac? Corrie tried to focus, but her partner swung her in the other direction. When they turned, Mac cut in and reached for her, enveloping her with the leather-and-wood scent of his aftershave. She stepped into his arms, his warm and dependable hug, and planted a kiss on his cheek. If that didn't make her intentions clear—

"Let's make plans," he whispered, his breath tickling from her ear all the way down to her toes.

"Yes! Let's!"

The bandleader cut off the tune. Instead of her waltz, he directed the party to the barn. Corrie moved through the crowd, greeting friends who wished her well on graduation. Somehow she lost Mac.

What could her present be? Every other year, Corrie tricked her brothers into spilling the beans. But this time, they'd been as tight lipped as spies.

Father grinned. Corrie untied the bow. The boys pulled the doors open and oh. Oh. Oh! An airplane! A red biplane with a five-cylinder engine. *Ohmygoodnessgracious.* Father had bought her an airplane. She gave him the biggest hug ever. "Thank you!"

"It's an Arrow Sport, built down the road in Lincoln." Father patted her back. "My little Amelia Earhart."

I'm not little. No time to argue. She had a plane to fly. She hurried inside the barn and almost bumped into a guy swinging a pair of goggles.

"Corrie, this is Bob Steele, your flight instructor."

She shook the hand of the skinny man with a thick mustache. "Pleased to meet you. Let's go!"

"Cordelia, you have guests!" Mother hissed. "And you can't climb on that thing in a dress."

Corrie raised her skirt. "I'm wearing shorts."

"Everyone at the party knows what you're wearing under your skirt. Lord, help us." Mother turned to Father. "I told you this was crazy."

Mr. Steele propped his hands on his hips and tipped his head toward the pasture. "Horse field's too short and rough to take off with both of us. I'll fly it back to my field. Meet me there tomorrow."

"But …" She had an airplane, but she couldn't fly it? A lump filled her throat and she fought an awful impulse to throw a temper tantrum.

"How about if Corrie sits in it while we push it out?" Artie asked.

"You're my favorite," she whispered as she hugged him. She climbed into the cockpit. The Arrow was smaller than the other biplanes she'd ridden in. She could see ahead over the engine. The seats were side by side instead of tandem, which should make it easier to hear the instructor. Corrie ran her fingers across the mahogany instrument panel. Fuel mixture, altimeter, compass, oil pressure and temperature, turn and bank, airspeed, tachometer, oil pressure, magnetos. Nothing to it.

Her brothers rolled the plane into the sunshine. One of the fellows raised his camera and yelled, "Amelia Earhart!" Corrie perched on the coaming and waved, posing like her heroine. "Goodbye America. Hello Paris!"

Evelyn ran her hand over the fuselage. "My favorite shade of red."

"Who cares what color it is. It's an *airplane*!" Ruth squealed.

"I'll pray for you," Mary Frances said solemnly, then grinned.

"Ride? Fly? Soar?" Thelma asked.

"As soon as I learn, I'll take you all up."

Jackie peeked inside. "One at a time. It's tighter than Mac's jalopy."

Mac? The airplane had pushed all thoughts of Mac out of her head. "Have you seen him?"

Lips clenched, Jackie nodded. "I'll tell you later."

Uh-oh.

———

When Miss Sackett drove Mac home from the party, she'd said, "You can't do anything to change Corrie or cure her airplane fever. But God loves her even more than you do. So don't fuss or fret or worry or nag. Give her to God, then step back and let Him work."

The rest of the weekend, Mac turned the idea over in his head. What else could he do? He gave Corrie to God.

Monday morning the boss peered over the slippery mound of paperwork on his desk. "How was your weekend?"

"Fine," Mac lied. His engine ran as rough as his Model T's. The girl he wanted to date, the girl he was crazy about, would die in a crash. And there was nothing he could do about it. "That list of new stores opening ..."

"Haven't seen it."

Lost in the haystack on his desk? Hidden? Or maybe "opportunity for advancement" talk was all a smoke screen. Mac stared, trying to keep his expression neutral. Neither of them blinked. Finally Mac said, "Tell Chicago I'm packed and ready now."

"Even if it's in a terrible place—"

"Like Chicago?" Mac would run a Ward's in Al Capone's basement.

"All right." A blank Western Union form emerged from the pile. He pointed Mac in the direction of a ranting customer out front. "See that fellow's satisfaction is guaranteed."

A couple hours later the boss called Mac into his office. "Training Monday at headquarters. Your store opens June twenty-ninth. You're not giving me long to find your replacement."

After six months of encouraging him to apply for a manager position, the boss gave him grief now? "The new automotive guy shows potential."

"He quit. Got a job working for Ford. Think twice about

Michigan." He handed him a telegram. "Auto plants snatch up all the good workers."

Michigan? Far enough. "Like you always say"—every time he dumped some sticky problem in Mac's lap—"great challenges build great careers."

CHAPTER
TEN

MRS. ZUKAS HANDED CORRIE a metal lunchbox. "I put in a second sandwich for your flying teacher."

"Thank you." Corrie hugged her. Knowing Mrs. Zukas, the sandwiches were braunschweiger with onion on rye. Good thing her plane had an open cockpit.

"Let me take a look at you." Mother fussed with the pleats of Corrie's tan trousers. "Where's your leather jacket and scarf? If you want to be Amelia Earhart, you have to look the part."

"It's too warm for a jacket." And she didn't want to be Amelia Earhart. She wanted to be herself, Corrie Tinley, pilot. "Are you ready? I don't want to be late."

"As much as Father's paying that fellow, he has nothing to complain about." Mother sauntered to the car with a swirl of her golf skirt.

Corrie dropped Mother at the country club. Omaha Municipal was under construction—improving drainage, building a hangar, installing lighting. So her plane had gone to Steele's airfield, which looked like a farm, except instead of a barn, it had a corrugated metal building with a windsock on top. She parked Mother's Oldsmobile and raced inside. Her plane's seats had been dumped by the tail. A skinny fellow stood on her wing with his head deep in her cockpit. "Don't take it apart! I want to fly."

The body unfolded. It was her flight instructor, Bob Steele. His beetle-brow scowl told her she'd said the wrong thing.

"What are you doing?" she asked. "You're supposed to teach me to fly." His scowl deepened, telling her *that* wasn't the right thing to say either.

"Trying to fix it so you *can* fly it."

"Fix it? It's brand new. What could be broken?"

A muscle jumped in his jaw. *What's eating him? Anyone who gets to fly all the time shouldn't be a sourhead.* "Too much friction on the cables. You won't have enough strength to work the controls."

Here we go again, another person underestimating her. "I'm strong. I played on Central's basketball team." If he hadn't heard of their record, and no one outside the team knew, he might be impressed.

Steele stepped off the wing and rummaged through his toolbox. "Yeah, you may be Jack Dempsey, but I'd rather fly than fight."

"If you loosen the cables, won't it be out of rig?"

He paused and gave her a narrow-eyed stare.

"I studied Clevenger's *Modern Flight*." Artie ordered a copy for her.

"Glorified Eaglerock sales brochure." He handed her a screwdriver. "Okay, Miss Expert, inside. You'll fit better anyway."

Corrie climbed in, breathing the heady aroma of oil and fabric-stiffening dope. "Do we have to remove the floor to reach the rudder and elevator cables?"

"No." Pointing with his flashlight, he shouted instructions.

"I'm not deaf," Corrie muttered as she adjusted the aileron pulleys.

"You will be once you start flying," he said at a lower volume.

Grease squirted everywhere except on the cable. "What if it's binding inside the wing?"

"Rip the fabric off."

Her heart started a ten-turn death spiral. "I'm never going to fly."

"Fortunately this plane was built with all its hardware showing. Already wrenched on the outboard ailerons."

"So we'll fly today?" *Pull up ... pull up.*

"Might. Here you go." He handed her a seat.

Straight and level. Corrie replaced the bolts and tightened them.

Two kids on bicycles rolled up. "New airplane, Mr. Steele?"

"It's mine." Corrie barely resisted the urge to stomp her foot.

The boys stared at her with wide eyes and open mouths.

"Show Miss Tinley where to get water. She's gonna wash her plane."

"Wash? But—"

Steele pointed a greasy finger at her. "This thing's got too much drag already. Don't need dirt or bugs adding to it. 'Sides, help you know your plane and build up arm muscles."

Her arms were strong enough, thank you, but pumping water and hauling buckets from Spangard's dairy barn told her otherwise.

Two hours later, she was drenched, filthy, and exhausted. But her Arrow Sport shone in the sun.

Mr. Steele finished tinkering with his biplane and closed his toolbox. "So what do you want to fly for anyway? You want to be another Lady Lindy?"

"I've wanted to fly since I was eight and took a ride at Aksarben."

"Barnstorming's a tough life."

"Lindbergh got his start that way." Corrie changed tacks, not wanting to alienate her instructor. "There's the Ford National Air Tour, speed and endurance records, The Women's Air Derby is coming up in August."

"They want a hundred hours of solo, twenty-five of cross-country."

"Let's get started, then!" She clapped.

"Should test fly it. And give the boys a ride since they washed my Eaglerock." He jabbed a thumb over his shoulder at the larger silver-and-blue biplane.

Screaming would merely prove she didn't have the emotional fortitude to be a pilot, so Corrie clamped her jaw shut.

Bobby and Ralphie looked up from scrubbing the oil beneath the Eaglerock's engine. Over the drudgery of the work and sharing lunch, she'd built a friendship with them. "Aw, c'mon, Mr. Steele. Take Miss Corrie up for her lesson. We got work to do yet."

Steele propped his fists on his hips and studied her. "You don't weigh much. Guess you could come along."

Sometimes being slim was an advantage.

"How are you doing on gasoline?"

"I didn't think I should open the tank while washing it."

"Okay." His scowl lessened. "It's the first thing you check as part of preflight. Second thing is the oil level."

Fueling the plane involved sticking a hose in the tank in the top wing while pumping from a barrel. A pint of oil from a can filled the engine.

"Next ..." Mr. Steele talked lift and drag, cantilevers and longerons, Glenn Curtiss and the Wright brothers. He explained humidity, dewpoint, and winds. He discussed the advantages of Kinner engines over LeBlonds.

Corrie figured he planned to talk until sundown.

Finally he said, "Get in."

He didn't have to ask her twice. Corrie climbed into the cockpit and got another lecture about brakes, magnetos, and throttle settings. After a long time he yelled, "Contact." The engine fired up with the first swing of the prop. What a great airplane!

"Scoot over. I want the brakes." The sweaty man squeezed beside her.

Flying would be better with Mac. Soon as she got her license, she'd take him up, and oh, the fun they'd have! How was he feeling today? Guilt gave her a poke—this was the first time all day she'd thought of him.

"Head in the clouds already and haven't taken off yet."

"Sorry." What had he said? *Engine speed is measured in RPM, revolutions per minute.* Corrie put on her helmet and goggles.

They taxied to the end of the field, checking the rudder along the way, then turned into the wind. Steele wiggled the stick, bumping her legs as he watched the ailerons and elevator. Then he jammed his feet on the brakes and pushed the throttle forward. The engine pounded, washing them with its hot breath. "Ready?"

Was she ever! But she couldn't speak over the lump in her throat, so she gave him a thumbs-up, then rested her hands on the stick and throttle.

They bumped down the field. Faster, faster, pressing her into the seat. A tip of the stick forward brought the tail up. But the plane still clung to the ground. Neither the Jenny nor the Standard took this long. As the end of the field approached, the wheels left the ground. The plane inched over the foot-high corn at the dairy, and they were flying!

"Whoopee!" Corrie yelled and finally got a grin out of her flight instructor.

———

"Left rudder! Pull back! Do you see the airfield?" Flying should be fun, but Mr. Steele seemed determined to make it hard work. "I've got it!"

Whew. Corrie shook out her cramped hands. Her legs were sore from working the rudder pedals. Prop wash battered her face.

The instructor brought the power back. The plane dropped to the field and bounced up like a basketball. Cursing the plane, her beautiful new Arrow, he shoved the throttle in and they roared back into the sky. He went around the patch again. This time he kept the power on and eased the Arrow onto the grass.

Muttering and grunting, he helped her hangar the plane. "Tomorrow."

Corrie glanced at her watch, then hurried to the country club. No time to stop by Ward's to see Mac. She was late to pick up Mother. Wouldn't it be fun to land on the golf course? The golfers would be so surprised! Waving to friends heading to the tennis court, she pulled up in front of the sprawling brick clubhouse.

Mother climbed in. "Cordelia Elizabeth. You are as filthy as a hobo."

What's a little oil and grease? "I've been flying."

"You must clean up before you come here. What if someone sees you? Amelia Earhart doesn't run around looking like a ... grease monkey."

Amelia must have posed, since pictures of other pilots usually showed a fair amount of grime. "Okay. I'll bring a bar of soap tomorrow."

"And a washcloth. And fresh clothes."

"There's no place to change."

"Never mind. I'll have Father pick me up tomorrow." Mother huffed. "Whatever possessed him ..."

Corrie parked in the garage, then headed for the telephone.

"Young lady, you do not make a call looking like a ragamuffin."

Why not? Mac wouldn't be able to see her. "But—"

"Upstairs. Now. Mrs. Zukas will be serving dinner any minute."

The bathroom mirror showed an oily brown face with white around her eyes. Lux spread the mess to an even layer, but Woodbury's took it off.

"My washcloth! I should have brought you a rag." Mother had already changed and washed. She handed Corrie a summer frock and a lemon half. "Jergens lotion. You're sun and wind burned. You should wear your complexion mask."

Nothing could be more uncomfortable or ugly than a sheet of rubber stretched across her face. "That's a thought." She parroted Mother's favorite evading phrase as the dinner bell rang. She hurried to the table.

"Corrie!" Father thumped her on the back. "How was your lesson? Did you fly over the house?"

Mrs. Zukas set the platter of fried chicken on the table. "No airplanes flew over this house. Not one."

"You didn't fly over Harry's office or the store." Ernie slid half the cucumbers off the relish tray.

"Where did you go?" Harry dug into the rice.

Where? Out in the country, over some farmland, but she wouldn't admit to being lost. "Up in the air!"

Artie grabbed her chin. "Betcha got bugs in your teeth."

"Three flies and a june bug, but Mother made me brush my teeth."

"Honestly." Mother downed her grapefruit cocktail. "She could wring out her clothes and fill an oil can."

"Mr. Steele says some cities have aviation country clubs. We could do that at the Omaha Country Club. All we'd need is a hangar and airplane. They could hire me as their instructor and I could teach all the members."

Harry frowned. "Golfers wouldn't like you landing on their fairways."

Corrie shook her head. "The course is too hilly. But that field along Seventy-Second Street would be perfect."

Father smiled at Corrie. "I'll discuss it with the board."

They talked about flying, then guessed what might have happened to the black diamond. Finally the meal ended and Corrie raced to the phone.

When Mac answered, she'd ask him how he was feeling, then give him the opportunity to ask her on a date. Corrie opened the phone book to Clara McFarland. If his mother answered, they could talk about basketball. But if Mr. Smooth— Oh no. No, she would not talk to that tomcat. Maybe one of her brothers could call. "Artie? Ernie? Harry?" They weren't upstairs, downstairs, or outside. "Horsefeathers!"

"Cordelia Elizabeth, watch your language." Mother caught her standing by the telephone. "Who are you calling at this late hour?"

Caught in the act without a handy fib. No way around, it, she had to tell the truth. "Mr. McFarland, the basketball coach. Another team member said he became ill at the party. I wanted to check on him, but–"

Mother snatched the receiver from her. "As the hostess, it's my responsibility." Mother dialed WA9037. Corrie held her breath as it rang and rang. "I'll call tomorrow. In the meantime, write your thank-you notes. I'll check your handwriting and spelling before I go to bed."

Corrie drew in a breath for an excuse, any excuse, but Mrs. Zukas waved behind Mother's shoulder. The housekeeper held up a plate with a slice of chocolate cake. Corrie winked at the housekeeper, then told Mother, "Okay, I'll get a wiggle on."

"And no slang!"

———

"This is lovely." Mom fingered the collar of the silk georgette dress Mr. Smooth had bought her. "A new dress. A night out on the town. So generous of your brother, isn't it, Mac?"

"Yes, Mom." He reached over the fancy china, silverware, and linen napkins, and squeezed her hand. *I'll miss you too.*

"Now that I'm home, I'll take you out to eat every week," Mr. Smooth vowed with a flourish of his knife.

Mom leaned in. "But the prices–"

"No more worrying about money." Boss Dennison's role in Mr. Smooth's newfound wealth remained unsaid. "From now on, we're putting on the Ritz."

Mac had no idea what the Ritz in Paris looked like, but Omaha's Hotel Fontenelle couldn't be far off. From chandeliers to inlaid flooring, it spelled swanky. Even the menu was in French. Would he ever be able to take Corrie to an elegant restaurant like this? Her father probably brought her here all the time.

His brother raised his goblet. The flush on his face signaled he drank something stronger than ginger ale. "No more wooden nickels."

Mac's jaw tightened, but he let the insult go. Montgomery Ward's had kept the family going while Mr. Smooth partied through college.

Since his brother was in a generous mood and Mom could referee, he asked, "Would you mind selling my car for me?"

"Sell it? Hope the junk man will haul it off."

"It still runs." *If the engine's not too hot and if it's pointing downhill with the tank full.*

Mr. Smooth handed a thick envelope to Mac. "Buy a new car when you get to Michigan."

Mom beamed. "Your father would be so proud of you boys."

"Wow. Thank you." Mac tucked the gift in his suit pocket. Maybe his big brother was a decent guy after all.

Mr. Smooth leered at a young lady crossing the room. Nope, still the same old weasel. The girl exited the restaurant on the arm of some swell, and Mr. Smooth went back to pretending to admire the woodwork and palm trees. "Say, wasn't this the place where they brought Lindbergh and the other pilot, Chamberlin?"

Mom breathed with a hissing sound. "The doctor said never to mention—"

"It's been years." Mr. Smooth smirked. "You must be over it."

Mom shook her head. "Mac's girl–"

"No." Mac's hand shot out. "It's none of his business."

"Your—?" Mr. Smooth choked on his hooch.

"No." He didn't know about Corrie? Had he danced with her by accident?

"*You* have a girl?" His eyes narrowed. "Then why are you leaving town? Unless … she's connected with airplanes somehow. Is she a pilot? She has an airplane and you think she likes *you*? Oh that's rich!" He hooted. "I have to meet this girl!"

"Why am I leaving? Because of you." Mac set his napkin beside his plate and stood. He removed the filthy lucre from the envelope and tossed it over Mr. Smooth's head. The air filled with pink, yellow, and blue play money. Mac turned to his mom, who had covered her face with both hands. He hadn't wanted to hurt her, but maybe she needed to see the truth about her oldest. Mac touched her shoulder. "I'll wait for you downstairs."

———

Thunderstorms rolled across Omaha, cutting short Corrie's lesson. Steele sent her home to study regulations and navigation. On the way, she stopped by Montgomery Ward's to see Mac. She didn't have basketball rules to give him, so what excuse could she use?

I'm here for more. *Dances, dates, airplane rides ...*

Corrie dashed inside. She recognized the lady in the clothing department. "Hello, Mrs. Eischied. Is Mr. McFarland working today?"

"He left this morning for a different job." The matron dabbed her eyes with a handkerchief. "We're going to miss him."

A different job? Corrie hadn't known he was looking. "So where ..."

"It's a big state starting with the letter *M*."

"He left Omaha?"

"Missouri? Montana? I don't rightly know. And the boss is out. Would you like to leave a note? He could call you."

And have Mother and Mrs. Zukas grill her on why the manager of Montgomery Ward's called the house? "No, thank you."

Mac gone? Heart aching, Corrie drove home. Mrs. Zukas met her at the door. "Your friend Ruth called from Clarkson Hospital."

"She doesn't start nursing school until next week."

The housekeeper usually hid a smile behind her stern expression, but not today. "Halleen had a miscarriage."

"But she crocheted her first pair of booties. Purple and white for Central High." No, it can't be. What more could go wrong?

Mrs. Zukas pushed her up the stairs. "I picked flowers before the rain started and ironed your good handkerchiefs. Wear something respectable. The head nurse will give you the bum's rush dressed like that."

Corrie washed, changed clothes, then drove to the hospital. Meager light from the rain-soaked windows dimmed the ward. Corrie tiptoed down the row of elderly patients. Could that be Halleen? Her lively teammate with a rosy complexion had turned so pale she blended into the sheets. The hospital gown rose a fraction of an inch. Yes, she still breathed. Corrie set the flowers on the windowsill and leaned close, not wanting to disturb the other patients and draw the wrath of the nurse. "Halleen?"

Not even a flicker of an eyelid.

Halleen hadn't planned to get pregnant in high school. She'd wanted a break from taking care of her younger brothers. She'd wanted a wedding and a honeymoon. But Corrie knew Halleen had not wanted this miscarriage.

What's this? A slip of paper stuck out from beneath the pillow, her name written in Ruth's loopy writing.

Corrie, Can't stay—have to take Grandma home after her surgery. Hope Halleen wakes up for you. Ruth

"Halleen? Talk to me." Corrie squeezed her hand. Her friend's fingers lay on hers, cold and limp. She unfolded the blanket from the foot of the bed and tucked it around her shoulders. At home, tears were met with taunts of "crybaby" from her brothers and "wash your face and count your blessings" from Mrs. Zukas. Corrie had learned early to hide her feelings. But today a tear snuck out.

The nurse swooped in. "Visiting hours are over. Patients need rest."

"But she …" Corrie gasped. "Isn't there anything …"

"Do not upset the other patients." The ward door closed behind Corrie.

What could she do for Halleen anyway? Corrie gave her friend one last look through the window, then dried her eyes and plodded down the steps. Mary Frances would say a prayer, but the convent wouldn't allow a phone call. Ruth was busy. Evelyn started business school yesterday. Thelma had gone to Des Moines to visit cousins. Jackie was on her way to stardom.

Dear Lord, this is Corrie. I know we haven't talked in a while, but I'm worried about Halleen—

In the lobby, she bumped into a woman in a blue uniform. "Excuse me."

"Are you one of the basketball players? Corrie?"

Not even friends at Central thought of her as a basketball player. She peered through the gloom at the very person she most wanted to see today—next to Mac, of course. "Mrs. McFarland?"

A bolt of lightning followed by a thunderclap shook the building. Everyone in the lobby flinched.

Mrs. McFarland put a steadying hand on Corrie's elbow. "What brings you to the hospital? I hope your brothers are all right."

"It's Halleen, our forward. She won't wake up." Corrie pressed her hand over her mouth, trying to keep from sobbing.

"Let's give the storm a moment." Mac's mother led her to the chapel. The floor, chairs, and altar were dark wood, but a faint glow through the stained-glass windows warmed the room.

"Go ahead. I'm not very good at praying."

"You can talk, and that's what prayer is, talking with God." Chapped hands clasped hers, then Mrs. McFarland asked God to heal Halleen.

"Thank you." Corrie's biggest worry had been put to rest. Now to work the conversation around to Mac without letting on she was goofy over him. "May I give you a ride home?"

"That would be lovely."

Corrie held the umbrella over their heads and they dashed to the car.

Mrs. McFarland must have been thinking about her son. "I don't know if Mac confided his plans to you ..."

Corrie dropped the key on the floor. "No, ma'am, he didn't."

"He took an assistant store manager position in Michigan." Were those tears or raindrops on her face?

"Oh, I'm so sorry. I mean, it's great that he'll be a store manager, but ... Omaha will miss him." *Especially me.* Corrie finally got the key into the ignition and the car started. "Was this a sudden decision?"

"He'd been hoping for a promotion. Then his brother moved home from college. They're different."

"And how, I mean, of course, my brothers are different too." She turned onto St. Mary's Avenue.

"Mac is more cautious, responsible, thoughtful. Herman—"

"Your older son's name is Herman?" Corrie missed the turn and had to backtrack a block. "Not that I thought you named him Mr. Smooth."

Mrs. McFarland chuckled. "Their father was quite a reader. He named his sons after Herman Melville and Horatio Alger, poor boys."

Corrie peered at the row of bungalows. "Which house is yours?"

"Third one on the right. You know where we live?"

Uh-oh. Her excuse came out in a tumble of words as she parked. "I looked you up in the telephone book. I called last night, to see if Mac was okay. He got sick at my party. Maybe the barbecue—"

"It wasn't your food." Instead of hurrying inside, Mrs. McFarland paused, as if she might be praying again. Then she turned toward Corrie, her eyebrows drawn together.

She knows. She knows I'm crazy about her son.

"A few years ago Mac's cousin built an airplane. When Mac went out to watch him fly, Henry crashed right in front of him. Mac pulled him from the wreckage, but he was dead, probably killed in the impact."

"Oh no." Corrie shivered against a sudden chill.

"The doctors prescribed rest. We had to hire a nurse and have the school send his work home. And … no airplanes."

"But … planes are safer now. I'm going to be the safest pilot ever." Now they were both crying. "He left because I got an airplane. Will he…"

"Keep praying." Mrs. McFarland gave her a hug, then ran to her house.

CHAPTER
ELEVEN

MAC KNEW ALL the statistics about Montgomery Ward's Mail Order House: the world's largest reinforced concrete building, two million square feet on eight floors, its own post office and railroad shipping platform. But the interior went way beyond the Santa's workshop scene Mac had imagined.

Train cars brought bags of orders. A machine slit open the envelopes. Each item moved by chutes and conveyor belts to the packing room so that the entire order arrived during a twenty-minute window. The packages were weighed, then sorted by parcel post or freight. The complexity and enormity of the task spun Mac's head. How did anyone get the right order?

Most of Mac's week in Chicago was spent inside the administration building, undergoing training with a large group of new managers. College classes without tuition. *Take that, Mr. Smooth.*

Occasionally office girls would sashay in with newly printed paperwork. Clothed in silk stockings and new dresses, they played the vamp with movie star glances of thin eyebrows and thick mascara. The other managers flirted back with compliments and smart remarks. All those feminine wiles couldn't keep Mac from thinking about Corrie. He said a prayer for her, that she'd stay safely grounded.

Mac hopped the early train to Detroit with a full load of confidence, a briefcase of training manuals, and a new boss Joe, with experience at Marshall Field's. Michigan Central Station boosted his mood even further. The bustle of passengers, elegant concourse, and vaulted ceilings of the waiting room said Detroit was the place to be.

Their taxi sped along broad Woodward Avenue with thousands of other would-be race car drivers. They left behind smoking factories and skyscrapers for the small town of Royal Oak. As recommended by the construction crew, he and his boss checked into the Brunswick Hotel, ate lunch next door at the appropriately named Royal Oak Lunch, then hauled their briefcases a couple blocks north. The downtown area consisted of small businesses in single-story buildings. The six-story-tall Washington Square Building towered over all. Across the street stood a new three-story building, yellow brick with limestone art deco accents. Gold lettering on a dark-red sign proclaimed *Montgomery Ward & Co.* On the glass door, a hand-written notice announced the store would open June 29.

Joe peered up through his round glasses. "This is it."

"Ten times the size of the Omaha store, which has ten times the population." Mac took a few steps north. No false front here. The building stretched as far on Fourth Street as it did on Washington. Uncertainty wormed up his spine. "Tell me the top floors are offices."

"It's all retail. And it's all ours."

Mac scanned the mom-and-pop stores. "So what do our neighbors think?"

"Most hope we'll bring more traffic. We don't compete with the meat market, drugstore, or cleaners." Joe tucked his straw boater under his arm, smoothed his hair, then elbowed Mac. "C'mon, old boy. Got a store to run."

The front door opened to the damp odor of wet paint. Fans and pendant lamps hung from tall ceilings. A double staircase led to the second floor. Only the back counter looked familiar to Mac. Would they have enough merchandise to fill this empty space?

"You can't put that here," yelled a female voice. "Wait until the painters finish. You don't want drips and spatters on these new desks."

"Don't want new desks rained on." The male spoke with an Italian accent. "Wood don't like wet."

"Oh yeah? Then keep them in the back."

"The back is full, I tell you. Full of shelves, display cases, cash registers, signs, tables. No room for nothing."

Joe hurried across the tile floor. "Good afternoon."

"Says you." The man's dark eyes studied them with suspicion.

The woman stood with hands on hips. Blond hair curled around her head like a halo, but her expression was anything but angelic. Through pinched lips, she said, "Sorry, fellows. The store doesn't open for two weeks."

Opening in two weeks. Could they pull that off?

The boss extended his hand. "Joe Avery, store manager, and Mac McFarland, assistant manager."

The woman's face softened into a smile. "Shirley Wendell, head cashier. I've been keeping an eye on expenses and checks paid out."

"Salvatore DiFlorio—I go by Sal—head delivery man, but right now king of chaos."

"Let's see what you got." Joe motioned for Sal to lead the way. Sal and Shirley gave the grand tour as Mac took notes for their to-do list. Joe found the painters having an extended lunch on the roof and sent them down to finish the offices. Mac and Sal moved the desks to the loading dock. Joe found the telephone and called the newspaper to announce interviews would start the next day. Which was how Mac found himself sitting in a freshly painted office behind the double-pedestal oak desk from page 331 of the catalog, talking to dozens of women the next morning.

When the noon whistle sounded, Joe asked, "Ready for lunch?"

"Am I ever." Mac stood and stretched.

"Find any good applicants?" Joe plopped his straw boater on and led Mac out into the fresh air.

"Sure. Mary worked her uncle's farm stand the past three summers. Another Mary ran the post office in her second-grade model city."

A half-smile twitched Joe's mouth. "Might know how to make change."

"Mary Elizabeth and Mary Margaret sew their own clothes."

"Good start for a fabric department. Any artists who can paint signs?"

Mac shook his head. "No artists, but a few with legible handwriting."

"How about wallpaper experience?"

"No one will admit to it."

"Ah, sounds like you've wallpapered before."

"Never again." Mac shuddered, remembering the slimy misery of Mom's dining room. "How did your interviews go?"

"A few have worked as store clerks. I thought automotive would be the hardest department to fill, what with Ford paying so well. But I found a few fellows whose injuries keep them off the assembly line. They know cars. Now all we need to do is teach them how to run a cash register and be friendly to customers."

Mac hoped Royal Oak's customers would be easier than Omaha's. "What's on this afternoon's agenda?"

"Moving and assembling furniture."

"That'll be a welcome change from interviewing."

Joe clapped his shoulder. "Sorry, old boy. You've got forty more interviewees."

Forty more women… none of whom are Corrie.

————

The sun's first rays peeked over Iowa's Loess Hills, lighting thin layers of altocumulus and the empty Steele Field. Corrie parked the Oldsmobile and shuffled to the hangar.

"You got my message." Mr. Steele sat on a camp chair. Mrs. Zukas had taken his call last night, then roused Corrie and sent her with coffee this morning.

Corrie handed over her Thermos. Any time at the airport was beautiful, dawn especially so, but the sun rose way too early at the summer solstice. "What's the rush?"

"Best time to fly. Air's cool and still. Thunderstorm this afternoon." Her tormentor poured his java. "Here's the deal. We've been flying every day for a month and you're still not ready to solo."

The fog of sleep dispersed in the heat of anger. "You won't *let* me."

"You can barely wrestle it into a turn. You bounce every landing."

He'd bounced a few, too, but she wouldn't mention that. Her fists tightened. "Nothing's broken."

"Yet. Landing gear and my ulcer can't take much more."

"What about replacing the pulleys and cables?"

"Don't want to waste good weather on maintenance."

Corrie didn't either, but this conversation had flown into a cumulus cloud. "So …"

Steele shook his head. "After yesterday's lesson, when you nearly dropped us into the trees, I called your father."

"What? No! I'll catch on. A little more time." Why didn't he talk to her first? Because she was a girl of course. She put her hands on the prop. They couldn't take away her beautiful plane. "I'll borrow my brothers' weights. Build up arm strength. Please–"

Mr. Steele made a chopping motion at his neck. In the air, that gesture meant "level off." "The Arrow Sport isn't a good plane for you. Even an Olympic weight lifter would have trouble."

Corrie clung to the prop, breathing in the engine smell. Her view down the cylinders, cowling, and fuselage blurred. She couldn't give up. A drop of liquid plopped between her feet. Pilots didn't cry. Maybe it was oil.

Steele emptied the last of the coffee. "Found a different aircraft. Your dad made a killing in the stock market yesterday, so he said yes."

Corrie let go of the Arrow. "A Travel Air?" Since Omaha had a Travel Air dealer.

"You are *not* ready for a Travel Air. Roy Furstenberg has a sweet little Overland for you."

She didn't want sweet and little. She wanted fast and fierce. She wanted to fly in the National Air Races. "What engine?"

"Sixty horsepower LeBlond, like the Arrow. And it's red," he said, as if that was the reason she liked the Arrow. He handed her a road map. "The Arrow factory's taking yours. Got a backlog of orders due to a fire at the engine factory. Plan the trip, preflight, and we'll go."

They took off and headed southwest.

"Two thousand feet." Steele tapped the altimeter. "Scan for traffic."

Traffic? *No one's up this early. Hello, Central, looking good.* If Mac was here, they'd swim at Peony Park. And they'd fly—passing cars on the road and dropping bags of flour into silos. Oh, the fun they'd have!

A greasy finger tapped the altimeter. Oops. *C'mon airplane, back where you belong.* Was it disloyal to be excited about a new, easier plane? She'd been telling everyone her lessons were going well, while wondering if she'd ever solo.

The needle on the altimeter zoomed down through two thousand feet. Corrie pulled back and added power. The Elkhorn River joined the Platte. A fisherman waved, and Corrie waggled her wings. Train tracks led past water towers announcing Ashland and Waverly. Where was Havelock?

"Stay north of the rails." Steele pointed. "The first one is Union Airport. Paved runways in the shape of an *N*. Flight school on southwest corner. Next is Arrow. Hangar on the east side."

"Where do I land?"

He gave her his you-have-got-to-be-kidding face.

"Never mind." A low pass over the hangar showed the windsock facing south. Corrie turned onto the downwind leg, then dipped the left wing to check the field for obstructions. Power back, turn onto base, then final.

"Got it," Steele yelled.

He could have it. No sense making a fool out of herself at the factory. The plane had its last hurrah, bouncing, dipping, and swerving before settling onto the grass.

"Gopher holes," Steele muttered. He parked at the hangar.

"Looks good." A man with a Swedish accent focused on the plane.

Mr. Steele started to introduce them, but the man motioned south. "Train over there."

Corrie hurried to catch up to her instructor. "Where's my plane?"

"Municipal."

They walked to the station. Corrie bought sandwiches and Cokes for both of them, then they caught the Burlington back to Omaha. "What do you know about it?"

"Two place, open cockpit. Stalls at thirty-eight. Cruises at eighty-five."

"Sounds a lot like the Arrow." No racehorse.

"Handles better." Steele slumped in the corner and snored away. What a flat tire. If Mac were here, they'd neck, or—since the other passengers looked like a bunch of bluenoses—talk and hold hands.

In the cab from Union Station to Omaha Municipal, Steele laid out the plan. "After tomorrow's lesson, report to Furstenberg's factory. You'll learn engine assembly, rigging, dope and fabric, valve timing, soldering and welding, magnetos, spark plugs, propellers. Expect to get greasy."

"Sounds wonderful."

"Evenings, you'll study weather, regulations, navigation."

"Of course." Everything she needed for a pilot's license.

On the apron sat a biplane with a red fuselage and gold wings, the word *Overland* emblazoned on the vertical stabilizer.

Corrie paid the driver and rushed over to the plane. "Let's fly!"

———

Mac surveyed the main sales floor from the top of the steps. Signs labeled each department: *Automotive, Hardware, Housewares*. Bolts of fabric stood at attention. Draperies hung from curtain rods. Watches and necklaces shone in glass cases. The linens clerk had tapped a creative streak to arrange Cannon towels in arches over the display tables.

Joe carried the sock display up the steps. "What are you doing?"

"Making sure we're ready."

"We are." Joe nodded toward Mac's feet. "Hamstring stretch?"

Oops. Caught in the act. "Old basketball habit."

"You play? We should have found a hoop."

"Played. And coached the girls' team. Trying to be a credit to the community and get promoted."

"Coached girls?" Joe scratched his head with the plaster toes. "Your first management experience."

"Mr. Avery, thanks for bringing my leg upstairs." The lingerie clerk covered her mouth and dipped her knees, a move that looked too practiced. "Oh dear, that didn't sound right."

"Here you go." Joe handed over the plaster leg, then checked his watch. "Showtime. Or in your case, jump ball. We're winners."

His Central team had always gotten a case of the pregame jitters. Jackie chain-smoked. Thelma strung endless synonyms. Mary Frances worked her rosary. But Corrie … Corrie gave him a grin, spun the basketball on her finger, and leaped into the game. With half her confidence, he'd—

Joe rang the bell, calling all the employees to the sidewalk in front of the store for a photograph. The women stood sideways, stretching from Kresge's to Fourth Street. The men sat on the curb in front of them. The photographer waited for a break in the traffic.

"What a fine group of employees!" Joe fanned himself with his hat. "Even found someone who knows wallpaper."

"Hope I can remember all their names."

"Start with your department managers. They'll learn names of the clerks in their sections."

The photographer yelled, "Look at me and say, 'Satisfaction guaranteed!'" He took a photo. "Now say 'Detroit Tigers!'" The smiles were bigger the second try.

The city council and manager lined up beside Mayor Storz to cut the grand-opening ribbon for another photo.

Joe clasped Mac on the shoulder. "Been great working with you."

"Pardon me?" Mac's jaw dropped. "You're leaving?"

"Telegram from headquarters this morning. I'm off to Toledo."

"They couldn't wait a month, a week, another day? Where's that padlock and chain?" Mac looked around, trying to keep a lid on his panic. "Are they sending help?"

"Chicago was impressed with how well you did during training. You've hired good people. Identify your best employee and promote him as your assistant. You don't need to know or do everything. Each department manager runs his own show and reports to you." Joe clapped Mac's shoulder. "Like coaching—you trained your team, practiced, and they're taking the court."

"More like the ringmaster of a circus." With too many clowns.

"Attaboy!" Joe plopped his hat onto his head and hopped into a waiting taxi. "Congratulations on your promotion!"

Two steps into the store, Shirley grabbed his arm. "That woman in draperies don't know nothing from nothing. She mixes up dimes and quarters, can't work the register, don't know how to use a tape measure."

Mac took a deep breath. "She's your employee. Review her training. If she doesn't come up to speed, send her to the children's department." Mac did a double take. "Thanks for wearing a Montgomery Ward's dress today."

All he needed was a clipboard and a whistle.

Sal caught him next. "Those boys you got unloading trucks keep getting their numbers flipped around. If they don't put orders in the right bins, I'll never get 'em to the customers."

"They're your employees. Show them how you want it done."

A clerk shouted from the back counter. "Boss, phone for you."

Coaching time. "Mary, please don't yell. Write a message and bring it to me." Mac hurried to his office. Boss? Promoted to exhaustion with no timeouts. He'd be too tired to worry about Corrie.

———

Yesterday's lesson had been her best yet. After ten hours in the Overland, Corrie managed smooth takeoffs, coordinated turns, and grease-job landings. Today Mr. Steele would let her solo.

A low sound disturbed the birdsong of the summer day. Corrie turned to her instructor. "I don't suppose you skipped breakfast this morning."

He frowned at the darkening sky to the northwest. A cool wind rippled the cottonwoods. A second rumble built into a boom. Definitely thunder. "Breakfast sounds like a good idea." He helped her push the biplane into the hangar, then headed to his jalopy.

"What about this afternoon?"

He shook his head. "Field will be muddy."

"Should I call you? What's your phone number?"

"No phone. Maybe I'll swing by later."

The clouds climbed. At home she'd get nagged into cleaning her room. At the country club, she'd be introduced to all the single sons of Mother's friends. Best to stay here and watch the weather.

A Travel Air buzzed the field and landed, shortly followed by a Waco.

Corrie helped the pilots squeeze their biplanes inside before the clouds let loose. "What brings you to Steele Field?"

"Construction mess at municipal." Jack climbed into Corrie's Overland without asking.

"Get your muddy feet out of my plane." His bootprints would end up on her jodhpurs.

"You know how to get mud out of your cockpit, don't you? Fly upside down." The big goof grinned.

"One good loop clears a season's worth of dead leaves off the floor." Chester leaned his greasy overalls on her fuselage.

As if her instructor would ever get around to teaching aerobatics.

Jack wiggled the controls. "So how do you like this little machine?"

"It's not that much smaller than yours." Corrie crossed her arms.

"Solo?"

Waves of rain pounded the field. "Supposed to today."

Chester found a recent *Omaha World-Herald* and sat in a camp chair. "When's Boeing coming to Omaha?"

Jack snorted. "Same day you have enough money to buy stock."

"When my ship comes in, I'll be at the airfield," Chester muttered.

Maybe Corrie could get a job with Boeing. Passenger traffic

increased every month. Or she could fly the mail. Or instruct—she'd be kinder to students than cranky old Mr. Steele.

"Some fellows are flying Chicago to Berlin."

"In what?" Jack finally removed his sorry carcass from her biplane. "Any photos?"

"Something called the Untin Bowler."

Corrie perched on a packing crate. "*Popular Aviation* says it's a twin-engine Sikorsky float plane. The *Chicago Tribune* is sponsoring the flight." Neither of the flyboys acknowledged her contribution to the conversation.

Chester kept reading. "Secretary of Commerce says airplanes are messengers of peace and goodwill. He hasn't talked to any of the girls who think I should be spending time and money on them instead of flying."

"He forgot the war." Jack asked. "Fokkers, Nieuports, Sopwith Camels."

Chester turned the page and laughed. "Some genius at Penn State figured out what the ideal husband ought to know. 'A lover, plumber, slayer of moths and flies. Manage furnace, raise children, sell old clothing and furniture.'"

"No one wants my old clothes." Jack rested on the doorframe.

Chester kept reading. "'Control his temper. No arguing. Hygiene and sanitation.' Well that knocks us out of the running."

Mac sounded like an ideal husband. She didn't know about his skills with furnaces and children, but he never showed a temper. He dressed neatly, shaved, and smelled good. Was that what marriage was about, a checklist of traits and skills?

Chester looked up. "Ability to sew. You know how to sew?"

"Buttons," Jack said.

"Rib stitching." Corrie had learned at the Overland factory.

Chester turned the page. "Air tour of Nebraska."

"When?" Corrie asked.

"Labor Day. Rapid Air Lines is sending its Ford Trimotor. Mid-West Aviation, Omaha Airways, Overland Airways, and Pioneer Airways are in. The manager of Omaha's municipal airport promises it will be ready."

They looked at the gully washer and laughed. Positioning the airfield between the Missouri River and Carter Lake meant constant mud.

"Where do I sign up?" Corrie reached for the newspaper.

Chester didn't let go. "Doesn't say."

"You're a student, Corrie." Jack shook his head. "You'll get lost."

"I'm not flying around this patch the rest of my life."

"Ask Steele to take you. Get some cross-country time."

Corrie resisted the urge to smack him. "It's two months from now. I'll be ready."

"Go with us as a ticket taker. Or wing walker." Jack leaned over Chester and pointed to another article three columns over. "What's that about a Cessna forced down?"

Flyboys. Corrie was sick of being underestimated. If Mac was here, he'd encourage her. Or at least respect her enough to listen.

CHAPTER
TWELVE

"PAYDAY!" Shirley slapped an envelope on Mac's desk. "Don't spend it all in one place." She wagged her finger and marched to the next employee.

Mac counted out the cash. Store manager pay, and oh boy, he'd earned every dime this week. He needed to find a place to live and move out of the hotel. And save up for a car. And …

And celebrate! He'd made store manager. They'd made it through the first week. He should take his staff out to dinner. Mac ran his thumb across Andrew Jackson's and Abe Lincoln's portraits. He was holding more money than he'd ever made, but no, it wasn't enough to buy dinner, or even Saunders ice cream sodas, for the whole crew.

He called the grocer he'd met earlier in the week and ordered a hundred ice pops.

After closing, the staff gathered on the loading dock for Popsicles. Employees clustered by department. Many of them knew each other. Working with friends made for good morale.

Mac stood off to the side, earning wary glances from his staff. As their boss, an out-of-towner with a different accent, he shouldn't expect to be buddies with his staff. He'd need to look elsewhere for friends.

Which made him miss Corrie all the more.

———

Corrie raced into the house waving her logbook. "I passed my check ride!" Mrs. Zukas wasn't in the kitchen. Her parents weren't in the living room. "I'm a pilot!" she yelled to no response.

No brothers in the basement or garage. She grabbed the telephone and called the store.

"Tinley Jewelers. How may I help you?" The saleslady spoke with the slow, refined voice Mother had tried to impose on Corrie.

"Hi, Mary. Is Father around?"

"I'm sorry, Miss Corrie. Mr. Tinley is unavailable. I will tell him you called."

"How about Ernie?" He worked for Father as a watchmaker.

"Mr. Ernest is with a customer. I'll tell him you called."

Corrie sighed. "Rats!"

"You have a rodent problem?" Mary whispered.

"No, not at all. It's an expression." If that rumor got around, Mother would cast a kitten. "I'll see them when they get home."

Now what? Corrie read the last entry in her logbook again. *31 July 1929 Private Pilot flight check satisfactory.* She wasn't allowed to call Harry at Union Pacific or Artie at Mutual. She could drive out to the country club to tell Mother... if she took a bath and changed into a dress. Jackie had moved to Hollywood. The convent didn't let Mary Frances talk on the phone and neither did the hospital where Ruth took her nurse's training. Thelma might be home, but Corrie wanted a conversation, not, "Congratulations, felicitations, bravo."

No fun having good news without someone to share it with. *Oh, Mac.*

———

Mac reached across the restaurant table and shook Dr. Joseph Jandali's hand. "Thank you for joining me."

The doctor undid his suit coat and settled into the adjacent chair. He had dark hair and glasses. Mac guessed he was in his early thirties. "I watched your building go up from my office window." His accent sounded European. "How is business?"

"Good." Like careening down Omaha's steepest hill after an ice storm.

The waitress filled their coffee mugs and took their orders.

Mac leaned on the table and launched into his spiel. "Montgomery

Ward's warehouses have medical departments to care for employees at work. After a year on the job, workers receive complete medical care at home too. But they're still figuring out how to apply those benefits to retail."

The doctor whistled. "Forward thinking. Healthy staff means less absenteeism. You'll attract and keep good people."

"Exactly. Would you be interested in providing medical service to the store? I have a hundred employees." If no one else had quit.

The doctor stroked his chin. "As busy as you are, with all those customers in and out, you could end up with a Typhoid Mary situation."

Mac shuddered. The publicity would shut the store down.

"For employees and for customers who have emergencies." Dr. Jandali smiled. "Yes. I'd like to be your medical department."

"If you write up a proposal, I'll send it to headquarters."

They spent the rest of the meal analyzing this year's Detroit Tigers, then the doctor returned to his office.

Since the store didn't have a cafeteria, Mac talked to the restaurant manager about feeding the employees. They decided on a selection of cold sandwiches and fruit delivered midday Saturday, their busiest day.

Most Montgomery Ward's warehouses had libraries. The Royal Oak library was across the street at the Washington Square Building. On the way back to the store, he'd stop in and see if they'd stay open a half hour later on Friday nights to accommodate his employees.

Finally, the warehouses had musical and athletic groups. The store didn't have practice space, but the Methodist church did. After the Sunday service, he'd ask. Then his thoughts, as always, found their way to Corrie.

CHAPTER
THIRTEEN

"BE BACK LONG BEFORE SUNSET"—MR. Steele crossed his arms and scowled–"or forget flying the Nebraska Air Tour."

"Yessir." Corrie would like to sass him, but she needed his instruction to prepare for her commercial license. All she had to do was follow the Missouri River to Kansas City and the Women's Air Tour. No chance of getting lost.

"Watch out for traffic, especially close to the airport. I can see the headlines now: 'Fifteen Flying Flappers in Fiasco.'" He'd missed his calling in journalism.

"I'd better go so I land before the race pilots." She took off at sunrise.

No one else in the sky. What was wrong with people, missing out on an opportunity like this? Both Mother and Mrs. Zukas had turned her down, Mother for a golf game, Mrs. Zukas with the old "if God wanted man to fly" nonsense. On this beautiful day? Of course God wanted this girl to fly.

Two glorious hours later, the skyscrapers of Kansas City poked through the haze. She saw grain elevators and trains but no air traffic. The airport sat north of the city, on the peninsula where the Kansas River joined the Missouri. The runways were paved and the terminal was a fancy new building. Omaha had some catching up to do.

Waves of heat rose from the concrete. Corrie landed and jumped out of the cockpit, yanked off her jacket and helmet, and stretched. Her poor little Overland looked like a toy next to the new Travel Air biplane. She stood on tiptoes, peeking around the propeller, trying to see what engine hid behind the large cowling. The smell of hot oil radiated from the cylinders—the pilot must be nearby.

A stubby fellow with dark hair sauntered from the nearby hangar.

"Good morning, sir. I need fuel." Corrie turned and realized it wasn't a fellow. "You're a girl."

A grin stretched across her round face. "So are you." Like Corrie, the woman wore jodhpurs, boots, and a white blouse. The imprint of goggles circled her eyes.

"You're a pilot," Corrie and the woman said in unison.

Corrie added, "Sorry. I didn't mean to mistake you for a line boy."

"If that's the worst anyone says about me, I'm having a great day." She shook Corrie's hand with a firm grip.

Corrie gasped. "You must be Pancho Barnes!"

"The one and only." The grin widened.

"The newspaper said you were out of the race."

Pancho called the race organizers an unrepeatable name. "They let some fellow drive onto the field. He lost the roof of his Chevy, and I lost my right wing. So I hitched a ride with the Travel Air rep, and I'm heading to Cleveland anyway. You coming?"

"In my plane? Be there next week."

"You beat the racers." She checked her watch. "They'll be here for lunch."

"You beat them too." Corrie nodded toward the biplane she'd been admiring. "What's under that cowling?"

"Three hundred horses."

Corrie whistled. "Is that Opal Kunz's, the one race officials said was too much for a woman to handle?"

"Same power, different plane. Since I'm out of the race, I can show those saps how it's done." Pancho grinned. "C'mon in out of the heat and I'll buy you a cold one."

"No hooch. I'm flying back to Omaha today."

The woman paused, head tilted back, one eyebrow raised. "Do I look like someone who'd entice you into illegal activity?" Before Corrie could apologize again, Pancho burst into a hearty laugh. "You betcha!"

In the restaurant, Pancho bought Coca-Colas and smoked a cigar.

They talked planes. Pancho had been flying a year longer than Corrie. She'd bought her Travel Air about the time Corrie had gotten her Overland, and developed a barnstorming act with friends. Union Oil Company paid her to advertise for them and fly their bosses around. She had won races, including one from San Francisco to Los Angeles against Roscoe Turner and his pet lion. Three different aircraft manufacturers had hired her to test their new planes. And she only had a student license.

Pancho looked left, then right, then leaned across the table and whispered, "Travel Air's new Mystery Ship is going to be in Cleveland."

"Mystery Ship?" Corrie whispered back. "What's the scoop?"

"Low-wing monoplane. Wright Whirlwind engine. Built for racing."

"Your next plane?"

Pancho gave a cat-who-swallowed-a-canary smile.

The cook said their order was ready. Pancho and Corrie took box lunches and a wagon full of Cokes on ice to the hangar.

The terminal's balcony filled with spectators. Race officials scanned the skies with binoculars.

"Travel Air." Pancho nodded at the sky. "Attagirl, Louise."

When the tall pilot landed, Pancho sent her inside to the restroom and watched the Travel Air refuel. "Fill the kid's too." She pointed her thumb at Corrie's Overland.

"Seen anything hinky?" Corrie asked in an undertone.

"I keep an eye out for my friends." She lowered her voice. "Thea had dirt in her gas tank. Claire had a flying wire eaten by acid. Someone put a lit ciggy in Blanche's baggage compartment. Since San Bernardino, we circle the planes each night and post guards."

Flying had enough hazards without sabotage. "Are you packing heat?"

The flier presented her with a fist. "Are you?"

Corrie returned her gesture. "I have three older brothers."

She looked away. "Lucky you."

Louise returned, and Pancho handed her a box lunch and a bottle of Coke. "This is the pilot of the little red-and-yellow plane, but I don't know her name."

Corrie introduced herself. "I'm rooting for you."

"Root for all the race pilots. The more we make Cleveland ..." Louise gave a weary sigh. "I'm too tired to make sense."

Corrie nodded. "It's a victory for all of us."

"You eat. I'll talk." Pancho told about Louise setting records for speed, altitude, and endurance when she sold Travel Airs in Oakland, California.

Gladys O'Donnell landed and the routine repeated. The Waco pilot lived in Long Beach, so Pancho knew about her too.

Ruth Nichols arrived in a Rearwin, a high-wing monoplane.

"I live in New York," Ruth told Corrie. "Pancho's making up stories."

"Would I do that?" Once again, a horrified expression stretched the round face. "Darn tootin'!" The pilots joined in the laughter. Corrie had learned a lot about throwing parties from her mother. Pancho raised the bar to a new level.

The rooftop crowd cheered. An orange high-wing plane turned final.

"Amelia." Out of the side of her mouth, Pancho said, "Don't get tangled with a publicity hound like Putnam. He's got Amelia strung like a marionette."

Corrie liked flying so much, she'd wished for a sugar daddy … but she wouldn't admit that. "Bet the Vega's comfortable to fly."

Mary Von Mach introduced herself, then said, "Enclosed cockpit seems like a better idea every time I go through rain and peel my skin off."

"Are either of you Neva Paris?" a reporter asked.

"She's over there powdering her nose." Pancho pointed to the woman emerging from her Curtiss Robin as reporters shouted questions and took photos. "Local girl makes good."

"Did anyone's relatives meet the derby along the route?" Corrie asked, thinking of her own family's lack of interest.

"Louise's folks met her in Wichita. And her boss, Walter Beech, gave her a pep talk." Pancho didn't mention her family. Hands on hips, she scanned the flight line and planes coming in for landing. She pointed to the low-wing monoplane on final. "Alexander Bullet. I want one of each, including your Overland, kiddo. Bet it does some sweet aerobatics."

Corrie hung her head. "My instructor won't let me try."

"Let's wring it out!" Pancho faked a step toward the red-and-yellow plane. "Whoo, scared you, didn't I? Admit it. I scare myself!"

"Aerobatics is essential." The heavily accented voice belonged to a sturdy woman in a white flying suit.

Pancho introduced Thea Rasche, who had a German aerobatics license.

"An aerobatic license?" Corrie asked. "I want one!"

"Don't we all!" Pancho and Thea laughed.

The rest of the pilots arrived. In spite of their exhaustion, they seemed happy to talk to Corrie. Mary asked about her engine, airspeed, and gallons per hour. Several promised to stop by Omaha for a visit.

What a privilege to meet so many female pilots. Corrie hardly took a breath in the excitement of it all. It was possible to make a life of flying. These women were like her. Well, Thea was from Germany and Jessie from Australia. And they all had a few years on her. Bobbi, at twenty-three the closest in age, had already set altitude and endurance records. Blanche, Phoebe, and Louise were married. Gladys, Edith, and May had children as well as husbands. Louise and Amelia were tall, about five foot eight. Vera announced with a grin she was four eleven and ninety-seven pounds. Amelia and Ruth Nichols had been flying over five years. Phoebe had barnstormed and flown the Ford Reliability Tour. Ruth Elder had flown the Atlantic with her flight instructor two years ago. The ink was still wet on Blanche's license and she had fewer hours than Corrie. All were smart and strong and thought flying was copacetic.

Race officials arrived with the weather report. They consulted stopwatches and clipboards, and waved red and white flags. The racers roared off to St. Louis.

"Aren't you going too?" Corrie asked.

"With that engine, I'll be there yesterday." Pancho tipped her head toward the remaining Travel Air. "Well, kiddo, what's your plan?"

"Learn aerobatics. Paint 'Skelly Oil' on the side of my plane and fly their executives around. Get hired as a demonstration pilot for Overland. And get a faster plane." Corrie thought of Mac. "Maybe get married."

"Only if he's rich and likes to nookie." Pancho wagged her finger.

Corrie blushed. "I'm flying the Nebraska Air Tour next month."

"Love those cross-countries. Kiss all the cowboys for me." Pancho sent the Travel Air rep into the passenger seat and climbed into the pilot's seat. "And find a crazy fellow with a pet cougar and beat him in an air race. Then move to California where the flying's great!"

"Visit me in Omaha!" After meeting Pancho, Mother would think Corrie was a saint.

Corrie grinned all the way home.

"That was my mad money."

"Five dollars for mad money? You crazy?"

Mac pushed back from his desk as the voices grew louder and two women burst into his office.

The lingerie saleslady, one of the Marys, carried a beaded handbag. She fluttered her eyelashes, the flapper version of a damsel in distress. "I had five dollars in my purse and someone stole it."

Shirley crossed her arms and parked her backside on Mac's desk, like she owned the place. "You were told not to bring valuables to work."

"I need it … after work." The handbag clicked like a bag of marbles.

"Why not keep your money in your pocket?" Mac asked.

"Dresses don't have pockets."

Shirley gave him her "poor little bunny" look. "She's right."

"Your dress has one."

Shirley slipped her fingertips into the shallow pocket at her waist and pulled out her handkerchief. "No room for a coin purse."

"I'll make a suggestion to headquarters." Mac shuffled through the piles, looking for the composition book where he kept notes.

"You change fashions with a two-cent stamp to Chicago, we'll call you a miracle worker." Shirley drummed her fingers on the wood. "So what'll we do while Ward's sews pockets in all our dresses?"

"Everyone could wear aprons."

The two women stared at him with identical expressions of horror. Shirley recovered first. "I thought you wanted Montgomery Ward's to be a high-class operation."

"I did. Okay, no aprons." He found a scratch pad and a pencil. "Let's see, at headquarters they have cloak rooms and parcel rooms."

"We don't have enough staff to keep a hat check girl busy."

Mary tipped her head. "What about lockers, like high school?"

"Now there's an idea." Mac grabbed his steel hundred-foot tape measure, page 616 in the catalog, and stepped into the hall. "In the break room. Maybe on the second and third floors, if we have space."

On the sales floor, someone yelled, "Stop! Come back here with that!"

A skinny kid dashed from the jewelry department carrying a ring display. He ran through dry goods, heading for the Fourth Street exit.

"Call the police!" Mac wound up and fired the tape measure over the stacks of fabric, hitting the thief between the shoulder blades. The fellow stumbled through the door and turned left. Dodging shoppers and displays, Mac raced after him. The ring display sailed overhead, landing in the street. As they reached Lafayette Avenue, the sap put on a burst of speed. *Can't have him running into traffic.* Mac leaped onto his back. The thief hit the sidewalk with an *oof.*

With a brother like Mr. Smooth, Mac had plenty of experience fighting dirty. Only this time he wasn't on the receiving end. He pressed a knee to the thief's back, pinning him, and grabbed both wrists.

"Ow! Get off!"

"Cops are on the way." Shirley retrieved the rings. "None missing."

"New display. Tight fit." But not as tight as the belt around the thief's wrists.

Across the street at the Royal Oak Theater, the matinee crowd applauded and cheered.

A motorcycle parked on the sidewalk. "You doing my job, Mac?"

"He's hurting me! He hit me and knocked me down!" the thief yelled.

"Good morning, Officer Hayward. I'll gladly turn him over to you."

"Let me get my handcuffs."

"Look over here, everybody! You too, punk." The *Tribune* photographer waved from the corner. "Shirley, move closer to Mac and hold up the rings. What a great shot!"

"You called the *Trib*?" Mac wasn't used to this small-town life, only a few blocks to the police station and newspaper office.

Shirley grinned like she was posing for a Pepsodent ad. "Sure. News flash to all robbers—crime doesn't pay. Our boss is a hero."

Hero? If the photo came out well, he'd send a copy to Mom. *Take that, Mr. Smooth.*

A police car pulled up. Officer Hayward cuffed the robber, shoved him inside, then followed Mac into the store to interview witnesses. They paused at the door as Shirley traced out the paths of criminal and pursuer and the location of every customer and clerk. Got to admire her memory.

Officer Hayward paused his notetaking. "Don't want to tell you how to run your business, Mac, but think about moving your jewelry case."

"Soon as we're done talking, it's coming back by the catalog desk." Chicago told him how to arrange the store, but they didn't say he had to keep it that way.

"Mr. McFarland." The lingerie clerk arrived with the clicking of her beaded purse. "You didn't have to call the police. My money wasn't stolen after all. It had slipped through a hole in the lining." She pulled out a five-dollar half-eagle coin with an apologetic shrug.

"Glad to hear we don't have a thief among us. Find a safe place for your cash, Mary, and I'll ask headquarters about lockers." Mac mopped his forehead.

"You look like you could use a drink." The officer elbowed Mac.

Mac gave him a sidelong glance. "Prohibition repealed and no one told me?"

"Diner up the road sells more than coffee, but you didn't hear it from me." Officer Hayward headed for the customers chatting by the front door.

Mac didn't need a drink. He needed … Corrie.

———

Beneath low clouds, Corrie landed the Overland on the muddy field at Omaha Municipal. She taxied down the row of planes and parked.

A man in a suit approached. "Are you here for the air tour?"

Corrie pulled off her goggles and helmet. "Yes I am."

He clenched his clipboard. "You're a girl!"

"I'm a pilot."

"Hold on, little lady. This is a serious air tour."

"To promote aviation throughout the state." Corrie swung out of the cockpit. "To demonstrate how airplanes can support business." She pulled the stick back and secured it with the seat belt. "To encourage cities to develop airfields." Her brothers had cut chunks of wood into triangles, painted them yellow, and engraved them with her airplane's number. She used these to chock her wheels. "And show the United States that Nebraska is ready for the twentieth century."

She strolled off to the large plane in the next spot. No wonder Braniff and Northwest chose it. The upholstered seats and enclosed cabin increased comfort for passengers. And the starter and wheel-brakes made life easier for pilots.

Mr. Clipboard followed. "Miss, you shouldn't be here."

"Why is that?"

He sputtered. "You're a girl."

A girl who had been accepted for the air tour. A girl who would not be given the bum's rush by some fellow who didn't know an aileron from an elevator. "You, sir, are standing under the wing of a Stinson Detroiter, made by Eddie Stinson, whose two older sisters are pilots."

"That's all well and good, but—"

"The sisters' flying school was so highly respected, the Canadian government sent their pilots to them for training. Katherine Stinson was the first girl to loop a plane and to carry mail, and she set bunches of endurance and distance records. Marjorie Stinson was the only female pilot in the army reserves, and she designed planes for the navy."

The fellow huffed. "I'll see what Major Houghland says about this."

"He's by the Douglas." The killjoy strutted off.

Like the Stinson and Lindbergh's Spirit of St. Louis, the Cessna Cantilever also was a high-wing monoplane. Increased visibility would be handy, especially on landings. With less drag and its big engine, it could really go. Oh, but the Travel Air biplane made Corrie's heart sing. Seeing so many in the Women's Air Derby confirmed a Travel Air was her next step.

Lawrence Enzminger, the head of Mid-West Aviation, dropped his duffel bag into the front seat. "Got your eye on my plane, Miss Corrie?"

"Louise Thaden won the Women's Air Derby in a Travel Air."

"And Marvel Crosson died in one."

"Louise thinks it was carbon monoxide poisoning. Hers gave her a dose before the race."

The man squinted. "Carbon monoxide in an open cockpit?"

"Could happen if she sits lower than you."

"I suppose." He glanced at his watch and nodded toward the hangar. "Pilots' meeting in five minutes. Any trouble getting your entry approved?"

"Mr. Steele wrote a letter of recommendation. And Mr. Furstenberg put in a good word."

"Hoping to sell planes"—he switched to his radio voice—"*so easy a girl can fly it.*"

"Exactly." Which was why he needed to hire Corrie.

The hangar filled with pilots in leather jackets and jodhpurs. Corrie was the only girl. Maybe she should give up on Mac—he'd left town without a word—and date one of these flyboys. Were any of them single? In the corner stood a group of women and children, the families of the pilots. Corrie's brothers and father couldn't leave work, and Mother wouldn't miss bridge.

Major Houghland assigned each plane a number. They'd fall in for takeoff, follow each other to the next airfield, and land in order. The field in Auburn was questionable, so only a few lighter planes would land there. The rest would go to Beatrice, then they'd all meet at Falls City.

Corrie and three other pilots volunteered for Auburn. The major pulled her aside. "What's your total time now, Miss Tinley?"

"Eighty-eight hours, sir."

"You've made your share of landings here in Omaha. You're used to setting down in a swamp." He gave each pilot a hard stare. "Make a low pass. If you don't like what you see, divert to Beatrice or Falls City. Even if the fellow in front of you decides to land. Got it?"

"Yessir." Houghland's military bearing had them all standing at attention.

As they returned to their planes, Bill and Myron flanked Corrie. "We'll take off first. Follow us so you won't get lost," Bill said.

"And if you do get lost, turn around and come back," Myron added.

"Sure." She couldn't wait to get up in the air and escape their baloney.

Her flight instructor and the Overland's builder stood next to her plane. "Everything running okay?" Mr. Furstenberg asked.

"Everything's jake."

Mr. Furstenberg followed her as she gave the Overland another preflight. "Heard rumors of sabotage at the Women's Air Derby. Keep an eye on fellows fueling you. My employees will meet you in Falls City, Lincoln, and Fremont. And here's a list of mechanics I trust at airfields in the rest of the state. They'll check in with you at least once."

"Thank you, Mr. Furstenberg." Surely vandals wouldn't mess with her little plane. She tucked the paper into the inner pocket of her flight jacket, then stowed her chocks.

"Got your map?" Mr. Steele had gone over the route and all its hazards a hundred times. "Finding Kansas City was easy compared to the lack of landmarks on this flight. And more planes in the sky than you're used to, so scan for traffic. No hotdogging."

Of course no hotdogging. The closest he'd come to teaching aerobatics was a steep turn. She climbed in.

As usual, Mr. Steele had more to say. "No racing. Don't let the wind push you into Iowa."

"Yessir. Nebraska Air Tour. No Iowa. I remember."

He cleared his throat and said her name for the first time. "Corrie ... one of these saps makes a mistake, he'll get a little ribbing, then everyone will forget. You make a mistake ..."

"My flying days are over and it's that much more difficult for the next girl." She looked him in the eye. "Ready for a prop."

"Safe flight." He marched around the wing to the engine.

The first plane took off and the rest rumbled across the grass. Mr. Furstenberg grinned. "Beautiful sight. Wish I could go with you."

Mr. Steele yelled, "Clear."

"Stick back," she called. "Brakes. Magnetos. Contact!"

Mr. Steele pulled the propeller down with a snap and the engine roared to life. He moved out of the way and gave a thumbs-up. Tachometer steady. Oil temperature and pressure good. *Here we go, little Overland. You and me into the sky.* She splashed through the muck, working her way around the deepest puddles, and lined up, watching the planes in front. *What's this lump in the throat? No crying with goggles on.*

A flagman waved her into position. She checked the windsock atop the hangar and pointed the nose a few degrees west. No sense dropping into everyone else's ruts. Best find her own path.

The plane leaped into the air, as happy as she was to be relieved of

Mr. Steele. They left the traffic pattern, climbed to altitude, and leveled off. Now where were Myron, Bill, and that other guy? Their planes weren't that much faster than the Overland. She ought to be able to see them. Two biplanes flew west down Dodge Street, but the southern sky was empty. *Well, who needs them?* Missouri River off the left wing, railroad tracks off the right, map in her lap. No getting lost today.

Corrie looked around and grinned. Tach, oil temp, oil pressure, and compass all held steady. A layer of clouds meant smooth air and no sunburn. A great day to fly. If only Mac were here to share this adventure. "Hello, Nebraska!" she yelled into the slipstream.

All quiet at Offutt Field this morning; the army wasn't training today. As the houses thinned out, the air cleared. Roads formed squares of farmland. She passed over the mouth of the Platte River and the appropriately named town of Plattsmouth. The next two villages were too small for Rand McNally to name. A big white house surrounded by orchards indicated Nebraska City. Corrie turned away from the Missouri and followed the highway, pointing the Overland's nose a few degrees into the wind, and checked her watch. A small river wound beneath her, then railroad tracks, so this must be Auburn. She spotted lines of cars and a haystack with a windsock! Found the airfield!

Corrie made a low pass. No airplane-eating puddles. The grass had been mowed short. Around the pattern. No traffic. Final. "C'mon, little Overland. This is your biggest audience yet. Give me a grease job."

The plane rolled onto the grass easy as you please. "Attagirl!"

Crowds around the field waved. *How many people live in this town anyway? There must be thousands here to see one little plane. Hope the others show up soon.* A flagman directed her to a parking spot. Corrie shut down the engine. Cheers and applause surrounded her.

Corrie pulled off her helmet and goggles, stood, and waved. "Hello, Auburn, and welcome to the All Nebraska Air Tour!"

"Where's the rest? We were told there'd be at least twenty planes!"

"Are you Amelia Earhart?"

"I'm Corrie Tinley from Omaha. Amelia's not a Nebraskan." Amelia was famous, taller, and blonder. Corrie climbed out. "The others will be along soon as they finish sightseeing." She hoped.

Someone bought her a Coke and a sandwich. Corrie signed autographs, handed out Overland brochures, and answered questions. Finally a low hum announced Bill and Myron had found the field.

"Where have you boys been?" Corrie asked after they shut down.

They exchanged glances. "Out looking for you."

Corrie crossed her arms. "By flying west? Tell it to Sweeney."

A Stinson Detroiter, not the Omaha one, landed. The crowd recognized Governor Weaver and applauded.

A Travel Air from Lincoln flew in to give rides, and an elderly man shuffled to the head of the line. "I arrived here in a covered wagon pulled by an ox team. Seems like I oughta try this flying business before I die."

Corrie helped the man step onto the wing, climb into the cockpit without hitting his head, and buckle in. "Where's your farm from here?"

"Northeast corner of where the highway crosses the river."

The pilot gave a thumbs-up. "We'll find it, old timer."

The farmer waved as they taxied out and headed north. He was still swinging his arms when they returned.

Corrie assisted him out. "How was your flight?"

"Delightful!" He grinned. "Them cows sure was surprised!"

Corrie grinned back. What fun to give people their first airplane rides. Next year she'd take up passengers.

Myron sauntered over as the fuel truck topped off her plane for departure. "If you see the Kansas border, turn around."

Corrie wagged her fuel stick at him. "And if you see the Colorado border, keep on going." She took off first and set a course southeast along the river. The governor's Stinson swept past. Corrie kept it in sight and followed it to Falls City.

"Okay, plane, another smooth landing." The crosswind threatened to push her into the trees. Corrie put the plane into a crab, straightened out at the last minute, and got it onto the ground. Not her prettiest landing. *Hope the major wasn't watching.*

Other planes joined those who'd started at Beatrice, for a total of twenty. The crowd was as big as Auburn's. The governor gave a speech dedicating the airfield. Corrie answered the Amelia question several more times, thinking she should have brought a sandwich board declaring her identity. Two pilots put on a show of loops and rolls. Next year Corrie would demonstrate her aerobatic skills. And write "Not Amelia" on the sky.

At the evening banquet, pilots were seated by horsepower, putting Corrie at the end. If they'd had a children's table, she'd sit there.

"Miss Tinley. How did you find Auburn?" Major Houghland asked.

"Short grass, well drained, helpful flagmen."

"Let me rephrase my question. How did you locate the airfield?" He shot a glare at Myron and Bill. "You were the first to arrive."

"The landmarks matched the map, especially the iron compass." Pilot slang for railroad tracks. "My calculated time aloft of forty-seven minutes brought me exactly to the airfield."

"Good airmanship."

"Thank you, sir." She resisted the urge to gloat.

Since the major had spoken to her, Jack and Chester decided they could too. They told her the crowd had been small at Beatrice—she hadn't missed anything. Well she hadn't missed Beatrice, but she did miss Mac.

CHAPTER
FOURTEEN

TUESDAY MORNING MAJOR Houghland announced that since the fleet had not maintained an attractive formation, they would depart in groups of three. Bill and Myron looked at Corrie, then shook their heads.

Jack and Chester sighed. "Guess we could slow down for you."

Forever the little sister, tagging along. "The Overland cruises at eighty-five. I hope you can keep up with me."

Bill and Myron stopped her as she walked down the flight line. "Hey, Corrie, we've got a great idea. Let's flour bomb the capitol. See who can hit the tower." They held out filled paper bags.

Tossing flour down an empty silo was great fun, but flour bombing the state capitol building, with the chance of hitting a construction worker or legislator? Thelma would say, "Reckless, thoughtless, irresponsible." The major would dishonorably discharge her. Corrie cupped her ear. "The jail called. Couple of delinquents missing."

The saps grumbled. Corrie braced to be hit by a sack of flour, but Clyde Ice, the Trimotor pilot, stopped the boys with a raised eyebrow. They headed for their planes.

From Corrie's position in the last group of three, a beautiful line of twenty planes stretched across the sky. They flew over the university and the state capitol, then landed at Lincoln Municipal. Lunch consisted of a bread pocket filled with ground beef and cabbage.

A helmet and goggles dropped onto the table. A pilot plopped into the next seat, radiating a wave of airplane smells. Corrie looked up, expecting to see a fellow. Instead an oval face surrounded by curls smiled at her. "You must be Evelyn Nicholas."

The young woman shook her hand. "And you must be Corrie Tinley."

"You made the newspapers, but I haven't. How did you know—"

"Pilots are the biggest gossips. I heard you returned your Arrow. What are you flying now?"

"An Overland. I'll show you." Corrie finished her sandwich. "How's your flying school for girls?"

"I'm still building time, barnstorming, trying to find a manufacturer who will hire me to demonstrate planes for buyers."

"Are you joining the air tour?"

"No plane."

"I've got room."

Evelyn shook her head. "I'd slow you down."

Corrie grinned. "I'm solidly in last place."

They strolled out to the flight line. Peeking into the cockpit, Evelyn noticed, "You already have a passenger."

A forked tongue took in the unfamiliar smells of leather, airplane dope, oil, and gasoline. Yellow stripes stretched from head to tail. Corrie pulled on her gloves. "Hello there. Who put you in my plane?" She climbed on the wing, scooped up the snake, and set it down beside the creek.

"What was that?" Mr. Enzminger looked over from his preflight, his eyebrows reaching for his hairline.

"Garter snake."

Evelyn had backed up ten steps. "You're awfully calm."

"My brothers gave me plenty of reptile experience." Screaming would delight whoever put the snake on her seat—and scare the snake. A scared snake in her flying cables could be disastrous. Corrie scanned the flight line, trying to guess which troublemaker had pulled this stunt.

"Now you have plenty of cross-country experience," Mr. Enzminger said.

"Much more fun," Evelyn agreed.

"Watch for me in the newspapers!" Corrie waved goodbye to her new friend. The fleet headed north to Fremont, passing over red-roofed houses, whitewashed barns, and green fields. On landing, a bump in the grass bounced her back into the sky. She powered up, pulled the stick back, and went around for a second try. This time she put the plane down in a three-point landing well before the bump and kept it on the ground. Thousands of people had seen her bounce. She hoped she wouldn't be sent home.

Corrie joined the fliers eating box lunches while the Veterans of Foreign Wars band played. The handsome pilot of the fastest plane took the seat beside her. "Nice save."

"Pardon me?" *Nerts! Chief Bowhan, Cessna Cantilever pilot and Osage Indian, is talking to me!*

"That hill in the middle of the landing field." His dark eyes glanced at her. "Caught me too. You're smart to go around."

"I learned on a short field. That's how my instructor taught me."

He nodded and concentrated on unwrapping his sandwich. "Mine too."

"Who was your instructor?"

"Walter Beech. He was building Swallows for Matty Laird."

"And now he's making Travel Airs. Did he teach you aerobatics?"

"Picked it up along the way." He turned, eyes wide, head shaking. "Not the best way to learn. Wait for your instructor to teach you."

When would Mr. Steele would get around to that? "Your wife didn't come with you on this trip?"

"No. Busy with family."

"You've got the life I want." Corrie sighed, thinking of Mac. "A spouse who likes planes. Air racing, test pilot for manufacturers, flying in the Ford Reliability Tour."

He rolled his apple between his fingers. "The world is changing. Your life won't be the same as mine. Maybe it will be better."

"Banana oil." Nothing could be better. "What's next for you?"

"Keep flying for Cessna until someone makes me a better offer."

"Let me know if there's an opening."

"At Cessna?"

"Why not? Travel Air has Louise Thaden. Elinor Smith flies for Bellanca."

Chief nodded. Did that mean he agreed to talk her up to Clyde Cessna or only that he'd heard of those other pilots?

Lunch finished, Major Houghland pulled Chief aside for a meeting. Corrie stretched out in the shade of her wing to watch others give rides and show off. The midfield bump surprised two more pilots.

"Whose plane is this?" A barefoot girl in a feedsack dress squatted by the Overland's front tire.

"It's mine."

Her eyes narrowed. "How'd it get here?"

"I flew it."

Head tilted, she pondered Corrie. "Where's your papa?"

"In Omaha."

"Got a husband?"

"No, but I have three brothers. Do you have any brothers?"

"Four brothers. And a niece."

Corrie whistled. "You're already an aunt."

"Yep." The girl nodded at the plane. "Can you learn me how to fly?"

"When I have more experience and you're tall enough to reach the pedals, I'll teach you how to fly."

Her grin revealed two missing teeth. "I'm gonna learn how to fly."

"Let me show you the inside." Corrie helped her climb onto the lower wing and told her what the instruments did.

On tiptoe, the girl touched the stick. "And this is how you steer."

"Right. You're smart!"

"Caboose." A kid in overalls motioned for the girl to follow. "Gotta head home for milking."

Arms outstretched, she jumped off the wing and ran in circles. "I'm going to fly."

"Nope." He grabbed her elbow. "You're going home to help Ma."

The girl pointed at Corrie. "She's a pilot. She said I can be one too. She flew here all by herself."

The kid looked back and spit onto the ground. "All by herself 'cause no fellow wants a girl who wears pants."

Corrie winked at the girl. "Hang onto your dream. Someday your brother will ask you for a ride."

The girl tried to wink back but ended up blinking, then waved.

Late afternoon the air tour flew to Norfolk, another long leg to the northwest. Thousands of people watched Jack fly the Waco as Chester hung from a ladder beneath it, then climbed onto the top wing. The boys had tried to persuade Corrie to be their wing walker, but she thought that was the screwiest idea ever.

As she covered her plane for the night, she found a skinny fellow studying her rudder. He kept his head down and hands in his pants pockets. "I am Gustave," he said slowly. "Roy sent me."

Gustave? Roy? Corrie pulled Mr. Furstenberg's penciled list from her jacket. "Gustave the mechanic? Pleased to meet you."

"Any problems?"

"Not a one." Other than Myron and Bill.

"May I?" Without a glance her way, he began a detailed inspection.

"It's flying well, not using oil." Corrie followed the mechanic around. Why wouldn't he look at her? Was she terribly greasy? Maybe he was shy. She stopped talking and hoped he'd fill the silence.

He headed to the hangar. "See you in the morning."

"Why? Is something wrong with my plane?"

"I will prop," he said over his shoulder. "To hear engine."

Norfolk asked the pilots to attend their Miss North Nebraska Beauty Contest. Corrie went to the hotel, washed her clothes in the sink, wrote a letter to Mac, and pretended she knew where to mail it.

Mac locked up his desk, stood, and stretched. Who was Corrie with on this Friday night? Some golfer from the country club or the boys' basketball team captain … anyone but Mr. Smooth. *Enough. You gave her to God. He's taking care of her.*

Shirley's frizzy head popped into the office. "Boss, got a situation."

"Situation" sounded better than going back to his hot room over the hardware store, falling into a squeaky bed, and being rocked to sleep by the Grand Trunk Railroad. "Spill it."

"Full truck pulled up. No one to unload."

The driver would hightail it back to headquarters with news of the fiasco in the Royal Oak store, bringing an end to his so-called management career. "Where's Walter?"

"College boy went back to Ann Arbor, looking for more prime numbers."

He scanned the schedule. A half dozen employees had left for school. Who was on tonight? "How about Sal?"

"Finished his last delivery and went home."

"Give the driver a cup of coffee." If they had any left. "I'll meet you on the dock in five." He hurried to the sales floor, past a good number of customers and well-ordered displays to dry goods. Plan B better work. He didn't have a plan C. "Helen, I need you to cover drapery tonight."

Before the older woman could argue, he motioned for the peppy brunette with the Dutch boy bob … What was her name? She'd nailed her interview with energy and enthusiasm that rivaled Corrie's. "Mary Jane, come with me please." The young woman set down a curtain and followed him. "You used to work at your father's gas station. I need to you cover automotive tonight."

"Hot dog! I mean, I'd be glad to, Mr. McFarland."

"Ralph, Mary Jane's going to hold the fort while you help me unload."

The older man's mouth pulled down. "Hey, Friday night's usually busy, people buying tools to work on their cars on Saturday."

"The sooner we empty this truck, the sooner you can get back to your department." Mac headed for the dock, hoping for teamwork. No time for a revolt.

Ralph rose to the occasion. They had the truck on its way in an hour. Mac walked the automotive manager back to his department. "Appreciate your help tonight."

"Good workout." The man rolled his shoulders. He rounded the tire display and stared. "What is she doing?"

Mary Jane stood behind the counter, pointing out features of Ward's various car heaters to a half dozen men. "For a Model A or Chevrolet Six, this cast-iron heater keeps you warm as toast. In summer, remove these two bolts, take off the cover, and it cools your engine like a racing manifold for better performance."

"She's getting our customers ready for winter."

Mary Jane looked over her shoulder. "We need more antifreeze."

"What happened to all the cans on the shelf?" Ralph asked.

"Sold. And we're down to our last zero testers."

Ralph took a deep breath. "I'll bring some fresh off the truck."

"Good teamwork." Mac gave them both a thumbs-up. Chicago had told him to hire men for automotive, but they didn't know Mary Jane. He crossed the store to see how it was going in dry goods.

"Smooth as silk." Helen glowed with excitement. "If a lady doesn't like our ready-made drapes, I show her how to make her own. Or she can jazz up our drapes with a valance, tie back, or ruffle. Or sew pillow covers—"

"Boss." Shirley pointed to the catalog desk where a dozen

customers swarmed one panic-stricken clerk. "They came out of the theater, saw the truck, and figured they'd pick up their orders. I haven't finished sorting."

"Can we pull someone from children's?"

She shook her head. "Busy selling school clothes. And two people in ladies' called in sick tonight."

Next week Mac would schedule more staff, but this week … He hurried behind the counter. "May I help the next person in line?"

Finally the rush ended and Mac sent Mary Louise on break. His stomach reminded him he'd missed supper. He found a Hershey bar by the cash register—who left chocolate behind?—and ate it. On the second floor, children's wound down as bedtime approached. Third floor was overrun by giggling girls trying on scarves and hats. He scanned the group, searching for Corrie's curls.

"Need help?" he asked the clerk, wishing he could remember her name.

She propped her chin on her fist. "They spent their first and last dime on the movie across the street. They have to be out front in a few minutes for their mamas and daddies to pick them up."

"Is it that time already?"

One of the girls looked his way, and suddenly he was surrounded.

"You're the fellow who caught the robber."

"I saw your picture in the newspaper."

"Mother was in line for the matinee. She said you looked like an Olympic runner."

Mac signed the girl's autograph book. "I'm a basketball player."

"We're a basketball team!"

The blonde propped a hand on her hip in a way that reminded him of Jackie. "You ought to watch us play."

"Y'all come," said the redhead.

"I'd enjoy that." Soon as he had the store under control. Mac glanced at the clock. Chaos made time fly. He hurried downstairs to the public address system and gave the closing announcement. He checked out a few straggling customers and locked the doors behind them.

Shirley swung her purse. "Good thing you know how to unload a truck, run a cash register, and wait on customers."

"The Omaha store is small. I did everything." Mac had learned a lot, although he still thought his boss's laziness was a bad example. "Do you know how late the diner's open?"

"Midnight. Got a speakeasy in the basement."

"That's what Officer Hayward said. What if they're raided?"

"Stay upstairs, get your supper, and you'll be fine."

Diner food filled his empty stomach, but not the empty spot in his heart for Corrie.

───────

Wednesday morning, Gustave propped and sent Corrie off from Norfolk without meeting her eye. Marrying a mechanic might have some advantages, but Corrie preferred someone who'd talk to her ... like Mac.

Flying in a group seemed easy. Children in schoolyards, women at clotheslines, and farmers in harvest fields all waved. Corrie wagged her wings. Her approach to Columbus was high and fast, forcing her to go around again, but her landing was smooth.

A congressman gave a speech dedicating the airfield. Speeches were her least favorite part of the air tour. Corrie plopped onto the grass beside her Overland and watched Lincoln pilot Frank Cropsey do aerobatics in his Arrow Sport. Engine roaring, he climbed to a thousand feet, then tipped the plane into a steep bank for a tight turn. Wings level, he dove. Why hadn't she been able to get her Arrow to maneuver? As soon as he landed, Corrie would ask—

A left wing snapped off. The plane dropped, struck the ground, rolled. A brown dust cloud rose, then filled with flames. Angry black smoke billowed. The wing fluttered to earth.

No! Somehow in the last few seconds Corrie had jumped to her feet. Her hands pressed to her mouth, holding in a scream. Breath caught in her chest and squeezed her heart. Wind roared through her head. *No, no, no ...*

An ambulance raced to the wreckage. No point in running over there—no one could survive that impact. Even if he had been wearing a parachute, he couldn't have bailed out.

"You okay?"

She glanced to her left, recognizing Chester's and Jack's boots. She nodded.

"You used to fly an Arrow." Bill's voice came from her right.

And Myron's beside him. "Was that yours?"

She shook her head.

"If you want to go home, everyone will understand," Chester said.

Myron gave her shoulder an awkward pat. "I'll fly you back to Omaha in my Waco, and Chester can bring your Overland later."

What? They assumed she would throw in her silk scarf because she was a girl? No, she was a pilot. She knew the risks. Corrie took a deep breath, straightened, and glanced at her watch. "Thank you for checking on me, but the mission hasn't changed. Let's eat. We leave for York soon."

In silence, they grabbed box lunches and found an empty table. Corrie choked down her sandwich, the bread sticking to her mouth. *It could have been me.* She'd tipped the Arrow into a forty-five degree steep turn, wrestling the stick to the side and back, pushing the rudder for all she was worth. The nose dropped and the bank angle steepened, spinning the farmland between her wings. Yanking the stick the opposite direction and kicking the other rudder didn't slow the turn. She pulled the stick back and added power, her weight pressing into the seat. The plane dove, spiraling toward the ground, threatening to flip over. Mr. Steele had wrenched the plane out of the turn, shoved the throttle in, and brought the nose up. He'd spent the rest of the lesson yelling that she was the worst student ever.

A local pilot joined them. "Saw the fire trucks. What happened?"

"Fellow doing aerobatics augered in." Bill studied his pickle as if trying to figure out how to eat it. "Dove into the ground."

"Bought the farm." Myron poked an apple with his pocket knife.

"No." Corrie set aside her sandwich and stared down the flyboys. Frank was no longer alive to defend himself, so she would. "Centrifugal force snapped the wing off."

They exchanged glances, then resumed eating.

Mr. Nielsen, the assistant flight commander, announced there would be no more stunt flying for the rest of the tour. He prayed for Frank and for the safety of the fleet. Without speaking, the fliers headed to their planes. This time Corrie wasn't the only one doing a preflight. All down the flight line, pilots grabbed wingtips and shook them. Flying wires and rigging were plucked. Struts, braces, and connectors received a thorough inspection. Oil and fuel were checked. Finally they took off.

The line of planes flew southwest. Wind played in the grass, pushing it one way then another, changing the color from green to gold. Every mile west meant fewer buildings, fewer trees, more cattle. Corrie's shoulders relaxed. The world was amazing, and an airplane was the best way to see it.

At York, the local radio station announced each arrival and interviewed several pilots.

A young girl in a plaid dress stared at Corrie. "Are you a pilot?"

"Yes I am. Would you like to learn to fly?"

"No, she would not." A woman wearing a matching plaid dress pulled her away, then hissed, "We heard about what happened in Columbus."

Corrie slumped against her plane's front tire. What was wrong with people, focusing on one accident instead of the many miles of safe flying?

"Aren't you a choice bit of calico?" asked a fellow in the slow manner of one on a toot. He leaned on her wing for balance.

Corrie stood. "Do not touch my plane." Were men this disrespectful to Amelia Earhart?

His friend, equally ossified, flapped at the sky. "We want to see some trick flying."

"Not today."

"Aw, don't be a Mrs. Grundy." He tried to cross his arms but couldn't manage which went on top. He settled for slapping his palms on his hips.

The beanpole snorted. "Maybe she don't know how."

"You afraid, little chick?" He waved a flask. "Got some courage."

Corrie sidestepped. "Go chase yourself."

"I'd rather you chase me."

"You heard the lady. Beat it." Andrew Risser, the Curtiss Robin pilot, pointed to a trio of police officers patrolling the flight line. "Those fellows will watch our planes tonight."

The police took the drunks away. Corrie thanked Andrew but wished she could fight her own battles. Maybe she should take boxing lessons.

Governor Weaver spoke that evening, his enthusiasm undimmed by the crash. The local hotel had run out of space, so Corrie ended up in a dorm room at York College. Her heart sore as if squeezed through a wringer, she dropped into bed. Frank Cropsey flew his Arrow across the inside of her eyelids, climbing, turning, and lining up for his final dive. "No." An electrical charge passed through her. She gasped and sat up in bed. She couldn't stop the crash. No one could. "No."

The streetlight shone on a print of Jesus standing at a door. "Dear Lord." Corrie folded her hands. "I know Mr. Nielsen already prayed about Frank, so I'm not sure what more I can add." *I hope he wasn't scared. I hope his family, if he has one, will be okay.* Would her family miss her if she crashed? Or say she died doing what she loved? Corrie put her head back on the pillow. "Thank You, God, for this chance to fly in the air tour and for the beautiful world You made."

Suddenly it was morning. Sunrise at their backs, they flew to Grand Island and the biggest crowd yet. While other pilots gave rides, Corrie talked to the locals and encouraged girls to give airplanes a try.

For an hour they followed the Lincoln Highway southwest, accompanied by the green ribbon of the Platte River valley off her left wing. The town of Kearney had pulled out all the stops to entertain, including a dance that evening. Unfortunately, the air tour had to leave for Broken Bow.

As they walked back to the flight line, Chester said, "Flat as it is, doesn't seem like it's over a thousand feet higher than Omaha Municipal."

Rats! Corrie had been so busy enjoying the trip, staying level with the others, she'd forgotten to reset her altimeter. Lazy beginner error. Mr. Steele would slap her with the checklist—and she'd deserve it. Corrie leaned into the cockpit. "So it's twenty-one hundred feet here?"

"Twenty-one thirty-one." Chester smiled. "Refill your canteen? Attagirl. Fly safe."

Under a clear sky, they followed a road north toward Broken Bow. Corrie had always lived in Omaha, a city of two hundred thousand. What if she'd been born in—she consulted the map—Pleasanton, Nebraska? Three churches, one school, no airport. Where was the nearest movie theater? Soda fountain? What did people do here? According to Rand McNally, the population was 262, less that her graduating class. Miles of cornfields stretched between farms. No stores nearby, so people would shop by catalog. Was Mac still working for Ward's?

A herd of animals with white rumps and antlers flowed across the hills. Antelope! Their hooves raised puffs of dust with every step. The shadow of the plane passed over them. Corrie glanced at her airspeed gauge and the way the wind beat the grass. Those antelope had to be running fifty miles an hour.

Friday the air tour passed over even more lonely and brown country until they reached a massive railyard where the two branches of the Platte River came together. They landed at North Platte, the westernmost location of the tour and a base for the transcontinental airmail route. In July, the newspaper had reported that a mob had chased two hundred Negroes out of town. Corrie wondered if she should warn Chief Bowhan. If Corrie could protect Chief from a mob, her parents would be proud of her, and Cessna would have to offer her a job. Wait … what was she thinking? She couldn't protect herself, much less Chief.

The pilots toured the university's experimental farm with its throngs of black-and-white cows, then had lunch in the airmail hangar. Lindbergh had built up time flying the mail. Maybe Corrie could be an airmail pilot.

In the afternoon, they crossed the Platte River, then flew over country as dry and rumpled as tree bark.

"This is the life," Corrie told the fellows that evening in McCook. "We should keep going, see Sidney and Scottsbluff and Chadron. You could flour bomb Chimney Rock."

"Good luck talking the major into changing the plan." Bill toasted her with his cup of coffee.

"Any airfields out that way?" Jack gnawed on a chicken leg.

Myron spit a watermelon seed. "Aren't you ready to go home, get a meal without a speech, clean clothes?"

"Are you kidding? Flying every day is the berries! Does Iowa have an air tour? Kansas? Let's tour the whole country!"

Chester waved a green bean at her. "Gotta give your hearing a rest from engine noise or you'll go deaf like Bill."

"How's that?" Bill cupped his ear.

Saturday they headed northeast through Holdredge, Hastings, then finally the emerald lawns and trees of Omaha. The fastest planes flew over the airfield in a V-formation. Next year …

Families and friends of the pilots cheered their arrival. Mr. Furstenberg met her as she shut down. After six solid days of flying, his mechanics would give the plane a thorough going-over and an oil change. "Looks good. Any problems?"

"Not a one. The Overland is nifty!" Corrie climbed out and

grabbed her traveling bag. "Your brochures were gone by Norfolk. Ranchers in Broken Bow and McCook seemed quite taken with the idea of flying. A plane this size and price would suit, but they'd prefer a high-wing monoplane."

"Whatever for?"

"So they can survey their cattle, check fences."

Mr. Furstenberg mulled that over.

"Bellanca hired Elinor Smith to tour the United States. I'd love to tour the Overland for you."

The airplane builder tipped his head sideways and squinted, as if he had a hard time imagining Corrie working for him. "I'll think about it."

Horsefeathers. Her parents' "think about it" meant "no." Somehow, Corrie had to prove herself. "See you Monday morning for the overhaul."

Mr. Steele marched up. "You survived."

"Yes sir." Her flight instructor had been annoying and nitpicky, catching every error, insisting on precision and perfection. He'd quizzed her on parts of the plane from tail wheel to nose cone. Under his critical eye, she'd changed the oil, gapped the spark plugs, and cleaned the carburetor. She'd learned cloud formations and reading the weather. She could spit out the Air Commerce Regulations in her sleep. This summer Mr. Steele had turned her into a pilot, a safe pilot. Corrie shook his hand. "Thanks to you."

Steele couldn't be happy for long. He frowned at the dark splotches dotting the leading edge of her wings. "Kill every bug in the state?"

"I did. Farmers appreciated it. I'll wash it after the overhaul."

He pointed. "Mrs. Tinley left the Oldsmobile by the hangar."

"Swell." It was Saturday. Couldn't one person in her family make time to celebrate with her? She'd flown the entire Nebraska Air Tour safely.

She raced home, noticing that pulling back on the steering wheel didn't lift her over potholes or trolley tracks.

She said hello to Mrs. Zukas, washed up, and suddenly she was tired. Should she skip this last banquet? No, she would not be left out of anything. She threw on her graduation dress and hurried out. Then had to come right back for her handbag.

At the Hotel Fontenelle, Mr. Clipboard asked, "Are you here with a pilot?"

Couldn't he see her sunburned nose and chin? "I am a pilot."

He gave her a blank look.

"Good gravy, Corrie. You look like a girl." Chester linked arms with her, choking her with hooch fumes. "Jack, did you know Corrie's a girl?"

The equally intoxicated Jack leaned toward Mr. Clipboard and stage-whispered, "She is a pilot."

Bill and Myron waved them to a table, where they sat with their girlfriends and flasks. Once again Corrie wished Mac was in Omaha.

"I thought you fellows were tired of banquets." Corrie sat herself.

"Can't beat free food." Bill put an olive on each finger.

"And free gas and oil. Hooray for Skelly." Myron heaped potato salad onto his plate.

None of the fellows seemed to remember their girlfriends' names, so Corrie introduced herself. They were anything but "pleased to meet you."

Mr. Nielsen stopped by the table so they could all sign a condolence card for Frank Cropsey's widow. Dinner was served, chicken again, followed by—what else?—speeches.

Major Houghland said Nebraskans should willingly spend money on national defense since the tour showed how easily enemy planes could wipe out every village in the state.

"Phonus balonus." Jack blinked through zozzled confusion. "I didn't drop even one flour bomb. Not a one."

"What enemy?" Corrie asked. "Who would want to bomb Nebraska?"

"Missouri," Bill declared, his voice thick, his index finger waving with feigned authority. "Because we beat them in football."

The head of the tour committee thanked the pilots. Sixty thousand spectators saw the air tour. Thirty-six hundred people took an airplane ride, including five hundred in one day who flew with Clyde Ice in the Ford Trimotor. And they had only one serious accident in twenty-five thousand combined air miles. The tour was a success.

Corrie counted it a success too. She had filled a logbook page with cross-country time, landed at all sorts of fields, and brought her plane back safely.

Warbling "I Can't Give You Anything but Love," the flyboys and their dates shuffled off. Corrie drove home alone. *Oh, Mac, I miss you.*

CHAPTER
FIFTEEN

THE STORE HAD BEEN quiet all afternoon, until the evening edition of the Detroit papers came out. Mac heard the newsboys yelling on the corner.

"What's going on?" Mac asked Shirley.

She twisted her imitation pearl beads until her fingers turned red. "I hope you don't have any money in the stock market."

"I don't, but our customers do." The stock market had been bouncing like a basketball since March. Bick at the diner said the banks were in trouble. Auto sales were down. Customers who used to pay cash now asked about Ward's Budget Plan. If sales dropped, would Montgomery Ward's close? He'd lose his job and have to crawl back home with his tail between his legs. Mr. Smooth would have a field day. Mac's gut lurched. He'd like to turn on the radio and see what WJR had to say, but he didn't want to scare the remaining shoppers—or his staff.

Margaret from the catalog desk knocked on the doorframe of Mac's office. "We need your help. Right away. Please."

Uh-oh. Mac raced to the floor. A rancid odor slapped him in the face, making his eyes water. He had no trouble identifying the source since only one customer stood at the counter. "I'm Mac, the store manager. How may I help you?"

"Heard Montgomery Ward's pays top dollar for furs." The fellow wore an army duck coat, hunting breeches, and boots. He slapped a stack of pelts onto the counter, letting loose a wave of spoiled meat and mustiness with a dash of skunk.

Margaret pressed a handkerchief over her face and dashed to the back.

"Yes, we do, through our Fur Receiving Depots." Breathing shallowly, Mac handed him the company brochure "Hints to Trappers" and a shipping tag. "There's all the instructions—"

"I need the money today." His mouth clamped, jaw hard and lips tight.

"I'm sorry. We don't handle furs here." He had to get these pelts out of the store before the stench drove the customers and staff away.

"Don't have money for postage." The hunter shifted his weight and gave him a hard stare.

"You can ship collect. Transportation charges will be deducted from the sale, then you'll receive a check." The animal on the top of the pile had a furless tail. Was it a rat or an opossum? Mac had grown up in the city, limiting his experience with wildlife.

"I need the money now." He gave the spot behind his ear a thorough scratching.

"Sir, I don't know anything about pricing furs. I wouldn't want to cheat you out of a good price."

The fellow grunted. He folded the brochure and shipping tag into his coat pocket, then hefted his pelts.

"When your check comes in, stop by for good deals on traps, ammunition, wool socks."

Over his shoulder, he asked, "Baby clothes? Cribs?"

Mac tried to hide his surprise. "Yes, sir. Second floor."

As soon as the door closed behind the fellow, Mac raced to the back. He filled a bucket of hot water and Lysol, then swabbed the counter. Shirley lit a match. Margaret set up the fan.

"Whoa, what died?" Clyde, the grocer, breathed through his collar.

"Did you know trapping is good in the city?"

He raised a finger. "Yet another reason why meat sales are down. Speaking of butchering, want to sell me a carving knife?"

"Sure do. Let me introduce you to Vera, our housewares manager."

As they crossed to a less odoriferous part of the store, Clyde asked in a low voice, "Did you hear? The Dow dropped below two hundred."

"So much for Durant and Rockefeller stopping the slide. Any word from the White House?"

"Hoover won't do anything. He's all about laissez-faire."

"Clyde, I didn't know you spoke French."

The grocer's mouth twitched as the joke fell flat. "We're all speaking economics now."

"Lessons from the school of hard knocks." Mac introduced him to Vera.

"Where is the fellow showed me the shock? Sewed my sock? Sold stock?" A heavyset fellow bounced off a Wardway washer into a gasoline range. "This is no bank. Where is the bank?"

"I'm sorry, sir." Mac steered him toward the door, trying not to choke on the beer breath gusting from his straggly mustache. Who would have guessed this job would be hard on a fellow's nose? "This is Montgomery Ward's. We don't sell stock here."

The man waved an envelope and moaned. "Good money. All gone." He grabbed Mac's collar. "I lost good money."

"I hope you find it soon." The fellow wouldn't find much of anything half seas over as he was. Mac held open the door, letting in a cold wind, and the man stumbled through.

Letters to the editor said repealing the Eighteenth Amendment would solve the economy's problems. Prohibition hadn't made any difference in the nation's alcohol consumption. Would ending it help the economy?

Mac stopped at the phonograph display and flipped through the demonstration records until he found one that would soothe worries. "It Is Well with My Soul" echoed through the store. Mac returned to his office and his weekly report to Chicago.

Sal stuck his head in. "You'd think Christmas was canceled all the gloom and doom on the streets. Want us to come to work tomorrow or what?"

With a glance at the clock, Mac pushed to his feet. "Meeting in the storeroom in five." The store had been empty of customers for a half hour. Mac locked the front doors, closed the safe, then headed to the back.

His staff shivered in overcoats and hats. The women clustered together and whispered. Some linked arms. He caught snatches of conversation "... started drinking again ..." "... have to drop out of college ..." "... we'll get by, if ..."

"Ford's laying off." Ralph, the automotive manager, scowled. "General Motors shut down Cadillac."

"Seems like people will be wanting parts and tools more than ever." William, the furniture manager, shuffled his feet. "Hope they still want furniture."

Sal whistled for attention.

Mac drew a deep breath. "I'll make this short since it's cold and late. I don't know anything more than you do about the stock market. We've had no word from Chicago. What I do know is we need customers more than ever. And they need our low prices. So tomorrow, as every day, we'll do our best. And pray for our country."

Vera asked, "Would you lead the prayer?"

"Please," William added.

Mac had never prayed in front of a group before. Headquarters hadn't said a word about it. But in times like these, surrounded by bad news, prayer seemed like the only answer. He cleared his throat, clamped his hands together, and closed his eyes. "Heavenly Father, we don't understand what's going on in Washington or on Wall Street. We don't know what to do. We're worried for ourselves, our jobs, our families, our neighbors, our nation. Guide our words and actions. Help us to trust in You and lean on Your wisdom in this troubled time. Amen."

"Amen." A few employees managed a smile.

Sal raised his fist. "Satisfaction guaranteed!"

Several others echoed his cry.

"I do have a happy announcement." The company advised ending every meeting on a positive note. Mac held up a message slip. "Many of you know Jim Dobie, Codling's jeweler."

Vera raised her arm. "He fixed my watch."

"And my cuckoo clock," Sal said.

Sal owned a cuckoo clock? Mac gave himself a shake and continued. "Jim and his wife Laurene are now the proud parents of a baby girl."

The employees applauded and cheered.

"Thanks," Shirley said. "We needed some good news."

———

"I thought I'd find you here."

"Miss Sackett! So good to see you." Corrie popped out of the cockpit, put down her grease gun and work gloves, and hugged her old basketball coach. "Would you like an airplane ride?"

Gray curls shivered under her wool hat. "Can I take a raincheck, or rather, a fair-weather check? It feels like snow."

The stratus layer and ice-crusted puddles on the taxiway agreed. Corrie had been so focused on the plane and bundled in fur-lined coveralls, she hadn't noticed the temperature drop.

"Next year I'll have a plane with an enclosed cockpit. Warmer and more comfortable." Rumors said Walter Beech had one under development.

Miss Sackett blinked and looked around the hangar. "Actually, I wondered if you've seen today's newspaper." She pulled a folded section of the *World-Herald* from her purse.

"No, I haven't." Corrie tilted the paper toward the light.

The headline read, "Omaha man stops robbery." The photograph showed a police officer waving handcuffs, a woman holding up a ring display, and a kid held down by a man in a business suit. Summer clothing and lack of snow indicated the photograph had been taken months ago.

"It's Mac!" Looking more handsome than ever. Corrie's heart revved.

"He's a store manager now." Miss Sackett pointed to the caption, which read, "Officer Hayward, clerk Shirley Wendell, and store manager Mac McFarland stop theft of jewelry from Montgomery Ward's in Michigan."

"And a hero." He'd accomplished so much. "I'd like to write to him, but it doesn't say what town he's in." Was it overly familiar to write to a fellow she wasn't related to? Corrie hurriedly added, "To congratulate him on his promotion. And on catching the thief. And since everyone gave me stationery for graduation—" Had Miss Sackett given her a box? She didn't mean to sound ungrateful.

"Perhaps the Omaha Montgomery Ward's would have his address." Miss Sackett dabbed her eyes with a red handkerchief.

"They weren't even sure what state he'd moved to," Corrie blurted. Nerts. She sounded completely stuck on Mac. Which she was.

"What about calling his family?" Miss Sackett asked as if Mother and Emily Post might allow it. As if Mr. Smooth might not answer the phone.

"This photo is a great excuse, er, reason to call." The wind rattled the newspaper. "Could I keep it, for my scrapbook?"

"Of course." The woman pulled her scarf higher over her face. "Do you hear from any of the other players?"

"The convent doesn't let Mary Frances write. Ruth is busy with nurses' training. Halleen thinks she's pregnant again. Jackie is auditioning for movies. Evelyn's at the business college, and Thelma's at the university."

"You're a pilot." Miss Sackett raised her hands with a proud smile.

"Yes, I am." Corrie grinned. Someone recognized her accomplishment. "I flew in the Nebraska Air Tour in September. Only three more flying hours and I can take my commercial test."

"I'm so glad you got to go on the tour." She wiped her nose.

Hope she isn't coming down with something.

"Come with me next year." If Corrie couldn't find Mac. "You can read the maps and be my navigator."

"At the moment, all I can think of is getting home to a hot cup of tea, but thank you for asking." She wiped her eyes again, hugged Corrie, then raced to her car.

Had Miss Sackett been crying? No, the cold wind made her tear up. Corrie pulled out her plane, preflighted, climbed in, and took off. Five hundred feet off the ground, wisps of snow blew past her wing. A few flakes stuck to her leading edges and windshield. So much for practice. She returned to the field and hangared her plane. An eerie quiet blanketed the airfield. Maybe the weather kept everyone away.

Corrie rubbed her face on the drive home, but the chill clung to her. She parked in the barn, rolled the newspaper so the snow wouldn't damage Mac's photo, and dashed inside. Why hadn't Mrs. Zukas turned on the lights? The smell of a roast confirmed she was here.

Corrie clicked on the wall sconce at the bottom of the stairs and found her brother sitting on the floor. He leaned against the wall, arms propped on bent knees. His face had even less color than usual.

"Hi, Artie. Would you make a phone call for me?"

He held his finger over his mouth.

"What are you doing?" She knelt on the oriental rug beside him. They hadn't eavesdropped like this for years. Raised voices of their parents penetrated the closed doors of the living room. "Why are they arguing?"

"Money." He wouldn't meet her gaze. "Father's been speculating. His investments took a dive."

"So he's a little behind the eight ball—"

Artie shook his head. "Booted out of the pool hall."

Uh-oh. Even fur-lined coveralls couldn't hold back the cold bite of this news. Corrie slid down the wall to sit beside her brother. "But I thought those Wall Street bankers fixed it."

"Stock market keeps diving." Artie groaned and dug his fingers into his hair. "The store's been dead. Christmas sales were pitiful. No one buys jewelry when they can't feed their children."

"Ernie's been bringing work home."

He bit his lip. "Repairs."

"We'll be okay, won't we? We cut back on Christmas gifts. Mother canceled our New Year's Eve party." And Corrie's subscriptions to *Popular Aviation* and *Flying*.

"Corrie." Artie put an arm over her shoulder. His Adam's apple jerked and his voice hoarsened as if he might be coming down with a cold. "Corrie, is there anyone at the country club or airport you might want to marry?"

"Marry?" The newspaper crinkled in her hand and she thought of Mac. He'd never called or written. "Is Mother on that bandwagon again?"

Artie shook his head. "Might be a way for you to keep your plane."

Her blood iced up. "What does my plane have to do with—"

"Father has three mortgages on this house. He's months behind on bills. The bank's going to foreclose."

The room spun. This wasn't supposed to happen. Foreclosure happened to other people, not to the Tinley family. "Can you and Harry pay?"

"Father owes too much." He leaned his head on hers. "We expect to be let go any day."

Corrie would find a job and save the family and then they'd realize she was a good egg. She'd worked too hard to let the airplane go. "I've been looking for work everywhere, writing letters, asking every visiting pilot if he knows of an opening." And they always said if they knew of a job, it would go to a man, not a girl. "Three more flight hours and I can—"

Raised voices and the crash of breaking glass in the parlor sent them dashing into the kitchen. Mrs. Zukas set out covered dishes. "*Paskubek*. Sit, eat. No sense letting good food go to waste."

Artie held out the chair at the head of the table. "Mrs. Zukas, please join us."

They took their usual seats, as if they were children again.

Foreclosure? Corrie twisted her napkin and glanced at the new gas stove, the cabinets full of silver and porcelain, the black-and-white tile floor. "What are they saying at Mutual?"

Her brother shrugged then served himself pork roast, mashed potatoes, and gravy. Mrs. Zukas filled Corrie's plate, then hers.

"What about Union Pacific? What's Harry think?"

Artie cut his meat into neat squares. How could he eat?

"Someone will do something." She couldn't lose her plane, not after all her hard work, not when she was flying so well. "Maybe the president, Congress, or the bankers. They won't let the country fall apart."

"Corrie, you're looking in the wrong place for help." Mrs. Zukas filled their milk glasses, then set the pitcher on the table with a thump. "Look to Jesus. And eat your supper."

Corrie sighed and stabbed her meat. If Father couldn't keep their family afloat, what was Jesus supposed to do about it?

CHAPTER
SIXTEEN

A YEAR *and a half later*

Mac found Corrie alone on the bluff, silhouetted against the sky. She had on the blue and white checked dress he'd admired in high school. A panama hat with a red ribbon shaded her face better than this year's silly cloches. Hair lightened to the color of honey curled down her back. She'd worn it short in high school to celebrate Amelia Earhart crossing the Atlantic. Mac was glad she'd let it grow.

Feet slipping on the loose soil, Mac grabbed a handful of prairie grass and climbed up the path. He paused at the crest of the hill.

Corrie turned, her startled expression blooming into the sparkling smile he'd been dreaming about. "Mac! Hot dog! Montgomery Ward's gave you time off for the air races!" She jumped up and hugged him. "I've missed you so much! You left without a word, no forwarding address. Where'd you go?"

"Michigan."

She motioned across the Missouri River where planes and cars crowded Omaha Municipal. "Can't you see better from your house?"

"View's best right here." The view of long athlete's legs that had raced across the wood floors of basketball courts.

"Have a seat." She patted the plaid blanket she'd been sitting on. "You missed the flour bombing and dead-stick landings. I can't tell from here who won. The newspaper will say. The light plane race is starting. Fifteen miles around pylons. You didn't happen to bring binoculars, did you?"

"Sorry." The airshow wasn't on his agenda, but he wished he'd brought them for Corrie's sake. "Where're your brothers?"

"Ernie's directing traffic. Artie somehow got a ticket from a city commissioner. Wish he'd bribed him for two. Here they come!" She stood.

Mac grabbed her elbow to keep her from falling off the bluff. A dozen planes, wobbling like drunken bumblebees, dove toward the giant flagpole at center field. Would they crash into the ground or each other? If he'd known about this plane craziness, he'd have picked a different weekend.

"It's Jack in his Waco. Come on, Elliot. Keep your Cirrus running! Where's Leon? His engine's been giving him fits." Corrie kept up the play-by-play as the planes buzzed to the field, not sitting until they'd all landed. Finally she turned to Mac. "So what brings you up here?"

"I stopped by the store ..."

"The store." Corrie's eyes darkened. "You know our bad news."

"It's not all bad."

"That's Mother's song, 'We've got our health, a hot meal in our bellies, and a place to live.' Let's not mention it's squeezed in with Aunt Florence and Uncle Chester." A large plane caught her attention. "Boeing Air Transport's Ford Trimotor. Have you seen the inside of one of those, Mac? Fancy. Washroom, clothes closet, table, kitchenette. Three Pratt and Whitney Wasp engines. Real smooth ride. Wish they'd let me fly it." Corrie watched it speed north.

"What have you been up to since I left?" *Tell me you're not dating anyone special.*

"Since my plane went in the auction, I became an airport bum. Last summer Halleen had twins. I've been helping her with the little scamps, adorable balls of energy." She flashed a smile. "She had a baby girl two weeks ago, but Eddie was laid off from Ford, so he'll help this time."

"Three children in two years. Wow."

A small biplane leaped into the air. "That's Dorothy Hester. Nineteen, younger than me, and she flies all over the country."

"You're old? When did that happen?"

Her dimple deepened, but her focus stayed on the plane circling higher over the field. "Great Lakes with a hundred horsepower Menasco engine. Nice acrobatic plane."

Finishing its climb, the little ship flipped over, upside down then right side up.

"One."

"What is she doing?" Mac's heart did its own flip. A crash would put a damper on his plans.

"Two. Three." Corrie counted as the plane continued its gyrations down, then zoomed back up. "Setting a world's record for inverted snap rolls." Corrie's voice sounded hoarse.

"Won't she get sick?"

"Four, five, six, seven." A tear formed at the corner of her eye. "No. Go fast enough, you don't even know you've been upside down."

"Are you okay?"

"Eight, nine, ten." She swallowed hard. "I miss it so much. That morning before the bank fellow came, I took one last circle around the field. Since I pumped that gas, I ought to get the fun out of it." She blinked at him, her expression soft. "Oh, Mac, it was perfect up there, smooth as silk. And the plane ran like a dream. Fourteen."

"So you're done with aviating?"

She wiped her eyes with her palms and blew out a deep breath. "It's over. Even if the economy perks up, people don't want to fly with a girl. Eighteen..." She glanced at him. "I'm sorry I didn't get to take you up."

"I'm not much on flying."

"Ever since you left, I'd wish you were riding with me, to show you how beautiful it is. We'd have so much fun. Twenty-one. Good going, Dorothy."

"You'd really want to fly all over the country like that?"

Corrie watched the biplane. "New designs to be flown, new engines to test, records to be broken. But I'm grounded. Missing it all. Twenty-two."

Mac shook his head. "Seems like there's a crash every other day. Look what happened to Knute Rockne. And Mother said last week some lady pilot crashed north of town." She had the same last name as Corrie. The news report had nearly stopped Mac's heart.

"Louise Tinley. And she didn't crash. She made a forced landing when her engine quit. Bent the prop, but she's fine. Twenty-five."

Corrie stretched her legs. "It's getting safer all the time. Look at all the flying that's been done today, and no one's augered in."

"None that you know of."

"Hmm." Corrie watched the next set of flip-flops without speaking. "Why did you stop by the store?"

"To see your dad about that black diamond he used to have."

"Twenty-nine. Remember that robbery while we played North High? We got everything back except that diamond."

"I remember. Jackie went downtown to some speakeasy, and the next thing you know, an unmarked package showed up at your door."

A dimple flashed. "Father's reward money took her to Hollywood."

"I haven't seen her on the silver screen."

"She runs the MGM office in Omaha, winding and splicing film. Making sure they're delivered to the right theater." As the girl pilot climbed back for another round, Corrie turned her sparkle Mac's way. "Whatever would you do with that diamond?"

"I thought it would make a nice engagement ring."

"Nice?" She shot him a worried look. "Do you know how long Father tried to sell that stone? Most people like diamonds without color. Your fiancée better be on the unconventional side."

He propped his elbow on his knee. "Well, I was hoping to get your slant on a few things."

"If you think a washed-up old flygirl would have any insight into your love life. Thirty-three."

He scraped a bead of sweat off his temple. "She's a local girl, so I'm not only asking her to marry me. I'm asking her to leave her hometown, move to Michigan."

"Any girl worth her salt has got to realize ..." Corrie ticked off each point on her fingers. "You've got a job, a good job. You're a handsome, healthy guy with the nicest mom in Omaha. We won't mention Mr. Smooth."

"Appreciate that." Thoughts of his brother, the notorious wiseguy, tended to ruin Mac's day.

"You haven't taken up drinking, smoking, or swearing now that you're away from home, have you? You're a good basketball player and coach. A girl who'd say no to you must be too immature to leave her mother's apron strings or must not care about you at all. Go ahead and ask her. Find out where you stand. Was that thirty-seven?"

Mac cleared his throat. "You think I'm handsome?"

"Forty-one." Biting her lower lip, she gave him a once-over. "You're in good shape. You used to have nice wave to your hair. Forty-one."

"New barber cuts it close." He ran a hand through his hair, wishing he hadn't gotten it cut before this trip. "There's the problem with my name..."

"Forty-five. She doesn't know?"

"She knows. But I sure don't want to be standing in front of a justice of the peace, answering the question 'Do you, Horatio ...' No one would hear the rest of the ceremony over all the snickering."

"Oh, Mac." She swatted his knee. "You charmed all the teachers at Central into using your nickname. One little judge will be a snap. Forty-eight. Go ahead and ask her."

"Without a ring?"

"Sure. Promise her one after the next election."

"What if Hoover stays in office?"

"Not a chance. I'd vote for our neighbor's schnauzer, what was his name, Roscoe, over Hoover." Corrie bounced to her feet. "Come on, Dorothy! Hang in there! Did you see that wobble? She's getting tired and sloppy. Fifty-four, fifty-five, fifty-six." The plane rolled right side up and stayed that way. "She's coming in for a landing. A good pilot knows when to quit. Way to fly it, Dorothy," she whispered.

"Is that a world record?"

"It's the most inverted snap rolls I've ever seen. Laura Ingalls did seven hundred fourteen barrel rolls over St. Louis. Are you coming back tomorrow? They're doing the balloon burst and the autogiro's supposed to fly. And Dorothy's going for the inverted loop record. You could bring your fiancée. By the way, which of your flock of girlfriends are you asking?" Corrie wrapped her hair into a knot and pinned it to her nape, then folded the plaid blanket. "Could it be someone from our basketball team? Wait a minute, let me go through the list. Halleen has Eddie and the babies. Mary Frances took her vows. Evelyn left a good job, doing the books at Capitol School of Hairstyling, and ran off with a vaudeville act. Thelma married a Joe College who works for Union Packing. You're running low on choices."

"Thelma wed, married, hitched?"

"One semester at the university cured her of that habit." Corrie stood above him, her face was level with his. "Okay, Mac, spill it. Who's getting your proposal?"

Mac took her hand to steady her on the steep path. "What would you think about moving to Michigan?"

Her mouth dropped open and her eyes widened.

"Corrie, will you marry me?"

———

"Mac! Let's make plans!" Corrie opened her arms and pulled him close, inhaling his wood and leather aftershave and watching a Curtiss Robin take off. "I've been goofy over you ever since I saw you play guard on Artie's team. And having you coach us girls but not be able to date you ... Then soon as we're out from under Klemfuss's eagle eye, you scram."

"You must think I'm a piker."

"Never." She leaned back and caught his face in her hands. "Your mom told me about Henry's crash."

"I couldn't lose you to an airplane." His eyebrows creased.

"You won't." Without her plane, she was grounded.

"Does that mean ..." His face relaxed into a smile.

"I've been waiting for you." She inched closer and looked at his mouth. He got the message and did his part. Unlike his brother, who was only interested in raising his score, Mac kissed like she was his best and only. He started out gently, not teasing, but his usual cautious self. Then he turned his head and gently took charge. Oooh, was that his tongue?

Mac broke contact. "Time to close the bank and throw a wedding."

"When do you have to be back in Michigan?"

"Sunday. Working Monday." Mac kept her hand in his and led her down the hill. He'd parked Mr. Smooth's breezer next to her bicycle. "Our train leaves in the morning, so we're getting married tonight."

"Tonight?"

"It's all arranged." He loaded her bicycle into the rumble seat. "Your father gave the okay."

"Awfully confident, are you?"

"Awfully hopeful." He paused for another kiss. His tongue brushed her lips as if tasting her. Whoopee! As fun as a loop!

Mac dropped her off at Aunt Florence's with a third kiss, more sedate this time, and the promise to pick her up in an hour.

Corrie threw open the front door. "I'm getting married!"

Mother leaned close to the radio. "But Father Coughlin is on."

Father pulled a "medicinal" bottle from between the davenport cushions and took a swig. Hadn't he told the family? Or had he forgotten?

Artie pounded up the basement steps. "You're getting married? Some airshow flyboy swept you off your feet?"

"No. Mac proposed!"

"Mac?" Artie swung her in a circle. "He's here?"

"Only for this weekend. He'll pick me up in an hour for the justice of the peace. I leave for Michigan tomorrow!"

Aunt Florence burst from the kitchen, wringing her apron. "Tonight?"

Mother turned down the radio. "Honestly, Cordelia. I need at least a year to plan."

"Congratulations." Aunt Florence's enthusiasm blossomed. "Wash up. Brush your hair. Your mother and I will find something for you to wear. Chester, make sure your camera has film and flashbulbs, and cut some flowers—keep the stems long."

Uncle Chester roused himself from his chair. "Didn't you hear about Bloody July? Gangsters shot up people in a hotel lobby in Detroit."

Corrie gave him a hug, glad someone cared what happened to her. "Mac's store is in Royal Oak, north of Detroit. I'll be fine."

"As long as the city doesn't have a roller coaster." Her aunt shuddered. An acquaintance had been killed when the Big Dipper roller coaster in Krug Park crashed last summer. Her focus shifted to Corrie's father. "Charles, call your sons. And see if you can reach Mrs. Zukas."

"The housekeeper?" Mother asked. "We can't afford her."

"She'll want to see Corrie get married."

Minutes later, Florence burst into the bathroom with a lavender chiffon dress Mother had worn to the country club. "My word, Corrie. You can't get married in rags."

"But no one will see—"

Florence was back in two shakes with Corrie's silk brassiere, bloomers, slip, and body powder—graduation presents she'd never used. "Your husband will." She closed the door behind her.

Husband? Corrie peeked at herself in the mirror. What would he think? What did she know about being a wife?

Down the hall, Mother whined, "My last pair of stockings."

"It's your daughter, Minnie. Your only daughter is getting married."

"Married? We should tell her about—"

"Have you been to the movies lately? These modern girls could teach us a few things."

"I suppose you're right. She took that personal hygiene class."

Which warned about venereal disease and expounded on the joys of motherhood, but didn't say anything about being a wife. *Lord, help!* Corrie was pretty sure praying about sex wasn't allowed. No Sunday school teacher had ever mentioned it—Corrie would have remembered *that*.

Wait … motherhood? Corrie would be the best mother ever. Her baby would know love every day.

After dressing, Corrie stood in front of the long mirror.

"That's no wedding gown." Mother pouted.

"It's the closest thing you've got." Florence pinned the lavender dress into decency. "Gathered skirt with fishtail hem and shoulder drape is almost like a wedding veil and train."

"Hardly." Mother snorted.

"Work on her hair and makeup while I find a hat," Florence ordered.

"Wish we could afford a hairdresser." Mother yanked a comb through Corrie's hair. It was the first time Mother had touched her since … since she'd put a hand on Corrie's five-year-old shoulder for their family photograph.

"I couldn't find a hat to match that dress, so we'll put lilac blossoms on this straw cloche."

"Good." Mother threw down the comb. "Cover her unruly hair."

Corrie rolled her hair into a knot at the base of her neck and pinned it.

Florence settled the hat in place and pulled a few curls in front of Corrie's ears. Her aunt stepped back and studied her face. "Let's not bother with makeup."

At least Mac didn't think she was a bother. "I should pack."

Florence pointed her toward the stairs. "Your mother and I will take care of that. Go eat an cookie, if your brothers left any. No fainting."

Uncle Chester handed her a bouquet of irises and tucked sprigs of lilacs in her hatband. "I'm driving. We'll meet Mac at the courthouse. Save your fellow from having to pay the bridge toll again."

Herded by Aunt Florence, who must have been descended from cowboys, the family packed the car and headed across Douglas Street Bridge to Omaha.

Mac stood on the courthouse steps with his mom, Mrs. Zukas, Corrie's brothers, and the judge. Corrie's best friend, Jackie, looked swanky in a new dress. Mac wore a double-breasted suit. Steady, dependable Mac. He tucked her hands in his. Corrie shivered.

A biplane flew west along Dodge Street. Awfully close to sunset to be starting cross-country. Maybe he was only taking a spin around the patch.

The judge said, "By the authority that I hold under the law of the state of Nebraska, I declare you as husband and wife."

Married? And she'd missed it. Mac leaned forward and wrapped one arm around her the small of her back and placed the other on her shoulders. He planted his lips on hers and tipped her back. The family cheered.

Uncle Chester invited the wedding party to dinner at Hotel Fontenelle. Mother and Father led the way to the sixteen-story hotel, through the mahogany doors, across the marble floors into the restaurant with white linen tablecloths, silverware, and a menu in French.

"They changed the carpet." Mother would let everyone know she'd been here before.

A waiter arrived with a tray of champagne glasses filled with bubbly, followed by a sashaying Mr. Smooth. "Don't worry. It's ginger ale."

Mac groaned.

"I'm here to kiss the bride." Mac's brother leaned close, way too close, to Corrie. "Congratulations, baby. I gave my little brother a few tips, but if he has any difficulty, call me."

"Scram," Mac said in a fierce voice.

"Mr. Smooth, I believe you're spifflicated." Corrie slipped the table knife under her elbow and poked. His kiss landed on her hat.

He sidestepped out of knife range, then waved a thick envelope, making sure everyone at the table noticed it. "Mazuma for my little brother to keep his bride in style." Mr. Smooth set it next to Mac's elbow. "Ta-ta, all!" He grabbed a giggling flapper in Theda Bara makeup and hustled out.

Mac's mom shook out the pastel notes. "Play money again. He pulled the same stunt at Mac's going-away dinner."

"He's a sore loser." Mac's warm arm stretched across her shoulders. "I caught the best girl."

Corrie tipped her head and winked. "And I caught the best fellow."

During the soup course, friends of her parents stopped to offer congratulations. After they left, Mother burst into tears. "We gave a silver gravy ladle, crystal relish tray, and a Lenox tureen to their daughters. But what does Corrie get? Nothing."

No loss since Corrie didn't know how to make gravy, relish, or soup. Mrs. Zukas, their former housekeeper, sat between Artie and Ernie. She knew about cooking. And laundry. And housekeeping. Maybe she'd move to Michigan. Corrie turned to ask Mac about a housekeeper, but the waiters cleared the main course and served a two-tiered white cake.

Uncle Chester handed Mac a room key and a small suitcase. "Meet you at Union Station in the morning."

"Thank you for everything." Mac shook his hand, then turned to Mother and Aunt Florence. "You couldn't have done better with a year's planning."

Given a year, Mother would have filled it with tea parties at the country club, dress fittings, and etiquette lessons. No thank you.

The elevator whisked them to their room. And finally they were alone.

Mac whirled her around. "I've been waiting a long time for this."

Corrie jumped into his arms. "Let's make whoopee!"

CHAPTER
SEVENTEEN

MAC'S BRIDE leaned out the window of the passenger car. "Goodbye, Mother!"

"You'd better write, Cordelia Elizabeth!"

"Of course I will. Where's Father?"

"Sitting in the shade." Corrie's mother motioned toward the depot, where the heavyset man sprawled on a bench. Even in the canopy's shadow, his face glowed with perspiration. "You know how he is about the heat."

Heat? Mac figured the temperature barely topped sixty.

"Bye, Father." Corrie blew a kiss over her brothers' heads. Mac stood behind her and waved.

"Now, Cordelia, be a good wife. No more of this airplane silliness."

"Oh, Mother. Mac's keen on planes. He watched the airshow with me."

What? No! He'd have to set her straight.

Her mother fluttered a lace handkerchief. "Father Coughlin's in Royal Oak. You might get to meet him."

"I suppose." Corrie and Mac shared an aversion to the radio preacher.

A railroad bull swinging a billy club patrolled the train, watching for hoboes trying to ride without paying. Corrie shuddered and looked away. "This economy ..."

The train whistled and pulled away. Corrie settled onto the seat. Mac closed the window, then joined her.

"So much fuss. We should have eloped." Corrie removed her black-and-tan cloche, setting free a jumble of curls, and dropped it on the picnic basket at their feet. The train crossed the Missouri River into Iowa.

"And miss all the fun?" He raised her hand and slid a kiss under the scalloped hem of her cotton glove. Marrying Corrie was better than all of his imaginings over the past two years. "Honeymoon at the Fontenelle ... wow. So generous of your uncle. I wouldn't have skipped that."

"Ooh la la, Mac." She flashed him a look under her eyelashes. "How'd you get to be such an expert? Easy Louisy?"

"Heck no. She wasn't easy at all. Slapped me a good one when I tried to sneak a kiss after the spring dance." He brushed imaginary dust off his homburg. "The dirty book section of the library."

Corrie tipped her head back and laughed. "If Omaha's library has a dirty book section, then I'm a Ziegfeld girl."

"Last night I was beginning to think you might be." Mac let out a long, satisfied sigh. "You put as much energy into loving as you do playing basketball."

"As if you minded." Her cheeks brightened to red. "It's like ... the best takeoff ever with loops and rolls thrown in for good measure."

"Without worrying about crashing." Mac nibbled her earlobe, earning a happy moan from his bride.

The train picked up speed, rolling through hills green with sprouting corn. A silent tear slid from the corner of her eye.

"Aw, Corrie." Mac squeezed her fingers. "They'll write. You can visit."

She shook her head. "I wish we were flying."

Not so good. "But, sweetheart, it's not practical."

"I know. Not enough time, too much luggage." She danced her fingers along the window glass, tracing the line where the sky met the trees. "But, Mac, we could be racing along, peeking down silos, scaring cows."

"Scaring me."

"We'd be fine. Could be a little bumpy in the afternoon with this heat, but no thunderstorms."

Enough pilot talk. "Let's see what your mother sent in the basket." He lifted the lid, releasing the aroma of fried pork.

"What didn't she send?" Corrie found apples, bridge mix, and bottles of root beer. "You'd think I'd married Richard Byrd instead of a Montgomery Ward's manager. There's enough food in here for a polar expedition."

He fidgeted with the buttons on his double-breasted jacket. "You'd rather be married to an explorer, a pilot, someone exciting."

"Oh, Mac. I didn't mean that." She pulled off a glove and touched her palm to his cheek. "If I'd known you were half interested in me, I'd have run off with you ages ago. But rumors had you chasing some other girl—Patricia Bowens, Helen Brunner, Margaret Sweton …"

He'd been interested all right. But Klemfuss, school secretary and all-around wet blanket, put the basketball team girls off limits. Then, scant hours after graduation, her father had given her an airplane. "Don't forget Violet Oberyl."

"How could I? Did you hear the latest? She had twins. In fact, so did Margaret. Oh my gosh… all your old girlfriends are *mothers*. I'm the last single girl from Central."

"Saved the best for last."

She leaned toward him as the train rounded a curve. He brushed a kiss across her temple, then headed down her neck. "I have so much to tell you."

She wiggled closer. "Two years of catching up to do."

"I have to warn you—I can't support you in the style you grew up in."

Corrie squeezed his hand. "Oh, Mac, that's all gone with the stock market crash. I'm not one for hosting fancy dinners, and decorating—"

"Mr. and Mrs. McFarland?" The conductor held out a note. "I've got some bad news. Mrs. McFarland's father has been taken to the hospital."

Mrs. McFarland's father? But Grandpa had died in the Great War. Oh… Corrie's father.

The conductor continued. "Next stop, Missouri Valley. A west-bound will be along twelve minutes after you disembark to take you back to Omaha."

"Thank you." Mac took the message slip. The timing couldn't be worse. The fellow who'd been covering for him was probably on his way back to Chicago by now. And Corrie. He'd waited so long, the idea of being separated made him ache. "Maybe I could get an extra day."

"Oh, no. You don't want Ward's thinking they can live without you." She pulled on her gloves and hat. "It's probably nothing. Mother and her worries. You have to work. Go on to Detroit. I'll see what the fuss is about." She grabbed her overnight case as the train slowed.

"Corrie." A half dozen "what ifs" and "when wills" clogged his throat. "Send me a telegram."

Her hand slipped from his. Then fearless Corrie turned back with a brave smile and a too-brief kiss. "I'll hurry to Michigan soon as I can."

———

Best guess, Father had been taken to St. Joseph's. Corrie joined the passengers exiting the station. The streetcar took her past warehouses, then through Little Italy's mix of workers' cottages and Victorian houses.

"Well I never." The nun in the next seat frowned at a group of nurses playing football on the hospital lawn. "They can't start without me."

Sister tucked a football under her arm and crossed the street to the game. Corrie grabbed her overnight case and handbag, and trailed closely, figuring no one would dare run over a nun. Her feet slowed as she passed the game. What fun to join in, to laugh and play with friends … No, as an old married lady, Corrie had to behave with dignity and worry about Father. She climbed the steps under the arch and pulled open the heavy door. A whiff of disinfectant took her back to that stormy day at Clarkson Hospital, visiting her teammate Halleen. The day Corrie found out Mac had left Omaha.

A clerk directed her up the grand stairway, through halls packed with nuns, nurses, and nursing students. Each room was furnished with a bed, dresser, and nightstand in mahogany. Drapes on the window coordinated with the coverlets. Swanky.

Father sat fully clothed on the bed. A white-coated man with round glasses loomed over him. "… complete bedrest, no exertion or excitement whatsoever, and a bland diet."

"The stress of a hospital bill will kill me." Father stood. "I'll rest at home."

Mother rose from the armchair and tried to hold him back. "But, dear—"

Her brothers chimed in with, "But, Father—"

The doctor spun on his heel and marched out. "It's your funeral."

"How are you feeling?" Corrie stepped into the room.

Father glared. "What are you doing here?"

"You collapsed at the station."

Harry said, "Not cardiac. Maybe gastric."

Whatever that meant.

"I'm fine." Father grabbed his suit coat and stomped out. "Let's get home before Chester eats the rest of that pineapple upside-down cake."

"I don't think that's on a bland diet." Mother scurried to catch up. "I'll make you milk toast and Jell-O."

"You can make it, but I won't eat it."

Harry drove, Father beside him, and the rest of the family piled in the back like the Keystone Cops. Corrie ended up on Artie's lap.

"You packing bricks?" Ernie balanced her overnight case on his legs.

"That's enough," Mother hissed. "Don't stress Father."

Corrie and her brothers had been picking on each other all their lives. If they stopped now, the shock might do him in.

Harry still had a job with the Union Pacific Railroad, so he paid the toll for the bridge to Council Bluffs. "The doctor wants Father to stay in bed, but his room is upstairs."

"I can climb the steps."

"No you can't," chorused the family.

"We could move your bed downstairs," Corrie suggested.

"We can't have a bed in the front room." Mother twisted her handkerchief. "What will people think?"

"The day bed in the sewing room came from the back porch." Harry parked in front of Uncle Chester's house. "We'll move it back down there. Most comfortable spot in the house during the summer."

"Then where will I sleep?" Corrie asked as they trooped inside.

"In Michigan," Mother said. "Father's supposed to avoid stress."

So they don't need me? Corrie stood by the front door and watched her brothers move her bed. *All I do is add to the stress around here?* She'd left dear Mac and raced back here for nothing?

"No sense standing around like Little Orphan Annie." Artie carried her overnight case to the car. "I'll drop you at the station."

The ticket agent had nothing but bad news. The next train for Chicago didn't leave until 6:00 p.m. He didn't believe her story about being on the earlier express, so she'd need to pay the fare again. Corrie closed her empty purse, shuffled across the checkerboard floor, and found an open spot on a long wooden bench. Important passengers hurried beneath the art deco ceiling. None of them had rushed off without a ticket or anything other than a few coins. Where would she get money for her fare? Father was so broke, he'd left the hospital against his doctor's advice. Harry's pay went for groceries. Ernie had lost his job when Father's store closed. Artie had been laid off by Mutual. She might cry after all.

"Tired of married life already?" asked a familiar hoarse voice.

"Jackie! Am I glad to see you." Corrie hugged her basketball team-mate and filled her in on her crazy morning. "What are you doing here?"

Her friend wore a swell new suit with a matching hat that framed her face perfectly. A job in movie distribution earned her a keen wardrobe, more fashionable than her patched-together high school clothes or the old sweater and skirt Corrie wore today. Jackie looped an arm through hers. "Picking up some Hollywood big shot who wants to see the air races. Hey, come with us. You know all the flyboys."

"And how! It's a great day for flying!" And she'd thought getting married would make her miss all the excitement.

"Good thing I taught you to flirt." Jackie caught her change of expression and winked. "You're married, not dead."

Jackie's guest turned out to be a tall Texan in his mid-twenties. Sweeping dark eyebrows gave him an intense stare. An exotic and expensive fragrance radiated from him. They worked their way through the traffic—the newspaper guessed an attendance of ten thou-sand—to Mid-West Aviation.

Instead of heading for the grandstand, Tex wanted to meet other pilots and see their planes. Corrie jumped out as soon as Jackie parked. She pointed to the biplane circling overhead. "It's Dorothy Hester. She did fifty-six inverted snap rolls in two hours yesterday." Shortly before Mac proposed on that bluff across the river. And now she was married. The last twenty-four hours seemed to belong to another person, as if a reel from a movie had dropped into her life. "Sorry. I babble when I'm excited."

"Airplanes are exciting." Tex asked smart questions about the planes she'd flown—stall speed, takeoff distance, fuel burn.

She told him she'd met the Women's Air Derby in Kansas City. "Have you thought about sponsoring another race pilot?" He'd backed Vera Dawn Walker.

"Perhaps."

Not the answer Corrie hoped for.

Dorothy flew inverted down the field, did two outside loops, and then returned with her wings nearly vertical. Corrie told him everything she knew about Dorothy and her plane. The Texan wrote down Dorothy's name, then the names of the top three finishers in the dead-stick landing contest.

During the first race, a Curtiss Robin suffered a broken left gear, but the pilot managed to land safely, without further damage. Tex recorded his name as well as the pilot who won the balloon-busting contest, and the top finishers of the next races.

An autogiro, a funny-looking thing with a low wing, a giant propeller on top and a regular prop in front, landed in front of the grandstand. Tex considered using one to film movies.

Speed Holman arrived in his hot biplane and showed them all how it was done for the third race.

"The best flying ever!" Corrie bounced up and down. "He must have been going two hundred miles an hour!"

"Impressive." Tex gave the Laird Speedwing a thorough inspection. "Think how fast it would be with retractable gear, flush rivets, and a bigger engine."

"Three hundred miles an hour." Corrie's feet announced they were tired of standing and her throat had dried out from narrating the air show over the roar of the engines. "Where'd Jackie run off to?"

Her friend sauntered up. "Sorry. Had to step away for a smoke. The pilots are going to a party at the Omaha Country Club. We'll give you a ride," she told Tex.

Corrie looked at her watch. Even if she had fare for the ticket to Detroit, she'd missed the last train today. Might as well join the fun.

The dining room at the club overlooked the golf course. Tex handed out business cards and talked aviation, from Zeppelins to Fokkers and Travel Airs. At the end of the evening, Corrie waited with Tex under the arched entrance as Jackie retrieved her car.

"Miss Corrie, I've enjoyed our time together." Tex focused his intense stare on her. "In Kansas City, did you meet Pancho Barnes?"

"Sure did! She flew a three-hundred horsepower Travel Air. Say, do you know her address? I want to congratulate her for beating Amelia's speed record."

A frown creased his brows. "She lives in San Marino."

"No number or street?"

He dropped his head to the side, exactly like Artie did when he was peeved. "You did say you'd met Pancho."

Her cheeks heated as his focus turned into a stare. "What am I thinking? Of course the mailman knows how to find her."

Tex shifted his weight. "You saw *Hell's Angels*?"

"Three times! Nifty flying." She gasped. "That was your movie?"

"Pancho flies for me. I've got a squadron of stunt pilots to fly in the movies. And you can too."

"I don't have a plane," she blurted.

"You'll be flying my fleet." He pressed a business card into her hand. "Join me in Hollywood, Corrie."

"But ..." The words on the card blurred. She choked. What had she done? Why hadn't he arrived a day earlier? "I can't. I'm married."

CHAPTER
EIGHTEEN

MAC GLARED at the piles of invoices, bills of lading, and receipts. Monday he'd gotten the front of the store in order. Today he'd tackle the back. He scooted his chair to the desk and started sorting. The manager who'd been pinch-hitting had been recalled to Chicago early, leaving Walter in charge. Walter's expertise in theoretical conundrums served him well at the University of Michigan but proved useless at Montgomery Ward's. He couldn't write a phone message without tallying the numbers.

Mac's stomach grumbled, reminding him he hadn't eaten today. Forget lunch. He'd give his right foot for an ice cold Vernors. Walter had forgotten to crank in the awning one night, and a hail storm had shredded it, leaving the store to bake in the sun all day. Then yesterday Mac had made the unhappy discovery that something had chewed the fan's cord over the winter. Fan repair. One more item for his list. Good thing Corrie hadn't come back with him—

"Mac, the toilet! Again!"

An ominous burbling sounded on the other side of the wall.

"Shut off the water, Walter, and use the plunger like I showed you." He opened the middle drawer. Where'd his pencils go? Did he have to lock his desk every time he left the room?

"It's still coming!" The bass voice trembled. "It's going to blow!"

Mac shoved through the crowded stockroom. "Turn the knob clockwise."

"I did!" The tall man backed out, vigorously wringing his hands.

Water gurgled to the top of the bowl. "Get some rags!" Mac tested the knob. Closed. But the water continued to rise. "Shirley, call the city. Find out what—"

"Delivery!" Salvatore DiFlorio banged the back door open. "Better shut that off, Mac. It's gonna overflow."

"Sal, did you see any utility crews in the neighborhood?" He stepped away from the ugly puddle seeping around the base.

"Buncha fellows standing around a manhole cover in the alley."

"No rags." Walter handed him a folded stack of new towels.

Mac took a deep breath and spoke slowly. "Go out in the alley. Tell the workers our store's filling with sewage."

Sal shook his head at the retreating man. "Better fire the cluck."

Mac handed him the towels, then rummaged through the broom closet. "That would put eight people on the dole. He's the only able-bodied one in the family." He found rags and twisted them into a dam around the fountaining fixture.

"That's not gonna hold it, Mac. You gonna have a mess on your hands, a real mess."

"Girl asking for you, Boss."

"I'm busy, Shirley. You wait on her."

"She says she'll wait. Eek! A dog!"

Mac groaned. "Walter must have left the back door open."

"You didn't tell him to close it." Sal swatted a buzzing fly. "Dog brought in his buddies."

A feminine voice, not Shirley's, commanded, "Sit. Stay. Good dog."

Mac's hands froze in mid-twist. It sounded like— Couldn't be. She was supposed to send a telegram.

Walter shuffled in. "The men say they're finished. Water will stop now."

The toilet gave an ominous belch, spurting up and out. Then with a loud sucking noise, it emptied.

Mac took inventory in the mirror as he washed his hands. An ugly stain spattered his tan slacks from the knees down. Yielding to the heat, he'd taken off his coat and tie. His hair stuck out in spikes, defying this morning's dose of Brilliantine. He ran damp hands over his head. Well, Corrie'd seen him in high school. "Walter, restock these towels. Sal, close the door. Please." He marched to the front.

"Mac!" Corrie straightened from patting a dog. She walked toward him, arms open, her smile wide. He was totally goofy over this girl.

"Corrie, you're here." He reached for her, his beautiful Corrie, the bee's knees of brides, his sheba. But wait—should a manager kiss his wife in front of the employees? An inhale reminded him of how he smelled. "Not too close. I'm a mess." He caught her hands. "I would have picked you up at the station if I'd known when you were coming." Over the reek of raw sewage, came a different smell. Not coal dust, but airplane dope and gasoline. His gaze took in his new bride, hair plastered to her head, greased-streaked face, leather jacket folded over her arm, slacks. A shiv struck his heart and choked him. "Except... you didn't take the train."

She grinned. "A pilot from Omaha Municipal had to ferry a Lockheed Vega to Joliet. Then I hopped a ride in a Stinson to their factory field. Fast trip and saved on train fare. Tex is right—monoplanes are the future."

Planes? Pilots? Tex? Mac didn't know what to worry about first.

Sal stepped around Mac. "You flew all the way from Omaha!"

"Flew?" Walter gasped. "In an airplane?"

"I always wanted to try that. What's it like up there?" Shirley asked.

"It's wonderful! Soon as I find a plane, I'll take you up."

"Shirley's a mother." Mac's alarm grew. Her children would be orphaned.

"I'll give your children a ride too."

Mac remembered his manners. "Corrie, this is Shirley Wendell, head cashier; Walter Purdue, head stockman; and Salvatore DiFlorio, head delivery man. Staff, Mrs. McFarland."

"The new missus! We thought he was waiting for Montgomery Ward's to deliver a bride." Salvatore pumped her hand. "Mac, you didn't tell us you'd married a regular Amelia Earhart!"

"You didn't get my telegram?" Corrie asked.

"I put it right here." Walter rummaged under the register, spilling piles of paper onto the floor.

"Sal, would you please lock up?" He grabbed Corrie's overnight case. "Let's go."

"What about the rabid mongrel?" Sal asked.

Corrie whistled, and the cocker spaniel followed.

"Corrie, you could have been killed!" Mac gripped her arm.

"No, I couldn't. The weather was great."

"But these deathtraps—"

"Stinson's been building planes since 1920. And the Lockheed really goes. We were getting ground speeds around one fifty."

"Miles per hour?" Mac wiped his brow. "And these flyboys you're riding around with, do they have any experience?"

She shrugged. "Who knows. I flew so they could catch up on sleep."

"Corrie." Mac groaned. "What were you thinking, taking a plane?"

"I wanted to be with you." Her shoulders drooped. "I didn't have a ticket or train fare."

So this was his fault. His heart hit the pavement. "I promised to take care of you but didn't give you train fare. I'm sorry."

"It worked out." She jumped straight up and swatted the drugstore's awning. "You'll never believe what happened, Mac! Jackie introduced me to the Hollywood big shot who made *Hell's Angels*. He offered me a job as a stunt pilot, flying his fleet. You can open a Ward's in California."

"Corrie." He caught her hands. Would he ever catch her spirit? "Didn't you hear about Speed Holman, Northwest Airline's number one pilot? He smashed into the ground and died in front of the crowd at the Air Races."

For a moment, she stilled. Her eyes closed and she nodded. "I was there." Then her eyes opened, blazing blue green. "People die from all sorts of things. I want to live."

"Yes. Live. Not end it all in a crash." Mac tightened his hold on her. Crossing the railroad tracks reminded him why she'd returned to Omaha. "How's your father?"

"It's not his heart. It's his stomach. He's recuperating at home."

"Good news."

"Unless you're trying to keep him on a diet. Uncle Chester's house was packed with relatives fighting for kitchen space. Aunt Florence's celery soup, Cousin Bertha's potato bread, Mrs. Zukas's rice pudding."

Mac's stomach growled. She was complaining about too much food?

Corrie glanced over her shoulder. "We're being followed."

He waved at the dog. "Go on. Go home, if you can find your way."

"People are letting their pets go." She blinked back a tear.

He guided his wife to an alley behind Mullen Wright Hardware and Lumber. The dog circled the garbage cans under the stairway, then plopped down in the shade of a Chevy.

"A new car. I didn't think the four-door came in red."

"The owner worked at the factory." He had so much to learn about his new bride. "Do you know how to drive?"

"Sure. My brothers taught me." She squeezed his hand. "You won't have to back up hills anymore. Remember your flivver? We had a lot of fun in that old jalopy."

"You, me, and the entire girls' basketball team. But now I have you all to myself." He pulled her into his arms. She leaned close for an enthusiastic kiss. Oh yes, they could do this all night ... except his gut reminded him about supper.

They climbed the wooden steps to the rickety landing and Mac unlocked the door. Tomato-red walls held in the heat of the day. The icebox had leaked, forming a puddle under Ward's Big Value card table in green and Ward's Will Not Tip folding chairs. The rest of his makeshift kitchen—a toaster, hot plate, and electric coffeepot—appeared to have behaved while he was gone. Laundry in various states of dirty covered Corrie's trunks.

Mac winced. Corrie had grown up in one of Omaha's most elegant mansions. "I've saved for a house. Pick out anything you like. Furniture too. Ward's has a good installment plan."

"I've been confined to a cot in Aunt Florence's sewing room for the past year. This is spacious."

"Let's wash up, change clothes, and I'll take you out for a nice supper." How could he suggest the wife of the Montgomery Ward's manager ought to wear a dress in public? "Uh, your face. All I've got is Lifebuoy."

"It works," she said as she entered the bathroom. "Good thing the Lockheed and the Stinson have closed cockpits. Can you imagine how dirty I'd be if I'd flown a Waco or Stearman?"

"No." He tried to avoid imagining Corrie in any airplane.

Her clean face peeked out of the bathroom. "How late are restaurants open in this town?"

"Eight, nine o'clock. You're not hungry?"

"Well ..." Corrie glanced from him to the bed and back. "Since you're taking your slacks off anyway ..."

———

Marriage would be great if they could stay in bed.

The springs screeched as Mac rolled to kiss her nose. "Suppertime, little bearcat." He climbed out.

Corrie grabbed onto the metal frame to keep from bouncing off. "Do we have to?"

"Ab-so-lute-ly. I'm bellybutton to backbone." He grabbed an undershirt and shorts from a stack of shipping crates. Two years had added muscles to his athletic body, broadening his shoulders. Watch out, Douglas Fairbanks. Mac snuck another kiss on his way to the bathroom. "Once we have our own house, we'll eat at home."

Who needs a house? Corrie dug through her trunks and found a rayon combination and a lightweight cotton shift dress in green plaid.

A loud whistle then the huffing and clanking of a train shook the building.

"Grand Trunk Railroad. Another reason to move," Mac yelled over the racket.

She danced across the brown tile, singing "This Train."

Mac frowned. "I should have hung up your clothes."

Corrie smoothed the wrinkles. "No one will notice this time of night."

"Hope not. I'll find something for the dog while you get ready."

Hearing the impatience in his tone, Corrie made a quick trip to the bathroom, then tied her shoes. "Let's paint the town."

He handed her a hat. "We can hold hands all the time now."

Corrie grabbed his warm one and spun to his chest for a quick kiss. "At long last, we're together."

The dog greeted them with a wagging tail at the bottom of the steps. Mac had put out a saucepan of water for him. "He finished the pork scraps."

"Hope he can make it home."

The dog followed, pausing at the intersection to cross with them.

"Spiffy place. Lots of trees, new buildings, brick streets." Like Omaha without the packing house odor.

"And the Detroit Zoo." He held her hand. "It's growing. Over twenty thousand last year. That's why Ward's built such a large store."

"Puts our little Omaha shop to shame."

"That's a display store. Customers were supposed to check the quality of our merchandise, then put in a mail order." He quirked a smile. "Who knew they'd want to take their purchases home with them?"

Mac pointed out theaters and grocery stores, hoping she wouldn't notice how many storefronts were empty. "Good-sized business district. Main Street behind us, Washington in front. This is Fourth. Streets are numbered north to south, Second to Seventh. To get you all balled up, the major roads start at Eight Mile Road at the Detroit city line and get bigger as you go north."

"How much bigger?"

"I don't know." His smile heated her engine. "I've been waiting for you to go exploring."

The dog padded beside them past a millinery store, bus station, and the Western Union office. The barber shop, shoe repair, and cleaner's had closed for the day, but the restaurant was still open.

Mac opened the door for Corrie. Dark wainscot covered the lower walls. An fellow looked up from his stool at the end of the long counter. Three men peeked out of the last booth. This establishment used to be a bar. No doubt they served something stronger than root beer in those Hires bottles.

To the right of the door stood a wooden case with a glass top. Two teenage boys sent a marble through a maze of nails and holes.

"What's that?" Corrie asked.

"It's called Whiffle, another way to separate a fellow from his nickel. The craze hasn't reached Omaha yet?"

"Some days I make more on Whiffle than I do selling food." The cook glanced up from scraping the grill. "Running late, Mac."

"Had to get my new bride settled in. Corrie, this is Bick, the finest hash slinger in Royal Oak."

"Congratulations, Mr. and Mrs. McFarland! Newlywed special coming right up." He set utensils and glasses of ginger ale on the counter. On the radio, a saxophonist played "You're the Cream in My Coffee."

Mac's glance said he'd been hoping for a little privacy too. He helped Corrie onto the stool. Their minute steaks came with onions, French fries, and a side of cantaloupe.

Parched, Corrie reached for her glass and took a big swallow.

"Careful, it's—" Mac said.

Too late. The cold liquid walloped her taste buds with intense flavor and she coughed. "What is it and is it legal?"

Bick laughed. "Welcome to Michigan and Vernors ginger ale! Good for what ails you. Ale for ails, get it?"

"It's legal," Mac said. "Aging in oak barrels gives it strong flavor."

"Wow." Corrie took a sip. "It's … potent."

Bick got her talking and before she knew it, she'd told him about flying from Omaha to Detroit.

"Never met a pilot before." He propped his elbows on the counter. "How'd a nice girl like you get bit by the flying bug?"

"I took a ride in a Jenny at the airmail field when I was little. The Ford Air Tour came to Omaha when I was fifteen. They landed at Fort Crook, the army's airfield, since the city's wasn't ready. Mostly Travel Airs, Wacos, Swallows, but they even had a Junkers, Fokker, and a Stout."

Mac pushed his plate aside. "And a Curtiss, which crashed."

"Some fool parked his motorcycle on the field. No one was hurt."

Bick refilled her glass. "You could fly in the air tour. They've had girl pilots."

Corrie nodded. "If I had a plane, I would."

Bick cleared their plates. "Wayne County airport's halfway to Ann Arbor. You called Mac to come get you?"

"No, one of the pilots drove me up here. He flies a Keystone-Loening Air Yacht. Detroit to Cleveland in less than an hour." She turned to Mac. "That's what we could do Sunday—check out an amphibian plane."

Mac turned a funny color. Maybe his supper hadn't agreed with him. He stood and put a dollar on the counter.

Bick pushed it back to him. "On the house, old man. Mrs. Mac, you're a hoot. Come back anytime."

They stepped into the cool evening. The dog had been waiting beside the door. Bright-brown eyes tracked Corrie's hand as she slipped him a piece of meat.

"Okay, little dog, that's enough. Find your way home now."

Mac cleared his throat as they walked back toward the apartment. "Corrie, you're from a retail family."

A retail family? Yes, Father owned a jewelry store. She nodded.

"In the past three years Ward's has gone from no stores to five hundred, from display shops like Omaha's to full-sized department stores. Between competition with Sears and the stock market crash, we're leaking millions." He wiped his hand across his forehead. "I'm the youngest manager in the country. While I appreciate the opportunity, there's a lot of pressure." He stopped at the intersection to let the theater traffic go by, then faced her. "I don't want to let you down."

Corrie raised up on tiptoes for a kiss, but he turned his head and it landed below his ear. "You're working so hard."

He continued, her hand tucked in his. "You're the wife of a Montgomery Ward's manager in a small town. So everything you say and do ..."

"Reflects on you." Horsefeathers. She'd already made a mess of things. What had she said? Slang. Mac was a stickler for proper speech. "I'll do better, Mac. I'll do my best."

The dog accompanied them into the alley.

Mac wrapped his arm around Corrie's shoulders and planted a real McCoy on her lips. "Thanks for understanding."

CHAPTER
NINETEEN

"CORRIE?" Morning light shone on her bare shoulder, a perfect place for a kiss.

She gave an appreciative hum, then fell back asleep.

More than anything, Mac wanted to join her. "Breakfast for my bearcat."

Her pert nose emerged from the feather pillow. "I thought you didn't have food here."

"Nothing fancy. Eggs fried in Crisco."

"And java! Swell!" Corrie bounded out of bed, showing her mighty fine chassis. She arrived at the table wearing a knee-length pink kimono, just as the toast popped. Where did all her energy come from?

"You can cook."

"Beats starving. Mom worked and Mr. Smooth—"

"Let me guess. He had no problem gobbling down whatever you made but wouldn't lift a finger for you."

Mac grinned. Moving out of his big brother's shadow had been a relief. "Most of the time he'd con the neighbors into feeding him."

"Speaking of moochers …"

"The pup's still outside. I saved him some eggs." Mac handed Corrie copies of the Royal Oak *Tribune*, the two Detroit newspapers, and a map. "Keep an eye out for lost-dog ads and signs when you're looking for our house. Here's the apartment key, car key, and enough money to keep the tank filled. I'm sorry I left you high and dry in Omaha."

"It's all copacetic." In other words, Corrie was happy to see the airshow and fly to Detroit. She tilted the venetian blind, exchanging the view of the street for the view of the sky. "A fan would move the air and cover up some of the traffic noise."

Mac studied his new wife. Fire trucks had wailed at midnight, the Twin Pines milkman clumped up the back steps just before dawn, and the Grand Trunk chugged through hourly, and the bedsprings squeaked with every breath. "You didn't get any sleep last night."

"Having too much fun." She kissed his cheek. "Maybe all we need is a different bed."

"In a house on a quiet street, with shade trees and cross ventilation."

"It's not so bad." She wiped a bead of perspiration from her brow and opened the *Free Press*.

Why was she digging in her heels? She couldn't possibly see any redeeming qualities in this apartment. Most girls would jump at the chance to pick out a house. Was she worried about money? "Corrie, we can afford—"

"Hot dog!" She held up the paper. "Mae Haizlip broke the light-plane altitude record yesterday—twenty-two thousand five hundred feet. Wonder what a Buhl Speedwing looks like."

"I have no idea." Mac set his plate in the sink, then slipped out the door. Corrie was thinking about airplanes. He might as well go.

"Woof!" The cocker spaniel sat at the bottom of the stairs, surrounded by trash from a tipped-over can. All the flies in town arrived to celebrate.

Corrie leaned over the railing. "Uh-oh. Don't get your work clothes dirty, Mac. I'll clean up. Here, boy."

The animal wagged his tail but didn't climb the steps.

"I think he's afraid." Mac bent, intending to pick him up until the stink hit.

"I'll get him. Can't have my favorite Montgomery Ward's manager smelling like a dog." Corrie descended the stairs, bare legs flashing like a dancer. Mac hoped no one wandered past.

"He'd like a house better, with a fenced yard."

Her eyes glowed. "We can keep him?"

"If no one's looking for him." Mac nodded. "He'll need a name."

"How about 'Monty'?" Corrie tucked Mac's tie under his collar, her touch spinning his head like a Wardway Gyrator.

"Might be taken as disrespect toward my esteemed employer. I'm thinking 'Lindy,' after your hero."

"Perfect! Lindbergh was born here in Detroit!" She gave Mac an off-to-work kiss tasting of coffee, then carried the cocker upstairs. "C'mon, Lindy. Breakfast, then a bath for you!"

Mac watched her disappear into the apartment. A dog. *Well, it's safer than flying. Anything's safer than flying.*

———

"We're all wet." Corrie dried herself, the dog, and the bathroom as best she could in the humidity. Her curls and the dog's fur lay in soggy clumps. "Let's go for a car ride."

Corrie grabbed Mac's newspapers and slid into the Chevy. Lindy hopped in the copilot's seat with a wag of his stubby tail and they headed west.

"You're a great dog, Lindy. Is anyone missing you?"

He panted but didn't answer.

Traffic eased as they left Royal Oak. Nothing but farms and open land out this way. Corrie turned south. Did that sign say Eight Mile Road? Mac had mentioned—

"Lindy, look!" A distinctive shape glided across the sky. "It's a Ford Trimotor, an all-metal, three-engine airliner. Let's see where it lands." Lindy gave a tongue-hanging grin, ready for adventure. "It's heading to Dearborn, where it was built. They fly back and forth to Chicago. Ford Airport has lights for night landing, paved runways, and radios to talk to the planes in flight—a first-rate airport."

Neighborhoods of two-story homes flanked the road. Factory smokestacks poked the sky. Traffic picked up and miles passed. West of the road stood a metal tower with a bucket at the top and a building at the base. "That's the dirigible mast, where the airships dock. Wish we could see one."

Corrie parked by the hangars, two buildings larger than football fields, built with light buff brick and tall windows. Henry Ford was all in for aviation.

The spaniel trotted beside her to a concrete airplane parking lot. "Stick with me, Lindy, and stay away from propellers. These are the first paved runways in the world. Keeps planes out of the muck."

Three all-metal Trimotors and a single-engine Air Pullman gleamed in the sunshine, making wood-and-fabric biplanes look old-fashioned.

"Now the first thing you do, Lindy, when you're picking up a new plane, is the preflight." Dog at her heels, she strolled around the closest Ford, telling him everything to check. She read the placard by the tail, "'Stout Metal Airplane Co. Division of Ford Motor Company.' A nice tribute to the man who designed this plane."

Corrie peeked inside. Large windows lit the wood-paneled interior. A man with thick curls and eyeglasses sat in the captain's seat. "Do you always teach dogs to preflight?"

Corrie walked up the aisle between the twelve wicker seats and introduced herself. "I learned to fly in a Lincoln Sport."

"Never heard of it." He shook her hand. "Name's Bill."

"It's like a Swallow. Flew a hundred hours in an Overland and a few more in Monocoupes, Stinsons, Lockheed Vega, whatever I could get my hands on." She should have brought her logbook.

"No time in a Ford? Today's your lucky day. Shut the door and let's go."

Corrie closed the door before he could change his mind. Lindy chose a starboard seat.

Next problem, how to clamber into the copilot's seat wearing a dress. Corrie pointed left. "Is that Henry Ford?"

Bill stuck his head out the window, and Corrie hopped over the brake levers and sat. Piercing eyes met hers. "You are too clever."

"We're sitting high." Thirteen gauges made this the most complex instrument panel she'd ever seen. Front and center sat a disk with an outline of a monoplane on a sky-blue background. "An artificial horizon!"

"Fuel and mixture controls forward. Engine gauges." He fired it up, then closed his window. "Mag check. You got the plane."

Whoopee! Corrie wanted to yell, but she didn't want Bill to think she was a rube. The cockpit filled with the engines' roar and the smell of hot oil and fuel. Bill worked the lever between the seats to brake and steer. Taxiing on the concrete was a dream—no stumps or gopher holes to worry about, although the big plane needed a lot of space to turn.

"Three throttles forward," Bill yelled as they reached the end of the runway. "Bring the tail up. Hold it on the deck until sixty-five."

Now she could see down the runway. Ten seconds later, Corrie pulled back the Model T steering wheel and the Trimotor lifted into the air. "Whoopee!" she yelled, unable to hold it in anymore. She turned crosswind. More aileron, a lot more rudder, push, push harder. C'mon, airplane. There, finally. "Where are we going?"

"Around the patch."

Rats. How could she stretch out the ride? "How's it stall?"

He grinned. "Take it up a couple thousand and find out."

At two thousand feet, Corrie did a clearing turn. She spotted another Trimotor on final and a Stinson in the distance. With the power back and both arms pulling on the wheel, the plane slowed. At sixty-three, the nose wallowed. Nice. Corrie powered up again but couldn't get the engines to synchronize. Bill tweaked the throttles into a harmonious rumble, then gestured for her to return to the airport.

"Follow me through." He took the controls on final. "Land on the mains, not the tail wheel."

The wheels touched five feet higher than Corrie expected. The tail settled, then they taxied to the hangar and shut down.

"Nice job, Miss Corrie."

"Do I get the job?"

"If I had one." He gave an apologetic shake of his head, then turned toward the port window. "This preacher's kid isn't looking at your legs."

"Thanks, Bill. You made a great airplane!" Corrie hurdled the brake lever and got halfway down the aisle when her hem caught on an armrest. Dumb dress. Without Mrs. Zukas, she'd have to sew it herself. She freed herself and grabbed Lindy. The mugginess of the cabin had the dog drooling furiously. Corrie mopped up with her handkerchief.

"Go see how we build it." Mr. Bill Stout waved toward the hangar. "Then stop by again and I'll find something you haven't flown."

"You got it!"

———

Mac trudged into the alley. His parking spot was empty. Corrie must be still out looking for a house. Hope she's found a good one.

The car zoomed around the corner, downshifting and braking into the parking spot with an *oo-ah* of the horn. The spaniel jumped out, circled Mac, then raced for the trash cans. Corrie emerged from the car, a grin lighting her face.

"You must have found a mansion."

After an enthusiastic hug and loud kiss, Corrie grabbed Mac's hand and danced a few Charleston kicks. "I found Ford Airport and got to fly a Trimotor with Bill Stout."

A hot jolt shot through his body and settled in his gut. Bill who? Flying? Which was worse—strange men or dangerous airplanes?

"It's so exciting." Corrie chattered about the flight, then the factory. "… huge sheets of aluminum, dip it, corrugate it, shape it on jigs. Then they bolt the pieces together, add the landing gear and engine, and roll it out for flight testing. Wouldn't that be a great job?"

"You went to Dearborn?" Mac fought to keep from yelling. "You didn't even look for a house." Oh no, another night in this steam bath. "And you rode in a Ford Trimotor? They crash all the time! Last June in the ocean near Boston. November and the previous March at Ford Airport. And Newark and San Diego and New Mexico."

"I flew with the fellow who built the Trimotor. Couldn't be safer." She dashed up the stairs. "It's the most modern aircraft factory in the world. They're using the wind tunnel to bring speed up to a hundred twenty-three miles an hour. And they're developing a bomber for the military. Besides, this place is fine."

"Fine?" Waves of heat billowed as the door opened. "You could bake bread on the windowsill. Noise from the street keeps us up all night."

"I'd say it's more than noise keeping you up all night." Corrie gave him a sassy smile and a wink.

"My cuddler." They kissed until the heat forced them apart.

They returned to the diner since it was cooler and had food. Mac made sure to sit at a table this time. Bick brought iced tea and took their order. Mac reached across the table and squeezed Corrie's hands. So much to tell her. "You won't believe what happened—"

"There she is!" Bick pointed out Corrie to the man walking in. The cook dragged another chair to their table. "I told John you flew all the way here from Omaha."

"And I said, I gotta meet this flygirl." The man pushed back the cuffs of his suit sleeves, shook hands, and sat himself down. "John of Royal Aircraft Corporation, manufacturer of the Royal Air Trainer."

No, no, no.

"The usual," the man said to Bick. He slapped a sales brochure in front of Corrie. "The Royal Air Trainer was designed by a University of Detroit professor, based on millions of dollars of experimental work by the military. High-wing and tandem cockpit." He tapped the photograph.

A sales presentation. An aircraft sales presentation. Mac groaned, but Corrie didn't hear him over the spiel.

"The Trainer's ninety horsepower LeBlond radial produces a max speed of one hundred five, cruises at eighty-five, stalls at thirty. Giving it a range of four hundred miles."

Corrie didn't look up from the brochure. "Have you considered using a tail wheel instead of a skid? And adding brakes?"

"We'll build it exactly the way you want it, to your specifications. What color would you like?"

Since the stock market crash, salesmen twitched, shook, and pleaded. Exactly like this.

"Where is your factory?" Corrie asked.

Mac gave his head a shake, signaling her to stop talking.

John broke out in a sweat. "I've got a building off Coolidge and Thirteen Mile."

This con man didn't have a factory; he had an old white barn.

"I'd like to see how it flies."

Mac shook his head more vigorously.

"Actually ..." The man's right leg bounced against the table, rattling the silverware. "The plane is in Lansing, where it was built."

Only one plane? That made it experimental. Even more dangerous.

Mac pulled the brochure from Corrie's fingers and handed it back. "We are not in the market for an airplane."

"Only two thousand eight hundred seventy-five dollars. We'll finance."

Mac stood and held out his hand, the businessman's version of the bum's rush. "Thank you for stopping by."

Bick brought their meals and joined the airplane talk. Never eating at this joint again. By the time the cook left, Corrie and John were deep in conversation about Ford's airplane factory. Mac stared at the ceiling. If he took a hike right now, would either of them notice?

A slender hand slipped into his and squeezed. She addressed the interloper. "John, it's been nice to hear about your project, but my husband and I need some time."

A warm glow eased his heart's chill.

"Sure, sure." John carried his meal to the lunch counter.

Mac returned to his seat and focused on his tuna salad. "Thanks."

"Four-flusher. He don't know from nothing," Corrie muttered and blew out a long breath. "John doesn't even have an airplane."

And neither did he.

———

"Keep an eye out for the Royal Aircraft Factory, Lindy. The fellow in the diner last night said it was out this way." Corrie drove down Thirteen Mile, passing houses and farms. The only building big enough was a white barn. She parked and, trailed by Lindy, headed up the rutted path.

The open doors revealed a radial engine attached to a dark-blue biplane missing a lower wing. A jig held the wing vertically.

"You're three weeks early for raspberries." A man in overalls sat on an apple crate beside the jig, holding a tangled ball of string.

"Need help?" Corrie asked.

He grimaced. "It's not hemming an apron."

"It's harder because you have to use a long thread for the whole rib."

Eyebrows raised, he gave her a once-over. "That so?"

"I worked in an airplane factory when I was building time toward my license." Corrie brushed a finger over the fabric. "You shrunk the cotton with a couple coats of dope, and now you're ready to rib stitch. It's easier if you have a second person on the other side."

"What do I got to lose?" He stood and gestured toward the apple crate. "Okay, smarty, all yours."

The steps were written out on a piece of paper tacked to the jig. "I would have never figured this out if another pilot hadn't showed me." Corrie took the foot-long needle and bent it an inch from the end. The man had started with a square knot and poked holes in the right places. "Up to the next hole, pull it through. Push it through the other side."

The man returned the needle.

"The top thread is your anchor, and the bottom is the tail." Corrie talked through the process. "The needle loops around, on top of the tail, under the anchor, making a figure eight. Keep holding the tail. Wiggle side to side to cinch it, put your thumb over the knot, pull the tail, and it tightens right where you want it."

"Says you." The man saluted. "Gil Hilzinger."

"Corrie McFarland," she said, proud she remembered her married name. She nodded at the dog snoozing in the shade. "And that's Lindy."

"Pleased to meet you. Show me again."

When he reached the end of the first rib, Corrie tipped her head toward the plane and asked, "What is this?"

"Hess Blue Bird, built in Wyandotte, south of Detroit." He started on the second rib. "One of these entered the Dole Race."

As Corrie recalled, the plane had made it to California but not to Hawaii.

Several ribs and many flying stories later, Lindy pushed against Corrie. "Out of the way, pup. Don't want to poke you." But he pressed a cold nose to her arm. "What do you want, silly dog?"

"Maybe he's thirsty. There's a bowl by the pump."

Outside, the shadows had lengthened. Her fingers were raw, her back sore, and her shoulders ached. Her dress looked like she'd cleaned the barn. Her stomach gurgled. Corrie checked her watch. Uh-oh. Mac would be in a lather. "I've got to run. C'mon, Lindy."

"Tomorrow?"

"I don't know." She hurried to the car.

"I owe you an airplane ride."

"You got a deal!"

———

Salvatore slapped the clipboard on Mac's desk. "That's it for my week."

"Wish I could say the same." Mac bent over the ledger, hoping his delivery man would take the hint. Managers shouldn't complain to their employees.

Sal propped an elbow on the rolltop. "Not much of a honeymoon, working so hard. At least you got a nice home-cooked meal every night."

"I wish."

"She no cook?"

The ledger slammed shut. "She *no do* anything but find every airport in Michigan. All she talks about is planes and flyboys. Bet they don't even know she's married—I didn't get her a wedding ring yet."

"You no want her to fly?"

"Would you want your wife up there?" Mac frowned at the mail stacked in his in-tray. "I raced to Omaha as soon as I heard her airplane was sold. But she hasn't given up on flying."

"Why did Amelia Earhart marry you anyway? You ain't no Lucky Lindy."

"I'm not even Tailspin Tommy," he said, referring to the comic strip hero who fought crime from his plane. "Guess she didn't want to be squeezed in with her aunt and uncle."

"Peter Pumpkin eater had a wife but could not keep her."

"I want to keep her safe." Mac glanced at his watch. Closing time. He stomped to the front door. "She came up with the screwy idea of skywriting to advertise the store. Ever heard of such a thing?"

"Keep up with the times, Mac." Shirley took down the day's sale signs. "It's the twentieth century, you know."

Walter brandished the awning crank to show he'd remembered his nightly job. "Montgomery Ward is fourteen letters long, if you don't count the space. At the rate of one letter per minute, factoring in an average wind speed of five miles per hour, the first six letters will be blown away by the time the last letter is finished."

"Thank you, Walter." What was he doing? His brain had gone blooey. "Skywriting smoke is made by spraying oil on the hot exhaust pipe. Where there's smoke ..." Henry's crash ran like a newsreel through his memory.

Sal trailed along. "Find something else to keep her busy."

Shirley looked up from the cash register. "Like a couple kids."

Walter straightened the doormat. "The average length of human gestation is two hundred eighty days."

"Private conversation. Beat it." Sal waved off his coworkers. "Yeah, get her in the family way. You need a little advice in that department?" he asked with a Groucho Marx eyebrow wiggle.

Never mind what Freud would say or that the regional director would string him up for discussing his sex life with his employees. Mac flipped the sign to *Closed*, locked the door, and tried to keep from grinning. "Actually … that's the berries."

CHAPTER
TWENTY

CORRIE SAT ON THE STEPS, pretty in her glad rags, even if her dress had the low waist and knee-high hems in fashion two years ago. She reached between the railings and let the wind take a tuft of yellow dog fur.

"You're not using your good brush?" Mac leaned over to kiss her forehead, breathing in her soap-clean smell.

"No, silly, it's yours." She tapped Mac on the shoulder with a metal comb he'd never seen before. "Doesn't he look handsome?"

Lindy's tail wiggled. He knew when he was getting a compliment.

"No lost-dog ads in the *Free Press*, *News*, or the *Tribune*. He's ours, so we'll definitely need a house. The landlord doesn't allow dogs." Mac helped her up off the floor. "Time for church."

"Okay, enough beating around the bush, Mac." Corrie sent the dog in. "Where are we going?"

"Shrine of the Little Flower?" He turned to lock the apartment door, so his face wouldn't give him away.

"Father Coughlin's radio show makes steam come out my ears!"

"I have better ways of steaming you up." Mac planted a kiss in her ear, turning her a delightful shade of pink. Maybe they should stay home. No, his customers expected to see them in church. And the single ladies of Royal Oak needed to scratch him off their flirt lists. He tucked her hand into his, so proud to show off his bride. "I've been going to the Methodist church with the jeweler from Codling's Department Store and his wife."

"Shirley said the Codling brothers are Jewish."

He shrugged. "Jim Dobie isn't."

Dozens of families converged on the Tudor-style brick building, calling greetings to each other. The medieval theme continued inside with dark beams holding the vaulted ceiling.

Corrie dragged her feet and fiddled with the cuffs on her gloves. "Who's the patron saint of grounded fliers? These women know each other. They'll talk crochet patterns and diaper rash. All I know is hangar talk."

"It's a friendly bunch." Whoa, this was a side of Corrie he'd never seen. She'd been everyone's favorite at Central. Until the stock market crash threw a wet blanket on all their lives. All through the service he prayed for a way to give back her joy and keep her on the ground.

"See, Mac," Corrie whispered as they filed out. "I don't have anything in common with these people."

He took her hand and plunged into the crowd, introducing her to everyone on their way to the narthex.

The minister pumped her arm. "Am I glad to see you! Our girls' basketball coach left for Cleveland, and we're up against the Presbyterians next week. Their forward is a five-foot-nine-inch free-throw ace. Mac tells me you play. We need you!"

———

Corrie stopped the Chevy in front of the white frame parsonage. The minister's wife wore a wide-brimmed hat and a dropped-waist dress in a floral pattern. Halfway down the steps, she raced back and locked the door.

"I keep forgetting." Lila got in the car. "With so many out of work, we have to lock up. Did you have that problem where you used to live?"

"No, there was always someone home." Mrs. Zukas had arrived before breakfast and left after supper. Then, when her family squeezed in with Aunt Florence, the house never emptied.

"Mac signed a blank lease and gave me deposit check." Lila waved a business envelope. "Get a wiggle on, he told me. Do you have a feel for what neighborhoods you might like?"

"No, but I know a quick way to check them all out." Corrie pointed the car east. "Let's go flying!"

"You're a pilot?" Lila dropped her jaw and the map. "I don't think my husband would let me learn to fly."

"Why not? Michigan's first commercial airport and first flight school is just east of here." Corrie told Lila about her flight time and experience so she'd know she was in good hands. "Who would have thought Michigan was such a hotbed of aviation activity? I should have moved here sooner." Mac should have asked her to marry him when he left Omaha. Why hadn't he?

Eleven Mile Road led directly to the airport, a grass field with five large hangars. Corrie walked Lila down the line of biplanes, telling her about each one.

A man in shirtsleeves wandered out of a hangar, wiping his hands on a rag. "Hello, dolls. I'm Al, the chief pilot. What can I do for you?"

Corrie made the introductions. "Let's go flying!"

"We're house-hunting." Lila glanced at her watch. "In Royal Oak."

"Got just the thing." He strolled down the line to a red high-wing plane. "The Stinson Junior is what you need. Perfect for sightseeing and it will hold all three of us."

Corrie handed him her logbook. "I have plenty of hours—"

He flipped through the pages. "Okay, you can sit in the left seat. We'll call this a lesson."

"How about a job interview?"

He made a wry face. "Soon as my students come back from the unemployment line."

As Lila buckled in back, Corrie completed the preflight. They fired up the engine, setting the windows wiggling in their frames, pointed the nose into the wind, and galloped across the grass and into the air. *Whoopee!*

An easy turn brought Lake St. Clair under the right wing. Another turn aligned the plane with Eleven Mile Road. No one could get lost in Michigan.

Lila pointed out the Shrine of the Little Flower to the north. Corrie cruised down Woodward Avenue, circled the zoo, then turned on Washington.

"There's the church!" Lila yelled. "And the Washington Square Building and Montgomery Ward's."

Corrie waggled the wings as they passed the store. Was that Mac out front? He'd be so excited. She held course another mile, giving Lila some houses to look at, then turned east. The left wing passed over a golf course, good for emergency landings if the golfers got out of the way. Too soon they were back at Gratiot Airport.

Al shook her hand. "Miss Corrie, wish I had a job to give you."

Corrie paid with the gas money Mac had given her, then she and Lila returned to Royal Oak. "Wasn't that the cat's meow?"

"It's kind of high … and fast … for looking at houses."

How Lila could have a beef against airplanes was beyond Corrie's comprehension. "Your first airplane ride! You want to learn to fly, right?"

Lila checked her watch. "We meet the basketball team at three. Mac said he was your coach. Did he teach?"

"No. He worked at Ward's. Mac helped out while our coach was benched with an injury." Corrie chuckled. "I've had a crush on Mac since his freshman year when I was an invisible sixth grader."

"How could he not notice you? How many students went to your school?"

"Over a thousand in all four grades. Your school was smaller?"

"Thirteen total, from first grade on up. Once the boys got big enough to help on the farm, we didn't see them anymore." As they reached the outskirts of town, Lila took out a compact and powdered her nose. "Did your school have a library?"

"Yes, but no gym. We played in a fourth-floor classroom with a tall ceiling, and changed clothes in a restroom half a flight down."

"You'll like this." The minister's wife showed her where to park. They walked into the Community House wing of the church, past the classrooms, kitchen, and fellowship hall. "The high school uses our space for graduation and for theater and musical productions." She opened the door to a quartet of girls in shorts and blouses shooting hoops. Lila introduced the girls. "Team, this is your new coach, Mrs. McFarland."

Mac's mother was here? Oh, *she* was Mrs. McFarland. Corrie faked a confident smile. "Call me Corrie." She gave the room an appreciative glance. "This place is the elephant's eyebrows. I'll need a rule book, clipboard, and whistle." She'd been too hopped up about flying to think about basketball earlier. Now where had Lila run off to, leaving her with these unfamiliar faces?

"McFarland? Are you related to Mr. Handsome over at Montgomery Ward's?" asked the brunette holding the ball.

"Yes," Corrie said with a spark of pride. "He's my husband."

Alice waved a typed sheet of rules at her. "You played before?"

She nodded. "I was a running center in Omaha. But every league has different rules: half court or full court, how many steps before you have to pass, that sort of thing."

"Omaha?" Alice snorted. "Play while you wait for the rodeo to start."

"She rides a bucking bronco to all her games," Irene said. "Or maybe she rides a bull while she plays."

"Lose two points for stepping in a cow patty."

"Girls—" Corrie had to get this practice on track.

"Time's a wasting." The short redhead introduced herself as Ruby. "Got to hurry up and play so's Gladys can get home and fix supper."

"Mother works second shift," said the one with the wavy hair.

"Welcome to Royal Oak." Mildred handed Corrie a clipboard and whistle. "Irene's behind the curtain, reading *Modern Screen.*"

"*Motion Picture.*" An arm waved a magazine with a red cover. "Let me know when we're ready to start."

"Now," Corrie said.

Mildred stuck her head out the door. "Dorothy, we're ready."

The girl sauntered in blowing a cloud of smoke.

What had Mac said about smoking? "That will slow your running game."

Dorothy scooped the ball, passed it behind her back, and shot it through the hoop. "Who needs to run?"

"Hot socks! The Presbyterians will never know what hit them." Corrie grinned. "Okay, pass and shoot drill to warm up. Show me your stuff, team!"

"We always play Monkey in the Middle first," Alice whined.

"Let's play Net Ball," Mildred said.

"Let's scrimmage." Ruby dribbled toward the net.

Had her team given Mac this much grief? Corrie blew the whistle, but no sound came out. Mildred giggled, Irene snickered, and Ruby dribbled. Corrie stuck her fingers in her mouth and whistled. "Pass and shoot. Now."

With a bit less heel dragging, the girls lined up for the drill. Most had a fair grasp of the fundamentals. Little Ruby had the speed, scooting under the other girls' elbows. Mildred always moved a beat behind. Alice and Dorothy argued constantly.

The lights flashed. An old bird pushed a dust mop across the floor. In a thick accent, he said, "Go see a man about a dog."

"Oh, no, Frank." Dorothy shimmied over to plant a kiss on his bald head. "You know good Methodist girls don't drink."

His face turned lipstick red. "Good Methodist girls go home so the janitor can do his job."

Corrie glanced at the clock. "Why the bum's rush?"

"So the boys can use the gym. Of course." Irene huffed.

"Recruit more players! See you tomorrow!" Corrie said.

The girls ignored her, talking to each other about movies and boys. Corrie had been born in Omaha, grew up there, and knew a good number of folks. She didn't have to work to make friends. Friends joined her group. Being an outsider was new … and lonely. Corrie folded the rules into her purse and drove home. Fortunately she had Mac.

———

Mac sauntered into work Monday with a big grin.

Sal called. "Bad news, Boss. Shipment of bees loose in the back of the truck. Got 'em shut up in there, and from the buzzing, they ain't happy."

"There's a beekeeper on Twelve Mile. Swing by there before you load up." Whistling "I Got Rhythm," Mac strolled to the office to open the safe.

"Not only we got bees, but we got us a load of snow skis." Sal followed him in. "In summer. What is Chicago thinking?"

"You heard about that article in *Fortune*? The skis originally went to a Florida store. In a few months, our customers will be begging for them and I'll be a hero to the distribution manager."

"If we have jobs then. Rumor says Sears is buying us out. I hear J.P. Morgan's cooking the deal."

Still whistling, Mac counted out a cash drawer.

Sal rolled up his sleeves. "Does Ward's know Sears is opening gas stations at their stores?"

"Both have headquarters in Chicago. Can't imagine they keep anything secret." Mac filled the register.

"Sorry I'm late, Boss." Walter shifted from one foot to the other.

Mac patted him on the back. "Don't worry about it."

"You're looking chipper this morning." Shirley polished the counter.

Sal crossed his arms. "Can't get a rise out of him for nothing."

"Thanks to the minister." Mac propped open the front door to the cool morning breeze. "His wife is a Realtor. She's taking Mrs. McFarland around to look at houses this morning. Then this afternoon my lovely bride will be coaching the Methodist girls' basketball team."

Sal raised his hands, fingers outstretched. "Well there you go. Percolating along in marital bliss."

Walter pointed with the awning crank. "Look!"

A low buzzing grew from the north. A high-winged plane, similar to Lindbergh's, made a low pass down Washington Street. Two people waved from the cockpit. *No! Hold on with both hands.* Mac leaned on the plate-glass window, hoping he didn't lose his breakfast in front of the employees.

Shirley pushed past him. "Is that who I think it is?"

"It's Mrs. McFarland!" Walter swung his arms wide.

"And the minister's wife." They would be thrown out of church.

"House-hunting from a plane!" Shirley said. "Who would have thought!"

Who else?

Good grief, the cereal bowls were still on the kitchen table. What kind of marriage was this? Mac turned the water on high, cleared the table, and rolled up his sleeves.

"Mac!" Corrie and the dog burst through the door. "Did you see us fly?" She hugged him from behind, choking him with her oily airplane smell.

Mac scrubbed the stripes off the bowl. "Yes, I saw you." His voice came out in a low growl.

"Sorry about the dishes. I would have done them when I got home."

He twisted his fists in the dishtowel. "You could have been killed."

"Honestly." She stomped to the window. "I gave the ship a thorough preflight."

"That's what went wrong with Speed Holman? He crashed because he missed something on preflight?"

She slumped to the floor and propped her forearms on her bent knees. "It happened so fast."

"He wasn't as experienced as you?"

She shook her head. "He was Northwest's chief pilot." She jumped up and paced from window to door. "Wiley Post flew around the world. And Amy Johnson flew from England to Japan." When he didn't say anything, she leaned her head against the sill, staring out through the grimy screen. "Why can't you be happy for me?"

"Why can't you find us a house?" Mac banged the saucepan on the hotplate, sending the dog under the bed. He'd better lower his voice before everyone in Royal Oak heard.

"I checked out every neighborhood in town."

"Too high up to see anything." He slumped in the chair and tried to rub his headache away. "Ever think the landlord we rent a house from might need our money? Food on his table, shoes for his kids. He might buy a car, another worker at Ford's stays employed. Might come in to Ward's, buy a washer so I can keep Shirley on payroll another day." He jabbed the can opener into the tuna can. "Maybe some poor slob needs this place."

After a long moment, she said softly, "When I'm up there, I can't see all the men out of work. I can't see the headlines about Hoover's latest foolishness. I can't see people lined up for relief. Just blue sky and white clouds, clean and unspoiled."

Didn't she hear me?

Corrie raised her chin. "If I had a plane, I could give rides, teach flying, take passengers around. I could tow a banner with 'Shop at Ward's!' I could fly orders in from Chicago. Then we could get a house next year."

Is she crazy? "The unemployment rate—"

"Look at all the people who do have jobs. They'll want to fly."

He slapped on the table. "Corrie, I don't have money for a plane."

"Sure you do. There's a used Stinson Junior in the *Free Press—* "

"For crying out loud." *She's going to get killed.* "No! No airplanes! Find us a house!" He stomped out. The screen door slammed behind him.

Mac reached the bottom of the stairs and stopped. Where could he go? Since arriving in Michigan, he'd spent all his time trying to stop the flood of red ink at the store, trying to keep from being replaced by one of the many unemployed fellows with experience. The other store managers in town were older and married to women who thought driving to Ferndale was daring. His employees knew too much about his life already. The local speakeasy would provide a sympathetic ear, but being seen there wouldn't help his career.

He sat on the second step and rubbed a bristly spot on his jaw. He'd have to shave before bed ... if Corrie would let him in. Corrie. She was supposed to help him extinguish Shirley's gossip-fed fires, to laugh at Walter's mishaps, to be his sounding board when corporate squeezed the nickel. She'd help him figure out how to extend credit to students for school shoes without the parents taking him to the cleaners. If she would ...

Lindy gave a quiet *woof* at the top of the stairs. Mac turned around. Corrie stood next to the dog. "Mac?" Her voice barely carried over the traffic noise. "Supper's ready."

He stood. "I don't want to fight."

"Me either." She nodded. "I'll go with Lila tomorrow and find a house."

Mac climbed the stairs. Soon as he got to work, he'd call the minister's wife, make sure they stayed away from airplanes. They sat at the table, set with tuna sandwiches, pickles, and canned peaches. He reached for Corrie's hand. "Thank You, Lord, for this food and for the one who prepared it. Amen."

She tried to pull away. "It's not much."

He brought her fingers to his mouth. "If we're together, it's enough."

She glanced up at him and managed a little smile.

He dug in. "How was basketball practice?"

"Awful. They're rude, can't follow directions, and talk back."

"Sounds familiar."

"We weren't that bad."

"You weren't, but the rest were determined to get my goat." He nodded.

"What did you do about it?"

"Don't you remember? You were there."

"I was too busy admiring my coach. Such a sheik." She fluttered her lashes and shrugged Clara Bow-style. "He had all the right moves."

He made his best Rudolph Valentino pose, hands on hips and chest out, then went back to leaning on the table. "Mom said coaching

Central's girls would teach me how to manage employees. So I kept showing up. Those girls are testing you, to make sure you'll stick with them, go the distance."

"Glutton for punishment." She finished eating and cleared the dishes without looking at him. "When I got home today... was that a test, to see if we can go the distance?"

"No, that was me being hungry and tired." He pulled her onto his lap and nuzzled her neck. "You're stuck with me forever."

———

Corrie entered Montgomery Ward's and scanned the sales floor.

"Mrs. McFarland." Walter dropped the broom he'd been pushing and dug into his shirt pocket. "Mac said you'd stop by. Here's your whistle, all paid for. Item number 60C5340, which is not a prime number since it can be divided by two, three, five, seven–"

"Thank you, Walter. Is he in?"

"Mr. McFarland went to a meeting. Goodbye." Walter grabbed his broom and swept toward the back of the store.

"Thank you," Corrie called after him. So ... was Mac still upset with her or did he really have a meeting? No time to worry about that now—she had a basketball team to whip into shape. Corrie headed down Washington Street, walking like a respectable store manager's wife.

Inside the gym, she changed into rubber-soled shoes. The girls dribbled furiously. Pleased to see two new players, Corrie blew her whistle to cut through the racket.

"You got the whistle working again?" Irene said.

Alice hushed her.

"Three-man defense." Corrie divided them into teams.

"I can't be on the same team as Alice," Irene said.

"Neither can I," Gladys said.

"Ah, but you are." Corrie threw the tipoff.

Ruby snatched it and sent it through the net.

"Defense?" Corrie asked.

"You said we're all on the same team."

"You said three-man–"

"Heard it all before." Corrie passed the rebound to Ruby, wishing Mac was here. And his mom, her brothers, and Mrs. Zukas. "Stop beating your gums and play. You four wearing white shirts keep Ruby from scoring."

The ball swished through the net before any of them took a step.

"My shoelace broke," Gladys wailed. "Anyone have a new one?"

Corrie grabbed the rebound again. "Make her work for it this time." She handed off to Mildred to give herself a few seconds to get into position. When Mildred bounce-passed in Ruby's direction, Corrie stole the ball, ran to the opposite net, and dunked it.

"Hey, the coach isn't supposed to play."

Corrie blew her whistle. "Who was your coach before me?"

"We didn't have one," Irene said. "We play too early, so our fathers are still at work. Our mothers are busy making dinner."

That explains a lot. "Coaches play to demonstrate techniques. And give directions which team members follow."

"No fair," Alice whined.

Corrie ignored her and threw the jump ball.

Frances took possession, ran the court, and fired at the hoop. Corrie swatted it to Helen, who scored. They went back and forth, running hard enough to keep the arguing to a dull roar, until Frank flashed the lights.

"Huddle." Corrie motioned them into a circle.

"This isn't football." Alice crossed her arms.

"Tomorrow we're playing the Presbyterians. Do we have uniforms?"

"Black shorts and white tops. Boring," Irene said.

"Do we have a team name?"

"Other than Methodist Girls' Basketball?" Dorothy looked down her patrician nose.

"Lock Horns?" Corrie stood hands on her hips. "Loggerheads?"

Irene giggled. "Bickering Babes."

"Squabbling Shebas." Frances's mouth twitched, almost forming a smile.

"I'm too tired to care." Mildred wiped her face on her shirttail and shuffled out. The others followed.

"See you tomorrow," Corrie said. Stick with it, Mac said. Hah.

Once again, they ignored her.

. . .

The Methodist team played well, but the Presbyterians had the height and the speed to beat them 28 to 17.

"If you'd pass to me." Alice snapped her towel at Dorothy.

"And give away the game?"

Corrie grabbed the towel. "Save your energy. We're playing the Catholics next week. We've got a lot of work to do."

Mac joined them, holding a cardboard box. "Would ice pops help?"

"Would it ever!"

"Thanks, Mr. Mac!"

The janitor stacked chairs. "All of youse, go chase yourself."

"You heard him." Mac opened the door, and the team galloped through.

Corrie linked her arm with Mac and gave him a saucy grin. "You, sir, are the elephant's eyebrows."

"And you, Coach, are the cat's whiskers." Mac grinned back.

CHAPTER
TWENTY-ONE

"CORRIE?" Mac called into the dark apartment. The car was here, but she wasn't. The afternoon had turned too muggy to stay inside with the door closed. Maybe Corrie had taken Lindy for a walk and found a shade tree. Maybe she stayed late at church. He glanced at his watch. No, the boys had the gym now. Hard-edged clouds marched assembly-line fashion across the sky. Clouds that chewed up airplanes and spit out the pilots. *Please let her be on the ground.*

He turned on the light. Emptiness hit him in the gut. No breakfast dishes stacked in the sink. No dog bowl dripped in the corner. No trunks lined the far wall.

Gone. He struggled to pull in a breath over the pain. *Oh, Corrie.* They'd been butting heads since she'd arrived. He hadn't handled her airplane obsession well. Had she gone off with one of those flyboys? Had he forgotten to say he loved her? Why hadn't he bought her a ring?

Empty. The closet was bare. All of Corrie's dresses were gone. Everything ... including his suits and winter coat.

What had she asked him this morning? Does this furniture belong to the landlord or to you? It seemed like an odd question, but he had been hurrying to work. No time to think. He yanked open the bathroom door. His car key and a note hung from the hook.

The McFarland family has moved! We're now located at 324 Aqua Court. Corrie had drawn a map from the hardware store.

Moved? Without saying a word. Without showing him the house.

The breath whooshed from his lungs as he closed the apartment door. Attagirl.

Grinning like the Marx Brothers, all of them, Mac hopped into the car. He drove north out of downtown. It wasn't country, this scattering of shops and houses, but there was room to breathe.

Aqua Court carried so little traffic, wildflowers thumped against the underside of the car. Saplings planted beside the street would provide shade in the summers to come. The houses were an attractive mix of styles, one- and two-storied brick and frame, only a few years old. Their house—he paused to grin—*their house* had been built in Tudor-revival style, red brick on the first floor, half-timbered on the second. Diamond mullions graced the upstairs windows and the three round-top windows of the entry gable. The driveway led to a garage in back.

Corrie stepped out the round-top door, as elegant as Janet Gaynor in her petal-print dress. The evening sun gilded her curls. Lindy dashed out and raced around him in circles.

"He's ecstatic. A yard to guard, squirrels to chase, and no open stairs." Corrie laughed, then reached out for Mac. "How's your back?"

"Need to move something heavy?"

"Me!" She tossed her curls with a tip of her head toward the door. "Over the threshold."

He glanced up and down the street.

"Yes, the neighbors are watching. Have been all day."

"Should make it worth the wait." He tackled her around the knees and flung her over his shoulder.

"Mac!" she shrieked.

He set her down inside and glanced over the living room. Sunlight from the bay window showed a jacquard-covered davenport and matching arm chair from the 1929 Ward's catalog, a rocking chair, and oak bookcases. Mac would bet good money the framed airplane pictures didn't belong to the previous owner, but he wasn't complaining. "It's the berries!" He swept his beautiful bride into a kiss. "How'd you pull this off?"

She kissed him back. "Do you know the Hamlins? Gladys is on the basketball team. Her uncle left for a job in Chicago. We've got their house, furniture, and a half dozen bottles of Vernors."

"One problem. Montgomery Ward's managers aren't allowed to live in Sears houses."

"Oh no!" Corrie gasped, eyes wide.

"I'm kidding. I don't know if it's a Sears house, and Ward's won't either." He leaned over for another kiss, and she tweaked his nose.

"You are a terrible tease, Mac McFarland. After I went to all that work to surprise you. The team spent all afternoon cleaning and arranging. Mr. DiFlorio hauled our stuff over here. If you'd made us move back—"

"To that steam bath? Not a chance."

"Speaking of the steam bath, when I told the hardware store manager we were moving, he said he'd turn off the heat. He'd been running the furnace to give you hot water."

"Are you kidding? I'd have washed in cold water to— Never mind. We're out." He gave himself a shake. "On with the grand tour!"

"If you behave yourself." She took him by the hand. "Living room and dining room here. Kitchen beyond."

He pushed open the swinging door, catching the aroma of meat loaf. "You had time to cook?"

"One of the mothers, Irene's I think, brought it over."

"Gas range, fridge stocked with Michigan's finest ginger ale."

One door led to the backyard, the other to the basement.

"The gas furnace is only two years old."

"Glad to hear it." Up the stairs, he found a bed made with his sheets and bedspread. The closet door opened to their clothes. The window view showed a generous lawn with a shade tree, and a row of green-knobbed tomato plants. Mac tried to stretch the shrunken curtain over the window.

"What are you doing?"

"I don't mind scandalizing the neighbors, but I draw the line at giving them heart attacks. Some might be my customers, you know."

"We'll turn off the lights."

"Aw, do we have to?"

Grinning, Corrie sashayed down the hall. "Here's the bathroom." Green tile and fixtures. "And Lindy's room." The small bedroom with tan walls held only an ironing board.

"Lindy, are you going to do some ironing?"

The dog tilted his head, as if considering Mac's sanity.

"He doesn't have an iron."

"I'll bring one home tomorrow."

"And…" Corrie stepped into a pale-yellow room with a crib in one corner and a rocking chair in the other.

"Corrie, are you trying to tell me something?" Mac's heart shifted into high gear. A house *and* a baby? So many reasons to celebrate!

"Well, no." She fidgeted with the doily on the dresser.

"Guess we haven't talked about children."

Holding very still, she whispered, "I never even thought of getting married until you asked me."

He wrapped his arms around her. "You'll make a terrific mother. Have as many kids as you want. Enough for our own basketball team."

"Well, I sure do enjoy the practice. And I'm not talking basketball." She turned in his arms, snuggling close. "Louise Thaden has a little boy."

"Who?"

"The winner of the 1929 Women's Air Derby."

He turned away. "Airplanes. It's always airplanes."

A voice behind him asked, "What else is there?"

———

Corrie fiddled with the tie on her kimono and studied the dark-green stove. All over the world, people made breakfast. How difficult could it be? She'd used the hot plate at the apartment to fry eggs, or rather, *burn* eggs. A turn of the beast's knob produced a hissing sound, but no heat.

Lindy backed toward the door with a worried *woof*.

Mac reached around her, planting a kiss on her neck and turning off the stove. "Try not to blow up the house on our first day."

"Blow up?"

He snuggled her from behind, his warmth welcome in the chill of the rainy morning, and fanned the air with the morning newspaper. "It's a gas range. Wait a moment for the air to clear."

He used the time for another kiss, heating her all the way to her toes. If he kept this up, they'd be facing a different type of explosion. He broke off the kiss, found a box of matches in the nearest cabinet, lit one, and held it near the burner. With a twist of the knob, the beast turned into a fire-breathing dragon. "I bet you've never used a gas range before. Call Consumers Power about their classes." In his best

Montgomery Ward's salesman voice, he said, "You'll appreciate the convenience."

Corrie had never used any stove before. She'd appreciate a housekeeper.

"Better roll up your sleeves or get dressed before you cook." Mac released her and opened the refrigerator. "This morning I'll make breakfast while you change."

Whew, got out of cooking today. Corrie pulled on a skirt and blouse. And tomorrow? Maybe she could persuade Mac to keep up his good work.

When she returned to the kitchen, Mac had coaxed the green beast into making toast. He set the table. "I need the car today. Meeting with county officials. You can take the streetcar to church for practice."

"Oh." How about the rest of the day? "What do you need me to do?"

"Let's see ... too wet for laundry. Your basketball team brought us a chicken casserole for tonight, so we're good on food. House seems clean. You could finish unpacking, set up housekeeping. Make a list of anything we might need. Groceries, cleaning supplies."

"What time will you be home tonight?" *Don't leave me!*

"After closing." Mac's kiss tasted of strawberry jam and coffee. He left. The Chevy sloshed out the driveway and down the road.

Lindy rolled onto his side and closed his eyes. Sleep the day away. Smart dog.

Corrie opened the newspaper. Oh no! Ruth Nichols, one of the Women's Air Derby pilots, had cracked up her Lockheed Vega in New Brunswick, on her way across the Atlantic. She was in the hospital with a broken back.

Leaving the sky clear for Amelia Earhart. She had a plane. And a husband who encouraged her flying. Why hadn't she tried already? Instead of heading to Paris, Corrie headed to the sink, washed the dishes, and set them in the drainer.

Lindy woofed to go out. Corrie watched him from the overhang as sheets of rain engulfed the house, concealing the rest of the neighborhood. The dog dashed back to the porch and shook, splashing a metal box labeled Twin Pines Farm Dairy in red letters with two trees in green. One of the basketball moms mentioned something about this. "Lindy, look!" Corrie pulled out a half-gallon bottle of milk, a carton of eggs, a pound of butter, and a quart of orange juice. She moved the haul to the refrigerator. "A magic box. What will it have for us tomorrow?"

Bright-brown eyes showed interest in the food, but he had no answers. He sat on the doormat, one paw raised. "Oh, I need to dry you." Corrie grabbed a dishrag, rubbed him down, then wiped his paws.

"Let's see … set up housekeeping. We've got seven dinner plates in a variety of designs, three tumblers in shades of green, and two heavy white coffee mugs." She opened the drawer. "A half dozen forks, knives, and teaspoons in various patterns. No butter knives, serving utensils, or salad forks. Mother would be appalled." Not the Gorham sterling silver set, Haviland place settings, and damask linen table-cloths she'd packed in Corrie's hope chest. All gone in the auction. "Know what that means, Lindy?" The dog's ears twitched. "That means no hosting luncheons for the other businessmen's wives." Corrie grinned. The thought of entertaining a flock of biddies gave her the heebie-jeebies. What did she have in common with other wives?

Wait … what if Mac brought home dishes and flatware from the store? Corrie paced the kitchen. Maybe people in Royal Oak didn't hold luncheons. Maybe nobody did since the stock market crash. She'd support Mac's career another way… like flying a banner over town. *That's the ticket!*

The dining and living rooms seemed swell. "Setting up housekeep-ing? Nothing to it, Lindy." Corrie climbed the steps two at a time, since Mother wasn't here to tell her to act like a lady. In the bathroom, her hair brush and Mac's razors and Mennen shaving cream hid in the medicine cabinet. In their bedroom, the drawers held Corrie's clothing and the chest held Mac's. Winter wear and trunks had been stowed in the second bedroom. And in the nursery …

Corrie sank into the rocking chair and put her hand over her abdomen. Was she pregnant? They'd certainly made every effort. So much fun. And oh, she did want children. Lots of little ones to love on and play with. Happy babies with their father's sparkling brown eyes. She'd teach her children to play basketball, and swim, and fly … Well, maybe hold off on the last until she got Mac up. He wanted an entire basketball team. Corrie glanced out the window at the unending rain. She might go screwy waiting.

Who could she ask about early signs? Corrie had scandalized the minister's wife taking her flying. The basketball girls' mothers seemed awfully proper. The team's girls were too young, unless one of them got pregnant like Halleen. Corrie jumped up, startling Lindy. "Halleen will know. She's on her third baby already."

Corrie threw open her trunk. Empty. Where would the girls put her stationery? In the desk! Corrie slid down the banister. Humph. Not much fun without someone fussing at her. "Lindy, you could bark at me."

He curled on the doormat with a heavy sigh.

The desk sat in a gloomy corner, so Corrie took the monogramed writing paper, address book, and a two-cent stamp to the kitchen. She dashed off a letter to Halleen and dropped it in the mailbox.

Her next letter went to Mary Frances, the nun in training. Corrie didn't know what to ask God for or even if He listened, but she figured it couldn't hurt to have a student nun put in a word on her behalf. She set it next to Halleen's letter. When did the postman come?

Was this her life now? Hoping for a conversation with the postman? Even if she was pregnant, it'd be ages before the baby could talk. What she wouldn't give for Artie to tease her, or Ernie to tell her a dumb joke, or Harry to explain internal combustion engines. Or Mrs. Zukas to cast a kitten about a mysterious stain on her shirt.

Mrs. Zukas knew her onions … and peas and carrots. Corrie scribbled a plea to her housekeeper for recipes and advice on cleaning. And would she be interested in moving to Michigan because Corrie missed her?

Word would get around that Corrie had written to their housekeeper, so the next letter went to Mother. *How is Father? And her brothers? How's your golf game? We have a new address.* Corrie looked around, trying to see the house as Mother would. New appliances wouldn't impress her. *The large yard has plenty of space for a rose garden.* Should she invite her family for a visit? No, too soon. She addressed the envelopes and put them in the mailbox. Still no postman. And still more rain.

The next letter went to Jackie. *What do you hear about Tex?* Out in Hollywood, Pancho Barnes and the flyboys zoomed across clear skies, made movies, and cooled off in the swimming pool every night.

Not like Michigan.

. . .

The basketball team got through practice with less arguing, more defense, and more accurate free shooting. And at the end of practice, when Corrie said "See you tomorrow." Dorothy sassed back with "Not if I see you first," then grinned.

———

"Lindy had a bath yesterday." Mac finished his toast.

Corrie studied her husband through the steam of her coffee. "How'd you know? Are you clairvoyant?"

"Nope." He kissed her head. "Muddy paw prints in the tub."

Rats. Add "cleaning the tub" to her list of duties.

"After you drop me off at the store, you can grocery shop," Mac said as he finished breakfast.

Shop? If he gave her more money, she'd fly!

But no, as if he'd read her mind, he said, "Put the bill on my account." The clock chimed the hour, and they hurried out the kitchen door.

Corrie opened the Twin Pines box. It was empty. "Speaking of groceries, I found eggs and milk in this yesterday."

"Was it still cold?"

"Yes. Where did it come from?"

"The milkman. When you get home, call and transfer the account to our name. We'll leave our order and money in the box." He held the car door open for her. "Didn't your family have Roberts Dairy deliver?"

"I don't know." There was so much she didn't know. She climbed into the car. "Mrs. Zukas took care of that."

"The Lithuanian basketball player."

"Yes. That was so fun when she and your mom helped our team." Back when life was good. "What time should I pick you up?"

"I'll ride the streetcar home. It's a nice day." Before Corrie could say the clear skies and light winds were perfect for flying, Mac said, "Nice enough to do laundry. There's a clothesline out back. Did the house come with a washing machine?"

"I think so." Lila might have mentioned something about a washer, but the spooky darkness of the basement had cut their tour short. Not that Corrie knew anything about laundry.

Mac parked behind Ward's and started in on a hotsy-totsy kiss.

Awooga! Awooga! The delivery truck pulled up next to them, and Mr. DiFlorio yelled, "Hey, lovebirds!"

"Supper in our new home. Can't wait."

So much for Corrie's hope they could eat at the diner indefinitely. Mac stepped out of the car.

Corrie parked in front of the market and contemplated the bins of produce. Did Mac like potatoes? She should buy some, but how many? And if she bought potatoes, she'd need butter and salt. No, the milkman brought butter. The green sticks in the next basket were asparagus. What meat went with asparagus? What meat could she figure out how to cook?

A woman marched into the market, holding a slip of paper. A grocery list. That was what she needed. No paper in her purse. Nothing in the car. Should she go back to Ward's and ask Mac for a list? No, that would embarrass him in front of his employees.

Corrie leaned forward until her forehead rested on the steering wheel. She'd never been so balled up. Four sunny years ago, she'd stepped out from her brothers' shadows. She'd been the sweetheart of Central, acing her classes, presiding over the French Club. She got a plane and her flying license, then ... Then the stock market crashed.

"Miss, are you all right?" asked a grocery clerk in a blue apron.

Corrie blinked. "I forgot my list."

"We'll figure it out. You're new in town? What brings you to Royal Oak?"

An airplane, she wanted to say. Instead she gulped and told him, "My husband manages Montgomery Ward's." She climbed out of the car.

"You must be Mac's new wife. Congratulations. I'm Clyde." He held the door open, then set a crate on the counter. "I'll pack his usual order. You pick out anything else you might need. Good price on peas and celery. Strawberries and rhubarb are in—Mac does love his pie."

Corrie had watched Mrs. Zukas make a pie once. The process seemed ridiculously complicated. "I don't have a recipe."

The clerk grabbed a book from a display. "Then you need Mabel Claire's *Busy Woman's Cookbook.*"

Corrie would rather be busy flying.

The clerk misinterpreted her hesitation. "If you'd rather, the bookstore has Fannie Farmer's cookbook."

Mrs. Zukas used Fannie Farmer's, so it was probably for expert cooks. Corrie nodded at the one in the clerk's hand. Its green cover matched the kitchen. "I'll take it."

He packed the book. "Crisco, flour, and salt for the crust."

"I might not have a pie pan."

"Have Mac bring one home from Ward's. Or make a strudel or a crisp."

"Sure," she said, but thought, *Fat chance.*

In no time, Clyde stacked crates of groceries into the back seat of the Chevy. "Remember, we deliver!"

"Thank you!" Corrie glanced over her shoulder before backing out, figuring they had enough food to last until Christmas. She hauled it home and loaded the refrigerator. Now what?

Lindy sniffed the crates, then scratched to be let out. Corrie opened a bottle of Vernors and her new cookbook. "The kitchen should be a workshop of color and charm," Mabel Claire advised. Mixing bowls, utensils, spice containers, serving platters, vinegar and oil flasks, and floor linoleum should be color coordinated. Corrie glanced up. The stove and linoleum were marbleized dark green, and the kitchen towels had a green border. Next? "Powder your nose," recommended the author. "The woman who serves roast bride with roast lamb is not a successful wife."

Corrie closed the book with a muttered, "Woof, woof." She ate a sandwich, then headed to basketball practice.

The girls resumed their surly mood. Corrie's prediction that they'd lose to the Catholics didn't scare them into cooperating. Before her head could explode, she cut practice short and returned to the house.

"Hi, Lindy. Did you do the laundry while I was gone?" The dog's blank stare indicated he hadn't even considered it. And now it was too late in the day. She opened the basement door and pulled the string to turn on the light. "I suppose we should find out if there is a washing machine."

Halfway down the steps, her face collided with a spider web. Corrie shrieked and raced upstairs, slapping her head and raking her fingers through her hair in case the spider had landed on her. She burst through the back door and collapsed onto the stoop.

Corrie curled into a ball, head on her knees. She missed her brothers, terrible teases but great defenders from eight-legged creepy-crawlies. She missed Mrs. Zukas, who cooked and cleaned and washed without breaking a sweat. Even Mother and a shopping trip would be welcome. But most of all ... A moan rose from her belly. She didn't want to let Mac down. Corrie had been stuck on him since she'd first seen him play basketball. Not a billboard or a star—he passed more than he shot—but he shone in his own way. As a coach, he'd been gentle and kind, no matter how much baloney the team dished out. Other girls said he was a flat tire, but Corrie knew—

Lindy streaked around the side of the house, eyes wide, ears back, tail between his legs.

"Ai-yi-yi!" A screeching black ball of fury followed on the dog's heels.

Corrie scooped up her quivering puppy, raced inside, and locked the door. But out in the yard, the screaming continued.

———

"Got another one, Boss," Shirley called.

Mac set the box in the Hazel Park bin—couldn't wait to meet the guy who ordered five accordions—and followed his clerk to the front of the store. The customer waited at the service counter, head down and shoulders hunched, as if she wanted to disappear. Behind her stood a Consolette. That radio weighed fifty pounds. How had this tiny woman carried it in? Mac scanned the store and spotted an equally skinny boy studying the bicycle display. "Yes, ma'am. How may I help you?"

The curve of her hat and a lock of hair hid her eyes. "I need to return this radio."

Tune in on happiness, the catalog said. But this lady looked anything but happy. "It's not working? Perhaps a new tube ..."

"No, I need a refund."

"Yes, ma'am. Satisfaction guaranteed or your money back." Best guess the radio satisfied her but the economy hadn't. "I'll look up your file."

The woman gave her name, but Mac couldn't find her payment card. "Could it be listed under someone else in the family?"

The woman fisted her hands over her middle and gave another name.

He tried adjacent sections, in case Walter had done the filing. "Did you finance it? Pay four dollars down and five fifty a month?"

She shook her head. "It was a cash purchase. Thirty-nine ninety-five."

Which she needed to feed her family or keep them from being evicted.

"Was it this store or—"

She swallowed and gave a nod.

Mac didn't think his customer was trying to trick him. But he needed paperwork to keep headquarters happy. "If you have a receipt …"

"I've looked everywhere," she said with a whimper. "It's gone." Probably fell out the hole in her cloth purse.

"Do you remember what month you bought it?"

"December. Around Christmas."

The file was thick but nowhere near as stuffed as 1929's. Mac flipped through, looking for the radio instead of the customer's name. "Could it be under the name of Sloniger?"

"Yes. That's it." She let out a big breath, and her knees wobbled. "My brother-in-law bought it the day after Christmas."

December 26. Finally a detail that matched his records. "Yes, ma'am. Paid in full." He opened the cash register and counted out her refund.

"Thank you so much." She clutched the money and finally glanced at him with dull, watery eyes. "The radio … works fine. I hope you find another buyer for it." She gathered her son from the camera display and rushed out.

"You're a sucker for anyone with a sob story." Shirley crossed her arms. "Hope they don't put us out of business."

You and me both. "I'll finish unloading."

"Just a second, buster. Whatcha wanna do with this radio?"

Walter trudged out. "The truck's unloaded. What next?"

Sal followed. "Whose radio?"

"Woman with a hungry kid," Shirley said.

"I'm hungry too." Walter plugged the radio in and tuned to "WJR Detroit, from the Golden Tower of the Fisher Building."

"Let's see. I got a radio. So's Walter. So's Shirley." Sal pointed at Mac. "Your turn, Boss. You need a radio for your new house."

"And your new bride." Shirley brightened.

"When does a bride become a wife?" Walter asked.

Good question. Mac figured Corrie wasn't there yet. "I don't know …"

Sal smacked his hands together. "Got a delivery up on Vinsetta. Load you and your new radio up, and I'll take you home."

Mac glanced at the clock. "It's early."

Shirley waved him off. "I'll close."

Sal loaded the radio in the truck. "Nice house your bride found."

"Sure is." He hoped Corrie thought so too. Marriage was a bigger adjustment than he expected. Mac sat beside his delivery man.

"Gonna be over the moon with that new radio." As Sal drove north, Mac's workday tension evaporated. Home. Dinner in the oven, laundry on the line, and happy Corrie in his arms. Life had finally fallen into place.

Mac unlocked the front door. No roast smell. Maybe she planned to pan fry meat, to keep the house from heating up. Where was she? And Lindy?

Sal hauled the radio into the living room and set it in the corner. "There's an electrical outlet here. You can run the antenna up the wall."

"Thanks, Sal. I'll take care of it." Mac steered him out. "Don't want to make you late for your last delivery. See you tomorrow!" He closed the door and called up the stairs, "Corrie?"

"Mac?" The bedroom door creaked open. She threw herself into his arms, shaking and cold. "Mac! I'm so glad you came home early."

Lindy leaned against his leg.

"What's wrong?"

She launched into a convoluted story about a giant spider who chased Lindy around the yard while yelling "ai-yi-yi!"

"So you didn't get the laundry done."

A thump on his chest told him that wasn't the right thing to say.

"Corrie, you're the bravest person I know, riding the winds in a kite with an engine spewing fire."

"I've never been this scared in an airplane."

Not the direction he wanted this conversation to go. "You're brave, so I'm surprised a spider scared you. I'll sweep the basement after supper."

"Supper." She moaned. "No grocery list. Clyde sold me stuff I don't know how to cook. I don't understand the cookbook or the stove."

He leaned over and tried to look her in the eye, but she burrowed into his shoulder. "Didn't you take household arts at Central?"

"I missed most of foods class when I got tonsillitis."

"And your mom—"

"Mrs. Zukas then Aunt Florence did all the cooking." She gave a big sniff. "Neither wanted me in the kitchen."

"A few gaps in your education. We'll figure it out." Mac kissed her forehead. Should he show her the radio or work on supper? His empty stomach set the priority. He opened the refrigerator. "Let's see what Clyde thinks we should eat this week."

"I don't want to ruin any more food. Maybe you could cook."

Mac gritted his teeth. Couldn't Corrie see how hard he worked? He glanced at his new bride. Her wide eyes didn't show laziness, but fear. The whole country had lost its confidence; why should Corrie be immune? "If you wait for me to get home, we'll be eating too late. I'll write up some instructions for simple recipes." He headed for the kitchen. "First step, open the door. Get the air moving in here."

"No!" Corrie threw herself against the door. "The screaming meemie!"

"The what?"

"A black thing chasing Lindy and howling." Corrie held her arm up about four feet high. "About this big."

Bigger and noisier than your average spider. "Was it an animal?"

"An old woman. She wasn't speaking English. Or French. Or Latin."

Mac's Irish granny would say it was a banshee.

Corrie sniffled. "I'm useless. Can't cook. Can't do laundry. Can't understand the screaming meemie."

"Lindy needs to go out. I'll see if it's safe." Mac slid Corrie out of the way, unlocked the door, and stepped out. Nothing in the backyard, side yards, or behind the garage. Corrie waited inside, face pressed to the window, eyes wide. She was crazy for planes. But was she also plain crazy?

CHAPTER
TWENTY-TWO

CORRIE STEPPED out of the bathroom the next morning and heard mellow band music. She rode the handrail down, landing in Mac's arms as he sang "Me and my girl, meant for each other."

"Where's the music coming from?"

He pointed to the Consolette in the corner. "I forgot to tell you."

"We have a radio!" She grabbed his hand and swung him into a two-step.

He steered her to the kitchen as the announcer gave the day's weather forecast, then played Fanny Brice singing "Cooking Breakfast for the One I Love." "When you have time today, fiddle with the antenna and dial, see what other stations it brings in. The newspaper lists the programs."

"The *School of Cookery* is at eleven." Corrie shimmied across the linoleum, got out the bacon, and lit the stove. "I hoped for a radio."

Mac ran his palm across her backside. "Hoping for anything else?"

An airplane, of course, but he didn't want to hear that. She planted a kiss on his cheek. "I've got you. What more could I need?"

They ate breakfast to the Rudy Vallee Orchestra. Then with a touch-and-go kiss, Mac dashed to work. "See you tonight, baby bearcat."

Corrie washed the dishes, then paused at the top of the basement steps. "Want to help?" she asked Lindy, but he dedicated his morning to napping on the back stoop.

Time to get a wiggle on. No, time to get in a lather. She set the laundry to soak, then told Lindy, "Let's blow this joint." She clipped on his leash and headed around the block. Little girls played dollies in the shade. Big girls raced down the sidewalk on skates. Boys pedaled bicycles. "Being a grown-up is overrated." Instead of being able to do what she wanted, she had to become Mrs. Zukas.

Once home, Corrie got the agitator beating the laundry into a froth. Following Mac's instructions and warnings, she managed to wring, rinse, and wring again without breaking an arm or crushing a finger.

Her brothers had worn wool vests and knee-length drawers in white. Mac had cotton knit undershirts and striped shorts. He looked like a sheik in them and even better without. And how!

The laundry basket doubled its weight for the trip outside. Corrie let it drop under the fancy clothesline, a square device like an umbrella frame. She grabbed one of Mac's shirts. The sleeve caught on the willow basket and the whole load tipped out. Fortunately, it landed on grass instead of dirt. "Good grief," she muttered as she righted it.

She tossed the shirt over the line. Hold on. Mrs. Zukas always used clothespins—Corrie had gotten her bottom paddled for playing with them. No clothespins hung on the line or sat in a bag by the back door or in a coffee can under the sink. *Who needs them anyway?* Toss shirts over the line, followed by undershirts and shorts, then ... oops, no room for bed linens. Move the little stuff toward the pole. Throw the sheet over. The wind picked up and slapped her across the face. "Hooey." She rotated the clothesline so the wind was at her back and managed to hang one sheet.

A woman in the next yard stared with half-closed Greta Garbo eyes. She'd pulled her blond hair into a knot at the back of her head and dressed in pink-and-white gingham. "Where you from, Dumb Dora?"

I'm no Dumb Dora. I'm a pilot!

The woman continued. "Somewhere they don't have wind, seeing as how you don't know to use clothespins. And don't know to hang sheets first so the rest of the decent world don't have to look at your unmentionables." Every *you* merited a finger point.

The resemblance jogged her memory. "Are you related to Miss Klemfuss?"

"Who? Never heard of her, and I know everyone around here, all the respectable ones." The woman's eyebrows twitched.

Lindy trotted up, carrying one of Mac's fancy Celanese socks.

"And keep your dog out of those people's trash." The woman jabbed her finger toward the house on the other side. "That old witch will put a hex on you, jinx you, and give you the evil eye. Heathen pagans. Beware."

"Read your Bible, Eunice. The disciples were first called Christians at Antioch. Eleventh chapter of Acts." A dark-haired woman sashayed across the yard. She handed Corrie a bag of clothespins. "Welcome to Aqua Court."

Eunice spun on her heel and stomped into her house.

"So this must be the fiendish over-turner of trash cans I heard so much about." The woman knelt and made kissing noises with her red lips. Her red dress had a low V-neck, high hem, and ruffled cap sleeves. Sculpted eyebrows arched over golden-brown eyes. Her words were spiced with an accent that sounded a little French, a bit English, and a heavy dose of something Corrie had never heard. "C'mere, old boy, and tell me your name."

"Lindy," Corrie said, wishing her faded Hooverette didn't make her look like a rube. "I'm sorry about your trash can. Was that your …"

"Grandmother of my husband. Did she give you the heebie-jeebies?"

"More like the screaming meemies."

She grinned. "You poor bunny. Do not worry. My mother-in-law took her back to Dearborn. We are safe." She stood and extended a hand. "Miriam. Your next-door neighbor."

Corrie introduced herself. "It's been a screwy week."

"And then Eunice casts a kitten." Miriam helped her secure the laundry. "I'd be a bluenose, too, married to that killjoy."

"Is Grandma…"

Miriam twirled a finger beside her ear. Her nail polish matched her lips and dress. "Grandmother's got a screw loose, all right. Still thinks she's in the old country."

"Which old country?" Which nation produced someone as exotic as Miriam?

"Have you heard of Syria?"

"Isn't that in the Bible?"

"Ding, ding, ding. Corrie paid attention in Sunday school. Our families left when war broke out six years ago. Grandmother wants to return, but the rest of us put the kibosh on that plan." Miriam hung the last washcloth. "Come over to my house. Keep me company."

"Thanks, but I've got to figure out how to cook supper."

"Nonsense. Our new neighbors eat with us tonight." Miriam took Corrie in hand.

They crossed the yard into another world. The walls were painted a warm yellow. Red-and-gold upholstery covered low couches. Colorful platters hung on the walls. Brass lamps sat on hexagonal tables decorated with lacy woodwork and inlays. An oriental rug graced the floor.

"It's the elephant's eyebrows."

"Some old hand-me-downs." Miriam dismissed the compliment with a wave, but her smile seemed pleased. She led the way into the kitchen. The counters held a few additions—a meat grinder, an unusual teakettle, and a mix of exotic bottles. "How long have you been married?" she asked.

"A month." Corrie sipped the iced mint tea Miriam handed her. "It's obvious?"

"It will get easier. The first month was a rude awakening. We used to have a housekeeper, a cook, a laundress—"

"So did we." Mrs. Zukas did it all.

"I knew nothing. One disaster after another. So I will teach you." Miriam's knife made quick work of parsley, tomatoes, an onion, and several ingredients Corrie didn't recognize.

"I'd appreciate the help."

"Of course. All done." Miriam shared a taste, then stored her creation in the packed refrigerator. "And now"—she flung off the apron—"I will teach you to belly dance."

Corrie glanced at her watch. "It'll have to be a short lesson. I coach basketball this afternoon. Do you play?"

Miriam shook her head. "Tennis is my game."

"Someday I'll teach you how to fly."

Miriam grinned and twirled her around. "I'm so glad your dog tipped over my trash can!"

———

Mac opened another letter from headquarters. Sales must increase, it proclaimed without a hint as to how to make that happen. Were any stores having a successful year? If the managers shared ideas—

Shirley yelled from the hallway, "Mac, got a situation."

An idea on training employees not to yell would be welcome. He kept his voice as low as possible. "What's the matter?"

"Lady passed out in Women's Shoes."

"Call Dr. Jandali." He raced up the steps. The Mary working in Women's Shoes had the customer on the floor, her feet propped on a stool. The right shoe had been resoled and the left needed it. "Is she coming around?"

"A bit groggy still." Mary held the customer's wrist. "Slow pulse."

"Maybe she got overheated," said the Mary from Lingerie.

The shoe clerk shook her head. "She sat, then tipped over."

"Might be drunk," said a customer.

"Or pregnant," suggested another.

"Please back up. Give her some air." Mac didn't recognize the customer. "Does anyone know her?"

The consensus seemed to be her name was Ethel or Edna, she lived by the zoo or in Ferndale, and had worked in the office of a machine shop or as a bank clerk.

"Good morning, Mac." Dr. Jandali knelt and pulled a blood pressure monitor from his black bag.

"Pulse is fifty-four and regular," Mary said. "She's cold and damp."

"She needs a glass of juice," the doctor said.

"I have a Thermos." The lingerie clerk hurried downstairs.

The squeeze of the blood pressure cuff roused the customer. The doctor introduced himself. "You fainted. Rest a moment longer."

The lingerie clerk handed her Thermos to the doctor. He poured a cup as the shoe clerk helped the patient sit up. "Thank you, my dear. Orange juice. Perfect. Sip slowly."

The customer took a swallow, then noticed the onlookers. She buried her face in her hands. "I'm so sorry."

"Thank you for your concern," Mac told the shoppers. *Now, beat it.* Spectacle over, they drifted off.

Dr. Jandali complimented the shoe clerk on her medical skills.

"I was an aide in a hospital during the war."

"If I could offer you a decent salary, I'd steal you away from Mac."

Then he turned to the customer, quietly asking her name, who she lived with, and what she'd had for breakfast.

She lowered her head. "I didn't mean to cause such a fuss."

"Of course." The doctor refilled the cup. As she drank, his glance moved from the lingerie clerk, to her lunch bag, to the customer, and back. At the clerk's nod, Dr. Jandali shook her hand, slipping her a dollar. He told the customer, "There's a chair in back where you could sit a moment."

The two Marys helped the woman wobble to the back room so she could eat lunch in private.

Mac accompanied Dr. Jandali down the steps. "She'll be okay?"

"Today." The doctor ran his hand over his thinning hair. "But if she doesn't have anything to eat tomorrow … Women don't go to the soup kitchens or stand in the bread lines. Family is supposed to take them in. But she doesn't have any."

"Wish I had a job for her."

Dr. Jandali clapped his shoulder. "Yes, that's what she needs."

"Time for coffee?" Mac poured two mugs, then they sat in his office. "How much do I owe you for this visit?"

"I shall add it to my bill." They both hoped Chicago would pay on time. "So. How is married life?"

"Not so good." A weight pressed his chest. "When I met her, Corrie was enthusiastic, confident, did well in school. But now she's … afraid. She struggles with the simple things, like grocery shopping and cooking. She didn't even know about milkmen."

"You didn't date. You didn't see her or hear from her for a year."

"Nearly two years."

"Have you changed in the past two years?"

"Same old nose-to-the-grindstone fellow. But she's changed."

Dr. Jandali raised an eyebrow. "When we left Syria, I grumbled that the food did not taste the same in France. Then we came to the US, where it is different again. So we adapt." He put the mug down and leaned forward.

"I moved and adapted."

"For you, perhaps Nebraska and Michigan are not so different. But for your wife …" He extended his arms. "Syria to Michigan."

Mac blew out a heavy breath. "Everything's changed."

"My prescription for you is patience." Dr. Jandali checked his watch, then headed out. "And for me, patients and prescriptions."

Mac hurried to the loading dock.

"Ay-yi-yi," echoed from the salesfloor.

Now what? Mac stowed five accordions into the Hamtramck band leader's truck, then followed the shrieking to the sales floor. An elderly woman, head to toe in black, scampered between stationery and typewriters. A middle-aged lady chased her and almost caught the old one when she paused to set off an alarm clock.

"Mama!"

"Ay-yi-yi."

"Foreigners," Shirley muttered.

The old woman stopped for a few seconds to dress down an oriental rug, then dove into the drapery display.

"Any idea what she's upset about?" Mac cringed as she nearly tipped over a lamp.

"The old bird lost her dentures."

"Why would she remove her teeth in Montgomery Ward's?" Walter asked.

"Ay-yi-yi." She wove through tables of bedding and made a beeline up to men's clothing, sending a stack of swim trunks flying. A fellow looking at work shirts locked himself in the dressing room.

Who cared why? Find the dentures and get her out of the store before she scared away the few remaining customers. "Shirley, check the ladies' restroom. Walter, look in the men's. I'll look out here." Mac threaded his way through the displays. Where would an old lady leave her dentures? She was only four foot tall. Couldn't reach too high.

Only four foot tall? Could this be Corrie's screaming meemie?

"No luck, Boss." Shirley said. "Doesn't the Washington Square Building have a dentist?"

"Check the china department." Montgomery Ward's couldn't afford to buy her another set of dentures on top of Dr. Jandali's visit today. Mac opened every suitcase and trunk in the travel display.

"Ay-yi-yi." For someone so advanced in years, she certainly had amazing speed, agility, and endurance. She popped out of the men's department and raced down the stairs and through toys, bicycles, and yard goods. Bolts of fabric toppled like dominos.

"Found them." Walter held open the egg tray of the chicken incubator.

Shirley peered into the drawer. The employees looked at each other, then at Mac. "Boss."

Mac glanced down. Yep, dentures. Uppers and lowers. A full set. Yellow with black stains and well-used. No one volunteered to pick them up. He waved at the two women, but they raced past kitchen-ware and, uh-oh, toward the lead-glass display. Mac grabbed an invoice, slid it under the teeth, and folded it into an envelope.

Shirley and Walter stepped backward. "Eww."

"See if you can corral her." He carried his burden across the store.

The old one cranked up a phonograph and her daughter caught her.

"Madam." Mac held out the teeth.

The old one shook her head, but the younger stuffed the package into her purse. "I'm so sorry. Please excuse—"

As the recording of "Please Don't Talk about Me When I'm Gone" filled the store, the daughter dragged her mother into a Ford Model A Town Sedan.

Mac turned down the volume and mopped his face with his hand-kerchief. "Tell me it's closing time."

"It's closing time," Shirley said.

"No, it's not." Walter cross-checked his watch with the store's clock. One of his duties was to wind up the clock at the noon whistle every day. "We have seventy-three minutes left to go."

Mac apologized to the customer in the dressing room and the couple hiding behind the roofing samples, then he retreated to his office. At least he could look forward to a quiet home-cooked meal with his bride.

But his arrival home wasn't met with any food smells. "Wash up quickly," Corrie told him. She had on one of her newer dresses. "The neighbors invited us to supper."

"Are any screaming meemies involved?" He told her about the experience in the store.

Corrie giggled and held his hand as they crossed the lawn. "The husband's grandmother. A visitor."

An attractive couple welcomed them at the door. Mac recognized the husband. "Dr. Jandali. We're neighbors! Wonderful!."

"Please call me Joseph." He turned to Corrie. "I am the doctor for Montgomery Ward's employees, who are blessed with excellent health. Please come in."

The living room looked like the set of a Rudolph Valentino movie. But remarkable cooking aromas captured Mac's attention. Food covered every inch of the dining room table, and he didn't recognize a single dish.

After asking blessing on their meal, the Jandalis said, "Please, eat."

Mac didn't need to be asked twice. Each bite intrigued his taste buds. Their hosts had grown up in Syria and lived in France before moving to Michigan. Miriam reminded him of Myrna Loy, graceful and exotic.

Mac bit into some sort of fritter, brown and crunchy but seasoned with onion, garlic, and parsley. Both the iced tea and the cucumbers had a refreshing dash of mint. Miriam knew her way around the kitchen. Maybe she'd teach Corrie, his beautiful wife. She had a glow about her, as if ... could she be pregnant? She was so animated, smiling and waving her hands around. What was she talking about?

"... As I lined up, ready for takeoff, a shadow crossed over me. It was no cloud. It was Costes and Bellonte hotdogging in their Breguet biplane."

"*Point d'Interrogation?*" Joseph leaned forward. "The plane that flew from Paris to New York? How exciting!"

The French flyboys nearly crashed into Corrie. Mac put down his fork.

———

Corrie opened the oven. Brown lumps of charcoal filled the muffin tin.

"Out of baking powder?" Mac asked over her shoulder.

"How'd you know?"

"I've made that mistake before."

"The recipe called for a teaspoon. I didn't think such a small amount would be missed."

"Baking powder makes the dough rise." Mac dropped the muffins into the trash bin. "They didn't stick to the pan."

"I passed greasing but failed baking."

"You'll get there." He tugged his collar. "This is my last clean shirt."

"But I washed a whole laundry basketful."

"They need to be ironed." He hesitated. "Do you know how to do that?"

"I've done my share of scorching." And he'd brought her a new iron, so she had no excuse.

He kissed her earlobe, sending shivery heat all over her. "I have an idea about the Jandalis."

"I know we're supposed to invite them to dinner. And I know sliced watermelon in the back yard doesn't equal the feasts they've fed us. But—"

"Homemade blueberry ice cream counts." Mac let Lindy out. "Let's ask the Jandalis if they'd like to go on a picnic on the Fourth of July. We could make fried chicken and potato salad. Or ham and baked beans."

"I don't know …"

"I'll help you cook the chicken." He took her in his arms and foxtrotted to the band playing on WJR. "We can take them to Belle Isle."

"Oh! I have a better idea." Corrie's hop-step was more basketball than ballroom. "The Ford Reliability Tour takes off from Dearborn Saturday."

"Reliable airplanes are the ultimate oxymoron." Mac turned her in a tight circle around the living room.

"Please, Mac. It's a chance to see history being made. We'll go to Belle Isle another day." If her cooking skills didn't impress, her knowledge of airplanes might.

He glanced up at the ceiling. His shoulder softened under her hand. "No riding with barnstormers."

"No barnstorming. Thank you so much, Mac." Corrie slid her hands under his waistband. "Later?"

"Absolutely," he promised with a slow kiss. As he went out the door, he said, "No wind. Good day to burn trash."

Corrie emptied the wastebaskets into the metal can behind the garage. Until now she'd never spared a thought for trash. It left the house and was never seen again. She tossed in a lit match.

No wind? No clouds? A perfect day for flying. Take off and explore the skies. Check out all the airfields. See what was hiding in hangars and barns. Lie under a wing for a nap. Wash the bugs off the leading edge. Anything but watching butcher paper turn to ash.

The phone rang. Corrie dashed inside and picked up. "Hello?" said a deep voice with a distinctive accent. "Corrie?"

"Tex?"

"Want to go flying?"

"Do I ever!"

"Meet me where St. Jean Street ends at the Detroit River."

"I'll be there in an hour." She let Lindy in, changed into slacks, grabbed her helmet, and headed into the city. Neighborhoods with thrift gardens became miles of smoky factories and high-rise buildings. Men lined up for work and food. She passed skyscrapers including J.L. Hudson's, the tallest store in the world. Not as exciting as flying. She followed the waterfront to the marina and parked by a large building. Tex's dark head rose above a half dozen men in suits. He spotted her and left the group.

"Corrie. Good to see you." He took her elbow and steered her toward an odd craft tied to the dock. It looked like someone had stuck a single-engine plane with a wing and a half on top of a metal boat.

"What is that?"

"Amphibious plane."

Heat radiated off the radial engine. "You've flown it."

"And had the tank topped off when I landed. Let's go." He motioned for her to climb aboard.

"Won't hurt to preflight again. Magnetos off?"

"Of course." His thick eyebrows lowered, and he scowled. Tex was used to bossing people around.

The prop looked smooth. The tires and pontoons were below the water. Struts and stringers held the wings in place.

"We're being intercepted." With a tip of his head, Tex motioned toward the approaching suits. "Get in."

Lettering on the tail proclaimed *Eastman Flying Yacht.* Corrie didn't know anything about yachts, but it seemed well built. She put her foot on the lower wing. The vessel dipped, reminding her it was floating. Before Tex could say "boo!" she swung into the pilot's seat.

Tex climbed into the passenger seat. "I've got it."

She buckled on her helmet. "Speeds?"

"Stalls at fifty. Cruises ninety." Tex fired up the engine, taxied into the river's channel, and brought the power up. Waves surged over the bow. Were they going to sink? Corrie swam well, but she didn't know if she could save someone as tall as Tex. How much time did he have in this amphibian? They picked up speed and left the river behind. Then at last, Tex's thumb wiggled over his shoulder.

Corrie took the controls and muscled it to a thousand feet. As they approached Belle Isle, she cranked the wings to a thirty-degree bank, and flew a straight line down the island, holding the plane at an angle. *Let me show you how it's done, flyboy.* Wings level, she followed the river and used the Ambassador Bridge for an eights-on-pylons maneuver. Tex motioned to go back. She executed a chandelle and all too soon they flew over the marina. The plane settled onto the water. They taxied in and shut down.

He swung the rope and lassoed the post. Eyebrows lowered, he turned and stared at Corrie. Was he angry because he'd gotten wet or because she'd showed off? "What were you doing over that island?"

"Looking for a spot to picnic. We're having one Saturday in Dearborn for the start of the Reliability Tour. Would you like to join us?"

His mouth twitched as if he wanted to say yes, but then he shook his head. "Back to work Monday." He pulled off his helmet and dried his face with his handkerchief. "When you headed for the bridge, I was afraid you were going to pull an Elinor Smith."

Corrie grinned, remembering the young woman who had flown under all four bridges in New York. "Tempting, but ..." She shook out her arms.

"Lacks maneuverability." Tex had wrung it out and found it wanting.

She removed her helmet. "What brings you to Detroit?"

"An aircraft company looking for an investor." He tipped his head toward the suits waiting in the shade of the building.

"Being able to operate on water and land seems like a good idea." Every airplane was a great idea. "But there's got to be a better place for a prop and engine than over your head."

"Two engines, outboard on the wings. Quieter, faster, safer." His dark eyes stared into the past. "My first airplane ride was in a Curtiss seaplane. I was fifteen."

"And you've wanted your own ever since."

"Think how fast Wiley Post could have flown around the world with a seaplane."

"He did it? He's back?"

"Yesterday. Eight days, fifteen hours, fifty-one minutes." Tex gave the Eastman plane a final glance. "Glenn Martin builds seaplanes near Baltimore. Pan Am and Lindbergh picked Sikorsky's amphibians for their South American routes. I'm afraid these Detroit fellows don't stand a chance." He jumped to the dock and held out a hand. The stare softened with a hint of a smile. "I need pilots in Hollywood. Flying sideways in a straight line takes skill. And eights on pylons—precise in spite of the wind and heavy control pressures. Corrie, you're hired."

She put her hand in his warm one and stepped out. "Unless you're making movies in Detroit ..."

Mr. Big Cheese didn't let go. Instead he turned the full force of his attention on her. He had a confident smile that said he always got what he wanted. "You'll love California. Good flying weather year round. Let me buy you a drink and tell you about my next movies."

Flying every day. Flying for a living. What could be better? And Tex ... If only ... Surely Mac would ...

The suits swarmed them. "Do we have a deal? One point nine million–"

Corrie raced to the Chevy before she threw herself into Tex's arms. What was she thinking?

She was thinking he was the wealthiest man in the world, and handsome to boot, and he'd pay her to fly for him. The whole drive back to Royal Oak, Corrie lined up her arguments. Surely Montgomery Ward's had a store in Hollywood that Mac could manage. Wouldn't that be the cat's pajamas?

But before she faced Mac, Miriam met her in the driveway. She unleashed a torrent of words, English, French, and at least one other language, sounding all too close to the screaming meemie. "Corrie, what were you thinking? I bring my laundry outside and there's smoke."

"What? I thought it was out. I'm glad you noticed it." She raced to the barrel. If the garage or the tree had caught on fire, the house might have burned down and killed Lindy. Once Tex called, every thought but flying had fled her brain.

"You must pour water on it or stay until it is finished. Be careful."

"I'm so sorry." The bin was cold to touch. The ashes looked exactly the same as when she left. No water dripped from the barrel. None of the leaves showed scorch marks. No smoke marred the garage. Corrie gave her neighbor a Tex-style stare. "The fire is out."

Miriam pouted. "Here I am without a car and you leave me. I thought we were friends. Where did you go, and why are you wearing slacks?"

Corrie crossed her arms. *So there's the fire.* Yes, she could have brought Miriam along, although her glamorous neighbor might have ended up in a movie. She drew in a breath. "C'mon in. I've got Vernors in the fridge." They sat in the kitchen and Corrie shared about her flight.

"I know who you're talking about." Miriam fluttered her hands. "He's in all the movie magazines. Corrie, stay away. He is a playboy. He dumped his wife and goes out with a different actress every night."

"With all those glamorous stars at his beck and call, he doesn't want me to be his sheba. He wants me to fly in his movies. Won't that be nifty?" Corrie finished her ginger ale.

"Your husband will think there was hanky-panky going on."

Corrie laughed. "Impossible. We were in separate cockpits." She had to get Miriam to stop saying bad things about Tex. "How about a picnic on the Fourth of July?"

Who cares about basketball? Corrie wondered as the girls missed every shot, dropped every pass, and argued with every instruction she gave. Flying made every day better!

———

"Miriam and I made a potato salad. And we've got ham, pickles, pretzels, and strawberries." Corrie pulled him to the sofa. "But I have something important to tell you."

Was she pregnant? She bounced on the edge of the couch, pulled his hands to her heart, and lit up with a smile. "Oh, Mac, it's the most amazing opportunity. Tex offered me a job flying in the movies. I'll learn all sorts of different planes and new maneuvers."

No! Mac's heart hit the floor. "I've got the straight scoop on that guy. He crashed during filming, and four people died making *Hell's Angels*. That's even more dangerous than barnstorming and wing walking and—"

She went on and on about a plane taking off in the river, which sounded like one more way to die. Henry's crash ran through his head like a Technicolor newsreel, only instead of Henry, Corrie flew the deathtrap. She screamed over the roar of the engine as the plane spiraled down. The earth shook. Mac ran through the dust. Smoke coiled from the fuselage. He found her pinned in the wreckage. Flames raced up her legs, blackening her jodhpurs, aiming for her face and hands. *Whoompf!* The gas exploded.

Mac grabbed Corrie. "No! No barnstorming."

"But I wasn't." Cool hands clasped his cheeks. "Mac? What's wrong?"

"Flying." Cold sweat ran into his eyes, but he couldn't let go to wipe his face. "My cousin—" He'd never wanted anyone to see him like this, especially Corrie. What fellow let fear get him all balled up?

"I know." She dried his face with her hanky. "Your mother told me."

A hot flare of frustration shot through him. "You know." How could she do this to him? "You *know*, yet you keep flying."

"If you'd go with me, you'd never be afraid again. It's so beautiful."

"Beautiful?" He released her and paced. "There's nothing beautiful about a crumpled—" It all came back to him on his next inhale: the bitter stench of burned hair and flesh, the bite of gasoline, woodsmoke. "Death. The worst kind of death."

"That's a crash. I'm talking about flying. You've never been flying."

"And I never will. Too dangerous. Too many crashes." He braced his elbows on the windowsill and rubbed the back of his neck. "For the last five years, Henry's death has been my nightmare. I'd never survive if anything happened to you."

Her palm touched his cheek. "Oh, Mac."

"Which is why we are not moving to Hollywood."

She stepped away from him and spread her arms. "What about me? What about what I want? Maybe you never had any big dreams, but this is mine."

"My dream isn't glamorous or flashy." He faced her. "It's to have a family with you."

"But I'm no good at it." She paced, chopping the air with her hands. "I mess up the grocery order and burn your toast. The vacuum hates me, and the washer eats the buttons off your shirts. And I killed off the African violet Eunice gave me."

"The only plant Eunice grows is poison ivy."

"You know her?"

"Every store manager in town has a Eunice story."

Corrie sniffled. "Tex has money. We could hire a housekeeper."

"No more talking about Tex. No more Tex, ever." He pulled her close, wishing his hug was enough to keep her safe. After a long moment, the stiffness left her body and she returned his embrace. For the millionth time, Mac wished his dad hadn't died. Although Dad never had to deal with a plane-crazy wife. Mom was sensible. No flying hokum for her. "Running a house is new to you. When I was nine, I started cooking with Mom's coaching, notes, and lessons on weekends. Still managed to burn meatloaf."

"Oops. What did Mr. Smooth say about that?"

"The neighbors invited him for pot roast."

Corrie sighed. "There's no justice in this world."

"None at all." Mac tickled her earlobe with his tongue. "But there is love."

CHAPTER
TWENTY-THREE

CORRIE WORKED the team hard all week. Dorothy called her a slave driver, and Mildred said she was a big meanie. Alice stomped out of practice but returned for the game. The Methodists Howling Cats, as Corrie dubbed them, beat St. Mary's 21 to 18. Mac took them to Cunningham's for ice cream cones.

Corrie watched him out of the corner of her eye. All the girls on the team thought he was the gnat's knees. Why did he have to be such a wet blanket about flying? Couldn't he see how important it was to her?

———

"This is the seventh National Air Tour," Corrie told Miriam and Joseph as Mac drove to Dearborn.

"Any girl pilots?" Miriam had decorated her red dress with a blue tie in honor of Independence Day.

"None this year. Phoebe Omlie was the first to join the tour in 1928, then Nancy Hopkins flew it in 1930." Corrie had on the outfit from her graduation party. She hadn't taken up Mac's offer of a new dress.

Joseph leaned over the car seat. "What's this about a nineteen-year-old in this year's race?"

"He flew last year too," Corrie confirmed. "Eddie Schneider. He's a record setter. Youngest commercial pilot's license, youngest airplane mechanic, transcontinental speed record." She pointed to a metal tower west of the road. "The dirigible mast. Take the next right."

Workers directed them to park in the grass beside the road. Red, white, and blue bunting decorated the hangars and terminal. Thousands of people strolled among the airplanes.

Joseph climbed out of the car and stretched. "Beautiful weather. Perfect for a picnic."

"Perfect for flying." Corrie had eyes only for the planes.

"What is that?" Miriam noticed the handsome red brick building across the street.

"The Dearborn Inn, the first airport hotel."

"You know so much." Miriam gestured toward the flight line. "Tell us about these airplanes."

Corrie didn't have to be asked twice. She led the way, introducing each plane. She talked about races, records set, and technical details like the importance of cowlings in reducing drag. Mac tried to catch Corrie's hand, to walk with her as Miriam and Joseph did, but she moved too quickly, darting among the airplanes, pointing out their parts. Mac trailed along, more lonely than ever.

Army planes from Selfridge Field flew in formation. Then the race started. Three planes, including a red one flown by the boy Corrie's age, took off on time. A fourth had a broken tail skid. After a while, two Ford Trimotors lumbered into the air. The smallest plane, a GeeBee, screamed away to the east. The next smallest, an Aeronca known as the *Flying Bathtub*, moved so slowly Mac wondered if it would make it off the airfield.

The oddest contraption had a long propeller on top, an awkward, evil-looking sort of bug.

Miriam asked, "What is that?"

"Pitcairn Autogiro, a new design. The *Detroit News* bought one in February for aerial photography. One landed on the White House lawn last year," Corrie said.

"Time for our picnic." Miriam's declaration earned agreement from Mac's empty stomach. They found a shade tree near their car, stretched out a blanket, and set out the food.

"So you could do this too, fly in the air tour?" Joseph asked Corrie.

Don't encourage her!

"If I had a plane." Corrie passed the fried chicken. "The Nebraska Air Tour was the bee's knees."

What? Her parents allowed it? Mac's jaw dropped as Corrie described wandering the state in 1929 with twenty other fliers.

"If only Mac had been there to share it with me." She squeezed his knee.

"How romantic." Miriam pressed her palm to her heart.

Romantic? No. The gut-wrenching opposite of romance.

———

Most of the after-church gum chewing concerned the shooting of some gang members in Detroit Wednesday. A different topic had three older men cornering Corrie and Mac. "Mrs. McFarland, we're pulling our daughters out of basketball until the reverend finds a new coach."

Mac turned to his wife, who had scooted behind him. "Corrie?"

The first man led the others in head shaking. "Didn't even tell her own husband. Shameful."

"Nothing shameful about it," Corrie said over Mac's shoulder.

"Then what—"

"She took our girls up in an airplane, that's what."

Again? Mac groaned. Was she off her nuts? Two of the men were wearing Ward's suits, and the third had bought a set of Riverside tires last week.

"For free!" Corrie's excited voice turned heads throughout the narthex. "Most barnstormers charge five dollars, but I took them up for free."

"Total disregard for their lives!" said the first man.

"Perfectly safe. A Stinson Junior like this finished third in Ford's National Air Tour. Stinson and Warner engines are both built here in Detroit, keeping more of our neighbors employed."

"Not even the airlines can keep those things in the air," the tire buyer couldn't wait to inform them. "Remember Knute Rockne."

Hundreds of people had been killed in crashes, but it took the death of the University of Notre Dame's football coach to interest the public in aviation safety.

The third man beat his hat against his leg. "Alice said you let her take off. Now she wants to learn."

"I offered to teach her. She's a natural! Do any of you want to try a flight or take lessons?"

One of the men raised a finger. Whether he wanted to ride in a deathtrap or ask a question, Mac couldn't tell, since the other two dragged him off. "The minister will hear about this!"

Jaw clenched, Mac escorted Corrie to the car. Instead of driving straight home, he pulled into the alley behind Montgomery Ward's.

"Why are we stopping here?"

Because, with the store closed for Sunday, it was quiet and no neighbors would bother them here. He shut off the motor and turned to face her. "Level with me. Where are you getting the money for all this flying?"

She twisted her purse handle. "Pilots look out for each other. Hold the brakes during propping. Help with a tie-down on windy days. Wash the bugs off the leading edges. That sort of thing."

"Are you telling me, all these pilots take you flying and loan you their planes out of the goodness of their hearts? You didn't have to pay to take up the basketball team? Or the minister's wife?"

"We all chipped in for the fuel. It was a short ride, a quick circle over their houses. The Stinson only burns twelve gallons an hour."

At ten cents a gallon, the fuel came to a dollar twenty. He waited.

Corrie shifted in the seat. "Sometimes I find change in your pockets."

And waited some more.

She fiddled with her hem. "We siphoned some gas out of the car."

Mac let out his breath. "I've tried to be understanding about flying, in my own Caspar Milquetoast way. You know about Henry's crash. You saw Northwest Airway's chief pilot die."

She started to protest, but he held up a hand and continued. "Auto production is down to a quarter of what it was in 1929. Do you have any idea how many people are unemployed?"

"I've seen the lines at the soup kitchens."

"Sixteen percent nationally, twenty-five percent here in Detroit. And how much do people get on welfare?"

She shook her head.

"Fifteen cents a day. Which explains the lines at the soup kitchens." He jabbed a thumb toward church. "Those three men, the fathers of your players, are my customers. This store cannot afford to lose even one of them. If I become a liability to the company, I'll be out of a job."

"I'm sorry." Tears formed on her lids. "I was trying to make friends."

The team fought more than they played. Riding in a plane wouldn't change that.

One Mississippi, two Mississippi, three... He counted to thirty before Corrie sniffed and said, "I'll stop."

Mac put his hand over hers. "Thank you."

She pulled her hand away, crossed her arms, and looked out the window. In a quiet voice, she said, "I've been flying with anyone, anywhere, since I got my license. Never had a problem. Last year I walked all over Council Bluffs and Omaha for a chance to fly."

"It's different now."

She continued as if she hadn't heard him. "I'm an adult. I'll be old enough to vote in the next election. Even before I started flying, when I learned to ride a bicycle and tell time, I rode all over Omaha. But now you want to confine me to the house like a child."

Would that be so bad? It's a nice house. "I'm trying to keep you safe."

She blew out a breath. "I'm not used to having someone worry about me."

"It's how I love."

She glanced at him from the corner of her eye. "Thank you."

Monday morning, as Mac attacked the paperwork, Shirley stuck her head into his office. "Got a visitor, Boss."

The fellow leaning on the catalog counter was the one who raised his finger at church yesterday. Mac braced for another dressing down.

"My daughter Mildred plays on the basketball team. Honestly, I don't have any beef with your wife. Mildred enjoyed her flight. Wish I could have sent my son along. He's crazy about airplanes."

Uh-oh. Corrie was right. People still wanted to learn how to fly. "I'm sure there's others who–"

"Tommy's eleven. Too young for flying lessons. His Scout troop would like to start a branch of the Airplane Model League. Would your wife be interested in helping? The boys could learn about flying from a real pilot. They meet Saturday mornings at church, starting in September."

"Would she ever. I'll donate the balsa wood. Let me know what else you need." Mac took down the leader's information and they shook hands again.

With the game against the Baptists looming, the reverend negotiated a cease-fire. Terms of surrender involved Corrie's promise to keep the girls out of airplanes. In exchange, she resumed her position as basketball coach. Overwhelmed with gratefulness, Mac donated a new Underwood typewriter to the church office.

Mac brought home a scrapbook for Corrie's expanding collection of *Free Press* and *News* articles about aviation. She collected yarn scraps from the neighbor ladies. But instead of learning to knit, she tacked a *National Geographic* world map to the dining room wall and traced out air routes. Purple for Miss Clara Livingston's flight from New York to Puerto Rico. Pink for Miss Peggy Salaman's trip from England to South Africa. Blue for Mr. and Mrs. Lindbergh's exploration of the Northwest Passage.

At least she was on the ground.

––––

The Baptists defeated the Methodists 14 to 13. Mac brought ice pops, which the team ate on the steps outside the gym. Since First Congregational had disbanded their basketball team out of concern for the health of their girls, Ruby arranged for them to play the boys next Friday.

The girls hurried off.

"They're getting along better," Mac said.

"Dorothy and Alice have been fighting over a thirty-year-old traveling salesman." Corrie picked up the ice pop sticks.

"Thirty? Why–"

"Boys their age don't have money for dates." She faced Mac. "I don't tell you enough, but thank you for working so hard."

"You're welcome." Mac looked left then right. The coast was clear. He leaned in for a grape-flavored kiss. "Thank you for being my girl."

––––

Joseph pulled into the last parking spot at the Detroit Zoo. "It's been packed since it opened."

"Everyone's looking for something free to do," Mac said. Something other than wandering around Montgomery Ward's, wishing for stuff they couldn't afford.

"The train costs a nickel, but unfortunately ..." Joseph pointed to the tracks. An old-fashioned locomotive pulled three open-air coaches, or would have if the last one hadn't jumped the rails. Employees jacked the wheels up and onto the track as passengers stood on the grass watching and offering unwelcome advice.

"It's a fine day for a walk." A perfect summer day, in the seventies with low humidity. Miriam slid out of the front seat, classy in her blue dress with the matching hat. "You haven't been to the zoo before?"

Here in the zoo, not an airplane in sight, Corrie held Mac's hand. "Nope. Been saving it, waiting for my baby bearcat to arrive." Only to discover she'd rather explore Michigan from the air. For today at least, she was safe on the ground.

Corrie gave him her warm smile. Her plaid dress had been around since high school, but she outshone every girl in the country.

"Is there a zoo in Omaha?" Joseph asked as they followed the crowds to the entrance.

Corrie nodded. "Riverview Park. A few bears and lions in cages."

Miriam stretched out her arms. "This zoo is without cages."

Mac's steps slowed. "No cages? How do they keep the animals from wandering?" And eating visitors?

"The exhibits are structured to keep the animals in. You will see." Miriam smiled. "When they dedicated the zoo, the mayor entered the wrong way. The polar bear jumped out in front of him. The mayor shook his paw and said something silly about a welcoming committee. Fortunately, the keepers got the bear away before any harm was done."

"Wouldn't want the poor bear to get indigestion from eating an elected official." Although Mac could think of a few who deserved that fate.

Crowds of families streamed past, pushing baby carriages and herding children. Someday soon he and Corrie would have a family—he hoped. They strolled past elaborate gardens and swans paddling in a small pond.

Monkeys scampered around an island in the middle of a water-filled moat. They swung from a tree, chased each other, and groomed their young.

When Mac was little, the summer before his dad died, his family had visited Riverview Park. Four baby monkeys had clung to the bars and chain-link fence of their dark cage. Adults paced behind them, three steps one way, thump the wall, and three steps back for another thump. The stench watered his eyes. Mac asked if they could take the monkeys home. The McFarlands didn't have a big yard, but he figured the animals would enjoy climbing their tree and playing ball, getting sunshine and fresh air. His brother said the monkeys couldn't leave, but Mac could stay with them. He pulled open the bottom of the cage and pushed Mac toward the poop and hay-filled slot. Mac yelled, the monkeys screamed, Dad swatted, and Mom said it was time to go home.

Mac blinked, bringing the Detroit Zoo back into focus. "This is a big improvement. It doesn't even smell bad."

"Much better for the animals," Corrie agreed.

Llamas grazed in a large open area enclosed by a moat. Buffalo and elk shared a similar space. Low fences kept visitors at a safe distance.

"This is the first wolverine born in captivity." Miriam pointed to a small bearlike creature dozing in front of a cave.

Joseph chimed in. "Since the wolverine is the state animal and mascot of the University of Michigan, news of the birth met with a bit of excitement."

"Aren't they supposed to be fierce?" Corrie asked. "It's not much bigger than Lindy."

The mammal yawned, displaying an impressive set of teeth.

"Never mind. I wouldn't want to run into one of those."

"None have been seen in the lower peninsula for over a hundred years." Miriam led the way to the next exhibit. "Now these fellows are more numerous, but they stay north of Saginaw."

The bear den held six Michigan black bears. They had been dozing in the shade, until the keeper rattled his bucket. Their ears perked up and noses twitched when he dropped hunks of meat into their enclosure.

"Can't remember the last time I had a steak," sighed a man with a mustache.

"Stop shaving a couple weeks," said his companion, "and move in with them."

The man didn't take his eyes off the meat. He swallowed and waved to the keeper. "Hey, throw some of that my way."

The keeper tipped his bucket to show it was empty. "Sorry, Charlie."

The man shuffled off, muttering, "Gonna fry me up some swan."

"Too many hungry people." Joseph shook his head.

"The food bill here is quite high," Miriam said. "The zoo sends extra animals to other zoos. And they have a garden for the herbivores, but bears cannot live on vegetables alone."

A group of children raced by, yelling, "Let's go see the giraffes!"

"Yes, let's!" Corrie pulled Mac along.

Two giraffes sauntered in sophisticated dignity across an open area backed by large rock formations and fronted by a deep canyon.

"Their names are Neck and Neck," Miriam explained. "They arrived here from New Hampshire in special train cars. When the track was clear, they could poke their heads out the hole in the roof. The keeper reeled in their heads when they came to a tunnel or bridge."

Joseph raised an eyebrow. "I thought giraffes were from Africa."

"Miriam, you know a lot about the zoo." Mac wondered if she could get Corrie interested.

"I volunteer."

"She's too modest," Joseph said. "Miriam studied biology and horticulture. She planted the zoo's vegetable garden."

"I'm glad to help." Miriam gestured toward an elephant. "Would you like a ride? Paulina aided the zoo construction and gives rides."

The pachyderm lumbered by, a load of six children on her back.

Corrie shook her head. "Paulina looks tired. She doesn't need to haul me around."

They passed the other side of the lake, relieved to see the swans hadn't been eaten.

The aviary's domed roof and mosaics over the arched entrance reminded Mac of a church. Tropical plants and musty air dripping with humidity greeted them.

Miriam pointed out each bird, giving its scientific name and land of origin. She whistled, and a red bird returned her call.

Mac rested his hand on Corrie's shoulder and felt her tremble. "What's wrong?"

"They're trapped," she whispered.

"Trapped? No, they're safe. Safe to enjoy life without the threat of predators or starvation."

"They're stuck." She shook her head. "They can't be happy."

"Sure they can. There goes one now." He tried to direct her attention to the yellow bird building a nest overhead.

"It's cruel." A tear seeped from the corner of her eye. She shuddered. "They can't fly."

Mac's heart sank and he wrapped an arm around Corrie's shoulders. He could ground his bride, but he couldn't keep her from thinking about airplanes. "Let's get some fresh air."

CHAPTER
TWENTY-FOUR

CLEAR SKIES and a light wind from the west made for a perfect flying day ... if Mac hadn't taken the car, confining her to the house. The mailbox clicked and Corrie hurried to see what the postman had brought.

Miss Sackett had sent clippings from the *Omaha World-Herald*. Corrie plopped onto the davenport and showed Lindy. "The air tour came through Omaha and I missed it. Photos of the pilots but not their planes. Although here's airplane builder Eddie Stinson. I should try to find him. See if he'll give me a job. Two pilots brought their wives. If I'd married a pilot ... A pilot with money, like Tex." The article said the air tour's stop in Omaha had been funded by a millionaire pilot from Council Bluffs. Corrie huffed. "I could have married Bernard, if I'd been able to find him. He's my age and owns lots of planes."

Lindy watched her with worried eyes. "But if I'd married someone else, I wouldn't have Mac. I'm goofy over him. And I wouldn't have you."

She put the articles away. "Let's see what Miriam is up to."

Miriam emerged from her house carrying a shallow basket. Her belted red dress with a wide collar made the most of her curves. "Would you mind if we share our meal tonight? Mother is bringing Grandmother tomorrow."

"As long as you show me how to cook chicken." Corrie followed her into the garden. Bees hovered over flowering plants, dipping into each blossom. Someday engineers would figure out how to make an aircraft fly like that.

"I have the perfect recipe." Miriam strolled through her garden, harvesting onions, carrots, and lettuce. Giant leaves with multicolored stems and a cucumber topped the pile.

"Is this for humans or zoo animals?"

"Both. We'll use it for our supper tonight. I'll drop off a box at the zoo. Cut that cabbage please." Miriam handed Corrie a knife.

Corrie cut it loose. It was the size of a basketball, but heavier. She tossed it high overhead and caught it.

Miriam gave a hearty laugh. "Oh, my friend. You may not know how to cook it, but you will find a use for it. Bring your chicken." Miriam sat her at the table with a paring knife and vegetables.

Corrie rolled a carrot. "Seems like it'd be easier to eat them whole."

"Not for this recipe. Cut them into coins. Then add the chicken, salt, pepper."

"Wait a minute. How big? How much salt and pepper?"

"How much spice does your husband prefer?" Miriam raised her shoulder like a French woman. "Cooking is another opportunity to be creative."

"Or really mess up." Corrie studied her friend. "You're creative with everything—decorating, cooking, clothing."

Miriam stared into the distance. "Living in France trains one to good design, good taste. A soupçon of effort makes a grand difference."

How could she afford such a swanky wardrobe? "Your dress is from Paris?"

"Unfortunately, no. One of mother's friends gave me this. It did not fit. Boxy shape. Belt across my hips. Buttons on the thighs. Made me look like a rube. So I took it apart, added a wider collar, moved the waist up, shaped it with darts, and saved the buttons for another project."

"Hotsy-totsy."

"Thank you." Miriam raised an elegant eyebrow. "Perhaps you would like a little help with your clothes?"

"I'd like a lot of help. I haven't bought anything since the stock market crashed. But I don't have a sewing machine."

"Ah, but I do. Such fun." She sprinkled spices without measuring, then assembled the dinner in a pot with a lid. "My refrigerator is full. Let's put this in yours, then see what we can do with your wardrobe. Mac will think you're a baby vamp. Oh, wait, he already does."

"Did you hear him yesterday? He called me a baby bearcat." Corrie held the door for Miriam.

"I thought it was endearing." A curl dipped over one eye, then she shook her head to spear Corrie with a glance. "If you did not, tell him."

"I don't know what I want." Corrie led her friend into her kitchen. "Do you ever feel like you're disappearing? Before you married, you had a name and you did things. Now you are the doctor's wife, Mrs. Jandali."

They climbed the stairs. Oh good, she'd made the bed this morning.

"Ah, but I'm still myself, Miriam Katabi, a student of biology and horticulture, a daughter and granddaughter. And now, also, wife of Joseph." Her friend clasped her wrist. In spite of mucking in the garden and kitchen, her hands were clean. "I do understand becoming invisible, losing a piece of yourself. I used to be Syrian, but now I am a citizen of the United States. This fact certain people have trouble accepting." She tipped her head toward Eunice's house.

"That's her problem, not yours." Corrie opened her closet door.

"Let's start with summer." Miriam pulled out a skirt in a green-and-white plaid with a coordinating white blouse with green trim. She held it up to Corrie. "Good-quality fabric. Even though you have narrow hips, the low belt is not flattering and dates the outfit. We'll loosen a few stitches, raise the belt to your waist, and—*voila*—you're in style."

"Mother always chose swell clothes." Corrie sat on the bed to watch Miriam work her magic. "Most parts of me are on account of other people. I'm a sister because I have brothers. I'm a basketball coach because the team needs one. I'm a wife because of Mac. But flying ... I'm a pilot. The credit is mine. And my flight instructor's, of course."

"This needs a longer hem." Miriam held up the lavender floral. "When you fly, you're in charge."

"In charge and important. People look up to me." Corrie slapped her forehead at her own pun. "They think I'm interesting. They respect me. Who am I if I'm not a pilot?"

"Amelia Earhart received many accolades from crossing the Atlantic."

"As a passenger. I'm guessing she'll fly a transatlantic solo next summer. I wish it was me."

"This needs gussets." Miriam added the two-tone green dress to the pile. "Life is short—"

"So I need to get into the record books now."

"Grass withers and flowers fade. Records will be broken, the ink will fade, and even Lindbergh will be forgotten. So consider eternity. You are a child of God, and He loves you." She held up the red with white dots. "Ooh la la, this flared skirt is chic. Let me see it on you."

Corrie tossed off her housedress and pulled on the red one.

Miriam turned her toward the mirror. "The twins of Aqua Court!"

Even in similar colors and styles, Miriam upstaged her in swanky. Corrie would save this for times her friend wasn't around. She tried to hang up the red dress, but her vision blurred.

Miriam put a gentle hand on her shoulder. "What's wrong, dear one?"

She pressed a hand to her lower belly. The words caught in her throat. "Shouldn't I be pregnant by now? We've been married three months."

"Give it six months, a year even." Miriam's tone soothed.

Corrie pulled on her housedress and found her handkerchief. "What about you? How long have you been married?"

"Six years. With emigrating, Joseph earning his US medical license, having to live with family, we decided to wait." A smile curved her ample lips. "Perhaps we will be pregnant at the same time."

Corrie wiped her eyes. "Oh yes, let's!"

———

All week, Ruby had been playing Mata Hari, gathering intelligence on the boys' strategy and strengths. The girls practiced enthusiastically, but the boys' height and competitiveness carried the day. They won 32 to 15.

"Good job." Ruby's father shook Corrie's hand. "Kept us on the run."

"We'd have won if the girls all played as well as Ruby."

He grinned. "She's speedy, all right."

The girls gathered their bags and left with the boys.

"No goodbye or thank you?" Corrie asked the closed door. She picked up her purse and pulled out the typed list of rules Alice had given her the first day. Might as well throw this away.

The door opened, and the girls returned.

"Boys distracted us," Alice said.

"We almost forgot about ice cream." Helen motioned for Corrie to follow her. "Our treat for coaching us."

Corrie pushed the rules back into her purse and joined them.

———

Mac inhaled the aromas of bacon and coffee as he hurried to breakfast. Married life kept getting better and better. He caught his wife as she packed sandwiches and planted a big kiss on her forehead.

She tickled his waist. "Eat up, Mac. We're going to be late."

He didn't mind taking the day off. It might be their last chance for an outing before winter set in and the holidays kept his hours long. This was the kind of occasion people told their grandchildren about: the most famous aviatrix of all was coming to town. Besides, with him along, his wife was less likely to do something foolish—like take to the skies.

Mac called Lindy inside and loaded the picnic basket into the Chevy. Corrie snuggled beside him, her hand warming his knee. She tried to keep a lid on her excitement with their sophisticated neighbors.

"Come along, my love," Joseph Jandali called to Miriam as he left the house. He sat behind Corrie and leaned over the back seat. "Did you hear the Cubs suspended Hack Wilson for fighting on the train?"

"Maybe the Tigers can pick him up," Mac said. "They need a good hitter."

"Unfortunately he hits more reporters than baseballs these days."

Miriam dashed to the car. Most women chose practical dark colors or tweeds, but Miriam dressed in an emerald-green jacket and skirt with a matching hat. Her contribution to their lunch filled the car with mouthwatering aromas.

"Sorry I'm late," she said breathlessly.

"For food smelling that good, we forgive you." Mac drove out of the neighborhood.

"It's nothing fancy like the Hoovers' meals in the White House." Miriam huffed. "My cousin sent a menu from one of their dinners."

"What did they eat?" Corrie turned in her seat.

"Don't ask." Joseph groaned.

"The main dish was tournedos Rossini."

Before Mac could ask what that was, Corrie piped up. "Tournedos? They're serving a fancy cut of beef while they tell the rest of the country to make supper with graham crackers and raisins?"

"As if that's not enough, grapefruit and strawberry delices, new peas, potatoes Georgette, bird-nest salad. And for dessert, bombe diable rose and friandises."

Everyone else seemed to recognize those foods. Mac kept his low-class mouth shut.

"Many of my patients are losing weight," Joseph said. "I never thought I'd see pellagra and scurvy in the United States. Yet the government says no food aid will be provided."

"Hoover says no one has starved. He's gone from portly to gross," Miriam said. "He needs to stop with his 'let them eat cake' and remember what happened to Marie Antoinette."

As Joseph predicted a communist revolution, Mac drove past the store. Walter had removed the awnings after Labor Day, since September brought cooler weather.

"Isn't Hoover a Christian?" Mac asked. "Seems like the Bible has a lot to say about sharing with those in need."

"We can raise money to feed people. We could have a charity basketball game. Play the boys again." Corrie rubbed her hands together.

Mac shook his head. "The boys' regular schedule will keep them busy until spring. We need to do something now."

"I know!" She bounced. "We can have a Harvest Hop with square dancing."

"I don't know that," Miriam said.

"A caller tells you the steps, so it's easy to learn. We had one at my high school, and it was a great way to get everyone out on the floor."

"Nifty," Miriam said. "Then after Thanksgiving, let's have a Christmas formal with the waltz and foxtrot."

"Many of my patients are from Eastern Europe. What about a polka?"

"I know a polka band with five new accordions. Great ideas, all."

Mac smiled as he crossed the Grand Trunk and Interurban tracks and turned onto Woodward Avenue. Corrie would be too busy to fly. "I know feeding people is the priority, but I'm worried about winter clothing. Between hand-me-downs and remaking last year's, most kids have a winter coat. But children grow out of their boots, can't keep their feet warm and dry, then miss school. Can we raise money for boots?"

Miriam said, "Call it Santa's Boot Ball."

"Ward's least expensive children's boot is a dollar twenty-nine—out of reach of many. I'll ask if we can drop the price to a dollar."

Corrie pulled a grocery list from her purse. "I'll talk to the church secretary, see what dates are available. Decorations, band with a fiddler, and dance band. We could serve cider at the Harvest Hop, hot chocolate at Santa's Boot Ball, and punch at the polka."

"We have a plan," Miriam said. "Tonight let's go the movies."

"Maybe they'll have a newsreel about the Lindbergh's flight to China or the air races in Cleveland," Corrie said. "Two fliers in GeeBees broke speed records. Phoebe Omlie, one of the race pilots I met in 1929, won several events, but the only photo I've seen is her powdering her nose."

Joseph tapped Corrie's shoulder. "I'm surprised you did not attend. Cleveland is not so far away."

"Maybe next year."

She'd wanted to go so badly that Mac was afraid she'd hitch a ride with some flyboy. So he'd called churches in neighboring towns until he filled the calendar with basketball games.

"I believe Miss Earhart made an altitude record in the plane we are to see today," Joseph said.

"Sure did—eighteen thousand four hundred fifteen feet." Of course Corrie knew exactly how high Lady Lindy had flown.

Mac shuddered. So much could go wrong at that height.

"She wanted to be the first to fly an autogiro coast to coast, but another pilot beat her to it."

"What do you know about her crash in Texas?"

"The winds changed."

Winds changed all the time. Flying would always be unsafe.

"We should pray for her," Miriam bowed her head. "Heavenly Father, hold Miss Earhart in the palm of Your hand and keep her safe. Amen."

Corrie reached over the back of the seat for her friend. "Great idea to pray for her. I should do that."

They parked at the state fair grounds and joined the crowds hurrying to the racetrack. Corrie stood on tiptoes to see over the milling people. "Amelia's husband's supposed to be here."

How did George Putnam stand it, his wife wandering the country in a deathtrap? "Probably that bald guy. Marrying a pilot will do that."

"*Humpf.* Like you've lost any hair."

"Is he concerned for his wife's safety?" Joseph asked, knowing Mac's position on the topic.

"He makes money from her celebrity."

"There's Ransom Olds. And the mayor." Miriam knew everyone. "And Clyde. If he's here, who's running the grocery?"

"And there's Bick the cook from the diner." Corrie raised on her toes and pointed overhead. "There's Amelia."

"The autogiro was invented by a Spaniard." Joseph Jandali trained his binoculars on the black dot. "The big blades on top generate lift, but they're not connected to the engine."

"What do you think Amelia will wear?" Miriam asked.

"A flying helmet and goggles." Corrie kept her focus on the sky. "At one hundred miles an hour, it's windy."

"I showed you the article Amelia wrote for *Cosmopolitan*: 'Your Next Garage May House an Autogiro.'"

Mac had thought, *No garage of mine!*

"How dependable are they?" Joseph asked.

"Very safe. John Miller flew one just like Amelia's from Pennsylvania to San Diego this summer."

The hornet's buzz of the engine grew to a roar. It circled the grandstands and lined up for the landing.

"High and fast." Corrie's fist closed over an imaginary stick. "Maybe it doesn't slip. Attagirl, AE, slow it down. No, no!"

The plane hit hard, one wheel folding underneath. The wing tipped, dug into the sod, and whipped in a circle. The rotors hit the dirt.

Corrie dashed toward the cloud of dust. The engine shut off. The tall, slender pilot climbed out, yanked off her helmet and threw it on the ground, and ran a hand through her blond curls. She squatted by the wing, examining the damaged gear.

Corrie reached the plane first. "Miss Earhart, are you all right? Guess this ship doesn't respond well to cross controls."

The woman glanced across the damaged wing at Corrie and winked. Then she waved to the approaching crowd. "Nothing to it," she called. "Entirely my fault. I'm not injured at all."

Two police officers ran up. "Are you hurt?"

Hands on hips, the pilot frowned at her broken plane. "Only my pride."

A fellow in a double-breasted suit raced across the field, tripped over a guy wire, and hit the ground. Calling for an ambulance, the aviatrix hurried to his side. Mac recognized the injured man from newspaper photos: George Putnam, Amelia's husband. Surprisingly, he had a full head of hair. Guess Miriam should have added him to her prayer.

Two more of the ugly planes circled the grandstand, waiting for the crowd to clear so they could land. Mac grabbed his wife and led her away. Now she'd have to admit aviation wasn't safe. Even Amelia Earhart crashed.

———

"Corrie, are you whispering sweet nothings in Mac's ear while he's at work?" Miriam popped in the kitchen door.

"I've got to go. Thanks for calling." Corrie hung up the phone. "Wow, lots of tomatoes. What a pretty dress. You're inspiring me to sew."

Her neighbor set a basket next to the sink, then drew circles in the air with a finger. "Wait a minute. Who was that on the phone? Are playing the vamp to someone who is not your husband?"

Corrie busied herself washing off the harvest. "Tex. We were talking about airplanes."

"I could hear you giggling all the way out in the garden." Miriam turned off the water. "I know flirting when I hear it."

"We talked about the Schneider trophy for the fastest plane. He thinks the British will win again." Corrie lit the gas under the kettle. "His new movie has a lot of flying."

Miriam set the tomatoes in the Dutch oven. "And a lot of Billie Dove. Did he tell you he proposed to her?"

Corrie hoped Miriam didn't notice her wince. "He doesn't gossip."

"Of course not. He's the reason for gossip." She poured hot water over the tomatoes, letting loose a fragrant steam. "You are playing with fire."

Corrie paced the kitchen. "Miriam, what if you had a really big dream, something wonderful that you always wanted to do, but Joseph didn't want—"

"No. Absolutely not." Miriam slipped the skins off, cut them in pieces, and put them in a big pot.

"If it was Mac's dream, we'd be out there already."

"It doesn't matter what foolish notions—"

"It's not foolish." But it might be desperate. This was her only chance. "I could support myself and Mac by flying."

Miriam slapped the knife on the counter and stomped out, startling Lindy.

"Where are you going? Are you coming back?" Basketball gave Corrie the speed to race across the lawn and grab her friend before she reached her house. The dog watched, but summer's heat curbed any urge to chase. "You're not leaving me in the middle of canning. What am I supposed to do next?"

"I'm leaving you in the lurch the way you're going to do to Mac."

"I'm trying to fulfill my destiny."

"What a load of hooey." Miriam speared her with a fierce look. "Do not think of running off to Hollywood, deserting your adoring husband."

"I'll come back after *Sky Devils*."

"It is the devil all right. His fingerprints are all over this." Miriam gave her a hard look. "You need to decide whose side you're on. What about your marriage vows?"

"Talking to someone on the phone isn't breaking any rules. Besides, who remembers their vows?"

"You've only been married four months? And you've forgotten already?"

"It was fast. No time to think." Except to wonder who was flying west.

Miriam gave her a shake. "You promised to stay true to Mac the rest of your life. Even if flying was sensible and safe, even if Mac would go along with it, it doesn't matter. What does matter is what God wants for you."

"What if ..." What if she was grounded for the rest of her life? "What if God wants me to fly?"

"And break your vows? I don't think so." Miriam looked over her shoulder and groaned.

"Don't you girls have anything better to do than stand around and chitchat?" Eunice shouted.

"Don't you dare leave me with that woman," Miriam whispered, then she hooked an arm through Corrie's and returned to the McFarland kitchen. "Back to work before your tomatoes burn."

Miriam finished canning with detached instruction of a Foods teacher, no joking, no teasing, and no meeting her gaze. "Please don't be mad," Corrie said as she set the last jar to boil.

"I don't want to lose you, my friend." Miriam held her face between her palms. Tears hung on her dark lashes. "And I don't want you to throw away the love of a good man. You're not just flirting with Tex. You're flirting with disaster."

No, I'm trying to find a way to keep flying.

CHAPTER
TWENTY-FIVE

"MONTGOMERY WARD'S, SHIRLEY SPEAKING." The head cashier put her hand over the mouthpiece. "Cops got your wife," she said in a voice loud enough to be heard at the corporate offices in Chicago.

"Oh no." Mac jumped to his feet. "What happened?"

"I'll send him right away." She hung up. "Go pick up your jailbird in Detroit. When this hits the papers, Sears will take all our business."

Mac's blood turned to ice. "May I borrow your car?"

"Sorry, Mac. My sister took her kids to Toledo."

"I'll run you down there." Sal ambled in from the stockroom, pointing both thumbs at his puffed chest. "I know how to deal with the cops. Take a wad of dough. You'll have to grease some palms to spring her."

By the time they'd reached downtown, Sal had filled him in on every criminal in Detroit. And Mac had convinced Sal that parking the Montgomery Ward's truck in front of police headquarters wouldn't do business any good. The delivery man let him out two blocks from the station.

"I'm here about Mrs. McFarland," Mac told the aged fellow at the desk. "Is she under arrest?"

Washed-out blue eyes under bushy eyebrows contemplated Mac in silence. Should he introduce himself, plead for mercy, show some of the cash his delivery man insisted he carry?

Sal burst through the door waving a fist full of dollar bills. "What's it gonna take to spring that lady pilot you got in your clink?"

The stocky clerk backed away from the counter.

Mac whispered to his delivery man, "The truck?"

"In the alley," he muttered. "No one can read the sides."

A gum-chewing man in a loose-fitting suit introduced himself as Detective Kobinski. "Mrs. McFarland's story checks out. She was the patsy."

"Yeah, well." Sal seemed disappointed over his lost chance at bribery.

Someone bellowed, "Hey, what sap's got a Monkey Ward's truck blocking the driveway?"

"Corrie and I can take the bus back." Mac waved his delivery man out, then turned back to the detective. "My wife?"

"City Airport. C'mon." On the way up Gratiot Avenue, the detective gave him the third degree.

"I don't know anything about flying," Mac said again and again, feeling sympathy for any criminal who had to face Beech-Nut breath. "I'm only a Montgomery Ward's manager. What happened?"

"Ever hear of Hymie Lebowitz?"

Mac shuffled through his memory. Not a customer. Not a baseball player or a boxer. Not someone from Omaha. "I don't think so."

The gum snapped. "Brown-Plaid Lebowitz, member of the Purple Gang."

"Wasn't the gang sent to prison after the Collingwood Manor Massacre?"

"A few minor players still loose." A thick hand pointed east. "They use speedboats for their bootlegging, but this time of year, they didn't want to chance the river. One of his battlers hired your wife to do the pickup in Ontario."

"Corrie wouldn't have anything to do with rum-running." She'd jump at the chance to fly though.

"Lebowitz told her she was hauling medical supplies, played on her sympathies. Case of Canadian Club might cure the shakes." He turned left into the airport. "After she loaded up, Mrs. McFarland got suspicious, diverted to City Airport, and called us. Elliot Ness's boys nabbed Lebowitz at the farm. Brave little wife you got there, McFarland."

"Brave? Will the mob be after us?"

"Not much chance of that with the Purple Gang and Capone in prison."

"Capone? I thought he was in Chicago."

The detective gave him an "anybody home?" scowl.

Corrie stood with another pilot next to a high-winged plane similar to Lindbergh's. A half dozen of Detroit's finest surrounded her. Wasn't she free to go? The officers parted to let him through.

"Mac! You'll never believe what happened." Corrie spoke quickly, keeping the other pilot between them, not looking him in the eye. "This is Mary Von Mach, Michigan's first woman pilot. She flew in the Women's Air Derby. We met in Kansas City. She teaches flying right here."

The woman had a long face and strong eyebrows. She shook his hand, then hugged Corrie. "This economy is giving all of us fits. I'm sorry I can't offer you a job."

A job? When half the men in the city were out of work?

One of the officers stepped forward. "Ladies? Could I have your autographs? I had Eastern Market patrol when Amelia Earhart came to town."

"Can't say we've flown the Atlantic…" The pilot signed his note-book, then passed it to Corrie.

Detective Beech-Nut waved. "Okay, boys, back to work."

Giving him the once-over, the officers shuffled off, while the other pilot hurried inside.

Mac kept his voice quiet. "You agreed to stop flying."

Corrie stared at the ground. "I thought I'd found a way to earn money." She shoved her hands in her pockets. "I told the police not to bother you."

He didn't know where to start. "I'm glad you're not hurt."

She took his hands. Hers were cold. "Now, don't get in a lather about this, but … This isn't Lebowitz's plane. He figured the owner wouldn't check on it over the winter. The police asked me to take it back to the hangar in St. Clair Shores, and they want you to ride along. I suggested Mary, but they don't believe she's really a pilot. They want a man to go with me. It won't be bumpy at all, I promise. Please …"

"What? We can't. We're taking the bus back!" Chips of paint were missing from the engine cover. Fabric rippled where the tail met the fuselage. The wires holding it together looked like they'd been stolen from an old piano. No doubt one of her grease-monkey friends had built it.

She nodded at the officers standing by their paddy wagon. "Never mind. I'll explain you don't fly. Maybe one of them will come with me."

He studied the sky. Not a single cloud. It'd be cold up there. Cold and noisy. The wing would tip, pointing toward the earth, and his stomach would sashay in the other direction. The plane would swoop and zoom. He'd hang upside down, only the fragile webbing of the safety belt between him and a ten-story death fall. His heart would flop up his throat, and his neck would stop holding his head straight. They'd spiral down, scaring birds, blowing the toupee off a fellow in a Pierce Arrow, and slam into the earth.

When Chicago found out about Corrie's run-in with the law, he might as well be dead.

A bead of sweat formed at his temple. He glanced at his wife, the smudge of grease on her chin, the shine of excitement in her eyes. For her he would take his first airplane ride. Unable to speak, he nodded.

"Great! Let me show you how I preflight." She started around the plane. Mac followed on shaking legs. "Move the ailerons. Hinges and cables work easily. The wing should be smooth, no dents or bulges. Tires evenly inflated. Stringers tight." She plucked the wires between the struts. Popping open a pair of suitcase latches on the engine cover, she examined the dipstick and plug wires and drained a squirt of gasoline onto the ground. Then she stood on the tire and peered into the gas tank. "Never trust a fuel gauge." She continued her circuit around the other wing and the tail, where she checked the tie-down. Then she motioned toward the cockpit. "Climb in."

Mac looked for a last-minute reprieve but saw only police officers. They lined the edge of the field with their arms crossed. Mac straightened his shoulders and approached the plane, trying to fake confidence. He put a toe in the stirrup and grabbed the seatback. Head in, backside toward the law, Mac realized he had started with the wrong foot. They'd notice if he backed out and started again. How hard could it be? Cross one leg over the— *Whomp!* He kicked the side of the plane.

"Careful. I don't want to be doing dope and fabric work the rest of the winter. Grab that tube by the windshield. Don't step on the doorframe." Corrie guided his foot by the ankle and pushed his hind end inside. "Find the safety belt? Good. Now pull the stick all the way back."

The interior had a musty odor of fabric, gasoline, and oil, like his Model T. He hoped it ran better. He pulled something that looked like it had been sawed off a broom. "Where are the brakes?"

"Aren't any." Corrie leaned into the cockpit. "Mac." She waited until he looked at her. "I understand your fear."

She couldn't understand.

Her eyebrows drew together. "Ever since I got my first airplane, I've been wanting to take you up, wanting to show you the joy of flying." She covered his hand with hers. "Please let me share this with you. My gift."

What was she asking? To pretend he wasn't terrified?

She pushed the throttle up a quarter of an inch. "Hold the stick back. When I say 'contact,' turn the magneto to 'on.'" She pointed to a black switch, then to the dashboard dials and the throttle. "When it starts, pull the throttle back so the RPMs are around nine hundred, but keep it running. Watch the oil pressure."

He might as well be sick now, get it over with. Breakfast coiled with a threatening pain in his gut.

Corrie turned the propeller counterclockwise three times, like winding up the rubber band on a model plane. The magnetos and throttle. *No, one hand has to stay on the stick.* When the engine starts— *What if she slips on the frozen grass?* He leaned out to check her shoes and the rope holding the tail. The policemen hadn't moved.

"Contact!" Corrie yelled. The magneto switch moved stiffly in the cold. He rested his hand on the wooden throttle knob, ready for soaring oil pressure and runaway RPMs, if not for flying.

Corrie put her palms on the end of the propeller and pulled down with a kick of her leg. Nothing. Not even a cough. Maybe it was broken. Maybe they'd take the bus after all. She stepped up to the prop again. Swing and a miss. Was this like baseball, three strikes and you're out? She wiped perspiration off her forehead. This propping business required some muscle. Maybe he should offer to switch places with her, if he could get out of the plane. She rubbed her hands on her flying suit, then yanked the prop through again. It caught with a roar.

The oil pressure needle jumped to life. Whoa, back to nine hundred

RPMs. *Easy, easy there, don't let it die.* Where'd she go? Mac stuck his head into the cold slipstream. Corrie yanked rope off the tail, jogged to the cockpit, and slid into her seat as if it were an easy chair.

"I got it!" she yelled over the engine noise. She wiggled the stick and he let go. With a growl and lurch, they left the parking space. Corrie leaned out to see where they were going. *What's wrong with airplane designers, building these things so you can't see out the front?* Gliding in giant nausea-inducing curves, she taxied to the end of the field, pointed into the wind, and closed the door. *Ah, that's better.* A degree or two above zero. The stick moved sideways, whacking him in the legs. He bent his knees to give it room and tightened the safety belt.

"Ready?" she yelled.

No! Let's take the train, walk, hitchhike! Anything but fly! Not trusting his voice, he stretched his arm forward and gave her a thumbs-up. The engine roared. The plane trembled like it was coming apart.

Let me out. Let me out now!

Corrie pushed the throttle all the way forward, and the engine thundered. Forward motion pressed him back into the seat. The tail bounced up, the stick shot forward, and hey, he could see out the windshield. They bumped along, faster and faster, until, no more bumps, they were up. Watching the ground made him dizzy, so he watched Corrie. Her head moved side to side. Her gloved left hand rested on the throttle. The slight decrease in noise indicated when she reduced the power. Mac looked out again. They were up, way up. Woodward Avenue cut a wide diagonal to the northwest. Cars glided between rows of offices and factories. Mac twisted around, looking over one shoulder, then the other.

"What?" Corrie yelled.

"The bridge?" he asked, then regretted it immediately. What if she thought he wanted her to fly under it?

She nodded and banked into a gentle turn, soaring over the mansions of Grosse Pointe. A lady pushing a baby carriage waved her handkerchief. A little boy and his dog raced along, trying to catch their shadow. Lake St. Clair narrowed into the Detroit River, then split to circle Belle Isle.

Gothic spires of downtown churches rose between factory smokestacks. And then, the longest suspension bridge in the world. The Ambassador Bridge draped the river like a jeweled bracelet.

Corrie circled back, picking up altitude. The Fisher Building, the most beautiful skyscraper of all, crowned the city with its granite-and-gold dome. Mac looked straight down. Detroit didn't look so bad from here.

They followed Gratiot Avenue northeast, flying high to stay out of the way of a biplane lining up for takeoff at City Airport. Hey, wonder what their house looked like from the air? And the store? If this plane held enough gas … He leaned over, trying to figure out the instruments. He recognized the compass, but the other two didn't seem to have anything to do with fuel.

Past Eight Mile Road, Corrie pulled the power back over an orchard and descended to a field. Mac knew they'd landed because the ride wasn't smooth any more. She taxied to the barn and did a sideways maneuver, bringing the tail close to the doors, then cut the power. Quiet, blessed quiet.

Corrie got out as easily as she'd climbed in. Mac bumped his head on the roof, missed the step, caught his heel on the lip of the door, and fell onto his backside with an *oof.*

"Land the plane better than your self," said a fellow in a tweed hat.

"Mac!" Corrie extricated his foot from the cockpit, helped him upright. She shook hands with the stranger and passed him some money. "You must be Mr. Carrington."

"Yup."

"I'm so sorry. I had no idea Mr. Lebowitz's operation wasn't legit. And that he didn't have permission to use your aircraft."

Mr. Carrington's jaw dropped. "You flew …"

"Your plane handles well, even in crosswinds." Corrie picked up the tail and pulled it into the hangar. "Keep an eye on the wingtip please," she told Mac.

"A flygirl. Do you know Amelia?"

"Yes I met Miss Earhart twice." Corrie chocked the tires. "Anytime you need a pilot, give me a call."

Mac curled around his wife as she slept, holding her warmth to his heart. Jagged stripes of moonlight slid across the wall, disappearing into the corner before dawn.

Corrie, Corrie. What am I going to do with you?

———

"... Then, instead of telling the customer her total, Walter told her it was a prime number—actually two primes, one to the left of the decimal point and the other to the right, but together they were a composite number. He couldn't stop himself. I had to take her money before she dropped the order and ran out of the store to escape the math." Mac leaned back in the kitchen chair and pressed his palm to his forehead.

"A numbers guy ought to be good at running a cash register." Corrie gave up on her fried chicken. She'd followed Miriam's instructions, but undercooked parts hid beneath the burned skin. How did that happen?

"If only he had this much skill in customer service." Mac held his index finger and thumb an inch apart. "I've got to find someplace to put him. Numbers in the stockroom send him into a calculating frenzy. Sal said he tried to load the delivery truck by order number instead of by address. He follows directions too rigidly, not setting priorities or dealing with problems, to be a good janitor. But I can't fire him. He's supporting who knows how many family members."

"Let's hope it's a prime number." Corrie dropped the undercooked meat into Lindy's bowl. It disappeared with a gulp.

"Or else he'd make someone move out." Mac chuckled and toasted her with his coffee cup. He took his plate to the sink and ran the hot water into the dishpan. "Any mail today?"

"Unfortunately, no new recipes from Mrs. Zukas." Corrie cleared the table. Artie had sent an article about Ruth Nichols setting a new distance record. Mac didn't want to hear that Ruth's plane had caught on fire afterward. "Mother sent my scrapbook, and a 'Central High boy made good' story from the *Omaha World-Herald*. Say, where's your yearbook?"

"Don't have one."

Yearbooks would have been a luxury for Mac's family. "This fellow's an actor. We saw him when Aunt Florence took us to the Omaha Playhouse last year. Did you know Henry Fonda?"

"Never heard of him, but then I missed a lot of school."

Corrie winced. Recovering from his cousin's plane crash had kept Mac out of school for a semester.

Mac set the last dish in the drainer. "How old is he?"

Corrie scanned the article. "Twenty-six."

"Mr. Smooth might know him." Mac dried his hands. "What play did you see?"

Corrie led the way into the living room. Mac turned on the lamp. The light through the mica shade created a warm glow by the davenport. Lindy slept on the hearth rug. A pianist played Gershwin's *Second Rhapsody* on WJR. Corrie hauled her scrapbook from the shelf and turned to the back page. "The play was called *A Kiss for Cinderella*."

"I'm more interested in *A Kiss for Corrie*." He pulled her onto the couch, his body heat welcome in the winter's chill, but the huge pages got in the way of serious necking.

"I'll put this away."

He held tight. "Let me check this out." He paged through concert and play programs, invitations to weddings and birthday parties, articles about her brothers from Central High's *Register* and the *Omaha World-Herald*, and her report cards. "Straight As. I married a smarty."

If only her parents had been as impressed. "All those years in school we work hard for good grades. Then when we graduate … nothing."

"No more homework, no more report cards. It's great." He leaned over to peek at her face and asked in a gentle voice, "What's eating you?"

Corrie closed her eyes, trying to sort through the hooey in her head. Unlike being fogged in at Omaha Municipal, she had no hope of a brisk Nebraska wind clearing the air. "When I was in school, I knew what was expected of me. English required a five-paragraph essay with correct spelling and grammar. Chemistry and math wanted decimal points lined up. My grades said I met the standards. When I flew, my logbook and less yelling from the flight instructor showed my progress. But now I don't even know what I am being graded on, much less how I'm doing." She turned to Mac. His warm brown eyes studied her as if she were the most interesting person on the planet, in spite of ruining the fried chicken. "I have no idea what I'm supposed to do and if I'm doing okay or not."

He traced her knuckles. "Your to-do list, your standards."

Could Mac really be so easy to please? Yes, as long as flying wasn't on the list. Her heart hit an air pocket, dropping for a moment. "I'll never cook as well as Miriam."

"Don't compare yourself with anyone else." He kissed her forehead. "It wasn't until the second or third time we ate with the Jandalis, since the food and company were so interesting, that I noticed the dust bunnies."

"Miriam has dust bunnies?" She wasn't perfect?

"A whole family, the size of groundhogs, under the couch."

"And they don't have a dog." Corrie tried to wipe the smile off her face before she turned to Mac. "Do you get report cards in your job?"

The corner of his mouth twitched as he clenched his jaw. "All headquarters wants is numbers. High sales, low labor cost, low complaints. Numbers don't get me excited about work every morning." He rested his head on hers and tightened his hold on her shoulder, the strain of his job tensing every muscle. "Becoming manager scared the socks off me. I was lonely for you, missed Omaha, didn't have another manager to share the load. So I talked to God."

Corrie ran her hand down his cheek, traces of whiskers brushing her palm. "I noticed … you seem different, more confident."

"Well, the bottom line"—he winked—"because business is always about the bottom line, is much of life is out of our control. Headquarters makes decisions without asking me. They could close the store. They could fire me. Whoa … sorry for the gloom and doom." He kissed the top of her head. "I decided to answer to a higher authority, to do my job the way God wants, to live in a way that points to Him. Sometimes employees and customers think I'm a pushover and try to take advantage, but—"

Corrie flipped to another page, the newspaper photo of Mac catching the robber soon after the store opened. "You nabbed the crook."

"My photo." He chuckled.

"Miss Sackett saved it for me."

"God is just. Letting that kid get away with theft would have encouraged a life of crime."

"God would give you a nifty report card."

"All our bad marks have been wiped clean. No grades needed."

Really? God was easy to please, like Mac? No worries about accomplishing something, getting her name in a record book, making her mark on history?

"This looks new." Mac found a business envelope in heavy linen bond paper clipped to the first page.

"I've never seen that before." Tinley Jewelers was printed on the return address. Her name was written in the elegant script Father used for engraving. He never wrote letters. "Father wrote me a letter?"

"Let's see what he has to say."

"'Dearest Corrie,'" she read out loud. "'Last summer all light in the house dimmed. All because my little ray of sunshine grew up and moved away. You may not believe this, since I spent so much time at the store, but I miss you!'"

"Aw, he misses you."

Her heart warmed until pricked by guilt. Corrie hardly ever thought about Father, but she missed the things his money had provided.

She continued reading. "'Before Mother packed your yearbook and scrapbook, I looked through the pages. I'm sorry I didn't see any of your games and performances. I wish I'd taken you up on your offer of an airplane ride. And I'm sorry my financial blunders led to the loss of the plane. But mostly, I want to tell you how proud I am of you. For all your amazing accomplishments and well-deserved accolades and for the way you embrace every day with gusto. Even in the grimmest situations, I could count on you to find the silver lining… or at least pewter (jeweler joke!).'"

Corrie explained, "Pewter is an alloy mostly made of tin, so it's less expensive." She returned to the letter. "'Thank God you never gave us any trouble.'"

Corrie winced. "Good thing he didn't hear about the time Jackie and I visited that speakeasy."

"He would have had a heart attack for sure. I almost did."

She read on, "'You were a friend to all. Your teachers told me they could count on you to manage the classroom if they had to step out, to welcome new students, to tutor anyone who struggled with home-work. Miss Sackett said you kept Central's basketball program going after the athletic department lost interest. Attagirl. You've grown into a wonderful young lady. I hope Mac knows what a gem he married. With all my love, Father.'"

Mac gave her a warm hug. "He's right. You are a gem."

"Father's proud of me. Even though I didn't set any records or win any races." Tears brimmed on her eyelids. "Mac, if you gave me a report card—"

"Absolutely not. Corrie, I love you. Forever. Always. No matter what." He set the scrapbook aside. "Let's do what God wants for our marriage—spoon, neck, and nookie, and enjoy being together."

CHAPTER
TWENTY-SIX

MONTGOMERY WARD'S marketing expert had talked nonstop from Mac's office all the way to downtown Detroit's Michigan Central Depot. He shook Corrie's hand again. "Here's where we part. Enjoy your visit to Hudson's, the world's tallest department store with the world's largest flag. Remember to go to their Thanksgiving Day parade." He went through the wrought iron gate and found another set of ears to tickle. "You going to Chicago? Same here. I work for Montgomery Ward's." His voice echoed down the ramp until he turned into the tunnel to the train sheds.

"Whew." Mac pretended to collapse. "That's a lot of jaw flapping."

"As Thelma would say, chatty, talkative, verbose." Corrie rose up on tiptoe to kiss each ear. "Poor bunny."

Loudspeakers announced trains to Toronto, Cleveland, and Chicago. Soon, Corrie thought, passengers would be flying to all those places.

Mac gave her an appreciative once-over. "You're all dolled up."

"Mother has been hammering the finer points of being the wife of a businessman." She pivoted. "Miriam helped me pull it together. What do you think?"

"Copacetic. I always think so"—he lowered his voice—"even when you're wearing nothing at all."

"Such a sheik." She gave him a Clara Bow smile, then looped her arm through his. "Give me a tour of this joint."

"The depot was designed by the fellows who did New York's Grand Central Station."

The skylit concourse connected to a smoking room, barber shop, drugstore, telegraph office, and newsstand. In the women's room, mothers fed babies as young children raced around the palm trees. The other side had a lunch counter, a café, and a reading room. Sunlight through massive arched windows lit the waiting room. Vaulted ceilings supported by marble columns soared over passengers on mahogany benches. Omaha had recently opened a new train station, but Michigan Central put it to shame. This was larger, fancier, and topped by an eighteen-story office building.

Corrie studied the green tiled ceiling. "It matches our bathroom."

Mac chuckled. "Maybe the builder got a discount on leftovers."

They exited through an enormous bronze door to wailing sirens, roaring car engines, and screeching tires. A rapid popping echoed. The second car made the same noise.

"Are they shooting?"

"Yes, and they're coming this way." Mac grabbed her hand. He dashed for the station's entrance. The crowd leaving blocked those scrambling to get back in. One yelled in German, another in Lithuanian. The cars raced closer, rat-a-tat-tats blasting. Mac tucked Corrie under his arm and ran around the front of the building into a corner. "Get down."

Heart pounding, she scrunched on a pile of brown leaves. Mac's arms clamped around her. His head rested on hers. "Help, Lord, hide us," he rasped. The world went dark.

Bullets pinged off the stone facade.

Tires squealed. Sirens grew louder, then passed. Then … only the thumping of her heart and Mac's.

Footsteps approached. An unfamiliar voice asked, "You okay?"

Mac's weight lifted off and Corrie blinked in the light. A taxi driver with a thick mustache stood on the curb.

Mac helped Corrie to her feet and held her with both arms, his muscles rigid. "I'm okay. Corrie?"

She nodded and leaned on him.

"Aw, I lost a tire." The driver switched to his native language, his whine and hand gestures asking, "Why me?"

Corrie traced a line from the tire to the dings in the building. The trail passed at head level.

The cabbie followed her gaze. "Say, very smart, coat matching the building. Although more shooting than aiming with them Tommy guns."

Mac's gray wool coat did blend in with the stone. Corrie brushed chips from his hat and his shoulders. When she tried to rub off a dark spot near the edge of his collar, her finger went through the sheepskin. "A bullet hole." Corrie gasped. "We almost got shot. What happened?"

Drivers climbed out of cab line. "Gang war," one said.

"The Licavoli brothers," said the next.

"No, it was the Purple Gang," said the one behind him.

The first driver noted, "Those guys all in jail. It was Irish in the second car. That Kennedy fellow."

"Looked like that Milazzo and Catalanotte to me."

"Both of them are dead. Don't you keep up? It was Zerilli and Tocco."

Hot anger straightened Corrie's spine. "Everyone in Detroit knows these gangsters? Are they on baseball cards?"

"Gangsters on baseball cards?" Mac blinked.

The first driver shrugged. "Can't turn down a paying fare."

"Next time drive them to the police station." Corrie turned to Mac. "Let's go."

He kept her close as they hurried to the car. His shaking hands dropped the key before fitting it into the ignition. "I just wanted to spend some time with you. I *never* intended—"

"Mac." She cupped his face, wiping away cold sweat, then gave him a gentle kiss. "You saved our lives. Thank you."

As they pulled away, Corrie looked over her shoulder. "Half-dozen police cars by the tracks. Looks like they caught the mobsters."

"You wanted to see Hudson's …"

"Another day." She settled into the seat. "Time to celebrate being alive. Let's go to Saunders for an ice cream soda!"

———

Corrie had breakfast on the table by the time Mac dressed.

"No paper today?" He spooned brown sugar onto his oatmeal.

She shrugged. "Expecting a busy day at the store?"

"All credit and no cash." He sipped his orange juice. "And you?"

"I should send out Christmas cards early, let everyone know our new address. Oh, look at the time! You'd better be going." She dashed out of the room, returning with his chesterfield and muffler.

"I've got twenty minutes."

"Get a head start on all those Christmas shoppers." She scurried off again, bringing back his galoshes and fedora.

He leaned over to nuzzle his wife.

"Mac!" She flicked a soap bubble at him. "You're going to be late!"

"I'm the boss." He looked her in the eye. "Something more going on?"

"Honestly!" She attacked the frying pan with a square of steel wool.

"Guess I shouldn't ask this close to Christmas."

"You certainly shouldn't!" The pan banged into the drainer. Her hug turned into a push toward the door. "Have a good day at the store!"

Mac patted Lindy and left the house. *Women. Are they all this... confusing?* Usually Corrie snatched up the *Free Press* for the flying news: who's setting records, how many passengers the airlines carried, what new planes were built. But today ... He paused at the corner and looked back. Every stoop, except his, held a newspaper. Hadn't he paid the paperboy?

Sal met him at the freight door, waving the front page. "Did your Amelia Earhart see this?"

Mac scanned the article under Sal's tapping finger. *Lowell Bayles ... Thompson Trophy at 236 mph ... GeeBee Model Z, made by Granville Brothers Aircraft of Springfield, Massachusetts ... flying barefoot ... record of 278 mph ... 3 kilometer course ... unofficial record of 281.9 mph at Wayne County Airport.* "We didn't get a paper this morning."

"Good thing. Corrie'd be out there proving girls can beat boys."

Mac stared at Sal for moment, then grabbed the phone. No answer at home. Too late. Unless ... No, he couldn't. Not in the middle of the Christmas rush. But ... it was his Corrie.

"I'm going to the airport!" he yelled, then realized he had no way to get there. At best, empty and down hills, the Montgomery Ward's truck rumbled along at twenty miles per hour. Sal had it packed with deliveries. He hurried to the credit office. "Shirley, can I use your car?"

"It's a hay burner," she cautioned.

"I'll fill it up."

Sal followed him. "You no want your wife to fly, you lay down the law. Show her who's boss. Smack her good."

"I don't hit women." Mac looked up from buttoning his coat. "Especially one who's been offered a flying job in Hollywood."

Sal whistled. "Sugar daddy with planes. Not looking good for you, Mac."

Don't I know it.

Cold air whistling around the window covers, Mac sped down Telegraph Road in the Model A station wagon. A cloud of gray smoke trailed. No wonder Shirley complained about it using gas and oil. It probably hadn't had a tune-up since her husband died.

He followed the traffic into the airport and parked at the end of a long line of cars. Wind sapped the heat from his body as his feet pounded on the frozen field. How would he find Corrie among all these people? Maybe she'd stayed in the Chevy, out of the cold. He shouldered through the men, looking for his car. "Corrie!"

Please let me find her in time.

A squat little plane, like a toy with a giant engine, trundled to the end of the runway. It paused, round nose into the wind. The tiny rudder waved goodbye. The motor screamed its death knell.

He grabbed a fellow. "Who's in that? Who's flying?"

The man shrugged him off. The engine roared louder, too loud for Mac to be heard. Then the plane raced down the field, the noise out of proportion to its size. It jumped into the sky, climbed toward the overcast, and circled the airport. Lining up with the pylons, it dove. Suddenly the plane twisted, rolled twice, and spiraled into the ground with a muffled thump. The crowd gasped. A puff of vapor and dust blew from the ditch, then with a boom, flames shot into the sky. Sirens blaring, a fire truck and ambulance sped toward the blaze. The crowd followed, boots thumping on hard earth.

Too late. Too late.

Gone. Dead. Like Henry. *No!*

"Corrie!" Mac yelled into the silence. Heart racing, he ran with the crowd toward the black smoke. Icy air scraped his eyes, throat, and lungs. He slipped and stumbled on the frost-slick grass. He reached the lip of the ravine. At the bottom, along the Wabash tracks, lay the smoldering pieces of the plane. No one could survive such a crash. Mac's blood turned to ice.

"Corrie!" Mac grabbed the man next to him, a short fellow with a handlebar mustache and porkpie hat. "Who was flying? Who was the pilot?"

"Is little guy," he said in heavily accented English. "Flies no shoes."

Mac had to be sure. "A man, right? Not a woman."

The mustache twitched. "No woman. Yah."

Mac thanked him and pushed through the mob. He had to find her. "Corrie!"

"Over here!" yelled a cluster of fellows in leather pilot jackets. The tall one stepped back. Corrie sat on the ground. Wind flapped the collar of her Spaulding wet-weather suit.

"Corrie!" He pushed through a slow-moving group of men without apologizing, dropped to the ground, and wrapped his arms around his wife, covering her with his body. Alive. Warm and wiggling. "You're safe."

"Of course. Except—"

"She stepped in a gopher hole and twisted her ankle when we ran to see if we could help." The skinny fellow in overalls introduced himself as Gil Hilzinger. He nodded toward the crash. "Is there anything we can do?"

Mac shook his head.

The aircraft salesman who'd accosted them in the diner watched the firemen. "Where's the nearest juice joint? I need a drink."

Mac turned to Corrie. "I'm taking you home."

"How're we gonna get back?" asked one of the flyboys.

"Here's a dollar. Fill up that Ford station wagon and drive it to Montgomery Ward's in Royal Oak." Mac pointed out Shirley's car, then scooped up his wife.

The fellow on her other side started to help.

"I've got her." Mac headed up the hill.

"Corrie, about that wing-walking job—"

Mac half-turned. "My wife does not wing walk."

Reaching the top of the slope, Mac set her down to catch his breath.

"You should let them help. I'm too heavy for you."

Anger gave him enough energy to make it to his Chevy.

A silent four miles up Telegraph Road, Corrie sniffled. He pulled over.

"Oh, Mac, he almost made history."

"What?"

"I bet he was going over three hundred miles an hour."

"Corrie, I thought it was you." Only a firm grip of the steering wheel kept his hands from shaking. "I thought you'd crashed."

She shook her head. "The GeeBee stalls at a hundred and ten. Its control surfaces are the size of postage stamps."

"You're wearing your flying clothes. What am I supposed to think?"

"They're warmer than a skirt."

He took a deep breath. Okay, he had to be clear about this. But diplomatic. Like dealing with a difficult customer. "No more flying."

"Of course not." She propped her swollen foot on the dashboard. "Not until this ankle heals."

––––––

Mac inched the front half of Shirley's Model A station wagon into his garage, thankful winter hadn't fully set in yet. He folded back the hood and groaned. What a mess. Lindy sniffed, then not finding anything edible, wandered the backyard.

"No sense letting you have all the fun." Corrie squeezed into the garage, wearing greasy coveralls and carrying a fistful of rags. "No gasket? Guess we can't clean the pan."

"Stay inside and let your ankle heal," Mac said. "Just an oil change."

"My ankle's fine." She squatted beside the front tire to examine the chassis. "This jalopy needs more than an oil change. I could see the wheels shimmy from the kitchen."

"I think Ford pays the state not to fix the roads, to make sure we all have to buy a new car every year or two." He slid under the engine and removed the drain plug. Oil oozed like Karo syrup into the waste can.

"Lumpier than the gravy I tried to make for Thanksgiving," Corrie said. "Has Shirley ever changed it?"

"Probably not." He crawled out as Corrie reached into the engine compartment. "It's dirty," he warned.

"Wish it was a little warmer so we could wash it." With a rag and a wrench from Mac's toolbox, Corrie wiped and tightened. She checked the brakes and cleaned the spark plugs. "Loose bushings, loose shafts, loose levers. Missing cotter pins. It's a wonder this flivver steers at all." She greased the hubs, steering box, fan, drive shaft, and universal joint. "At least the tires are good."

"How'd you learn to do this?" He replaced the drain plug and refilled the engine with Ward's Runrite oil.

"My brothers love to tinker." She oiled the springs and steering linkages. "My flight instructor had me work at the Overland Sport factory, thinking if I knew how my plane was built, I'd be a better pilot. Engines are pretty much the same."

"I should introduce you to Mary Jane. She'd be the assistant manager of my automotive department if I had the budget to promote her. Learned cars by helping at her dad's gas station."

"See if she'd like to come over for dinner next week."

"Great idea." Mac closed the hood. They went inside to scrub and change clothes. "I'll swap cars and be right back."

Corrie handed him a bar of Ward's hand soap. "How about if Lindy and I ride with you?"

Mac leaned over and kissed her cheek. "Glad to have your company." He whistled for the dog. Lindy rode on the seat with his paws on the door, pressing his nose to the gap where the window cover and frame met.

The engine ran smoother and without smoke. The car managed bumps and turns with a lot less shaking. They pulled into Shirley's driveway.

A pile of kids surrounded the dog. "He looks like the Magers' cocker." The tallest boy slapped his leg and called, "Here, Butch."

The dog's ears twitched.

"We figured he was someone's pet. Would they want—" Corrie's voice wobbled. "If you'll tell us where they live, we'll take him back."

"They moved last spring." Shirley came down the kitchen steps, arms wrapped in her apron. "Back to the family farm in Kentucky. They'd be glad to know he's well cared for."

Corrie let out her breath, then smiled.

Shirley thanked Mac for working on the car and said she'd see him Monday. They headed for home.

Mac gave Corrie's hand a squeeze. "You learned a lot after graduation."

She faced away from him, her right hand keeping Lindy from sliding off the seat. "I enjoyed flying, and I was proud of being a pilot, of all the hard work I put in to get my license. It's painful giving it up. If I'm not a pilot, who am I? A nobody. Another girl without a job."

Mac felt a chill unrelated to December in Michigan. Was she laying out the case for her move to California? "You're my wife."

"Only because you're incredibly patient and have a cast-iron stomach."

"I didn't marry you for your cooking skills."

"Hah. I didn't have any."

"I married you because you're you—smart, lively, enthusiastic Corrie."

She groaned. "Not so much lately."

They paused for a Grand Trunk freight train to chug past. Like everything else since the stock market crashed, it moved sluggishly. Mac wrapped an arm around Corrie and pulled her close. "I've been thinking about this, with so many out of work. You are more than an occupation."

"But that's the first thing people ask, what do you do?"

"But that's not what God asks. He took Moses from the desert to leading Israel out of Egypt. David went from shepherd to a king. The apostle Paul from persecutor to evangelist."

"What will God do with me?" Blue-green eyes shot him a glance. "If I'm not flying or looking for a flying job, am I giving up?"

"No. You're being realistic."

"Might feel good to stop banging my head on that brick wall."

He brushed his lips across her temple. "Poor head. It needs a break."

"Taking a break from flying sounds more hopeful than giving up."

"I don't know what God has planned, but I hope we do it together." He rested his cheek on her warm forehead. Her curls tickled his face. Was she wondering why she wasn't pregnant? "Being with you, even doing things like changing the oil together, it's the best."

She flicked his earlobe with her tongue, warming him more thoroughly than the Chevy's heater. "Any plans for tonight?"

"With you? Positively, absolutely." He bobbed his eyebrows like Groucho Marx. The caboose passed. Mac checked both ways, then drove across the tracks. "Have you been working on our car too? It's handling railroad crossings and potholes, starts easier, hasn't stalled for months."

"Of course. Got it ready for winter."

"You are the berries." Mac grinned. "Why'd you marry this Montgomery Ward's manager anyway?"

Her smile sparkled. "Because you're a lot more than what you do."

CHAPTER
TWENTY-SEVEN

MIRIAM BURST INTO THE KITCHEN. "Father Coughlin blames Jewish communists for the Depression and the Russian revolution."

Corrie poured her friend a cup of coffee. "I have a lot of Jewish friends in Omaha. They didn't cause either of those things."

Her friend hung up her coat and stomped to the living room, scaring Lindy into hiding behind the chair. "I'm afraid gullible people will believe Coughlin and attack my friends who are Jewish. We must pray for their safety. And pray that demagogue is struck with laryngitis."

"Permanent laryngitis." Corrie joined her on the couch and picked up her knitting.

"Did you hear Hoover's latest? As lines at soup kitchens grow longer, charities run out of money, men fight over restaurant trash, he says 'No one need go hungry or cold.'"

"Don't blame me. I was too young to vote for him." Corrie started another row of knit 1, purl 2. How could Miriam do something as complicated as making a sock while talking politics?

"I was not a US citizen, but we will vote in the next election." Miriam measured Corrie's project. "The cuff is long enough. Start on the heel."

Corrie released the breath she'd been holding as she tried to make the unruly yarn behave. "How about you do the heels and I'll do the cuffs?"

"Because Mr. Blue Serge wants a pair of socks from the loving hands of his beautiful bride." Miriam talked her through the stitches.

On the radio students from Longfellow Elementary sang "Up on the Housetop."

"Reindeer? Every boy and girl in Syria knows the smallest camel brings presents."

"A camel?" Corrie giggled. "Camels pull Santa's sleigh?"

Her friend grinned. "How many camels fit on top of a roof? And the noise of their big feet! No one could sleep through that."

"And all they brought was Camel cigarettes."

"No, no, no. They bring gold, frankincense, and myrrh. The Bible says so." Miriam put away her knitting. "And I have to put supper on the table. We shall finish the heel tomorrow."

Corrie pulled the curtain back, wiped a hole in the condensation, and watched her friend slog home through the gloom. Between the clouds, the lack of snow, and December's short days, it had been a dark month. Miriam's friendship was the only sunshine these gloomy days.

Thinking of friends ... Corrie started a letter to Jackie. Maybe she knew the latest about Tex.

Lindy woofed as Mac's car chugged into the driveway. Corrie sealed her letter and met him at the kitchen door. He pulled her into his embrace with a low hum.

"It's only meatloaf."

"Who's talking about food?" He warmed his cold nose on her neck, giving her the shivers, then Mac pulled the pan from the oven. "This does smell good. Whose recipe?"

"Your mother's. Don't feel too safe though. Aunt Sammy's blackberry flummery is in the refrigerator."

"She hasn't killed us yet."

"Her lima bean loaf came close. Not even Uncle Sam would eat that."

"And neither would Lindy. Maybe Aunt Sammy missed an ingredient when she read the recipe over the radio."

"Very kind of you to chalk up my disaster to the Department of Agriculture. From now on, I'm sticking with Mabel Clare's cookbook." She took a bite. "Seems dry."

"Mom usually tops it with ketchup." Mac grabbed the bottle. "I've got good news. Montgomery Ward's wants to keep their Wardway building crews busy and advertise their houses, so they're offering help with financing. If we tighten our belts a little, we can buy our own home." He set a catalog in front of her.

Their own home? "But …"

"Ours might not be as big as the one you grew up in, but it'll have the latest appliances and kitchen cabinets." He flipped the pages. "Book nook, folding ironing board, built-in phone cabinet, clothes chute."

She shook her head. "But I like this house."

"If the owners move back, we'll be out on the street."

"I like this neighborhood."

"Me too. I'll see if any empty lots are for sale." Mac finished his meatloaf and started in on the blackberry flummery. "Swell. Tastes like pie filling." He squeezed her hand. "You're becoming quite the cook."

"You are the cat's pajamas."

"I'll check out *your* pajamas later." He grinned and planted a kiss on her knuckles. "Look through the catalog and see what catches your eye. Let me give you the house you want."

Since it was important to Mac, Corrie nodded. "How much belt tightening are we talking about?"

————

Sales had been dismal all year, and Santa Claus hadn't brought much improvement. Chicago demanded workforce reductions to balance the budget. In other companies, seniority or merit guided cuts. But here, everyone had been hired in the spring of 1929. Most employees worked their fingers to the bone. What to do? Mac had tossed and turned all night and still hadn't found a solution.

Shirley stuck her head in the office. "It's time."

Mac pushed back from his desk. The rumble of voices from his employees quieted as soon as he stepped out. Headquarters had warned employees could get violent; he should ask the police to stand by. Mac had gauged the mood and elected not to call Officer Hayward. He hoped he was right. "Ladies and gentlemen."

Someone in the back sniffled. "Is the store going to close?"

"This Montgomery Ward's store will stay in business. That's the good news. But headquarters says employee hours must be reduced to meet our low sales."

"But if no clerks wait on customers, sales will take a dive," said one of the fellows from the shoe department.

Ralph from automotive seconded his opinion. "People got no clue what size tires to buy."

"I told them that." Mac nodded. "I told them this is the best group of employees on the planet and I hate to let even one of you go."

"So who's getting fired?"

"And when?"

Mac raised his arms for quiet. "I have to make the change by January 1. So I'm asking, if anyone's planning to leave or would like fewer hours, come talk to me. And if anyone has any ideas to increase sales and cut expenses, come talk to me. Let's figure this out together. And ..." He swallowed. "Thank you all for working so hard."

Gershwin's *Rhapsody in Blue* wound from the radio, pulling Mac into the house. The mouthwatering fragrance of roast beef nearly brought him to his knees. "Corrie?"

"Hello, handsome." His wife sauntered across the kitchen. Instead of her usual getup of sweater and skirt, she wore a dark-brown dress with a red scarf. A wave of marcelled hair dipped over one eye.

"Wow!" A cold draft reminded him to shut the door.

"Welcome home." She slipped a hand under his lapel to help him out of his coat. He caught the flowery scent of perfume. Candlelight reflected off a white tablecloth.

"Putting on the Ritz." Was she giving up on her harebrained Hollywood scheme? Or was this a last-ditch attempt to win him over?

"Just for you."

His foot bumped the dog as he sat down. He peeked under the tablecloth. Lindy raised a hopeful eyebrow. *Take a number, buddy.*

Corrie moved platters and covered dishes from the oven, then perched on the edge of her chair. Steam from the mashed potatoes haloed her glowing face. She flashed him a look, a secretive smile, as she passed him the glazed carrots. *We're having a baby!* He could see it now, father and son strolling around the zoo, watching the Tigers play at Navin Field, learning the retail business from the ground up.

"So what's the occasion?"

"I figured you'd need a good dinner after a rough day. How did it go?"

No baby? Mac's heart hit his empty stomach. "Grim. At first." The roast melted on his tongue. "Wow. This is delicious."

"Thank you," she said with a flash of blue-green eyes.

"One of the drapery clerks is leaving after Christmas, moving back to the farm, but otherwise everyone wants to keep their hours. As the day wore on, the ideas started to roll in. Some were unrealistic. But others … How's this sound? If you buy a pair of shoes, you get a nickel off a pair of socks. A set of tires gets you a discount on a quart of oil. A new mattress earns a coupon for ten percent off sheets."

"Buy a new dress, get a deal on stockings. You're moving the merchandise by encouraging people to spend a little more but not break the bank." Corrie knew.

"We'll have a different sale every week, keep the foot traffic up. But I still have to reduce payroll. The only fair way to cut is across the board. Everyone, including me." Mac leaned on the table and squeezed Corrie's hand. "It's just the two of us. We're not stretching my pay to support a heap of relatives. Can we manage?"

"Absolutely."

"It will take longer to save up for a trip to Omaha."

She shrugged. "You probably shouldn't be away from the store."

"I was hoping to have a house built, but you'd rather stay here."

"No moving? Now you're on the trolley." She grinned.

"And meals like this …"

"Clyde gave me a good price, and Miriam taught me how to make it tender." Corrie took another bite. "It's not as good as hers though."

Mac's fork paused in midair as he stared at Miriam's hairstyle, Miriam's clothing style, Miriam's recipes.

"Corrie." He reached across the table. The calendar should have labeled this *Difficult Conversation Day*. "You don't have to be Miriam—"

"I don't know how to help you." She stabbed a carrot.

He kissed her knuckles. "You're my one and only, no matter how you do your hair, what you make for dinner, what you wear … or don't wear."

His wink set off her blush. "Finish your dinner."

"Got something in mind for dessert?"

She flashed a smile. "Do I ever."

———

"Mac wants to put the kibosh on my flying." Corrie paced to the kitchen window and scowled at the low clouds. "Even this weather is on his side."

"Skies clear when the lakes freeze over." Miriam tied red yarn around a pine cone. "Come help. We have much to do."

Making decorations for the Boot Ball required patience, and Corrie didn't have any today. "Maybe we should take Lindy for a walk."

The dog opened one eye, sighed, then went back to sleep.

"Dogs know better than to go out in this weather." Miriam whipped together another centerpiece. "If you need something to fuss about, let me tell you Hoover's latest. He said, 'Many persons left their jobs for the more profitable one of selling apples.'"

Corrie blinked. "Is he off his nuts? Who would leave his job, any job, to stand on a corner in winter?"

"Someone who lives in an ivory tower called the White House." Miriam's voice lowered. "Anti-immigrant sentiment is rising. Los Angeles deported ten thousand people to Mexico."

"You're a US citizen. They can't do that to you."

"Hungry, angry people attack without asking to see paperwork." Miriam started another pine cone, but the yarn snarled into a knot. Instead of working the tangle out, she attacked it with scissors. "Father Coughlin yells about America first, saving America for Americans. Does he want to give it back to the Indians?" She wiped her eyes.

"I won't let anyone take you away." Corrie wrapped an arm around her friend's shoulder and breathed in her exotic scent. "You and Joseph are treasured members of this community."

Miriam leaned on Corrie. "We cannot go to Florida this winter. Joseph's patients pay with vegetables if they pay at all. I am thankful, but—"

"What would I do if you went to Florida?"

"Knit yourself into a corner." Miriam wiped her eyes and kissed Corrie's cheek. "Enough. We must do the good work God has prepared for us."

Corrie paced the living room. What good work had God prepared for her?

"Are you watching for the postman?" Miriam asked.

Corrie hadn't heard from Tex in twenty-nine days. No doubt he flew with a different movie star every day and had forgotten all about her. "I asked Mrs. Zukas to send her cookie recipes."

"I wish I got letters." Miriam nodded at the envelopes on the buffet. "Mail between here and Syria is slow and expensive. What do people write?"

"Mother reminds me to be a good businessman's wife, as if the world hasn't gone blooey. Ruth tells me about her work in the hospital. Jackie knows all the gossip." She said Tex was busy making a movie about Al Capone. "Thelma is having a swell time at college. Halleen is taking in boarders and chasing little ones. Sister Mary Frances writes sermons."

"Why don't you read one to me while I finish these."

Was that the mailbox? She raced for the front door. Christmas card, another card … then a business-sized envelope postmarked Hollywood containing train tickets. Corrie's breath caught. Here it was, her chance to be someone, to get her name in the record books, and to finally make her parents proud.

"Did the recipes come?" Miriam called from the dining room.

Corrie slid the envelope under the davenport cushion. "Oh yes. Bohemian Christmas cookies, cheese ball, eggnog, gingerbread cookies." The radio played Christmas music, but Corrie's heart sang "California, Here I Come."

CHAPTER
TWENTY-EIGHT

CORRIE AND MIRIAM had gone to church early for last-minute dance preparations. Mac had five minutes before he left with Joseph. He filled Lindy's water bowl, turned off the radio, then dashed upstairs. What should he get Corrie for Christmas? Shaker cardigans were in fashion and warm. Her drawer held green, red, camel, and blue sweaters. The way she was knitting, maybe he should give her yarn. Or… what about a sewing machine? She could make all kinds of clothes. Yes, an electric model with a new cabinet. Mom loved hers. Corrie would be thrilled.

"Ready, old boy?" called Joseph from the entry. "No need to wear boots to Santa's Boot Ball."

"On my way." Mac turned out the light and hurried downstairs.

The fine cashmere and close fit of Joseph's coat said he didn't shop at Montgomery Ward's. "Did you hear the Cubs traded Bud Teachout and Hack Wilson to the Cardinals?"

Mac grabbed his shoes and sat on the davenport. Crunch.

Joseph paused his recitation of sports news. "What was that?"

Mac reached under the cushion and pulled out an envelope. Addressed to Corrie. From Hollywood. Containing train tickets. His friend's voice faded like a lost radio signal. The room dimmed.

"Mac? Mac!" Cool fingers pressed Mac's wrist. "Take a breath."

A giant spear jabbed between his shoulder blades and out the front of his chest. It slashed his heart, sending the pieces to the floor.

A firm hand shook his shoulder. "Breathe or you go to the hospital."

"Corrie." Mac gasped, curling into the pain. "She–"

"Dear Heavenly Father," Joseph prayed, "bring Your Spirit of calm and peace to my brother. Deliver us from evil."

"She's leaving." He gasped out his words.

"She's at church with Miriam." Joseph pulled the envelope from Mac's shaking fingers. "Typed address. No note. Are you sure it is from Tex?"

"He wants her to fly in his movies."

"He has pilots." Joseph made a low sound in his throat and tucked the envelope in his pocket. "I will burn this."

"He'll send another. He's a millionaire." Mac squeezed his head. "A sugar daddy with airplanes. He can give her what she wants— flying. And me? I'm only a regular fellow, a rube, a Joe Palooka."

"You're the man she loves. Put on your shoes."

"I can't go to the dance."

"Palooka is a fighter. You must fight for your wife, for your marriage." Joseph shoved the shoes onto Mac's feet.

If his thoughts would pull into some sort of order. "Raising money for boots is foolish when the weather's so warm."

"Winter always comes. Tonight, above freezing and no rain, we will have great attendance."

"Take me to the diner."

"To the speakeasy? You don't drink. And even if you did, alcohol is the last thing you need." Joseph bundled him up and dragged him into the car. "And prayer is the first thing you need. Start praying."

"God doesn't want to hear from a small-town Ward's manager."

"God is on your side. David was a shepherd, a younger brother like you, but he conquered Goliath, won many battles, and became king."

"David wasn't married to a pilot." He wiped his face. In spite of winter's chill, he'd broken out in a sweat. "Maybe … I should let her fly, move to Hollywood, ask Montgomery Ward's if they need me out there." But no, he couldn't watch Corrie die in a ball of flame.

"Talk to God first, my friend."

"Prayers can't stop her."

"How shall I explain this? We pray for wisdom in this battle. We pray God will guide her. We pray she will listen to Him and obey, that she will honor her vows, that she will see how much you love her." Joseph turned toward Mac with a serious expression. "In the end, though, whether to stay or go is Corrie's choice."

Montgomery Ward's guaranteed satisfaction. Why didn't God? "I'm giving Corrie a sewing machine for Christmas. An electric model with a cabinet."

Joseph's gloved hand left the steering wheel to chop the air. "This is not a time to be practical. This is a time for romance, for convincing Corrie your love is worth more than every airplane in the world. Give her a symbol of your commitment. Give her a ring."

"Montgomery Ward's sells rings."

Joseph raised his eyebrows and lowered his chin, making Mac feel all of three years old. "Monday morning, stop by Wilfred and Tom–"

Now Mac's eyebrows raised. "The men's pants store?"

"Jim Dobie, the jeweler who used to work at Codling's, has a bench there. See what he can do for you." His friend took a deep breath. "Your wife … is one of a kind. You need to find a gem as rare as she."

They passed Ward's, closed for the night. What would Chicago say? He'd keep them from finding out as long as possible. How much time did he have before Corrie left? "Married only six months. And I failed."

"You did not fail, my friend."

He rubbed his aching chest. "Can a fellow die from a broken heart?"

"You are too young for that." Joseph parked across from the church.

The gym's windows glowed. Happy music scraped his heart. Giggling couples hurried to the door. "I can't face her. I'm going home. The Boot Ball is almost over anyway." He bent his wrist to check his watch.

"You have time. Time to put away anger and fear. Time to sweep her off her feet, remind her why she fell in love with you."

"I'm not sure she loves me."

"She does. I am sure of it."

Ka-thump, ka-thump.

"What's that?" Joseph wiped condensation from the windshield.

Ka-thump, ka-thump. A boy trudged by in man-sized boots. At the intersection, he tripped, falling into the street. One bare foot kicked in the frigid air. Joseph bolted from the car, but the boy hopped up, shoved his foot into his boot, and continued ka-thumping along.

Mac climbed out. "Get a refund for those tickets and buy socks."

"God has work for us." Joseph marched Mac into the gym, humming "Onward, Christian Soldiers."

Wall lights shone on a full dance floor. A dozen people clustered around the hot chocolate table. Garland decorated with pine cones draped the walls. A tinsel-covered Christmas tree glowed on the stage beside the band. The pianist, guitar player, and cellist shopped at Ward's, but the fellows on trumpet and sax weren't familiar.

Mac spotted Corrie right away. She danced the Lindy Hop, of course. She'd partnered with Walter, raising the question why the stockman didn't move this fast in the store. Corrie's face glowed, and her legs kicked with athletic energy. The crowd drew back, giving them space to show off their moves. She wore a red dress with a cowl neck and fishtail hem. It had been the height of fashion three years ago, but nobody bought new gowns these days. And nobody paid attention to her clothes with all her fancy footwork. How had he ever thought—

"The song after next will be a waltz. You will ask your bride to dance. Pour on the charm, old boy. I am praying." Joseph sauntered to the band leader and slipped him a tip large enough to raise his eyebrows.

Then Joseph claimed his wife for a foxtrot. Miriam's beaded green dress glittered against the European cut of his black suit. The elegant couple moved gracefully, with lots of spins and turns, making the dance look effortless. Unlike him, a lousy heeler to Corrie's peppy hopper, a flat tire to the flygirl.

The fast song wound to a close. Now, now, to capture Corrie's heart. For Tex, Corrie was another girl, another pilot, disposable. But for Mac, she was the one who held his heart.

Onward, Christian soldier. Mac marched across the floor, shoulders back, spine straight, chin up. Several people called out to him. He nodded but kept his eyes on Corrie. He touched her shoulder, then extended his arm. "Mrs. McFarland, may I have the next dance?"

"Mac! Ab-so-lute-ly!" Nothing about her smile hinted of a plan to leave. "You were so late, I was afraid Joseph had a patient."

"I'll never miss a dance with you." *Please, Lord, let this be the first of a lifetime of dances.* The opening chords of the Skaters' Waltz sounded. Mac swirled her across the floor.

Corrie had left the house with her hair in sedate marcel waves close to her head. Hours of dancing rearranged it into the tumble of curls he loved. Blue-green eyes sparkled beneath long dark lashes. A healthy shade of pink tinted her cheeks. "You're staring. Did my mascara flake off?"

"Admiring my favorite view." His hand drew circles on her back, and he paraphrased the Woodbury soap advertisement, "The skin I love to touch."

Her smile grew into a sassy grin. "Aren't you the live wire?"

"That's me." He snuggled her closer, inhaling a whiff of Coty powder.

"Ooh, Mac. The chaperones will street us."

"We're married," he murmured. "We're allowed all sorts of whoopee. Which I'll show you soon as we get home."

"Hot socks!"

"Hot everything." He swept her into a turn and whispered his plans in her ear.

The overhead lights came on, ending the dance. Mac kept his hand on Corrie's waist, tucking her in close.

The minister took the stage. "Dear friends, the churches of Royal Oak joined together to make sure every child in town arrives at school with warm, dry feet this winter. I'm pleased to announce that we've raised eighty-six dollars." As he waited for the applause to die down, the treasurer hurried up and whispered in his ear. "Make that ninety-two dollars. I'd like to thank Miriam Jandali and Corrie McFarland for organizing this dance. And Mac McFarland for negotiating a discount with Montgomery Ward's, so ninety-two children—" The treasurer stopped him again. "One hundred children will have new boots! Now that's the Christmas spirit in action! We'll see all of you in January for the Polka Party."

The crowd cheered and applauded.

Joseph clapped Mac's shoulder. "What a team you make, Corrie's energy and Mac's business skill."

"Don't forget Miriam's nifty decorations. And I'm guessing you paid for more than one pair of boots tonight." Corrie wagged a finger at Joseph.

"We all do our part, but I wonder who must clean up."

Mac hoped it wasn't Corrie. They had plans.

"The decorations are staying for the children's Christmas pageant. And the refreshment committee washes their own dishes."

The janitor flashed the lights and made a threatening sweep of his push broom. "All of youse, beat it!"

Corrie linked arms with Mac. "Let's get a wiggle on!"

―――――

Where was it? Corrie pulled out the davenport cushions. No envelope of tickets to California. Nothing on the floor. Or stuck to its underside. Not under the chair cushion either. Rolling up the rug released clouds of dog hair but no train tickets. What happened to them?

Cold air snaked across the floor and up Corrie's spine. If Mac had found them… he would have said something. And he wouldn't have been acting like a sheik, lots of necking, cuddling, and spooning. How could she leave him? No, she must. California had it all—a flying job, great weather, races, and record setting. If she didn't show, Tex would think she wasn't interested and give up.

Corrie pushed off the icy floor, grabbed her logbook, and crawled onto the davenport. Every page told of the best days of her life: first lesson, first cross-country, earning her license.

"Merry Christmas!" Miriam hurried through the kitchen door.

"Christmas isn't until Friday."

"We're off to Dearborn." She plopped next to Corrie and pointed to the logbook. "Reminiscing about the happy days when the sun always shone and your fuel tank was always full? You were never cold or scared or–"

"Hah. Froze my face off plenty of times in an open cockpit biplane. And scared?" Corrie pointed to a notation, *Never again!*

"What happened?"

She closed her eyes. "We took off on a perfect Indian-summer evening—clear sky, light winds, unlimited visibility. One of the hotshot flyboys wanted a ride in the Overland. Our flight path intersected with a flock of geese. Birds can do some serious damage. You don't want to hit one, much less a group of them."

"I should think not."

"He dove instead of climbing. The geese dove too. I grabbed the stick and yanked, but he wouldn't let go. I yelled through the Gosport tube—no response. Then he pulled the power back. My poor Overland wallowed through the air, heading for the trees and the ground. If the geese didn't take us down, he'd stall and we'd auger in." The memory had her heart racing.

"What did you do?"

"We were only a few hundred feet up. No time to think. I whipped off my helmet and whacked him. Finally he let go. I poured on the coal, executed a chandelle, and got us out of the flock. When we landed, the sap yelled at me for scratching his pretty face. He thought he was in charge since he's a fellow, even though it was my plane and I had more hours."

"You fought for control." Miriam propped her elbow on the back of the davenport. "Like your marriage."

"What? Mac and I don't fight." *Oh here it comes.* Corrie crossed her arms and refused to meet her gaze. "I suppose the Bible says the husband has to be in charge all the time."

"Not so much." Miriam tilted her head toward the logbook. "Let me see if I can explain this. When you fly, are you ever surprised by something you see? Perhaps a building that looks large but actually has a false front? Or an elegant house with mess behind a tall fence?"

"Our neighbors drained their swimming pool and turned their backyard into a vegetable patch. Their fence hid it from the street."

"Exactly." Miriam nodded. "And perhaps in science class you looked through a magnifying glass or a microscope and also received a surprise."

"Mosquitos look like monsters." Corrie shuddered.

"God sees more than we can. He knows all. Talk to Him, you and Mac together. Becoming one is more than making whoopee." Miriam winked, then extended her arms. "Pulling in different directions will destroy your marriage."

"If we moved to California or if he let me fly–" Corrie glanced at Miriam. Had she found those tickets? No, she'd have said so.

"He said no."

Corrie tapped her logbook. "I should give up the most fun ever to scrub burnt oatmeal, scorch shirts, and mop muddy floors?"

"Don't forget the Boot Ball." Miriam closed the logbook. "No, dear one, give it up for love." Her friend wished her Merry Christmas and left.

The mailbox clanked with Christmas cards from Mac's friends and

—hot dog!—a thick envelope from Jackie. A clipping from *the Hollywood Reporter* said Tex had finished two new flying movies. Finished? Without her? The rest of the clippings matched Tex with various starlets. Where were the photos of Tex and his airplane?

"Yoo-hoo!" Eunice barged through the kitchen door and stomped into the living room. The fabric of her pink coat looked like the blanket on Corrie's bed back home. "Such mess. You are sick?" Her hooded eyes took in the unfinished Christmas cards, the open photo album, white ink for labeling, and bottle of mucilage. "Thrifty housekeepers make glue from flour and water."

"Good morning, Eunice." Anyone else would get an invitation to sit and visit, but not this waspish neighbor.

"I bring Christmas stollen for you." The heavy package hit the table.

"I'm sure Mac will enjoy it very much."

Probing fingers flipped through photos of daring young men with their flying machines and Corrie with hers. Newspaper clippings reported her pilot's license, the Women's Air Derby, and the Omaha Air Race. Eunice ought to be impressed, if not with Corrie's aerial prowess, at least with her swell photo album.

The woman closed the back cover with a thud. "No photo of you and Mr. McFarland on your wedding day. Are you living in sin?"

"This is for airplanes, not wedding photos." Corrie closed the album. "You're right, I am feeling sick. You better go home before you catch it."

"*Humpf.* If that's the thanks I get …" The house shook with heavy footsteps and the slamming door.

Whew. Except … *Had* anyone taken a photo at their wedding? The rush of the day blurred her memories. A lump rose in her throat and an odd pressure built behind her eyes. Was that a tear? No, she never cried. Of course she didn't have a handkerchief. She sniffed and wiped her eyes on her sleeve.

WJR finished the weather forecast—more clouds—and began "Puppy Hour, Where They Teach Dogs to Talk."

"Lindy? Time for your radio show."

No toenails clicking on the linoleum. No dog on the kitchen rug.

"Lindy?" Uh-oh. Eunice must have let him out. Calling from the back door got her a face full of cold dampness, but no dog. Corrie pulled on her coat, hat, and galoshes. "Lindy!"

Eunice crossed the street, returning from ruining another neighbor's morning. "Not sick after all."

"Please help me. Lindy is lost."

"Like the prodigal son, he will return when he's hungry."

"He's a dog, not a fellow." She waved mittened hands. "The ground is frozen. I can't find his tracks."

"Fool's errand." The door slammed on hope for a kernel of kindness.

"Lindy!" Drivers wouldn't see him in the gloom. He'd be hit by a car and his little body would lie in the gutter until spring. Corrie started down the block. "Lindy?" Her foot slid on the ice and she landed in a puddle, wrenching her ankle again. She couldn't stand. Hopping would only lead to another fall, so she crawled. Ice water seeped into the gap between her mittens and her coat sleeves. The knees of her long drawers soaked through. Snow pants would have been helpful, but Corrie hadn't taken the time to put on hers. When she reached the house, she called Lindy again. No answer. She hauled herself inside.

Corrie crept to her bedroom on hands and knees, changed into dry drawers, then went down the stairs on her bottom. Every sound echoed. She opened the curtains and perched on the arm of the chair to keep an eye out for the dog. "Please, God, please bring Lindy home."

Corrie had never come home to an empty house. Mrs. Zukas had rattled in the kitchen, Father had read the paper in the living room, noisy brothers had played, mother and her friends had gossiped over bridge. She had never known silence or loneliness. Was this what it would be like for Mac if she left? She didn't want to hurt Mac, but what if she never flew again?

Another tear snuck out.

Three sharp barks sounded from the back of the house. Corrie hopped to the kitchen, opened the door, and a damp cocker spaniel raced inside. "Lindy! Am I ever glad you came home!" She dried him.

Lindy was home, safe and sound. Corrie should be happy, but instead her throat tightened and her eyes watered. She wiped her face on the last clean dish towel. Lindy nuzzled her hand.

Her tears wouldn't stop. "I'm sorry. So sorry. I can't ..." Who was she talking to? Was she praying? Miriam recommended it, but praying was another skill Corrie didn't have. "Now I lay me down to sleep."

No. Not bedtime. "The Lord is my shepherd." Was that a prayer? Well, she needed a shepherd, but she couldn't remember the rest. "Dear Jesus, thank You for bringing Lindy home. About those train tickets…"

———

Corrie pushed the fried eggs around her plate.

"Feeling poorly?" Mac put a hand on her forehead. No fever.

"Fine." She took a bite of toast. Low clouds and the lack of snow gave everyone the blues. And three small gifts under a scrawny pine couldn't match the extravaganza her big family had put on when she was growing up.

Or was she upset about the missing train tickets?

Leaving her breakfast, Corrie shuffled to the living room.

Mac found her curled in the easy chair listening to a mediocre rendition of "Jingle Bells" on a wheezy accordion. At least the accordionist didn't attempt to sing along. Mac covered her with the afghan his mother had crocheted for their wedding gift. "Stay home and rest. No need for you to go out."

"The announcer said we might get a break in the clouds today." Corrie lifted her face for his kiss. "I'll try to finish the Christmas cards."

"Take care of Corrie," he told Lindy, knowing the dog would take care of her eggs first.

Mac headed into the dark chill. If Corrie wasn't better this evening, he'd ask Joseph to check her. After the polio outbreak last summer, he wasn't taking any chances. Diseases ran unchecked when people couldn't afford to take care of themselves.

Shirley waved as he climbed onto the streetcar. "Stop frowning or your face will freeze like that."

"Too late." He slid onto the seat. "How's everyone at your house?"

"In their usual state of screwy. Grandpa's trying to make it warmer by wearing out his 'Aloha Oe' record and hula dancing. Grandma carved a bar of Lifebuoy into a sheep to replace the lost one in our nativity set. The children are playing Peter Pan and pirates in the yard, but instead of Neverland, it's mud land."

"Sound messy." Would he and Corrie have children? Or would she leave? "How much rain have we gotten this month?"

"Less than an inch. Don't worry. You'll get to use your snow shovel soon enough." Shirley twisted an errant curl around a finger. "Never thought I'd say this, but I miss snow. Brightens up these short days and covers up dead grass."

All along the business district, holiday decorations hung next to signs announcing price cuts. Were the other merchants in trouble too? Christmas sales barely put his store in the black.

"Well, Boss, Ward's going to make it to 1932?" Shirley asked as they exited the streetcar.

"Of course." No need to worry his employees or any customers in earshot. "We're swell."

Shirley nodded at the steamed window of the flower shop across the street. "They're shutting down December thirty-first. Not even waiting for Valentine's Day." She knew the scoop on every business downtown, a one-woman news agency. If Corrie left, it wouldn't be a secret for an hour.

Shirley paused at Wilfred and Tom's store. "Got to make sure they're not undercutting Ward's."

No one in yet. They opened an hour after Ward's. "Know anything about Jim Dobie working here?"

"Yep. Codling's jeweler has a bench in back. Nothing he can't fix. He got Grandpa's pocket watch ticking and my alarm clock ringing. I don't know how he supports his family on what little as he charges." She moved to the next window. One light shone on a half dozen pieces of jewelry. "Here's his display case."

Mac leaned close to the plate-glass, holding his breath so he wouldn't fog the window. Could it be? He'd found a gift for Corrie.

CHAPTER
TWENTY-NINE

"KNOW THIS GANGSTER FROM OMAHA?" Sal read the *Detroit News*. "On the lam since May. Police gunned him down Sunday night. No Christmas for him."

"Montgomery Ward's managers don't usually cross paths with criminals." Mac worked the numbers. How many employees he could he keep on payroll?

The delivery man turned the page. "Cops found a cable running under the river, pulling a submarine full of whiskey from Canada."

"Yeah? Says here, customs had to hire more matrons since eighty-five percent of the smugglers are women." The front page of the *Free Press* lowered, revealing hair permed like a Brillo pad. "Your little Corrie was ahead of the craze."

"Corrie's no smuggler." Mac accidentally hit the repeat key on the adding machine. He groaned and started over again. "Much as I appreciate well-informed employees, I'd rather you wait on some customers."

Shirley wheeled her chair to the door and gave the sales floor a once-over. "A few sad sacks. Women finished shopping weeks ago. All's left are desperate husbands hunting a gift for their wives."

"In need of feminine guidance. Help them buy bath salts or slippers—"

"I'm Baptist. You can't make me sell that Buddha statue."

"Wouldn't dare. How about a sewing kit or a compact or–"

The phone rang. Shirley answered, then hung up. "Bad news, Boss. The jeweler says no ring in the afternoon mail. What are you giving Corrie?"

"No idea." He pushed away the accounts that wouldn't balance and walked out of the office. The store closed in less than an hour.

His head cashier tapped her nails on the metal cover of an appliance. "The ads say every woman wants 'the glorious freedom of an Ironrite.' And it's made in Michigan."

"Much as I'd like to keep my neighbors employed ..." Mom used a mangle every day in her work at the hospital laundry, so an automatic ironer seemed even less romantic than a sewing machine. Mac raised a skeptical eyebrow. "You've met Corrie."

"Unless she could iron her wings ..."

"Exactly." He walked up to the third floor, women's clothing and accessories. Dresses, blouses, sweaters, vests, stockings, gloves, boots. She had all those. Clothing seemed too ordinary for Corrie.

"Merry Christmas, Mr. Mac." The clerk straightened displays. "We've had a run on handkerchiefs and gloves. Sold a few tapestry bags and bracelets too."

"Well done. Have a wonderful Christmas everyone." *Hope we still have jobs in 1932.*

Second floor had menswear and children's. He strolled through, greeting the employees. Baby clothes... Shouldn't they have started a family by now?

He couldn't go home empty handed. What about a Murray Bay wool blanket in blue-and-white plaid? Although he and Corrie had no trouble keeping each other warm.

As he reached the first floor, a now-familiar clatter echoed. Walter had bumped the skis again.

"Sorry, Boss."

It didn't matter where Mac displayed them—wedged between tires in automotive, behind the couches in the furniture department, or with the towels and bedding–Walter managed to topple them. Mac even moved them to the toys, hoping a child would knock them over for variety. But no, it was always Walter. The stockman dropped them again as he tried to right the display, tangling them in his feet, threatening to take out a lamp.

"You know, Boss." Sal slurped on a candy cane. "You could get rid of some of those skis."

Shirley put her hand on her hip. "Pair for you, pair for her. Corrie's peppy. She'd like to ski."

"She might. Except, there's a reason why they haven't sold." The view out the big windows showed Washington and Fourth Streets were dry and clear, not a snowflake in sight.

"Detroit is experiencing its warmest December since 1881." Walter dropped three more pairs. "We had an inch of snow on the ninth, three-tenths on the fourteenth. Today's high was fifty-seven degrees."

Mac tapped the counter. "Do we have any basketball goals?"

"You betcha!" Sal found a hoop with a net in the sporting goods department and waved it overhead. "Corrie has quite a jump shot. Saw her practicing at the church."

Shirley pulled a large box off the shelf. "An official Dutch Lonborg ball to go with it. Comes with its own pump."

"Last season, Northwestern's basketball team, under Coach Lonborg, won sixteen games and lost one, first place in the Big Ten Conference." Walter braced skis on the rack holding all-weather hunting coats.

"Okay." Mac sighed. Their first Christmas together and all he could come up with was this dud of a gift. "Corrie has a present."

"Attaboy. I'll wrap it." Shirley headed for the cash register.

"Only the ball. I'll hang the goal in the morning." Mac couldn't give her an airplane like Tex, but he could hang a goal on her garage. And hope she'd stay to use it. "Merry Christmas to all and to all a good night."

Corrie slept in Christmas Day. With the sun coming up so late, she'd been sleeping more. Mac had plenty of time to hang the goal on the garage. Looked fine, too, like their house had become a home. Using Corrie's menu plan on the refrigerator, he mixed up blueberry muffins and put them in the oven, started a pot of coffee, and fed Lindy.

He found Sleeping Beauty where he'd left her, wild curls spilling over her pillow. He played the prince and awakened her with a kiss. "Merry Christmas, Corrie."

"Is it morning already? Your ears are cold." Corrie grabbed his shoulders and pulled him in. Ah, a warm and cozy way to start the—

Brrrring! said the timer.

Her hands stilled.

"Muffins." He stood and helped her to her feet. "Sorry."

"Never apologize for cooking." She grinned, then tipped her head toward the bed. "Later?"

"Absolutely!"

Taking their time over breakfast seemed like a luxurious indulgence. As they lingered, Mac slid his hand over Corrie's. He took a deep breath. "I've been wanting to talk to you about something for a while."

Her eyebrows creased, and she sent him a sidelong glance.

He squeezed her hand and rushed on to ease her worries. "Joseph recommended that we pray together. You and I haven't talked much about spiritual stuff. What do you think about praying?"

She nodded. "Everyone tells me to pray—Miriam, our former forward and future nun Mary Frances, and Mrs. Zukas."

"Your housekeeper told you to pray?"

"Well actually, I think her words were 'You haven't got a prayer when it comes to cooking.'" Corrie grinned.

"I disagree. Everything's jake in the kitchen." Mac chuckled. "Christmas seems like a good time to pray. Shall we?"

"And how!" Corrie put her other hand in his and bowed her head. "You start and I'll finish."

"Dear Jesus, thank You for coming into this world and thank You for bringing Corrie into my life. We ask You to help us become the family You want us to be."

Corrie cleared her throat. "Bring Miriam and Joseph back safely. And ... happy birthday! Amen!"

Mac planted a big one on her sassy lips. "You are the cat's meow."

"Ooh la la, Mac." She kissed him back. "Let's open our gifts."

While Mac plugged in the Christmas tree lights, Corrie tuned the radio. A brass quintet played "Hark, the Herald Angels Sing."

Mac opened his gift, peacock blue socks with white stripes. "Nifty! I didn't know you could do fancy knitting."

"I can't. Not without a lot of coaching from Miriam."

He tried them on. One was tighter in the cuff and the other bunched by his little toe. A few weeks' wear and washing would even them out.

Knitting must have been the theme for the year, as Mac's mom had sent them matching red stocking caps and scarves.

Corrie opened a silver candy dish from her folks. "This used to hide in our china cabinet. I'm surprised it didn't sell in the auction."

Mac passed his gift. "To my best bearcat."

Corrie shook the square box. "Oh, Mac, a bicycle!"

His heart skipped a beat. "You wanted a bike?"

"I'm teasing, silly. Big, but it's light … what could it be?" She tore the paper. "A Dutch Lonborg basketball! Hot dog!"

Lindy wandered over to join in the excitement.

"Where can we play? Is there a hoop at the park? Where's the nearest school with a court?"

Mac led her to the kitchen, pulled aside the curtain, and pointed.

She posed like Betty Boop, hands on hips, held tilted, peering at him from the corner of her eyes. "Clever boy! You asked my ring size to throw me off what kind of ring you were giving me. Well, let's take advantage of this snowless winter!" She hugged him with her free arm. "That's why you were up so early this morning."

"You found me out. I'll air up the ball while you get dressed."

Did she like his gift? Or was she stringing him along until she heard from Tex? Oops, he'd overfilled the ball. The gift was pitiful enough. He didn't need to explode it. He released some air.

Corrie was back in a flash, wearing slacks, a cardigan, and her high-top Keds. Mac passed her the ball. "Loser in H-O-R-S-E cooks dinner."

"You're on!"

They both sunk baskets one handed. Corrie made a two-handed, overhead, backward shot that Mac missed, earning an *H*.

"Well I never," Eunice hollered from her stoop. "Desecrating this holy day with–" She paused for a flap of her hand. "Sports."

"Join us," Corrie said, knowing Eunice would never.

"'We wish you a Merry Christmas,'" Mac sang, and Corrie chimed in, sending Eunice inside before the third line.

Lindy gave a *woof*. Two kids emerged from the house across the street and came their way. Up close the pair looked to be Mac's and Corrie's ages. "We finished opening our presents. Can we play?" The young woman had dark bobbed hair like Colleen Moore. "I'm Mollie, and this is my husband Freddie. We moved in last week."

Corrie bounce-passed to Mollie, then introduced herself and Mac. "I thought everyone had left town."

"I'm a Michigan Bell manager." Freddie had a Douglas Fairbanks grin, complete with a pencil mustache. "The telephone company never closes."

"Mac manages Montgomery Ward's. This is his only day off," Corrie said. "Well, let's play then."

Mollie produced a piece of chalk and marked off the half-court and free-throw lines. "I was a teacher before we got married."

"You're not teaching anymore?"

Mollie nodded. "I had to resign."

So Corrie hadn't been the only one to trade a career for a husband. Although begging rides from any pilot with an empty seat wasn't a career.

"Red hats versus blue hats?" Freddie suggested.

"You're on!"

Corrie and Mollie were evenly matched in height and skill. The inch Mac had on Freddie didn't give him much of an advantage. All four played to win, working up a sweat and breathing hard. He couldn't wait to introduce them to Joseph and Miriam.

"Glad the snow held off so we can play," Freddie said when they paused for a drink of water.

"The Methodist church has a swell gym." Corrie dried her face. "Let's get a group together and play."

"Count us in!" Freddie and Mollie said in unison.

They played a few more minutes, then a woman with gray curls called, "Time's up! Who won?"

They looked at each other and shrugged.

"All I know is I worked up an appetite." Mollie retrieved her sweater from the pile on the stoop. "This is my mom. She thought I would ruin dinner, so she took over the kitchen." The young woman pressed her hands to her ruddy cheeks, opening her eyes and mouth wide.

"Enough ham already." Her mother wagged her finger. "You bought a turkey, remember? Plenty for everyone. C'mon over."

Freddie handed the ball to Mac. "What do you say?"

Mac exchanged a glance with Corrie. She was game for anything that got her out of the kitchen. "Be glad to. May we bring anything?"

"I made a plum pudding," Corrie volunteered.

"Hot socks!"

Corrie and Mac hurried inside to wash up. He caught her at the bathroom sink. "Marriage to you isn't quite what I expected."

Her eyes widened. "I can put the pork roast in if you'd rather—"

"No, we'll have it tomorrow night. Marriage to you"–he gathered her in his arms and kissed the damp tip of her nose–"is a lot more fun than I ever imagined." Fun yes, but uncertain.

CHAPTER
THIRTY

THE FIRST CUP of coffee hadn't sparked her ignition, so Corrie poured a second. She hadn't felt this lousy since the morning after the speakeasy.

Sun lightened the kitchen. Perfect for flying. She'd pull her plane from the hangar, breathing in the smells of butyrate dope, gasoline, and oil. The cockpit surrounded her like a hug. With a swing of the prop, the engine fired. Point into the wind, scan for traffic, power up—

Lindy gave her a hopeful snuffle.

Corrie rubbed his ears. "Roscoe Turner flew around with a lion, so of course you can fly with me." Someday …

Why not now? If Tex ever called, she'd take him up on his offer. Millionaires must pay well. She could save her earnings and bring them home for Mac. They'd buy this house. Or maybe he'd figure out a way to join her in California. She'd send money to his mother so she could visit. Then she'd buy a house for her own parents. Wouldn't they be proud? They could take their friends to see her on the silver screen. Little Corrie finally made it big.

For now, laundry. She hauled the pile downstairs and filled the washtub. The phone rang. Some fellow who proclaimed himself as Tex's assistant said, "A car is on the way for you. Be ready in fifteen minutes."

"Pardon me?" Corrie pulled the phone away from her ear and frowned, as if some explanation might emerge from the handset. "Let me talk to Tex."

"Fourteen minutes, miss."

"Goodbye," Corrie said to the dial tone. She turned to Lindy, who sat by her feet. "I was thinking how wonderful it would be to have a flying job, and guess who calls?" She propped her hands on her hips. "Although Tex needs a lesson in manners."

She hurried through the house, shutting off the washer, double-checking the stove, filling Lindy's water bowl. Time to follow her dream. "California, here I come!"

She rubbed Lindy's ears. "I'll be back." Dark-brown eyes asked when, but she didn't know. Corrie tossed a dog biscuit to keep him from staring. A lump in her throat threatened to choke her. What was she doing? How could she leave? She started to write a note, but a horn honked outside. She'd send a telegram–Tex could afford it.

A midnight-blue Cadillac limousine idled at the curb. Good thing Miriam wasn't home. She'd throw a hissy when she found out Corrie had gone. Maybe she and Mollie could be friends. Corrie hurried out.

A uniformed driver opened the back door for her. Corrie told the man her name, startling him into introducing himself.

"What's our destination, Mr. O'Brien?"

"Ford Airport in Dearborn, miss. We're in a bit of a hurry." The driver waved for her to enter the car. "Might you be bringing any luggage?"

"No, I'm not." Mr. Got Bucks could afford to outfit her.

The back seat sat six feet away from the driver. "Mind if I sit up front?" She slipped into the copilot seat before he could say no.

The cockpit had the same levers, knobs, and instruments as Mac's Chevy, but polished aluminum and rosewood trim made it fancy. The car negotiated Twelve Mile's potholes with barely a wobble. Once they reached the highway, O'Brien gave it full throttle. Since it was a Saturday and the day after Christmas, few got in his way.

Corrie pressed back into the seat. "What have you got under the hood?"

"A V-16. Biggest engine in any car."

"Add wings and a tail, and we could fly."

O'Brien grinned. "Like Lindbergh."

Except they were ground bound, eye level with stores decorated for Christmas. On side streets, children played ball and bicycled, making the best of a snowless winter. The low sun shadowed grass muted to a dull brown. In California, flowers bloomed and palm trees–

What about Mac?

"So Mr. O'Brien, how was your Christmas?" Corrie explored that topic and his entire family history until they arrived.

Last summer, when Corrie visited the airport, she'd hardly noticed the cream brick building where O'Brien parked. A sign labeled it *Passenger Terminal,* but it was smaller than Aunt Florence's house in Council Bluffs. The half-sized second story formed a balcony, a great place to watch airplanes.

Fatigue held Corrie to the seat. What was she doing? Following her dream! Taking charge of her destiny! The driver opened the door and she stepped out. "Thank you, Mr. O'Brien."

Inside, large aerial photographs of Ford Trimotors decorated the waiting room. A businessman wrote at a desk and another man smoked in a wicker chair. The ticket window was empty. Corrie asked the porter, "Have you seen a tall pilot with a Texas accent?"

He pointed up.

"Thank you, sir."

Corrie hurried up the stairs and yanked open the door. Leather davenports and chairs, a large radio, and a thick rug filled the room. A map of the United States, larger than any at Central, stretched across the back wall. If the Omaha Country Club decorated a pilot's lounge, it would look exactly like this.

"Kiddo!" A stubby figure in a flight suit and beret stepped away from the window and grabbed Corrie.

"Pancho! What a wonderful surprise!" Corrie hugged her back. "Congratulations on your new speed record. What brings you to Michigan?"

"You. Take off your coat and stay awhile." Pancho sprawled on a davenport and motioned Corrie into the nearest chair. "You wrote me asking about Tex. Took a while for the letter to find me since I live in San Marino and you'd addressed it to Santa Monica." Pancho waved her cigar. "San? Santa? All the same if you're not from California. Fortunately they know me in Santa Monica too. The next time I landed at Clover Field, your letter was waiting for me." She leaned forward, elbows on knees. "Let me tell you about Tex, the two-bit four-flusher."

"Well–" A whiff of cigar smoke sent her stomach rolling. Corrie adjusted her position out of its path.

"Here's the straight scoop, kid." Pancho's eyebrows lowered, and all trace of her smile disappeared. "Tex hires desperate fools with only a handful of hours in their logbooks, gets them flying dangerous stunts, and pays five bucks a day for the chance to die. That piker survived a crash during *Hell's Angels*, so he thinks he's a tough guy and expects everyone else to push his luck. Meanwhile he puts professional stunt pilots, the fellows who know what they're doing, out of work." Pancho called Tex a cheapskate, Scrooge, and several more offensive names.

"I don't want to take anyone's job." Or be Tex's rube.

Pancho blew a smoke ring. "How's your aerobatic training going?"

"It's not. No airplane."

"Same here." Pancho cursed the economy, then she gave Corrie a looking over. "Maybe there's something other than flying between you two."

"I'm no gold digger." Corrie flicked her hands down her torso. "Why would he be interested my fuselage when he can have any starlet in Hollywood? Besides, I'm married."

"Married? Yeah, I got a husband somewhere, but I don't let that stop the party." Pointing her cigar toward her round face, Pancho shimmied her shoulders. "Ask me how often I go to bed alone."

From the davenport facing the map, a low voice said, "*You* never go to bed."

Pancho flopped back, hooting and laughing hard. "On the bear rug, on the piano, in front of the fireplace. Who needs a bed?"

"Tex is here?" Corrie whispered as heat rose in her face. Had he been listening to their entire conversation? What had she said? What *hadn't* Pancho said? She tiptoed across the room, leaned over the back of the davenport, and came face to face with Tex. "What are you doing here?"

"You're going to make a movie for me." He closed his eyes and rubbed the space between his thick eyebrows.

"Are you ill? There's a new hotel across the street, if you need to rest." Maybe she shouldn't mention the hotel if he wanted to be her sugar daddy. "Could it be carbon monoxide?"

"Thirteen thousand feet to catch tailwinds." He groaned. "I ordered an oxygen tank for the return."

No oxygen at that altitude? Reckless.

"We're testing new planes for Lockheed and decided to balls-out race. I won, of course, so pretty boy came down with the vapors." Pancho jabbed her thumb toward the large windows overlooking the airport.

"New planes?" Corrie couldn't resist a peek. She opened the window, inhaling smoke-free air. Below on the concrete sat a Vega like Amelia Earhart's. The other aircraft, a low-wing, looked similar to the Lindberghs' seaplane except it had a row of windows below the pilot's seat. "Is that the one that flew in the Bendix race?"

"Yep, it's an Orion." Pancho nodded. "Retractable landing gear. Room for six passengers. Four-hundred-fifty-horse Pratt and Whitney."

Corrie whistled. "Two hundred miles an hour?"

"Without breaking a sweat." Pancho gave a satisfied smile. "Better visibility than the Vega. When the canopy's closed, it's more comfortable than the Mystery Ship. So kiddo, if you want to go to California, escape the cold, and seek your fortune, I've got room for you."

Corrie gave the planes one final look, then closed the window and pushed away. She had her answer, actually more than one answer, delivered by the oddest messenger God had ever used. Time to figure out how to get home. Home? Corrie liked the sound of that word better and better.

Someone knocked on the door.

"That will be my oxygen tank," Tex said.

"Well, thanks for your offers, both of you." Corrie hugged Pancho. "But I'm staying here with my husband."

"Is he good in bed and everywhere else?" Pancho asked.

Her heart filled with memories of Mac's touch, his patience, the way he appreciated and celebrated her every effort. Corrie glanced at the davenport where Tex lay and raised her voice. "Absolutely the best." She grinned. "I'm stuck on him for good."

"No sense taking wooden nickels from that drugstore cowboy." Pancho jabbed her thumb toward Tex, then yanked open the door. Her voice lowered. "Hello, handsome." She leaned a shoulder on the door-frame and propped a hand on her hip. "Interested in girls?"

Mac paced the empty store, shuffling past phonographs, bicycles, and skis marked down to two dollars a pair. Rotten economy. Making another circuit, he wandered by the cash register where Shirley read the January *Life* magazine, then up front to the plate-glass window. The guy who sold apples on Main was trying his luck on Washington. What if Ward's closed this store? What if Tex—

The phone rang. Mac spun, catching his shoe on a washing machine.

Shirley held the handset out to him, "Fellow with a Scottish accent."

Mac lunged for it. "McFarland here."

"Hello, Mac," said the distinguished voice of Jim Dobie. "The mounting's in. You can stop in and see the ring anytime."

"How about now?"

Jim chuckled. "Ward's must be slow too. See you soon."

Mac found the tall Scot at his jeweler's bench, magnifying lenses perched on his blade of a nose. "I wondered what happened to you after Codling's went into receivership."

Jim folded his glasses. "Thought I was out of work. Didn't have enough money to start my own shop. But the auctioneer was impressed with the inventory." Jim glanced up from his tools. "Loose diamonds tend to disappear, but Codling's were all there. So he auctioned the jewelry repair department separately. I raised my hand to bid, and he said, 'Sold!'"

Mac returned the man's grin, stowing the lesson in how to land on your feet and hoping he'd never have to use it. "Then Wilfred and Tom opened …"

"And asked me to help with rent. Repairs keep me busy, and every once in a while, I sell something." He put a small white box on the bench and opened it. "The platinum sets off the stone's color well."

Mac turned the ring under the jeweler's lamp and watched the gem's facets flash. "It's beautiful."

"I'm curious," he said. "This is an unusual stone. Neither you nor Mrs. Mac came in to look at it."

"Corrie's father had a jewelry store in Omaha. He had a black diamond she admired, but it was stolen in a robbery."

"A true black? Hope she's not disappointed. Most black diamonds are full of particles, iron, graphite, other minerals. Not only is this stone clear, but it looks blue when it's worn. And I wouldn't say this to sell it, but there's a legend that goes with it. You'll find it in the box."

Mac sent up another prayer that Corrie would love the gift ... and the husband who gave it to her. "I should have asked earlier, but how much does the ring cost?"

"Since the gas line came through our neighborhood, I'd like to get my wife a new stove. Do you suppose we could work that out?"

"Absolutely." With the cash shortage, barter had become a way of life. Mac returned the ring to its box. "I hope your new Desoto Windsor gas range is every bit as satisfying as this ring."

"Do you and your wife play pinochle?" Jim wrote his phone number on the back of his business card. "We're a bit homebound these days, with little ones, but we enjoy guests."

"We'd love to." Mac gave him their number.

"Are you Mac McFarland?" yelled one of the pants salesmen across the store. "Shirley called to tell you WJR announced that Texas millionaire landed at Henry Ford's airport."

Oh no. His heart hit the floor. The salesmen, the jeweler, and three customers stared, waiting for Mac to do something. But what?

The telephone rang again. The salesman listened a moment, then hung up. "Shirley again. She heard from Eunice." He shuddered. "A limousine picked up your wife."

Eunice? The whole town would know. No, between Shirley and Eunice, the whole town already knew.

Mac held onto the jeweler's bench. He couldn't move, couldn't breathe. If Corrie had already left him, no sense taking the ring. But ... he'd do anything for Corrie. Even if he looked like the biggest sap in the world.

"You have your gift." Jim set the box in Mac's hand. "Go then."

Mac's legs listened. He dashed out of Wilfred and Tom's to his car. No need to tell Shirley where he'd gone; she already knew. He glanced at the clear sky, wishing it was covered with clouds full of ice and snow, grounding airplanes. Even now Tex could be scooping up Corrie and heading to California. He raced south. What could he say to convince her to stay? Would the ring be enough? Driving by the church reminded him to stop worrying and start praying. *Help!* he choked out. A particle of calm seeped into his heart. God heard his prayer.

Mac found the airport and parked. No planes in the air. No blue limousine, only a Dearborn Airport Taxi. The sign over the door said *Passenger Terminal.* Inside, two fellows in suits filled the air with cigarette smoke. Mac burst through the north door to the aircraft parking area, ran to the first plane, and peeked inside. Empty. Same with the other. Concrete stretched in every direction. Ford trimotors sat in front of a hangar. Airplane factories stretched as long as Montgomery Ward's warehouses in Chicago. At the west end of the airport stood Henry Ford's museum, a building resembling Philadelphia's Independence Hall. No planes or people. If Corrie was still here, how would he find her?

Back inside, Mac asked the porter, "Excuse me, sir. I'm looking for a young lady with curly hair, light brown." Like maple syrup. "She might be with a man from Texas."

The porter gestured toward the stairs.

Halfway up, Mac heard a woman with a deep voice speak, then laugh. Another replied. Was that Corrie? He listened under the transom window. Yes, it was! She was still here! Mac's knees gave out and he grabbed the handrail.

Thank You, God!

Wait … a man's voice? Tex? She still planned to leave? Mac patted his pocket. He had the ring, Corrie's ring, but would it outshine a fancy new airplane? Guts churning like a Wardway washer, he knocked.

Corrie's voice carried. "I'm staying here with my husband."

Attagirl!

The woman asked, "Is he good in bed and everywhere else?"

Mac took a step back. Corrie knew someone who would ask that?

His wife said, "Absolutely the best. I'm stuck on him for good."

My baby bearcat!

The deep voice muttered, then the door flung open with a whoosh of cigar smoke.

"Hello, handsome." A wide-shouldered woman in a beret scanned him head to toe. She struck a pose and licked her lips. "Interested in girls?"

From behind the funny old bird, another person stepped out. Corrie, his love. Her mouth curved into a smile. Mac held her gaze as he said, "I'm interested in only one girl, and there she is."

The woman stepped aside and said to Corrie, "You know how to pick 'em, kiddo."

"Thanks, Pancho. Blue skies." Corrie joined Mac on the landing and pulled the door shut behind her. She'd been pale this morning, but her cheeks had a bit a color now. One eyebrow raised. "Take me home?"

Mac opened his arms and she stepped into them. "Absolutely!"

She hugged Mac. "Am I glad to see you," she whispered as the two on the other side of the door traded insults. "Let's go."

Hand in hand, they raced to the car. The faster they got away, the happier he'd be. *Corrie had chosen him over a millionaire flyboy! Whoopee!*

"How did you know where to find me?" Corrie asked as they headed home.

"Shirley and Eunice."

She groaned. "I'm so sorry."

"Joseph and I found the train tickets. We turned them in for cash, and he bought socks to go with the boots from the Boot Ball."

"Joseph knows? He must not have said anything to Miriam, or I would have gotten an earful." She pressed her palms to her head. "I cleaned under the couch for nothing."

"Lindy will have it full of fur in no time."

"Pancho's right. Tex is a piker." She shared what Pancho had told her.

"Hollywood's Mr. Smooth, leaving a trail of broken wherever he goes."

Corrie slipped her hand into his. "Thanks for picking me up."

"Anytime."

"No more times. He won't call again."

Should he pull over now? No, not on a grimy city street. Mac nibbled her knuckles, promising more, much more, as soon as they got home.

As he turned into the driveway, the postman hailed them. Corrie took the letter. "It's from Halleen. Hope Santa brought Eddie a job."

Lindy met them at the door with a wag of his stubby tail. Corrie hung up her coat. "I suppose you have to hotfoot it back to work."

He locked the door and pulled Corrie close. "I have a better plan. Let me check in with the store, then meet you in the living room."

Mac rang up the office.

"Spill it, Boss," Shirley said. "Did you bump off the Texas flyboy? Turn into Jack Dempsey and give him a black eye?"

"Nothing like that."

"A limousine was involved. I need details."

"Corrie went to Dearborn to look at friends' planes. She's home now. As they say at the end of the cartoons, 'That's all, folks.'"

"You, Mr. McFarland, are a terrible storyteller."

"And you, Mrs. Wendell, are a terrible gossip." He got a laugh out of her. "How's business?"

"Watching the dust settle."

"See you on Monday." Mac hung up. Now was the time to set aside every plane crash. He sat beside Corrie and wrapped an arm around her.

She dropped the letter and squeezed him back. "About my flying …"

He swallowed. "It means a lot to you. When you flew me over the city … everything does look better from up high. And …" He looked her in the eye. "If you're careful, if the weather's good, and if you find a safe plane…" *Safe plane? There's an oxymoron.* "You could do a little flying. Short trips. No stunts or races. When the weather's good."

"I do love you. So very much." She knuckled a tear from the corner of her eye and smiled. "But I'm hanging up my helmet and goggles for a while. We've got to make a new plan. Mac, I'm pregnant!"

"Really?" He scooped her into his lap. "You're sure?"

She fanned herself with the letter. "Halleen told me the signs. I've got all of them." She wiped her eyes and Mac passed her his handkerchief. "Especially weepiness."

"A baby." *Thank You, Lord.* He hung on tighter.

Corrie snuggled deeper into his hug. Her gaze met his, watery with more tears. "I'm going to do better, I promise. I'll be the best mother."

"You are the best in my heart." He kissed her until she revved like a big six. "Especially when it comes to spooning."

He ran a hand down her legs, pulling off her boots, wishing he'd worked up a romantic speech for this moment. "I'm sorry I didn't have this when I proposed." He slipped the box into her palms.

"Oh, Mac, you didn't …" Corrie lifted the lid and gasped. Her wide eyes blinked. Was she happy with it? She slid it on her finger, then showed it to Mac. "A black diamond."

The stone glowed deep indigo. "Like the world—a dark place, but if you look carefully, there's hope." Now where did that come from? He was too young to wax philosophical.

A folded paper, brown and crisp with age, sprang out of the box.

"When love is true," she read, "the color is blue." Corrie held up the ring, catching the light in the facets. "It is blue, like when the sun comes up in the morning. So is it true? You love me, the last single girl in Omaha?"

He took her hands. "I've loved you since the first time I saw you play basketball, racing around the gym, sinking every basket."

"Not every basket." Her cheeks pinked. "I've been stuck on you since you coached us. You never raised your voice, even when the other team cheated or the referee made a bad call."

He pressed his lips to her warm temple. "I would have proposed then, but we had the team as a chaperone."

Corrie rubbed her palm down Mac's jaw. "Then you disappeared after graduation."

"You got an airplane. I figured one of those flying circus fellows …"

"Oh, Mac, I wouldn't trade you for a thousand flyboys." She planted her lips on his for a let's-hit-the-sheets kiss. "I love you."

"And how!"

CHAPTER
THIRTY-ONE

MAC ROLLED OVER IN BED, reached for his soft, warm wife, and came up empty. The drapes swayed, letting in a gentle breeze, birdsong, and sunlight. Retirement was the berries.

The quick slap-slap of flip-flops heralded Corrie's arrival. He opened his arms, and she swooped in for a morning cuddle. Her curls, maple-syrup swirl over vanilla ice cream, tickled his chin.

"You're up early." Mac tugged her hot pink T-shirt from the waistband of her matching shorts and popped the waistband hook.

Corrie caught his hand. "Take a check. Heather's on her way."

Heather? For some reason he couldn't fathom, seeing as how the Vietnam War ended a few years ago, the US Navy had signed up one of his favorite grandchildren. He'd blame those Village People for their "In the Navy" song, but it came out after Heather enlisted.

Mac resumed his exploration of the silken skin along Corrie's ribs. "Pensacola's hours away."

"Not if you're flying."

Flying? Not so good. "We'll have noise complaints if she lands a Phantom here."

"We'd need an arresting cable to stop an F-4." Corrie slipped away and straightened her clothes. Decent again. Rats. "Fortunately, the navy doesn't rent fighter jets. She's flying a Skyhawk. Cessna, not Douglas."

"Skyhawks aren't that fast."

"ETA is twenty-eight minutes."

Mac groaned. "Winds aloft must be straight out of the west."

Corrie bent to look under the bed, giving him a chance to pat her round bottom. She wiggled away and removed a flat carton. "Miscellaneous? Which one of our daughters labeled all our boxes 'Misc.'?"

"When we find out, let's disinherit her." Mac stood and stretched. "What are you looking for?"

"My airplane album."

"Shelf of our closet." Her most precious possessions earned the most secure spot in the house. He headed for the shower. "You didn't show it to Heather when she learned to fly?"

"Too self-involved at sixteen."

Mac washed, then combed his white hair with a dab of Brylcreem, and dressed in his retirement uniform of shorts and tee. In honor of Heather, he chose his Blue Angels shirt.

An Australian shepherd greeted him with a wagging tush and a food dance. "Not buying it, Piper. Corrie fed you. No second breakfast from me."

Piper raced outside. The hum of an airplane engine added a bass note to the birdsong. Corrie called, "Piper, *paskubek*." Bounding down the grass, the dog sent gulls and canvasback ducks to the safety of the water.

A high-wing, single-engine plane entered downwind. If she came in hot, dumped the power, and slammed it on, the pilot would hear from her flight instructor. Mac twisted two grapefruits off the tree, then watched the Skyhawk execute precise turns onto crosswind and final. Landing light on, left wing a few degrees down to compensate for the wind, power back, nose up, full-stall landing. "You taught her well, Nana."

Her lips curved. "Best student ever."

Heather taxied and parked as Mac went inside. Pilots liked to sit in the Florida room to watch planes go by. When they'd moved here, Mac had painted the dark-pine living room set sky blue. Corrie had covered the earth-toned farm scenes in a tropical print. Nothing fancy, but it held up to grandchildren and hurricanes. He moved recent issues of *Life*, *Flying*, and *Southern Living* from the couch to the end table, and returned the Audubon bird book and binoculars to the drawer. There, ready for visitors.

Now, for breakfast. Dishes in the drainer said Corrie had already eaten and Heather was smart enough to fuel herself before takeoff. Scrambled eggs for one then.

The kitchen door burst open, and Miriam blew in on a cloud of allspice and pepper. "I heard a plane. Who's here?" With light steps, she crossed to the window. The sun glowed on waves of chestnut hair, culottes and a blouse in green-and-white seersucker.

"Heather. The navy's giving her a hard time."

"Poor girl. I'll pray for her."

Heather climbed out and fell into her grandmother's arms.

Joseph stuck his head in. "Good morning, Mac. Miriam, tee time–"

"Yes, my love, I'm coming." Miriam squeezed Mac's hand, then headed for the door. "Are we still on for mahjong tonight?"

"Absolutely." Mac slid his eggs to his plate, then dropped a bit into Piper's bowl. "Supposed to keep your coat shiny."

Piper gulped the egg, then joined the pilots outside. Under the wing, Heather moved flat hands through the air. Hangar flying. Mac put Heather's grapefruit in the fridge.

The radio said something about trouble in Iran. *Dear Lord, please end war. And keep my grandchildren safe.*

Herded by Piper, Corrie and Heather strolled toward the house. Heather towered over her nana, even more now that the navy had spit shined her posture. Montgomery Ward's didn't make slacks in her length.

Mac held the door open. "There's my favorite granddaughter."

Heather had a strong hug. "How's my favorite grandpa?"

"On top of the world. Ready for a grapefruit?"

"Not yet. Nana wants to show me photos. I'd love coffee though."

He looked up at her. "Didn't anyone tell you coffee will stunt your growth?"

She straightened, the sparkle in her eyes pure Corrie. "Bring me two cups then."

The dog stretched on the tile and the girls settled onto the love seat. Mac served the brew in a Pitts Special mug for Heather and a Christen Eagle mug for Corrie. The aerobatic biplanes were pretty, but these two better not get any ideas about a nana-granddaughter airshow act.

He sat where he could watch for other flashes of Corrie in their granddaughter. None of their children or grands looked like him, although Heather had gotten his straight hair. It was cut as if the navy had plopped a bowl on her head and trimmed around it. Regulation off the collar. Or maybe they were going for the ice-skater look like Dorothy Hamill.

Corrie opened the box, unleashing a whiff of butyrate dope, the fabric stiffener for airplanes back in the old days. She removed her all-weather suit, her leather jacket, helmet, and goggles.

Piper cocked her head, then pushed through the screen door and raced down the runway. Corrie followed. *"Paskubek."*

Heather opened a logbook. "Did you and Nana meet at an airport?"

He shook his head. "Coached her basketball team in high school. She had a swell layup." He wiggled his Groucho Marx eyebrows. "And great legs."

"Grandpa!" Her cheeks pinked.

Mac nodded at the low-wing plane with a double tail bouncing down their runway. "JC Penney's and Macy's used to sell Ercoupes."

"Did Nana teach you to fly?"

"No. I didn't have the stomach for it."

Her head shifted side to side. "You fly all the time with Nana."

Corrie and Piper returned. "Your grandpa pulled his cousin from an airplane crash."

"Nineteen twenty-seven. Home-built. Biplane." Pilots wanted to know about the plane, not about Henry dying.

"He overcame a lot for me." Corrie's smile held a mix of pride and gentleness.

"Flying's safer nowadays." He pulled Corrie close for a kiss. "I stopped worrying about death and enjoyed every day God lets us live."

"Enough with the PDA." Heather hid her grin behind a framed airplane ad, the art deco colors still bright.

Corrie slipped into her spot on the love seat and put her photo album in her granddaughter's lap. "Here you go."

Heather opened the black cover, her face taking on the same glow Corrie's held when she looked at planes. "A Jenny and a Standard. Barnstormers. Cool beans!"

"Your nana was the only girl in her family and her father doted—"

"Doted?" Corrie muttered. "Ignored."

Mac continued, "When she caught Lindbergh fever, he bought her a biplane for graduation."

"A biplane? All I got was a Cross pen and a calculator." Heather studied the photo. "What kind of biplane?"

"Started in an Arrow. Got my license in an Overland. That's me in the helmet and leather jacket."

Heather's mouth quirked. "Everyone's in a helmet and leather jacket."

Blue diamond flashing, Corrie pointed. "Everyone was flying higher, faster, farther. Crossing oceans and continents. Starting airlines. I was going to get my name in the record books. Then the stock market crashed, and my plane was auctioned off."

"I took advantage of the situation and married her,"

"Best revised flight plan ever." Corrie winked, warming his blood. "Then I met a Texas millionaire looking for stunt pilots to make movies in Hollywood."

"You went to California?"

"No. I was married," Corrie said matter of factly, not showing the pull Tex and his planes had held. "I tried to talk your grandpa into moving–"

"Why not?" Heather spread her hands. "We could have grown up in sunny California instead of chilly Nebraska."

"More likely we'd have ended up like the Joads in the *Grapes of Wrath*, sleeping in our car and starving," Mac said. "It was 1931. People who had jobs hung on with both hands."

"I decided to go without Grandpa, grab my fame and fortune, not knowing Tex would never make another airplane movie." Corrie turned to the scrapbook page with a magazine photo of the Lockheeds. "God spoke through straight-talking Pancho Barnes. Her warning confirmed what my heart knew, the right choice in every way. Even though it was painful, I told Tex no."

"Whoa. Nana loved Grandpa enough to turn down a flying job!" Heather tilted her head, giving him a sassy expression that was pure Corrie, then said to her grandmother, "Did you wonder if you'd ever fly again?"

"Absolutely. God had better plans than any I imagined. Years later, I became an instructor with the Civilian Pilot Training Program. I was too old for the WASPs, but I worked at the Martin Bomber plant."

Heather blinked. "Were you a test pilot?"

"Those positions were held by military officers," Corrie said primly.

Heather glanced at Mac, and he nodded. Yeah, he figured as much.

His granddaughter flopped back. "I'm a chump."

Corrie wrapped an arm around her granddaughter. "No. You've been put in a difficult position by a higher-ranking lowlife."

Mac straightened. "Do I need to make him an offer he can't refuse?"

Heather shot back in her best Mafia imitation, "Cement overshoes are too good for him."

He leaned forward, elbows on knees. "Miriam's on a first-name basis with our congressmen. We'll hire a lawyer. We'll fight this."

"No chance, Grandpa. The navy is a boys' club, and the pilots are the elite. They'll close ranks and fight any action against their best and the brightest." She shook her head, her hair lifting then falling back into place. "It's put out and shut up, or drive a honey wagon in Iceland the rest of my enlistment."

Honeywagon? Mac mouthed to Corrie.

Lav truck. Corrie mouthed back. Her voice firmed with conviction as she turned to her granddaughter. "You read *God Is My Co-Pilot*?"

"The summer you taught me to fly. You told me God should be my captain. I'm His child first and foremost." She rested her head on her nana's shoulder. "I thought my dream of becoming an airline pilot or astronaut was from Him. But maybe prestige set my course."

Corrie clasped her hands. "My dream of flying didn't come from God but from trying to win my parents' approval. God was with me after the stock market crashed. And I guarantee He's with you in this battle." She turned to the photo from the 1929 Women's Air Derby. "We all tried so hard to wrest a career out of aviation. How many of these pilots can you name?"

"Amelia Earhart."

"Disappeared in 1937." She pointed to the woman with the big grin. "Pancho Barnes. Kept me from throwing away my marriage. Set speed records. Died alone and broke a few years ago. Ruth Nichols almost died trying to beat Amelia across the pond. Louise Thaden held the women's altitude, speed, and endurance records. She won the Derby in 1929 and the Bendix in 1936. Louise, Phoebe, and Blanche marked the airways back when navigation involved arrows painted on barn roofs." She continued down the row. "All of these women made history and set records, an uphill battle during the Great

Depression. Every flight we take today is safer because of these trail-blazers. Yet no one remembers them."

"Andy Warhol's fifteen minutes of fame."

"Accomplishments, like getting in the record books or a photo in the newspaper, don't last. Applause fades to nothing."

"But faith, hope, and love last forever." Heather quoted the Bible, then teared up. "As much as I love flying, it doesn't love me back."

"You need a person for that." Corrie squeezed her hand. "If God brings love into your life, give the best of yourself. Don't let anything, not another person, not aviation, come before your spouse. Keep your vows. Live honorably."

"You and Grandpa always play kissy-face in the kitchen, hold hands in church. So embarrassing." She wiped her eyes. "I hope I find that kind of love."

So much fun. Mac grinned. If he had it to do all over again, he'd do more of the kissy-face part. And spooning. A lot more.

ACKNOWLEDGMENTS

With special thanks to Grandpa Dobie for the black diamond story, and to Mom and Aunt Carolyn for Royal Oak history. Angela Kroeger shared her extensive library on women in aviation and joined me for a Ford Trimotor flight. Nebraska Novelists continues to hone my writing chops. Elaine Quinn, Chris McIvor, and Central staff proudly shared their experience at this historic high school. Omaha's Centennial Model T Club contributed expertise for Mac's Tin Lizzie. And to everyone who encouraged me to continue writing, especially Steve and Cheryl Roberts, thank you.

ALSO BY CATHERINE RICHMOND

Spring for Susannah
Third Strand of the Cord
Through Rushing Waters
Gilding the Waters
The Shelter of Each Other

I love to hear from readers! Please write to me at https://www.facebook.-com/catherinerichmondfans/ or my website CatherineRichmond.com. If you enjoyed *Off the Ground*, a review would make this author as happy as chocolate!

www.ingramcontent.com/pod-product-compliance
Lightning Source LLC
Chambersburg PA
CBHW031119210626
46816CB00016B/1719